Salish Myths and Legends

NATIVE LITERATURES OF THE AMERICAS

Salish Myths and Legends

One People's Stories

Edited by M. Terry Thompson *and* Steven M. Egesdal

UNIVERSITY OF NEBRASKA PRESS • LINCOLN AND LONDON

© 2008 by the Board of Regents of
the University of Nebraska
All rights reserved
Manufactured in the United States of America

Library of Congress Cataloging-in-Publication Data

Salish myths and legends : one people's
stories / edited by M. Terry Thompson and
Steven M. Egesdal.   p. cm.
Includes bibliographical references and index.
ISBN 978-0-8032-1089-9 (pbk. : alk. paper)
1. Salishan mythology. 2. Salishan Indians—
Folklore. 3. Tales—Northwest, Pacific.
4. Legends—Northwest, Pacific. I. Thompson,
M. Terry. II. Egesdal, Steven M.
E99.S21.S35 2008
398.209795—dc22
2007052085

Set in Times New Roman by Bob Reitz.

Contents

Maps

Tables

Acknowledgments

Several colleagues helped us with the Introduction and other aspects of *Salish Myths and Legends: One People's Stories* M. Dale Kinkade (University of British Columbia), Thom Hess (University of Victoria), and Dell Hymes (University of Virginia). The view is always better riding on the shoulders of such giants.

Laurence C. Thompson always will have our gratitude for his help and his mentoring to both of us. Salishan studies miss his gently guiding hand since his massive stroke in 1983.

Of course, we accept full responsibility for any errors that remain, despite their valuable advice. To all of you, *néxʷm tək kʷukʷstéyp*. (Thompson River Salish, "Thank you very much.")

We also must express our utmost appreciation and gratitude to the many Native speakers and storytellers with whom we have worked over the years: Martha Abbott (Lummi), Louis Adams (Flathead), Angeline Alexander (Lummi), Hilda Austin (Thompson/Nłeʔkepmx), Chauncey Beaverhead (Pend d'Oreille), Anna Bennett (Klallam), Alice Camel (Pend d'Oreille), Aloysius Charles (Lummi), Bea Charles (Klallam), Irene Charles (Klallam), Tom Charles (Klallam), Elizabeth Combs (Flathead), Mary Coutlee (Thompson/Nłeʔkepmx), Joe Cullooyah (Flathead), Margaret Finley (Flathead), Tony Finley (Flathead), Louise George (Lushootseed), Mamie Henry (Thompson/Nłeʔkepmx), Tony Incashola (Pend d'Oreille), Mandy Jimmie (Thompson/Nłeʔkepmx), Mabel Joe (Thompson/Nłeʔkepmx), Martha Charles John (Klallam), Mary (Dolly) Linesbiegler (Pend d'Oreille), Sophie Mays (Pend d'Oreille), Felicite McDonald (Flathead), Louis McDonald (Pend d'Oreille), Louise McDonald (Pend d'Oreille), Agnes Paul (Flathead), John Peter Paul (Pend d'Oreille), Pat Pierre (Kalispel), Louis Phillips (Thompson/Nłeʔkepmx), Elizabeth Prince (Klallam), Alex Quequesah (Pend d'Oreille), William Samson (Thompson/Nłeʔkepmx), Minnie Adams Scovell (Tillamook), Margaret Sherwood (Spokane), Adeline Smith

(Klallam), Shirley Trahan (Pend d'Oreille), Eneas Vanderburg, (Flathead), Francis Vanderburg (Flathead), Lucy Vanderburg (Flathead), Harriet Whitworth (Flathead), Josephine (Tony) Williams (Klallam), Clarence Woodcock (Pend d'Oreille), and especially Annie York (Thompson/Nɬeʔkepmx, Spuzzum).

We also wish to thank those people who assisted us during fieldwork, without whose encouragement and cultural facilitation much of our work would not have been possible. They are Harold and Pamela Amoss (University of Washington); Jo Antonioli (Missoula MT) and her family; Geoffrey and Hilary Bursill-Hall (Simon Fraser University); Collin Dickson (Anglican priest, Lytton, B.C.); Barbara Efrat (Royal Museum of British Columbia); Thomas Hess (University of Victoria); Vi and Don Hilbert (Lushootseed, University of Washington); Melville and Elizabeth Jacobs (University of Washington); Andrea Laforet (Canadian Museum of Civilization, Ottawa); Anthony and Nancy Mattina and family (University of Montana); William Seaburg (University of Washington, Bothell); Joyce Silverthorne (Salish Kootenai College); Tom Smith (Salish Culture Committee); Terry Tanner (Pend d'Oreille); Rob Taylor (Victoria, B.C.); Nancy Turner and her family (University of Victoria); Arthur Urquhart (Thompson/Nɬeʔkepmx, Spuzzum); Germaine White (Pend d'Oreille); and Suzanne Young (University of Washington).

There were those special people who, in addition to being our teachers, fed us, housed us, and loved us: Annie York and her younger cousin Arthur Urquhart at Spuzzum, B.C.; Mandy Jimmie and her family at Merritt, B.C.; Mabel Joe and her family at Merritt, B.C.; Martha Charles John at Little Boston, Washington; Elizabeth Prince and her family at Port Angeles, Washington; and Minnie Scovell and her family at Garibaldi, Oregon.

Special recognition goes to Robert Hsu, Mariana Maduell, and Judith Wang of the University of Hawaii, who gave irreplaceable support with computer programming. Thomas Powell (Honolulu) also helped in the early phases of *Salish Myths and Legends: One People's Stories*.

During the years of our fieldwork we were both supported by grants to Laurence C. Thompson, and more recently to M. Terry Thompson, from the National Science Foundation and the National Endowment for the Humanities, through the University of Hawaii. Both of us were supported by grants from the Jacobs Research Funds, and Terry was also supported by a grant from the Royal Museum of British Columbia.

Introduction

Salish Myths and Legends: One People's Stories presents selections of literature from a group of culturally diverse people who trace their origins to a common source from long ago—the Proto-Salish of northwest North America. Their narratives reveal recurring motifs and similarities across linguistic and cultural boundaries, which suggest interesting patterns of diffusion through contact and borrowing, or independent retention over millennia. This book draws its subtitle from that common linguistic heritage and those shared elements of oral literature. The twenty-three Salishan languages can be organized as shown in Table 1.[1] This linguistic organization largely reflects the tribal groups' geographical locations, which in turn ultimately reflect history.

Origins and Migrations
The early ancestors of the Salishan people probably settled in a homeland south of the lower part of the Fraser River in southwestern British Columbia, extending southward to the Skagit River and possibly as far south as the Skykomish River, both in northwestern Washington.[2] Pressure from increasing population, favored by a bountiful food supply, probably caused the Salishan ancestors to expand along the Gulf of Georgia (British Columbia) to the north and Puget Sound (Washington) to the south. That early and rapid expansion fostered the development of regional ways of speaking (i.e., early dialects) within a larger language continuum of Central Salish, as contact among the groups lessened due to geographic barriers and as many of the groups encountered peoples speaking various non-Salishan languages.

A large group left the main body of Central Salish and migrated across the Cascade Mountains into the interior plateau. The languages of that group, the original Interior Salish, eventually developed into seven distinct languages, stretching from parts of south-central British Columbia into eastern Washington, northern Idaho, and then farther into western Montana. Interior

Table 1. The Salishan Language Family

Interior Salish	Lillooet [Li]
	Shuswap [Sh]
	Thompson (River Salish) [Th]
	Columbian [Cl]
	Okanagan-Colville [Ok]
	Spokane-Kalispel-Pend d'Oreille(s)-Flathead [Sp, Ka, Pd'O, Fl]
	Coeur d'Alene [Cr]
Bella Coola [Be]	
Tsamosan	Upper Chehalis [Ch]
	Cowlitz [Cz]
	Quinault [Qn]
	Lower Chehalis [Lo]
Central Coast Salish	Comox [Cx]
	Pentlatch [Pt]
	Sechelt [Se]
	Squamish [Sq]
	Nooksack [Nk]
	Halkomelem [Hl]
	Lushootseed [Ld]
	Twana [Tw]
	Straits Salish [St]
	Klallam [Kl]
	Northern Straits [NS]
Tillamook [Ti]	

Salish separates into northern and southern branches. The northern branch includes three languages—Shuswap, Lillooet, and Thompson—which spread along the river valleys and lakeshores of south-central British Columbia. The southern branch includes four languages: Okanagan-Colville sweeping southward from south-central British Columbia into Washington; Moses-Columbian in what is now central Washington State; Coeur d'Alene, occupying parts of northern Idaho; and the dialect continuum of Spokane-Kalispel-Pend d'Oreille(s)-Flathead, which extends from eastern Washington through northern Idaho into western Montana.

The ancestors of the Bella Coola became isolated far to the north of the body of Central Salish. That isolation may have been caused by an original migration to a distant village site or through separation by encroaching Wakashan people. Perhaps more likely, however, is an Interior origin for Bella Coola (Kinkade 1990:204–5). That is, the Bella Coola were part of an Interior Salish expansion, with subsequent further separation. Linguistically, Bella Coola is not closer to Central Salish than to Interior Salish. The Bella Coola eventually occupied the shores of the Bella Coola River and the inland waterways into which it empties (North and South Bentick Arm), and the connected Dean Channel and the lower reaches of the Dean and Kimsquit rivers that feed it.

The Bella Coola would have been at the northern end of a continuum, but not necessarily in the "Interior" as Salishanists now use that term (i.e., not on the Plateau). The Bella Coola then migrated to their present location, passing through territory now occupied by the Chilcotin. The Bella Coola migration does not need to have had anything to do with the Interior Salish migration onto the Plateau. It does suggest, however, that the ancestors of the Interior Salish were next downriver (the Fraser) to the Bella Coola, thus accounting for Bella Coola–Interior Salish similarities (see Kinkade 1990:204–05). Some Salishanists oppose Bella Coola to all the rest of the Salishan languages (Central Salish, Tsamosan, Tillamook, and Interior Salish), while others (Aert Kuipers and Stanley Newman) accord Interior Salish a special status vis-à-vis the others (including Bella Coola) (Kuipers 1996a:209–10). Bella Coola also shares certain linguistic characteristics with Interior Salish not shared with Central Salish, such as retention of Proto-Salish velars *x, *k, *kʼ. (Linguists use the asterisk (*) to indicate an earlier or reconstructed sound or part of a language or distinct language group.) Bella Coola also shows interesting cognate words with Interior Salish, including that for "fisher" (*Martes pennanti*) with distant Coeur d'Alene. Kinkade (1990:205) presents a cogent argument for an Interior origin for Bella Coola.

Probably before the migration of the early Interior Salish, another group moved from the southern part of Central Salish and spread onto the flat woodlands and prairies to the south of Puget Sound in southwestern Washington, eventually expanding toward the open ocean and occupying the Pacific littoral. That group developed four languages known as Tsamosan (also referred to in earlier publications as the Olympic Branch of Coast Salish). The Tsamosan languages included two sets of closely related languages: inland Upper Chehalis and Lower Cowlitz and maritime (downriver/coastal) Lower Chehalis and Quinault.

Yet another group, ancestors of the Tillamook, became isolated from the southern end of the main body of Central Salish and eventually were situated south of the Columbia River on the north Oregon coast. Like the Bella Coola, they established an enclave separated from the main body of Salishan. It is unclear whether the Tillamook migrated across alien territory to reach their present location, or whether an earlier Salishan continuum was broken by Chinookan expansion. Some recent Tillamook speakers have said they heard that the Tillamook migrated by sea from the western coast of the Olympic Peninsula,[3] but there is no clear indication of that migration, and the myth included in this volume indicates a long history on the Oregon coast. The Tillamook commanded the north Oregon coast from the mouth of the Nehalem River south to that of the Siletz River. Tillamook is clearly closer to the languages of Central Salish than to those of Tsamosan or Interior Salish.[4]

After the separation of the Interior Salish, Bella Coola, Tsamosan, and Tillamook from the main body of Central Salish, the Central Salish group diversified, ultimately developing into ten languages strung out along the inland waterway. At the southern end of Central Salish were two branches, Twana, along the western shore of Puget Sound; and Lushootseed (or Puget Sound Salish), having several mildly differentiated dialects along the shores of Puget Sound in the Seattle area.

Farther west and north of Twana and Lushootseed lay the closely related Straits Salish languages, with Klallam on the northern shores of the Olympic Peninsula, and the Northern Straits language, an intergrading set of dialects, extending along the southern end of Vancouver Island and the San Juan Islands to the mainland around Bellingham, Washington. The major Northern Straits dialects are: Saanich, Sooke, Songish, and Lummi.

Next, there were the Nooksack, which was south of the long dialect continuum of Halkomelem that stretched from just north of the head of navigation for the Fraser River at Yale, British Columbia (upriver Halkomelem, including Chilliwack, Hope, and Yale dialects), down to its mouth (Musqueam), and across to the southeastern littoral of Vancouver Island, including the islands of the Gulf of Georgia between (Cowichan and Nanaimo). Just north of the Chilliwack were the Squamish. Finally, the northernmost group of Central Salish included Sechelt, just north of Squamish on the British Columbia mainland; Pentlatch, on the east shore of Vancouver Island north of Halkomelem; and a considerable dialect spread of Comox-Sliammon from Powell River to Bute Inlet on the mainland and from Courtenay to Campbell River on Vancouver Island.

The Salishan Cultural Landscape
The Salishan peoples represent a large, complex language family. One might envision the following snapshot of the Salishan landscape in about A.D. 1800 (L. C. Thompson 1974:981–82). The main body of Salishan lay in Washington and southern British Columbia, extending from the Pacific Coast straight across the Cascade Mountains and the Plateau beyond to the Rocky Mountains in Montana, and into the Plains. The Cascades divided the Salishan people into two culture areas, two distinct ecological areas, and two great language divisions (sixteen Coast Salishan languages to the west and seven Interior Salishan languages to the east). The Coast Salish belonged to the Northwest Coast culture area, ecologically a temperate, productive coastal zone. The Interior Salish belonged to the Plateau culture area, ecologically forested mountain and semidesert.

The Northwest Coast culture area, including Salishan, generally includes the coastline from the panhandle of southeastern Alaska through British Columbia, Washington and Oregon, to the northwestern corner of California (Driver 1961:15). Its aboriginal inhabitants were able seafarers and most notably fishermen. Many were also whalers and hunters of seal, sea lion, and otter. They typically subsisted primarily on fish (especially salmon), were expert woodcrafters living in cedar plank houses, and enjoyed a considerable surplus of the necessities of life. Perhaps the most distinctive characteristics of the area were a great emphasis on the acquisition of material goods to be given away, display on public occasions, emergence of social classes, and the taking and keeping of slaves (including hereditary slavery). One of the Lummi speakers with whom L. C. Thompson worked was a child of slaves (probably Haida), who belonged to the family of another Lummi speaker with whom Thompson worked.

Although most Coast Salish perhaps were not truly ocean-going, their villages often clustered around river mouths opening into the salt water, usually in sheltered bays and inlets, and by extension they also settled at the mouths of creeks emptying into the large rivers. Probably only the Klallam and Quinault were whalers among the Coast Salish. Some of the other groups were happy to "harvest" any whale that happened to wash ashore.

They were quintessential water people, with the canoe a basic element in their lives. Salmon was the staple food, but they also hunted game and fowl, killing with a variety of means. Women gathered plant foods, including roots and bulbs (for example, camas, wapato), berries, and so on; they also gathered a variety of shellfish (clams, cockles, mussels, and oysters). They seem to have been oriented more toward the inland waterways than toward the open ocean, although they used the prolific fruits of the sea extensively. Those people who lived at river mouths on the salt water traded dried fish, clams, mussels, and such, to the groups living farther inland for fruits, roots, and such, which were not so plentiful nearer the ocean.

Property rights and the status associated therewith largely defined the cultural personality of all of the Northwest Coast peoples, including the Salishan. With ownership and title came rank and privilege. Those notions permeated the cultural milieu—from the celebrating of potlatches, to the taking and keeping of slaves, to the performance of myths. Rainy winters were spent in permanent villages, during which potlatches were held to celebrate important events. Through a potlatch, a village headman could affirm his social status by giving away material goods, from which he also expected to reap a substantial economic return, when his donees reciprocated in kind, plus the culturally mandated interest. The potlatch was especially beneficial in reaffirming social and kinship bonds among the different groups. When the Northwest Coast peoples warred on one another, captives were taken as slaves; the slaves, in turn, became property, enhancing the owners' prestige. Some of this characterization perhaps most closely applies to northern non-Salish peoples of the Northwest Coast. However, to some extent, it fairly describes Salishan groups as well.

Ownership rights covered the tangible and intangible; even some myths could be owned and told only by their owners. That Native perspective on property rights has led, in some groups, to the politicization of the publication of myths and stories by persons other than the perceived owner. Because this knowledge has, in many cases, been lost, along with so much of the other culture, some groups feel that all myths must belong to the tribe and they refuse to give permission for their publication in any form, by any person, including their own tribal members. That accounts for the absence of some well-known Salishanists among the authors in this volume. They did not want to chance offending the groups where they have studied in the past, or where they are currently studying.

The Plateau culture area was different. It is named after the Columbia Plateau. It embraces most of the Fraser River drainage and the Columbia River drainage and includes parts of British Columbia, Washington, Idaho, Oregon, and Montana. The Plateau culture area lacked the stratified society of the Northwest Coast. Rivers played a key role in the lives of the peoples of the Plateau, perhaps allowing an analogy with the Northwest Coast in that both were oriented toward bodies of water and the fruit they bore. Fish (principally several species of salmon, although fewer than on the coast) and roots were the staple foods over much of the Plateau. A wide variety of game and wild food also was hunted, including buffalo for certain southern Interior Salish.

The Interior Salish lived in a domain of relatively little geographic diversity—forested mountain and semidesert. They occupied the area between the Cascade Range and the Rocky Mountains. The severity of cold winters on the high Plateau and its often semidesert environs forced the Interior Salish to develop different dwellings, clothing, and lifestyles from those of their relatives on the more temperate Northwest Coast. Many groups wintered in villages of semi-subterranean houses (e.g., Thompson s ʔístkn, lit. "winter-house"),[5] and they summered in encampments of reed or mat lodges near fishing spots, good hunting, and where berries and roots were plentiful. They tended to be more nomadic than their coastal cousins, as the quest for food often required greater movement to and from gathering places, fishing stations, or hunting grounds. They gathered roots (principally camas and bitter-root), berries, nuts, and lichen, which were prepared or dried and then stored for the winter. Fish and game similarly were dried for winter use. Still other animals, such as beaver, were trapped for their pelts.

Perhaps the Plateau is not a truly distinct culture area, but one showing a mixture of Plains and Northwest Coast cultures. It might be argued that for Salishan people of the eastern fringe (i.e., Flathead), influences from the Plains began to blur somewhat the nature of aboriginal Salishan culture. Importantly, there were routes along which some Plateau people interacted with some Coastal people, and along which stories as well as trade items moved. The Interior Salish typically also had complex kinship systems, more likely resembling the Proto-Salish system than those of other Salish groups. The Interior Salish kinship systems often show reciprocal terms, differentiation by gender (i.e., different terms depending on the speaker's gender). Reciprocal terms and death replacement terms also figure in the Coast languages. The difference between the two systems generally lies in the Interior being bifurcate collateral, and the Coast being lineal.[6] Lineal kinship systems do not distinguish between a parent's sibling or a parent's parent, according to the sex of the connecting relative; bifurcate collateral systems do.

There is an episode of one humorous Spokane myth (versions of which occur throughout the Salish groups) reflecting the complexity of a bifurcate collateral system. It involves two young and handsome hunters who approach a village during a rainstorm. The fires are out in all the skin lodges but one, where Toad Woman sits. They attempt to enter her lodge, calling her a number of terms for female kin (father's mother, mother's mother, father's sister, mother's sister, etc.), all of which she rejects. One finally calls her his wife, whereupon she jumps upon his face and fixes herself there. He is ashamed and becomes the Moon, which explains why the moon's surface resembles toadskin.[7]

Other typical elements of both Interior and Coast Salishan culture were: (1) the first fruits rite in the spring, such as the Flathead bitterroot feast, to honor the first plant gathered and assure the orderly fruition of other plants gathered thereafter; or the Tillamook first salmon feast, with ritual return of the bones to the river or to the fire to insure the future runs of salmon; (2) guardian spirit quest at puberty; (3) shamanism (e.g., healing, bewitching, and divining); (4) expert basketry (especially famous were the Thompson); (5) stick game gambling, wherein one could show the strength of one's spirit power to "hide" the gambling bones or "see" an opponent's bones; and (6) importance of the sweathouse for spiritual health (described by one Pend d'Oreille elder as the "church" of his people). The smokehouse was the Coast Salish analogue to the sweathouse of the Interior.

Imperiled Status of Salishan Languages
Many Salishan languages have no longer been spoken as a means of daily communication for many years (Nooksack, Pentlatch, Tillamook, and Twana). Many languages no longer have any fluent speakers. Most are nearly in that condition. All are at serious risk of vanishing by the middle of this century, despite often valiant efforts to perpetuate them. In fact, it is quite difficult to determine just how many speakers of Salishan languages there are, even

assuming people can agree on what "speaker" means. Kinkade (1992:362) provided rough estimates of the number of speakers of Salishan languages, based on the best estimates of people in a position to know. Sadly, some of those numbers may be unrealistically optimistic. For instance, Kinkade estimated eight hundred speakers of Kalispel-Flathead in 1977. In 2006 there probably were fewer than twenty *fluent* speakers of Kalispel-Flathead. Similarly, Kinkade also reported twenty or fewer fluent speakers of Klallam in 1990; today, that number probably is closer to none.

There are commendable attempts by many Salishan groups to recover or revive languages no longer spoken as a first language. Some groups are attempting to create a new generation of speakers through immersion programs, language classes in the local schools, and sometimes as extracurricular activities drawing on the whole community as participants. Survival will be difficult, however, especially for fledgling language programs in communities under siege by poverty and still living with the legacy of broken treaties and failed government policies. Perhaps best equipped for survival well into the next century are the Salishan groups that have developed a working relationship and mutual respect between Native speakers and Native and non-Native linguists. The editors, having spent considerable time on such projects, are encouraged by the valiant efforts of many groups to recover or perpetuate their languages.

The remaining speakers of Salishan languages almost invariably are elderly, especially on the Coast. Almost without exception, they are bilingual in English, if not living lives dominated by English. For most, using their Native language is a special, even unusual, event isolated from a natural speech community. Indeed, for some it is the linguist with microphone and tape recorder who prompts use of the language. Unfortunately, Salishan languages largely have devolved into something akin to museum artifacts— objects for preservation, not perpetuation—whose linguistic destiny often falls to an "outsider" as caretaker. Speech acts, including the performance of myths (except in English), have become anthropological events, not natural communicative ones.

That reality helps to explain certain selections in this book. Most of the traditional stories were told, written, or recorded on sound equipment, in the original language and then translated into English. This explains the large number of linguists among the authors in this volume. Some selections were originally conceived in English, however, notably the contributions by two Native poets. Their origin in English reflects the loss of the Native medium, though the poets retain their Native American character and viewpoint, and the poems are authentic contemporary examples of Native American culture.

When possible, the name of the person telling the story has been included here. In some cases of stories told many years ago, when the language was still used actively, the person writing down the story did not give the name of the storyteller. This may have been because the story was widely known and was told and retold by several people, because the teller did not want to be publicly identified, or it may have been simple neglect. We have no way of knowing. So far as we know, none of those storytellers claimed "possession" or "family rights" to these stories. The widespread repetition of major motifs in most of these tales shows the significance of borrowing and transmission from one group to another, so that actual "ownership" of any of these stories is questionable.

Most of the storytellers working with linguists within the past thirty years or more have felt a responsibility for saving their language and their stories for posterity, at a time when most tribal groups had no sure means of safe preservation. Martha Charles John, a Klallam woman who worked extensively with Laurence C. and M. Terry Thompson, was extremely happy that, through her, the Klallam language would be preserved for "young Klallams a hundred years from now."

Aloysius Charles, a Lummi chief who worked with the Thompsons, William Seaburg, and Elizabeth Bowman (Western Washington State University), was extremely anxious to preserve the locations of the traditional fishing grounds of the Lummi. He had drawn a map of specific areas in the ocean, with their names and descriptions of how the Lummi could ride the tide and ocean currents out to those specific places and then ride back in again.

Annie York, a Lower Thompson woman who worked with the Thompsons, Egesdal, and Andrea Laforet, among others, was most anxious that her language not disappear. She was an expert with the tape recorder, and she insisted on recording stories whenever she remembered one, sometimes recording the same story or song several times when additional bits were recalled.

Hilda Austin, a Central Thompson woman from Lytton, British Columbia, shared her stories with Egesdal and Laforet so that her grandchildren would know them.

All of these elders were very pleased that this information was being preserved in the archives at the University of Washington, where it would always be available to their people. These are persons known to us, and we have heard similar stories from many of the authors in this volume.

Writing Salishan Languages

Most Salishanists and literate speakers use a special alphabet to write the languages; it is an Americanist adaptation of the International Phonetic Alphabet. Some linguists and some Native groups use so-called practical alphabets. In the following selections, some authors use such practical alphabets. Where possible, we have attempted to translate these alternate alphabets into the Americanist orthography. Each language may have particular characteristics of its own that require writing it somewhat differently from other languages. If symbols for writing each language are chosen from a common set, it is easier for others to understand them. Native Americans from different language backgrounds will have easier access to one anothers' materials. This is sometimes, however, a political decision.

A more technical examination of some of the characteristics of Salishan languages follows this Introduction.

Mythographic Presentation and Features of Narration

The authors use differing means to put the oral stories on the written page. Some use an ethnopoetic approach (following principally Hymes 1981); they use a verse format, divided into acts, scenes, and so on, to capture something of the performative structure of the oral literature. Other authors use a more familiar prose format. Still other authors use a format to capture something about the performance itself, highlighting characters' lines, to draw attention to the playlike nature of the story, with the raconteur playing narrator and all of the parts. The quality of the oral material generously allows such richness and difference in written interpretation.

Melville Jacobs's (1959) revolutionary study of Clackamas Chinook (Oregon) oral literature sensitized Amerindianists to the notion that Native American oral literature could best be understood as performed art. It was to be seen as something more of the stage than for a book. "Folklorists have tended to treat oral literatures of non-Western peoples as if their subject matter were analogous to novels, short stories, or poetry. I believe that stress upon Chinook literature as a kind of theatre does better justice to its content, designs, and functions. Therefore emphases are upon actors, acts, scenes, epilogues, and the like, rather than on plots, motifs, and episodes" (M. Jacobs 1959:7). For readers used to Western (Euro-American) literature, adjusting to that cultural paradigm shift is crucial to understanding and then appreciating the selections in this book. Otherwise, the Western reader may find many stories seemingly lacking, sparingly detailed, or perhaps almost artfully unadorned.

Jacobs also introduced the notion that Northwest Amerindian narratives could be described as "terse, staccato, or rapid moving," and not overly embellished with narrative description. In what he termed "tersely delineated" narratives, narration lines compress expressions of content and are limited to giving only a succinct description of setting, movement in time or space, and characters. Any important feelings or ideas concerning the dramatis personae are conveyed through the mouths of the actors. Jacobs (1960:x) wrote: "A recitalist never once verbalized a motivation, feeling, or mood of the actors of a myth or tale . . . the succinct recitation of actors' deeds and discourse alone revealed sentiments meant to be expressed and the response meant to be elicited." Jacobs's description of such tersely delineated texts fits Salishan oral literature well, but perhaps his comment is not entirely correct. He is largely correct if "verbalization" is understood as commentary by the narrator apart from speech by characters. But nonquoted accounts of what actors felt do occur. Most—but not all—are handled in characters' speech and thought (silent speech).

Jacobs thus provides readers with an important insight for understanding these stories: Characters' lines have greater relevancy than narration lines in the "performance" of a narrative. The reader should look to characters' lines to carry the story. They bear the performative load of the myth. Essential elements of the plot are carried in the characters' quoted speech. Narration lines, by contrast, ordinarily set the background for the characters' lines, offering interstitial descriptions of place, person, or passage of time.

Characters' quoted speech (and their thoughts as silent speech), play a critical role in Salishan traditional narratives. Indeed, the use of direct quoted speech casts the narrative as traditional in style and content. One component of that speech is abnormal, unusual, or stylistic ways of talking by characters. Egesdal (1992) discussed the stylized speech of characters in Thompson River Salish, also referring to material from other Salishan languages and beyond. In Lushootseed (which lost nasal consonants historically), Raven uses nasals and nasalizes vowels; that sort of nasalization characterizes Raven exclusively (Hess 1982:93). In Lushootseed, Rotten Log palatalizes consonants (*s* becomes *š*), and it sometimes changes *ł* to *p* (Hess 1982:90, 94). In Thompson River Salish, Coyote has a special suffix $=\acute{o}l\acute{k}$ added to certain of his words, which marks such speech as his alone. Thompson

River Salish Grizzly Woman has a peculiar lateral and garbled quality to her speech.[8] Such abnormal bear speech suggests comparisons with the phenomenon covered in Hymes (1979), where he discusses how to talk like a bear in (non-Salishan) Takelma. Thompson River Salish Meadowlark sings her speech to the same melody throughout narratives, again, uniquely her own. Similar examples of affected speech are numerous.

Another salient feature of Salishan narrative is "pattern number." Pattern number is that culturally "right" number into which persons or things are grouped or occurrences of events "naturally" fall. Pattern number influences both the content and style of Salishan narratives. Examples offer the best explanation. In Flathead or Thompson River Salish, for instance, things or events are patterned into sets or cycles of four. The Flathead culture hero Coyote has four sons. In Thompson River Salish, when Coyote's son descends from the Skyworld, he stops four times, hitting four barriers. When Coyote encounters (and abuses) maidens during his journeys, there are four of them (usually sisters). If the story of Goldilocks were adapted into Northern Interior Salish, one could expect her to confront four Bears; and she would have four bowls of porridge to try, four chairs to sit in, four beds to test, and some fourth activity to perform four times.

The concept of pattern number extends beyond Salishan narrative. Indeed, pattern number is a natural extension from Salishan culture more generally into the content and style of its oral literature. In Salishan languages where four is the pattern number, it is considered special in terms of how the world and life within it are organized. There are four directions, four seasons, four principal times of day, four primary elements (earth, air/wind, water, and fire), four kinds of animals (classified according to their locomotion: swimming, flying, crawling, and walking), four stages of a man's life, and so on.

Pattern number also varies across Salishan languages, and even within dialects of the same language. In Northern Lushootseed, the pattern number is four; in Southern Lushootseed, the pattern number is five (Hess 1995:140). In Columbian, the pattern number is five, and Coyote expectedly has five sons. In neighboring Spokane, where the pattern number is four, Coyote has four sons. In Upper Chehalis, where the pattern number is five, there are five Cougar brothers, five daughters of fire, and five baskets of water are given to Bluejay to put out the fires on the five prairies he must cross (in this volume; also see Kinkade 1994:41). In Tillamook, pattern number seems to add another twist based on the gender of the character involved: four for females and five for males (see the South Wind story in this volume).

Pattern number affects the structure of the narratives. Events occur the requisite or expected number of times, which shapes the narrative. Some Salishanists believe that pattern number plays an even greater role in determining the organization of verses, stanzas, scenes, or acts within a narrative (e.g., Kinkade 1983a; 1984; 1987). The narrative structure is marked by linguistic cues: particles, segment lengthening, and morpho-syntax. For those ethnopoetic presenters of Salishan narrative, organization of the narrative is crucial to their interpretation. For them, narratives are measured verse and should be represented on the page as such.

Other Salishanists (e.g., Mattina 1987) have questioned whether such a formalized "ethnopoetic" structure exists. "Not all of North American Indian narrative is verse, any more than all of English literature is dialogue" (Mattina 1987:137). Mattina concludes by arguing against the then pervasive (ethnopoetic) mythographic approaches of Dell Hymes and Dennis Tedlock: "Let the texts come forth, in whatever typographic arrangement the editor deems appropriate. Given an understanding of the tradition and context of the text, I expect that the worthiest texts will require the least architectural support" (Mattina 1987:143).

Without entering that interesting debate over mythographic presentation, it has been our general experience that Thompson River Salish raconteurs rarely performed a narrative the same way every time. Instead, they varied the content or themes depending on the performative context—the audience and the occasion. A raconteur could expand or abridge certain episodes to fit the particular purpose of the performance or interests of the audience. That variance perhaps was most prominent when a narrative was told first to a non-Native linguist and then later to a Native speaking audience. (Or when the same narrative was told to the same linguist before and after he or she gained some knowledge of the language and culture of the raconteur.)

A version of a story told to a non-Native linguist often would contain explanatory cultural background, which knowledge the raconteur normally could (and would) presuppose the audience to possess. Traditionally, Tillamook listeners "culturally" knew that snails had keen eyesight in the Myth Age. Without that fact being noted during the narrative, they understood that was why, when Bald Eagle lost his eyes, he chose Snail's eyes as substitutes. Traditionally, every Thompson River Salish person knew that Mole was Coyote's wife, she worked very hard, and she was a polyglot. Similarly, Flathead listeners would know that Fox was Coyote's older, wiser, brother—his "partner" in Indian English—and they could expect Fox sometime in the narrative to bring Coyote back to life after Coyote once again fell victim to his own foolishness. They also knew Fox was a powerful medicine man, and they were familiar with the shamanistic practices Fox would use to revive Coyote. Those respective Salishan audiences would have heard such facts since childhood; they did not need to be reminded of the background. In some narratives, however, those facts might be important, so the raconteur might include them as cues or background information.

For instance, in the story of Nx̌íksmtm in this volume, Coyote disguises himself as a medicine man from the Plains, and he pretends to speak a foreign language. Only Mole can understand him. The raconteur explains that she spoke many languages, because she had husbands from many lands. That fact explains why the People consulted Mole, when all others failed to communicate with Coyote, and why Mole could interpret his feigned gibberish.

Humor is another salient feature of Salishan narratives. Indeed, quite often humor is their quintessential feature. The focal point of such humor often is the main character of the narratives, such as Coyote in Interior Salish, Mink or Raven in the Coast Salish, and South Wind in Tillamook. When such leading characters play the role of tricksters or transformers, they often are the victims of their own mischief or foolishness. Coyote on one hand is responsible for imposing order on the world to make it ready for humankind, while on the other hand he seems to run afoul of or break all of the culture's mores. In the same narrative, he can vacillate between trickster and dupe, punishing others for their wrongdoing but also being punished for his own follies. Western readers might find that combined duality of trickster-dupe unfamiliar, if not unsettling. To the Salishan audience, such duality and antics make perfect sense.

Melville Jacobs (1959) pointed out that Coyote's ribald behavior and breaking of cultural taboos had a healthy effect on the Native audience. It acted as a psychological safety valve. For Jacobs, Native American oral literature reflected something deeper about a culture than its everyday practices and concerns. He believed that as a "fantasy screen," oral literature could provide an outlet for the release of fears, anxieties, and tensions brought about by certain strained relationships in tribal culture. Acting as a psychological safety valve, then, oral literature safeguarded against the consequences of emotional turbulence and insured personal and cultural stability. Moreover, in the humorous context of traditional narrative, Coyote actually was reinforcing the very rules of Salishan society he was breaking in the narratives.

Genres of Salishan Oral Literature

Salishan narratives generally are of two types: traditional stories and ordinary or historic stories (often akin to news or historical accounts).[9] Languages generally have two different words for those types; for example, Thompson River Salish *sptékʷɬ* "traditional story" and *spíləx̣m* "news, information, story"; Flathead *sqʷllú(m̓t)* "traditional (or Coyote) story" and *sm̓iʔm̓íy'* "news, story"; Klallam *sx̣ʷiʔám̓* "traditional story," and *syə́cəm* "news, information." Most of the narratives in this collection are of the traditional type.

What we have written elsewhere concerning Thompson River Salish traditional narrative (*sptékʷɬ*) applies more broadly to Salishan traditional narrative: "*Sptékʷɬ* perhaps is not so much a time or place as a dimension, another reality, in which elements of the landscape—fauna, flora, and even natural phenomena, such as Thunder and Ice—are anthropomorphized. As 'real people' of the *sptékʷɬ* stage, legendary dramatis personae act out the quintessence of their personalities, wearing different skins on transformed shapes. Coyote always was Coyote; he just looks more doglike in the here and now" (Egesdal and M. T. Thompson 1994:314–15).

Traditional narratives are set in the Myth Age, before things became like the modern era. A time before the world had been made ready (or perhaps more accurately, put in order) for humankind, and a place where animals were people (and people were animals). But this was no fairyland or fantasy world. There were benevolent grandmothers and beautiful women, to be sure, but there also were kidnapping basket ogresses and maidens with toothed vaginas. It was different—indeed, remarkably odd—but nonetheless real. Hilda Austin, a Thompson River Salish elder, rejected the translation of "myth" for *sptékʷɬ*, because, she explained, "myth means it is not true." For her and numerous other elders with whom we have worked, the events occurring in the *sptékʷɬ* "are true." (Hilda Austin therefore preferred the term "legend" for *sptékʷɬ*.)

That insight marks an important distinction between Salishan traditional narrative and Western literature. Salishan traditional stories are not considered to be imaginative fiction, nor are they appreciated as such. A traditional narrative is not intended to be the product of an individual's creativity. The raconteur (who in more recent times has most frequently been a raconteuse) instead is relating a legendary event, the details of which have been handed down across many generations. Traditional narratives belong to the group, as a sort of collectively held history of the events and beings of the Myth Age.

The raconteur does not own it any more than he can own the language he shares with his audience. Neither the narrative nor the language is a product of individual invention. Creative expression does play a role, however, in how the raconteur interprets the "script" handed down from generation to generation and possessed collectively.

The notion that traditional stories are not the product of creative invention perhaps has a broader significance for Salishan culture, particularly concerning song. In the West, musicians compose songs; it is a product of their creative genius (classically, at most aided by some muse). Western music derives from an internal voice. For the Salish, however, songs are the product of discovery or revelation vis-à-vis creation. As one elder explained, all the songs were created at the beginning of the world, and they must be discovered by the singer or revealed to him or her. That discovery or revelation is facilitated by animals (or one's other guardian spirit). Much of Salishan music, then, apparently derives from an external calling. The intimate magical nature of Salish song often stopped outsiders from gathering even a modest amount of song. One does not share secrets with strangers, especially powerful ones.

Songs connected people on this side of the world with the other side—the spirit side—typically to effect some change on this side. Songs come from the other side.

Characters in many stories sing songs, reflecting the importance of songs in Salish culture. As in Salish life, songs in Salish stories have a variety of functions. In this volume in Amoss's "Beaver and Mouse," for instance, Beaver's spirit song is used to punish Mouse with flooding after he fails in his attempt to woo her. Short, repetitive, and very effective. In Elmendorf's "Star Husband," an old lady, feeling sorry for letting someone kidnap a baby, sings a sad mourning song. When the baby later is found, the old lady helps to celebrate with a happy song. Kinkade's "Kidnapping the Moon" has a version of the same story where an old woman sings a lullaby.

When South Wind or Coyote's Son goes to the Skyworld, these are not Salishan analogues to Jack and the Beanstalk. Instead, it is much more like the recounting of the successful Apollo mission to the moon. Indeed, following Neil Armstrong's "giant leap for mankind," Thompson River Salish elders commented that Coyote's Son (Nx̣íksmtm) already had accomplished a similar lunar trip some time ago. Coyote's Son had been there and done that, in the Myth Age.[10] And because the stories are considered to be true, raconteurs are especially sensitive about "getting them right." Some even will decline to tell traditional narratives because they cannot remember certain parts or details. Others considered it bad luck to tell only part of a traditional narrative. Interestingly, the advent of tape-recording traditional narratives has led to situations in which raconteurs now will "edit" a performance, to add corrective comments or make improvements for the final written text (even in some cases in which the raconteurs are illiterate).

Reverence for Traditional Narrative

There was a reverence for traditional narratives. As one Flathead elder, Joe Cullooyah, shared, "Everything you need to know about life is in the Coyote stories—if you just listen carefully." That reverence was reflected in several ways.[11] It still can be seen clearly with certain tribes, where even today traditional stories will not be told "out of season." Winter is that special season, defined (at least by some) as the time from the first snowfall (in late autumn) to the first thunderstorm (in early spring). Within at least Interior Salishan, telling traditional stories out of season was thought to bring cold weather. Thompson River Salish elder Louis Phillips explained that if one told traditional stories in the summer, Coyote would pull the foreskin on his penis back, and a mist would come out and cause cold weather. For the Flathead, telling Coyote stories in the summer risked the mauling by a grizzly bear or being attacked by snakes. Similar penalties existed for other Salishan groups. For most groups today, however, the custom of telling traditional stories only in winter is remembered but no longer followed.

The reverence the tellers have for traditional stories can be seen in a dialogue Egesdal had with a Flathead elder, Joe Cullooyah. Egesdal asked Joe (one winter) whatever happened to Coyote. Joe, accustomed to if not amused by such probing, thought about it for a while and then thoughtfully replied: "You believe that Christ is coming back some day, right? Well, Coyote is coming back some day, too." Christ and Coyote, as kindred entities. The analogical linkage of Coyote and Christ aptly reflects the reverence that Mr. Cullooyah (and his people) had for traditional narratives. From such comments one can infer that Coyote stories are more akin to the whiteman's biblical truths than to his fairy tales.

When elders speak of "the Coyote stories" or "the stories the old people used to tell," they mean a collective canon of interconnected narratives, only pieces of which remain. When raconteurs begin a Coyote story, Coyote usually is walking along somewhere. And that is how the story usually also ends. (Salishan Tricksters and Transformers were perpetual travelers.) Each narrative, therefore, is framed at both ends to connect with other adventures not told at that sitting. The same holds for other Salishan traditional narratives concerning culture heroes, transformers, tricksters, and the like. Thompson River Salish raconteurs frequently added the disclaimer in ending a traditional narrative concerning Coyote (or some other culture hero) that the preceding was only a part of a larger story, and that it was all they could remember of that greater whole. Cycles of Salishan traditional narratives might have taken several lengthy performances, or perhaps a whole winter season, to complete. Thompson River Salish and Flathead/Pend d'Oreille elders have shared childhood memories of Coyote stories that spanned several winter evenings. The Tillamook "South Wind" epic in this volume gives an idea of the geographical progression of such stories.

Importantly, a story was never THE story. There might be many versions of it, perhaps inserted into other stories as an incidental bit, or it might be told alone with embellishments from other stories. Sometimes a raconteur would give an abridgement, other times it would be greatly embellished. Variables in the context led to varied performances.

In this volume many of the themes are repeated, but with different characters, different locations, different motivations, and with more or fewer details, as the situation demands. Some of the themes become long involved stories that stand alone, while showing up only as a minor incident in some other long story.

We are pleased to have the unusual opportunity to present two samples of traditional oratory. Since this was often done on special occasions not attended by a person with a tape recorder, there are few recordings of such speeches. One such was recorded by a Thompson chief, in his native language, at the national museum in Canada early in the twentieth century specifically as a sample of oratory, and was probably from a remembered occasion. It was very short because of the limitations of sound recording equipment at that time. The other was a public speech given near the end of the twentieth century. It was given in English, because by that time there were so few speakers of the Colville language. Then there is the ubiquitous speech of Chief Seattle, which is not known to have been recorded at all, but has been quoted (in English) over the years in many versions, styled to fit many different occasions.

The Performative Context

One of the problems with a Western audience understanding, let alone appreciating, Salishan narratives is that often they are decontextualized to the point of being incomprehensible. The narratives seem terse, laconic, and spare, because much if not most presupposed cultural knowledge is missing. That leaves outsiders with a problem grasping the actual themes of the narratives. They just do not get it, because they are not culturally prepared to understand. In preparing this collection for publication, for example, we had such an experience with the Sliammon narrative from Honoré Watanabe. The narrative involves a drowning that occurs during a seal hunt. The force of the narrative was lost on us until Watanabe did additional fieldwork and added an explanation of traditional sealing practice to the introduction of that narrative.

Not all Native speakers tell traditional narratives. Nor do all those who tell traditional narratives tell them equally well. Those may seem like simplistic observations; however, such insights can be missed when the number of true speakers for any given tribe drops into the dozens or less. Sometimes inexperienced or unaware linguists expect all gray-haired Native speakers to be proficient at telling traditional narratives. Of course, that is not the case. It can be fairly said, however, that those who are culture-bearers for a tribe generally tend to be experts on a number of topics, often including traditional narratives. Annie York and Hilda Austin (Thompson River Salish elders with whom both the editors worked) were both expert herbalists and expert raconteurs. They also knew traditional songs and prayers and a wide variety of other cultural information (place names, personal names and genealogy, history, proverbs, customs, practices, fishing areas, and so on).

One setting for traditional narrative was nighttime around a winter fire, the season when nights were especially long. Another setting for the traditional narrative was bedtime stories for children. Several languages have a formulaic reply that children were supposed to say to let the raconteur know that the child still was awake (and even to urge the raconteur to continue). For instance, Thompson River Salish children were to say *ʔéy ʔéy*, or the telling of the narrative would stop. When Lushootseed narratives were told, children similarly were expected to show their attentiveness by uttering a formulaic response: *həmuʔ kayʔ həmuʔ kayʔkawič*; if they did not, they were warned they would become hunchbacked (Hess 1976:178).

Today, most traditional Salishan narratives are not told within the traditional performative context. As mentioned above, the prohibition against telling outside of winter has been lost or been weakened for most groups. The loss of the languages has reduced the potential audience. And great changes in lifestyle have undermined the opportunities and reasons for telling the stories. Domination by English, in print or on the radio, television, and film, has relegated traditional narratives to staged events, Elders' Day celebrations, or storytelling contests (most occurring during the summer). And sadly, except for such special events, all too often the non-Native linguist's microphone is the primary audience for what remains of traditional narratives.

One notable exception is Vi Taqʷšəblu Hilbert, a Lushootseed elder who became an internationally famous storyteller. She perfected a remarkably satisfying technique of smoothly interweaving Lushootseed sentences and their English translation. She introduces her performance by saying Lushootseed is such a beautiful language that she wants to share it with her audience, but she also wants them to grasp the meaning of the story so she will give them that in English. A number of others have now adopted her technique.

History of Collecting Salishan Oral Literature

Western anthropologists and linguists started collecting Salishan narratives in the late 1800s. Until relatively recently and with a few notable exceptions, almost all of the published materials were in English. The most significant early work was done by Franz Boas personally or at his urging and direction. Boas (1898a, b, c) published myths of the Bella Coola and of the Tillamook, and James Teit (1898; other dates) published material on the Thompson, Lillooet, and Shuswap. The works of those two are set forth in detail in the bibliography. Contemporaneously with Boas and Teit, Charles Hill-Tout (1899, 1900, 1904, 1911) collected Salishan materials in British Columbia (Thompson River Salish, Okanagan, Halkomelem, Squamish, Lillooet, and Seshelt), published in English and reprinted in Maud 1978.

Later, other publications in English included Erna Gunther's (1925) Klallam narratives, Thelma Adamson's (1934) narratives for certain Coast Salish tribes, and Verne Ray's (1933) Sanpoil (Colville-Okanagan) narratives.

Gladys Reichard (1947:57–212) published a comparative study of Salishan narrative, with Coeur d'Alene material, in English. Elizabeth Jacobs (1959) published a collection of Tillamook narratives in English. William Elmendorf (1961) published a collection of Twana and some other Coast Salish narratives in English. (Versions of two of those Twana narratives are included in this collection.) Snyder (1968) published a collection of Lushootseed narratives (his Southern Puget Sound Salish).

Vi Hilbert (1980, 1985) has published several collections of Lushootseed narratives in English. Bouchard and Kennedy (1977, 1979) have published Lillooet and Shuswap narratives in English. Darwin Hanna and Mamie Henry (1995) have published a collection of Nɬheʔképmx (Thompson River Salish) narratives in English. Portions of some of E. Jacobs's (1959) stories, combined with portions of some of the Edel (1931 ms.) stories, and one of Boas's stories are included in Deur and M. T. Thompson's "South Wind," in this volume.

Linguists and anthropologists have published narratives in several Native languages as papers of the annual International Conference on Salish and Neighboring Languages (e.g., Kinkade 1986; Egesdal 1991).

There have been some publications of narratives in both the Native language and in English translation. May Mandelbaum Edel (1939) published a Tillamook narrative as a short illustrative text for her Tillamook grammar, and readied a collection of Tillamook narratives for publication (Edel 1931 ms.). Gladys Reichard (1938:694–707) included a short illustrative narrative as part of her Coeur d'Alene grammar. Hans Vogt (1940:80–135) included numerous texts (in the Native language and translated) as part of his Kalispel grammar. Aert H. Kuipers published Squamish narratives (1967:219–42, 1969:19–31), and he also published narratives in Shuswap (1974:91–130). Barbara Efrat's dissertation (1969) included a narrative that is in English here. Barry Carlson (1978:3–14) published a humorous Coyote story in Spokane. Dale Kinkade (1978:15–20) published a Coyote story in Columbian in that same volume. Anthony Mattina (1985) published a long narrative in Colville (Okanagan) and English. L. C. and M. T. Thompson published a Thompson River Salish narrative with their grammar (1992).

Publication of materials, in English translation or the original, almost invariably has lagged far behind collection. Indeed, most narrative material remains in field notebooks, gathering dust on bookshelves or filling boxes in archives. Those materials await proper attention and treatment. The severe exigencies posed by the imperiled state of almost all the languages fairly and frequently has led many researchers to err on the side of gathering more material instead of working thoroughly with material already collected. Collection of narratives in the Native languages continues; however, for most Salishan languages few speakers remain, and even fewer raconteurs exist among them.

For many years there was little interest, or little time, for the Salishan people to concentrate on the preservation of their cultural and linguistic heritage. The elders were very happy to have us (as professional linguists) ask to preserve their languages for posterity. We heard complaints from elders about "lack of interest" among the younger members of their groups, and we always tried to make soothing comments about their young lives being so busy. When the younger people began to take an interest in preserving the culture and the language, linguists became very supportive, and have spent a great deal of time working with local and areal language programs. The editors have both spent many happy hours working with these languages, their speakers, and their would-be speakers.

What Melville Jacobs (1967:20) said about Pacific Northwest Indian folk lores applies at least doubly today: "Therefore, the small oral literature collections that we have remain for us something like ancient Egypt's Sphinx. That treasure is badly worn and chipped. We can no longer gather information about everything that it signified to the people who lived when it was fashioned. To be sure, we will preserve it, just as we guard Upper Paleolithic cave drawings and paintings about whose roles, when they were made, we can never learn a thing. We will remain burdened with regrets that our non-linguist forbears were not sufficiently civilized to interest themselves in the creativity and values of peoples whose communities were not included in some restricted inventory of 'great civilizations.'"

Organization of the Collection

Salish Myths and Legends: One People's Stories presents its material within twelve sections. Those sections are not intended to reflect Native topics, or to correspond to anything akin to Native genres. As stated above, Salishan narrative is bifurcated largely into the traditional and the ordinary or historical. And the material herein includes more than narrative. Instead, we have tried to bring together similar types of oral literature and other material for the reader's enjoyment. For instance, sometimes the type of leading actor brings narratives under a single heading (e.g., Basket Ogress or Tricksters). In other cases, headings are intended to reflect something of the content of the narrative or overall structure of the narrative (e.g., epics, journeys to other worlds, why things are the way they are, when the animals were people). Still other headings bring together nontraditional narratives and other material, such as historical events, viewing the whiteman as "other," real life stories, songs, and oratory. The sections are undoubtedly artificial. Many stories represent several of these categories, but they serve to present in some orderly fashion a manuscript that was originally several hundred pages of unorganized material.

Some might question whether *Salish Myths and Legends: One People's Stories* fairly represents what is actually out there in terms of Salishan traditional literature. And that would be a very good question, deserving a good answer. To begin, one must realize that most significant folkloric and ethnographic work with Salishan peoples (and in the Northwest more broadly) since the 1960s has been done by (anthropological) linguists. Many were students of the Salishan troika of Aert H. Kuipers, Laurence C. Thompson, and M. Dale Kinkade. Not surprisingly, they and their students account for much of the material in *Salish Myths and Legends: One People's Stories*.

Those interested in Salishan linguistics and ethnography form a small and tight community—Native and non-Native. When we began this project, it was relatively easy to contact all persons, Native and non-Native alike, who had shown an interest in Salishan oral literature over the last thirty years. Indeed, it was like old home week. As good editors must do, we asked, asked again, and then charmed, coaxed, prodded, searched for current addresses, and otherwise did whatever was necessary to obtain the best and widest representation of Salishan traditional literature available.

We do not attempt to discuss contemporary Salishan literature, written in English. Several Salishan writers are or have been prominent in the renaissance of Native American writing. Sherman Alexie (Spokane/Coeur d'Alene), Duane Niatum (Klallam), D'Arcy McNickle (Flathead), and Mourning Dove [Christine Quintasket] (Colville-Okanagan) are several examples. We list some of their works in the bibliography.[12]

We believe we have accomplished what we set out to do. Every Salishan language but one (Lower Chehalis) is represented in some fashion (twenty-two of the twenty-three languages), and some language groups have selections from more than one dialect represented. That feat is noteworthy for two reasons: first, most Salishan languages are no longer spoken actively; second, delicate political issues often arise concerning just who holds intellectual property rights to traditional Native literatures—the tribe or the individual raconteur. When traditional or non-Native notions of individual ownership or lack of ownership for narratives collide with current Native notions of collective ownership, the conflict can stifle attempts to obtain permission to publish narratives.

In sum, we are confident that this collection fairly reflects what is currently available in terms of Salishan traditional literature. That having been said, much more traditional Salishan material of this type awaits publication. We hope that *Salish Myths and Legends: One People's Stories* will stimulate reader demand and publisher interest toward salvaging it from notebooks and archives and putting it into print.

Notes

1. See L. C. Thompson 1979:693; Kinkade 1992:360. We acknowledge that there are various spellings of certain tribal names, and that certain groups use Native terms (often not widely known). We use the traditional English names for many of the Salishan tribes or groups, however, in addition to the traditional Salishan names, because these English names will be familiar to the widest readership.

2. See L. C. Thompson 1979:694; Kinkade 1991 1992:408, using comparative linguistic data, investigates the Proto-Salish homeland, which he places as south of the lower part of the Fraser River.

3. L. C. Thompson, personal communication.

4. Egesdal and M. T. Thompson 1998.

5. Laforet and York (1981) provide a description and sketch of the Thompson subterranean pithouse.

6. Collateral ascendants are distinguished from lineal ones, and from one another; e.g., mother, mother's sister, and father's sister all have different terms.

7. See Elmendorf 1961:373. In other stories, Frog is Moon's sister or wife and is seen as Frog herself on his face.

8. Egesdal 1992:10n3.

9. M. Dale Kinkade (1994) provides an excellent discussion of the Native literature of the Northwest Coast and Plateau. Dell Hymes (1989) discusses the mythology of the Northwest Coast culture area. Ralph Maud (1982) discusses the history of myth collecting in British Columbia.

10. For a complete rendition of one version of this story, see Thompson and Thompson 1992:199–227.

11. Upper Chehalis audiences could not ask for food during a narrative performance; the performance would end, if that rule was broken (Kinkade 1994:39–40).

12. More generally, there are a number of books that document the history and development of Native American literature. The reader might wish to consult Fleck (1993), K. Kroeber (1981), Krupat (1993), Lerner (1990), Lincoln (1983), Riley (1993), Ruoff (1990a, b), Swann (1983, 1992, 1994, 1996, 2004), Swann and Krupat (1987), Vizenor (1993), and Wiget (1985, 1994).

Language Characteristics

Steven M. Egesdal

Salishan languages have a number of features that make them unusually complex and distinctive.[1] One of the most striking features of Salishan languages is their elaborate consonant inventories.[2] The following phoneme inventory from Flathead, or *Séliš* (from which the entire language family ultimately derives its name), is fairly representative of Interior Salish:[3]

ʔ a c č č̓ e h i (k k̓) kʷk̓ʷ l l̓ ƛ̓ ɬ λ̓ m m̓ n n̓ o p p̓ q qʷ q̓ q̓ʷ s š t t̓ u w w̓ xʷ x̣ x̣ʷ y y̓ ʕ ʕ̓ ʕʷ ʕ̓ʷ

Contrasting with a typically elaborate consonant system is a usually small inventory of vowels. Proto-Salish may be reconstructed with four vowels: *i, *u, *a, *ə.

Salishan languages have a tendency to delete unstressed underlying vowels, often resulting in long and complex consonant clusters. A good example of this is Bella Coola. There is a story about the famous German anthropologist Franz Boas, early in his research in North America, sending an article about this extreme example to a German journal. The article was dismissed as fiction.

Salishan includes certain "oddities," such as languages with no Native labials (e.g., Klallam and Northern Straits) and languages without nasals (e.g., Lushootseed and Twana).

Salishan languages, like many Amerindian languages, are polysynthetic. They typically show morphologically complex word-forms, which contain a large number of affixes (generally suffixes as opposed to prefixes) to express syntactic relationships and meanings. A Salishan full word contains a root-stem (indicated by a preceding slanted bar [/]), which may be expanded by a variety of grammatical affixes (indicated by a hyphen following the affix for prefixes; preceding the affix for suffixes). Grammatical affixes may show transitivity (relation between agent and patient), voice, aspect, number, degree of control over the action, and other grammatical categories. A number of the grammatical affixes are reduplicative, indicated by a raised

Table 2. Pronunciation Guide

The following symbols from Salishan languages may be found in the selections. The pronunciation of those symbols can be made as follows.

ʷ   following a consonant (k^w, q^w, x^w, x̣ʷ, ʕʷ) marks lip rounding that accompanies the consonant.

ʾ   following or accompanying an obstruent (for example, *p'*, *t'*, *c̓*, *č'*, *k'*, *q̇*, *λ̓*, *t'*) marks an "ejective consonant," which is immediately followed by a popping sound made by the forceful expulsion of air at the point of closure (see note 2 below). Following a resonant (*l*, *l'*, *ẏ*, *ẇ*) or a nasal (*ṁ*, *ṅ*, *ŋ*), this symbol signals an accompanying glottalic constriction (which can precede or interrupt).[1]

á   acute accented vowel (also *é*, *ɜ́*, *í*, *ó*, *ú*) marks the most prominent (or stressed) vowel of a word.

ʔ   (called "glottal stop") is similar to the catch in the middle of "unh-unh" (meaning "no"), or "oh-oh!"

a   as in English "father."

c   is similar to the *ts* sound in English "bats."

c̓   is like *c*, described above, with a sharp popping sound. One makes the popping sound by preparing to make a ʔ (glottal stop), holding it, and then saying *c* simultaneously with the release of the glottal stop. (In linguistic jargon, *c̓* is a glottalic ejective, articulated with the glottalic airstream mechanism.)[2]

č   is like the *ch* in English "church."

č'   is like *č* but with the sharp popping sound described for *c̓*.

e   as in English "bet."

ə   (called a "schwa") represents a central vowel sound like that of the last vowel (the *u*) in English "halibut."

h   as in English "hit."

i   as in English "beet."

k   as in English "kick."

k'   is like *k* in English, but has the same popping sound described for *c̓*.

k^w is like the *qu* in English "quick."

k̓ʷ   is like *kw*, but has the same popping sound (i.e., glottalic ejective) described for *c̓*.

l   as in English "let."

l'	is like the *l* in English, with a catch in it.
ł	is like the English *l* but very breathy. One should whisper "please," holding the *l*. As the air is released past the sides of the tongue, the sound should then approximate ł.
λ̓	is similar to English *kl*,[3] with the same popping sound i.e., glottal-ic ejective) described for *c̓*. One should place the tongue to say *t*, keeping it closed against the roof of the mouth. The air should then be released quickly past the sides of the tongue, with a pop.
m	as in English "mom."
m̓	as in the English *m* with a catch in it.
n	as in English "nut."
n̓	as in the English *n* with a catch in it.
ŋ	is the nasal sound *ng* as in English "sing."
o	is like the *ou* in English "bought."
p	as in English "pop."
p̓	as in English *p* with the same popping sound described for *c̓*.
q	represents a *k*-like consonant produced with the back of the tongue against the uvular region (farther back in the mouth than the *k*).
q̓	is like *k'*, except produced with the back of the tongue farther back in the mouth.
qʷ	is like *q*, produced with the lips rounded.
q̓ʷ	is like *k̓ʷ*, except produced with the back of the tongue farther back in the mouth.
s	as in English "sop."
š	is like the *sh* sound in English "she."
t	as in English "tot."
t'	is like the *t*, with same the popping sound described for *c̓*.
θ	is like the *th* sound in English "think."
u	as in the *oo* in English "boot."
w	as in English "wow."
w̓	is like *w*, with a catch in it.
x	is like the sound of the *ch* in German "ich," a prevelar, but not "ish" or "itch."
xʷ	is like *x*, except produced with the lips rounded.
x̣	is pronounced farther back in the mouth than *x*, like the *ch* in German Bach.
x̣ʷ	is like *x̣*, except produced with the lips rounded.
ʕ	represents a voiced pharyngeal resonant, which shows varying de-

grees of friction or even trilling, across Interior Salish languages. One makes the sound by constricting or narrowing the pharynx and uttering an "*a*" sound (described above).

ʕ'   is like ʕ, by with a type of constriction or catch.

ʕʷ   is like ʕ, with rounded lips. One makes this sound by constricting or narrowing the pharynx and uttering an "o" sound (described above).

ʕ'ʷ   is like ʕʷ, with a type of constriction or catch.

Notes

1. Some consonants combine more than one diacritical mark: *ƙʷ, q̓ʷ, x̣ʷ, ʕ'ʷ*.

2. For the nonlinguist: Imagine that you have a watermelon seed between your lips. Imagine also that you are still six years old and can get away with this. Now, while holding the breath, spit the seed out by contracting the muscles of the throat. That is the glottalic airstream mechanism. Now, while holding your breath, from the *c* (the *ts* as in *bats*) and, still holding the breath, eject the *c* just like you did the melon seed. *Voila!* You have just pronounced č̓.

3. The cluster *kl* is used here to describe this sound, because the cluster *tl* does not occur in English; *tl* would be more accurate phonetically.

bullet (•), "copying" all or part of a root (or other part of a word) and affixing it as a prefix, suffix, or infix. Transitive words may contain pretransitive suffixes (e.g., relational, ditransitive, noncontrol), with the obligatory transitive marking, followed by patient and agent marking (in that order). For example, Thompson /zo ʕʷ-mí-x-cm-s "he took care of it for me" (underlying ///zo ʕʷ-mí-xi-t-sem-es// : /strong-RELATIONAL-INDIRECTIVE-TRANSITIVE-1S. PATIENT-3AGENT). In that word, -*t* and -*sem* coalesce and are reduced to a single "portmanteau" morpheme -*cm*.

A Salishan word also may contain one or more lexical suffixes, indicated by a preceding double hyphen (=). An example is Thompson *čuʼ/čúm=ks-e-s* "she is sucking on its paw" (underlying //čuʼ/čúm=ekst-n-t-ø-es// : AFFEC-TIVE•/suck=hand-DIRECT-TRANSITIVE-3PATIENT-3AGENT). Lexical suffixes are unique to the aboriginal Northwest (found only in the Salishan, Chemakuan, Wakashan families). They are suffixes that carry specific lexical meaning, usually with no directly apparent phonological relationship with their correlate independent word (e.g., Flathead /*čéls* "hand," =*ečst* "hand"; /*ɫw̓=éčst* "he got his hand pricked"). A Salishan language may have more than a hundred lexical suffixes, covering a wide semantic range, such as body parts (e.g., head, foot, mouth), elements of nature (e.g., sky, fire, star, water), various artifacts (e.g., handle, rope, horse, weapon), and some concepts often by metaphorical extension of a lexical suffix's more basic meaning often with locative prefixes (e.g., Flathead *=éple?* "handle" extended to "permission," or Flathead *=úlexʷ* "ground" extended to "bread").

Salishan languages also show a wide variety of infixes, affixes inserted within the body of an element to which it is added (e.g., Flathead /kʷúp-i-s "(s)he pushed it" versus /kʷú[?]p-i-s "they pushed it" [or "(s)he pushed them]"; Thompson *s/xénx* "rock" versus *s/xé[•x]n̓x* "small rock"). Infixes can impart notions of aspect (e.g., inchoative, repetitive, out-of-control), size (e.g., diminutive, proportional), or quantity and quality (e.g., distributive, augmentative, characteristic, affective).

Stress is distinctive in Salishan, except for Comox and Bella Coola. Interior Salishan languages generally show a complex system of stress assignment, involving strong and weak roots (i.e., stress-salient versus stress-aversive), and strong, weak, and variable stress suffixes (lexical and grammatical). That hierarchy likely reflects the earlier pattern for the language family, which languages outside the Interior have not preserved as systematically. After assignment of stress to the word's prominent vowel, according to that stress hierarchy, the other unstressed vowels usually are deleted (or reduced to schwa), consonants often are deleted or adjusted, and some resonants are vocalized (e.g., *y* to *i*, *w* to *u*, *ʕ* to a, *ʕʷ* to *ɔ*; and *n* to *ɛ* [Thompson], *n* and *m* to *ɛ* [Shuswap, eastern dialect], *n* and historically *m* to *i* [Flathead]). Compare two morphologically parallel forms from Flathead, one with a strong root and the other with a weak root: /kʷú[?]p-i-s "they pushed it" ///kʷú[?]p-n-t-ø-es// /push[PLURAL]-DIRECT-TRANSITIVE-3PATIENT-3AGENT; /šl-n-t-é[?] s, "they chopped it" // /šil-n-t-ø-é[?]s// /chop-DIRECT-TRANSITIVE-3PATIENT-3AGENT[PLURAL]. Those Flathead examples also show that placement of the plural infix [?] is determined by stress: it is inserted directly after the word's stressed vowel.

A Salishan full word, then, can incorporate numerous semantically discrete ideas; and elaborate, regularly conditioned sound (i.e., morphophonemic) changes often obscure the underlying shape of the word's root and affixes, as exemplified above. The combination of those word elements (or morphemes) in a single word often is equivalent to a sentence in English.

Salishan grammar is likewise complex. Words are divided into two general types, full words that can appear as predicates, and particles that cannot. Particles supply aspectual, modal, temporal, and existential nuances and deictic and discourse orientation for full words (and their expanded clauses). Salishan languages have been characterized as lacking meaningful distinctions among nouns, verbs, and adjectives.[4] The familiar, discrete opposition of those word-class types seems alien for Salishan, where they are, at most, only marginally developed. Clauses usually begin with a full word (or predicate) the only obligatory element in a Salishan sentence. That predicate can be expanded by optional lexical arguments, which elaborate references implicit in the predicate or provide additional information. Those lexical arguments themselves may be predicates, inflected and modified by particles as the main predicate. Expansion of the main predicate by more than one lexical argument per clause is uncommon.

The following are the first lines of a well-known Thompson River Salish legend, "Nx̌ík'smtm," fully presented in English elsewhere in this volume. They fairly exemplify the orthographical look and grammatical structure of a Salishan language. The first line is in Thompson, unanalyzed. The second line is analyzed, using the following devices: Stems, the surface representation of roots, are preceded by a slash (/). Prefixes are followed by a hyphen (-), unless they precede a stem directly. A reduplicative prefix, however, is followed by a bullet (•). Two kinds of suffixes are distinguished: grammatical suffixes are preceded by a hyphen (-), or a bullet (•) for reduplicating suffixes, while lexical suffixes are preceded by a double hyphen (=). Infixes are enclosed in square brackets [...], and reduplicating infixes also have a bullet [•...] or [...•] connecting them with the portion of the stem that is copied. Pauses are indicated by the pound/numerical sign (#). The third line is a morpheme-by-morpheme translation,[5] and the fourth line is a translation into English.

   1   húm'eł. xʷuy' ptékʷłetimn ł snk'y'ép.
            húm'eł # xʷuy' /ptékʷ ł -e-t-im-n ł s-n/k'y'ép #
            ALL.RIGHT FUT /legend-DRV-TR-2POBJ-1SSBJ EP NOM-LCL/Coyote
            All right. I'm going to tell you a legend about Coyote.

   2   Ɂe xeɁ ł snk'y'ép tək sptékʷł.
            /Ɂe xeɁ ł s-n/k'y'ép tək s/ptékʷł #
            /INT NEARBY EP NOM-LCL/coyote DSCR NOM/legend
            This is the Coyote legend.

   3   Ɂe xeɁ ł nx̌ík'smtm tək sptékʷł.
            /Ɂe xeɁ ł n/x̌ík'-s-m-t-m tək s/ptékʷł #
            /INT NEARBY EP LCL/squint-CAU-RLT-TR-IDF DSCR NOM/legend
            This is the Nx̌ík'smtm legend.

4   Ɂe · · · x ekʷu néɁ ɬ snk'y'ép.
     /Ɂe · · · x ekʷu néɁ ɬ s-n/k'y'ép #
     /exist RPRT EST.CTX EP NOM-LCL/Coyote
     Coyote was there.

5   Ɂe skʷózeɁs te sqâyxʷ.
     /Ɂe s/kʷózeɁ-s te s/qâyxʷ #
     /INT NOM/child-3PSV OBL NOM/male
     He had a male child.

6   Ɂe swɁexs téɁ ɬ skʷóze · · · Ɂs
     /Ɂe s/wɁex-s téɁ ɬ s/kʷóze· · · · Ɂ-s
     /INT NOM/exist-3PSV PART EP NOM/child-3PSV
     His child was there

7   ƛuɁ qəɬmín,
     ƛuɁ /qəɬmín
     PER /old
     until he was grown up,

8   ƛuɁ pút k Ɂesm Ɂéms.
     ƛuɁ /pút k Ɂes/mɁ-ém-s #
     PER /appropriate UNR ST/wife-MDL-3PSV
     until he was ready for marriage.

9   Ɂe Ɂsm Ɂéms ɬ twíw't ɬ snk̓y̓ép.
     /Ɂe Ɂs/mɁ-ém-s ɬ /twí[•w']t ɬ s-n/k̓y̓ép #
     /INT ST/wife-MDL-3PSV EP /young.man[•DIM] EP NOM-LCL/
       coyote
     Young Coyote got married.

Notes

1. For excellent descriptions of Salishan languages, see Thompson (1979) and Kinkade (1992b).

2. See Thompson et al. 1993:636.

3. Proto-Salish *k, *k' have become Flathead č, č', respectively; likewise Proto-Salish *x has become Flathead š. Most other Interior Salishan languages have retained these Proto-Salish sounds. Flathead k has been reintroduced in borrowings from French (*likók* "rooster") or English (*kasalín* "gasoline"), and Flathead k k' have been retained exceptionally in certain onomatopoeic words. Flathead ḷ, ḷ' correspond with r, r̓ in Spokane, Columbian, Coeur d'Alene, and Okanagan-Colville.

4. See Kinkade 1983; Thompson 1979:669.

5. A number of abbreviations are used for grammatical labels: AUX auxiliary, CAU causative, DIM diminutive, DRV directive, DSCR descriptive, EP established in the past, EST.CTX established in context, FUT future, IDF indefinite subject, INT introductory predicate, LCL localizer, MDL (control) middle, NEARBY near speaker and hearer, NOM nominalizer, OBJ object, OBL oblique complement, P (used with 1, 2, 3) plural, PART particular, PER persistent, PSV possessive, RLT relational, RPRT reportive, S (used with 1, 2, 3) singular, SBJ subject, ST stative, TR (control) transitive, UNR unrealized (Thompson and Thompson 1992:xxii–xxvi).

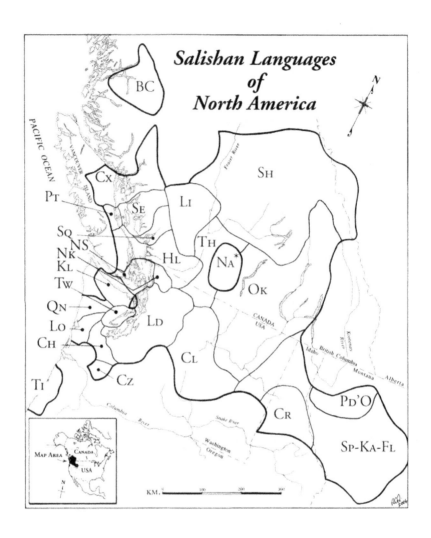

Map 1. Salishan languages
of North America and Salish
Territory. Drawn and edited
by Robert D. Turner.

Names and Abbreviations

Bella Coola (BC) (Nuxalk)
Coeur d'Alene (Cr)
Columbian (Cl)
Comox (Cx) (Sliammon)
Cowlitz (Cz)
Flathead (Fl)
Halkomelem (Hl)
Kalispel (Ka)
Klallam (Kl) (Clallam)
Lillooet (Li) (Stl'atl'imx)
Lower Chehalis (Lo)
Lushootseed (Ld)
Nooksack (Nk)
Northern Straits (NS)
Okanagan-Colville (Ok)
Pend'Oreille(s) (Pd'O)
Pentlatch (Pt)
Quinault (Qn)
Sechelt (Se)
Shuswap (Sh) (Secwepemc)
Spokane (Sp)
Squamish (Sq)
Straits Salish (St)
Thompson (River Salish) (Th), Nlhe7kepmx
Tillamook (Ti)
Twana (Tw)
Upper Chehalis (Ch)

Other Languages Noted on Map

Nicola Valley Athapaskan (Na*)
(An isolated Athapaskan language,
now considered extinct)

Epic Stories

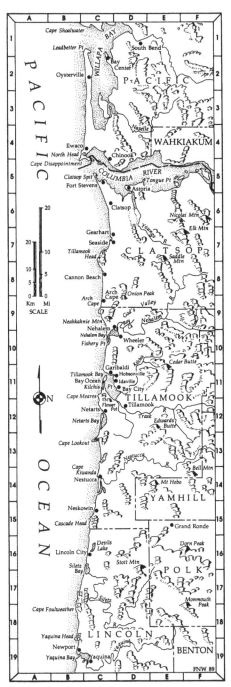

Map 2. Tillamook Territory. From *Nehalem Tillamook Tales*, published by Oregon State University Press. Reproduced by permission.

South Wind's Journeys

A Tillamook Epic Reconstructed from Several Sources

Compiled by Douglas E. Deur and M. Terry Thompson

He came from the south making and naming places—South Wind the Trickster, South Wind the Transformer. In the transformation era of the Tillamook, at the intersection of myth time and historical time, South Wind both walked and shaped the land.

Although he traveled alone through the land of the Tillamook, South Wind was not a lone traveler in the Salishan world. Throughout this world, and across the Americas, there were beings living during the myth time who were able to change the physical world. In English, they have been called the Transformer, sometimes the Trickster, and sometimes the Changer, and much has been written about them. They took a number of different forms, the most famous in North America being Coyote. Coyotes were scarce on the pre-European coast of British Columbia, Washington, and Oregon, but other powerful figures fulfilled this mission of changing the myth-time world of the coast into what we know today: Raven among the peoples of the central and northern coast; Bluejay, Dukʷibał, Moon (as Transformer) or x̣ʷéni the Trickster on portions of the southern coast; South Wind, Ice, and Wild Woman among the Tillamook. Like other Transformers, the Tillamook South Wind was certainly a hero figure in some instances, but he was also a Trickster—unpredictable, bungling, and gluttonous, often lewd and lascivious. Through his actions he shaped the land, originated customs, and commented—often by negative example—on Tillamook conceptions of morality. For the Tillamook, the tales of South Wind would have both instructed and entertained.

The tale that follows is an epic saga of South Wind's travels through Tillamook country along the northern Oregon and southern Washington coast. In this tale, South Wind behaves in many respects like his fellow Transformers to the east, north, and south; still, his personality and actions are inextricably rooted in the distinctive lands and lifeways of the Tillamook. The English version presented here represents a synthesis of tales recorded by Franz Boas, May Mandelbaum Edel, and Elizabeth Derr Jacobs. It combines a version found in Boas's publication of thirteen stories in English (Boas 1898b:140–46) with stories in Edel's manuscript collection (1931 ms.), and with stories from Elizabeth Derr Jacobs's (1933 ms.) manuscript collection as well as her published (1959) version. Boas's version was recorded in a southern dialect of Tillamook, probably Salmon River, while Edel's and Jacobs's versions were recorded in Nehalem, the northernmost dialect of the language. The manuscripts in the Edel collection include some stories in Tillamook, with English translations, from Franz Boas's Tillamook fieldwork in 1890, as well as tales collected by Edel during her 1931 dissertation studies of Tillamook grammar under Boas's supervision. The people who originally told these stories in the Tillamook language probably included Jane and Lizzie Adams and Jane's daughter, Nora Goff; Louie Fuller; Ellen Center; and Clara Pearson. While Louie Fuller resided on the Siletz Reservation, the rest of these storytellers resided in Hobsonville, or "Squawtown," across Miami Cove from Garibaldi. It consisted of people of mixed Nehalem, Clatsop, and southern Tillamook ancestry, but was not part of a reservation or any federally recognized Indian tribe. Chief Illga Adams purchased the village site in 1890, and the site continued to be occupied by individuals of Nehalem-Tillamook and Clatsop ancestry into the 1940s. Clara Pearson told this and other stories to Elizabeth Derr Jacobs in English only, while Ms. Jacobs's husband, Melville Jacobs, was collecting information from other speakers on the Tillamook language to aid Edel in preparation of her dissertation. The published version of these field notes was edited by both Melville and Elizabeth Derr Jacobs (E. D. Jacobs 1959:123–47). Melville Jacobs also collected one short story (not included here) in Tillamook from Clara Pearson, a story that she had originally told to Mrs. Jacobs in English. On the basis of this, the Jacobses both concluded that Pearson's English versions of the tales were *direct* translations from the Tillamook (E. D. Jacobs 1959:viii). Clara Pearson heard these stories regularly from her parents, who lived in her home until she was in her forties (Seaburg 2003, E. D. Jacobs 2003). In light of these observations, it is likely that all of the tales synthesized here, including those originally told in English, are reasonably faithful, if fragmentary, versions of the original Tillamook.

The saga presented here is a combination of South Wind stories from all of these sources—each of the versions contained minor variations not included in the others. We have arranged episodes of the tale from these multiple sources to cohere thematically and geographically. We have also cross-checked episodes of the South Wind tales with the tales and ethnographic data collected by John Peabody Harrington (1942–43). In a search for ethnogeographic data, Harrington consulted with Louie Fuller, Mrs. Louie Fuller, Sammy Jackson, and Clara Pearson. Harrington asked these people to recount tales associated with specific landmarks and environmental phenomena, and many of these episodes appear to have been derived from South Wind tales. Although Boas, Jacobs, and Edel had sought full tale narratives, the fragmentary episodes provided by Harrington are remarkably similar in content to the more complete tale sequences provided by these earlier researchers. It is likely that both approaches are true to Tillamook tradition: the Tillamook almost certainly invoked *fragmentary* episodes of the South Wind cycle within everyday speech as they navigated the sites and social conundrums mentioned or created in the epic tale, while longer tale sequences were told, in more ritualized form, only as a part of the Tillamook winter ceremonials.

We are deeply indebted to the storytellers, as well as the ethnographers and linguists who recorded these tales. They gave us a glimpse of Tillamook lifeways that had largely disappeared and were increasingly forgotten as the Tillamook entered the twentieth century. The language has not been spoken actively at least since the 1950s, and so far as can be determined there are no proficient speakers of Tillamook still living, though a few remain who grew up hearing the language and who know some words or sentences. Through their combined efforts, and their deep concern with recording Native tales, Boas, Edel, Harrington, and Jacobs, as well as the Adamses, Center, Jackson, Pearson, and the Fullers, did much to enhance our understanding of the Tillamook world, and to preserve some portion of the aboriginal Tillamook worldview for future generations.

In order to conserve space while we present as much of this epic tale as possible, we have elected to do no poetic or other type of line arrangement.

The composite tale we have compiled from these multiple sources should be seen as only a part of the larger epic told aboriginally, during many blustery winter nights, often accompanied by ceremonial dancing and singing. Much of the context of the oral presentation is lost to contemporary readers; we are relegated to reading fragmentary tales. We cannot hear the orator's use of different voices, or other contextual cues; we cannot see the responses of the audience. Although it is a fragment, the individual episodes are almost certainly faithful representations of the precontact oral tradition surrounding South Wind, issues of translation notwithstanding. As Edel (1944) noted, there was remarkably little variation in the content of individual Tillamook tales told to different ethnographers in the early twentieth century. The Tillamook were conservative tale-tellers, and little premium was placed on orators' deviation from the rote "text" for the sake of stylistic innovation or elaboration. Different individuals provided consistent retellings of these tales, even when they were of different gender, had experienced varying levels of continued exposure to Tillamook traditions, and the telling times were separated by decades. It is a testament to this "stability in Tillamook folklore" (Edel 1944) that we have been able to compile a South Wind epic from these multiple sources, with only minor differences in the episodes, and that missing episodes in one version can be easily interpolated (usually geographically) from other versions. And importantly, we can be assured that when we read this rendering of the Tillamook South Wind tale, we are reading a story that has come to us in a fragmentary but largely unmitigated form. It consists of parts of the tale as it was told around fires on long winter nights before the arrival of Europeans; it is something of the remote past.

Told during the shortest, stormiest, darkest days of winter, such tales and ceremonies served a certain "world renewal" function among the Tillamook: they ushered in the new year, preparing people for the end of winter and the return of fish, game, food plants, and calm weather. It is probable, though not entirely certain, that in the dead of winter the Tillamook viewed the telling of tales as a precondition for the return of these things, and felt that they were, in part, responsible for ushering these things back to the Tillamook world through ceremonial intervention. The Tillamook did conceive of some natural events as being a product of tale-tellings. Unseasonably rainy weather (and other, worse, forms of deprivation) were thought to be the outcome of tale-telling out of season. Oral performances thus were potent and transcendent events, capable of resetting the cosmological clock to wintertime. Transformer tales that depicted the creation of landscapes, animals, plants, and customs would have stood out among other tale-types in this reconstructive ceremonial function. Transformer tales were presumably central to any world-renewal function the larger corpus of tales was thought to possess.

As a faithful relic of past speech events, these tales provide valuable insights into how the Tillamook traditionally made sense of their world. While we cannot say with authority what the pre-European Tillamook people thought about their world or what went on in their minds, we can still hear their words— and such words reveal a great deal. Arguably, tales are a form of discourse; though often depicted as intact and autonomous artifacts, there is little doubt that many tales—Transformer tales among them—were performances, public utterances that presumed a listener, with social functions wholly contingent upon listeners' presence (see M. Jacobs 1959). Public comments, questions, clarifications, assessments, and feedback were possibly a part of the tale-telling. As statements about the world and its workings, these tales were shaped through countless exchanges between orators and listeners—listeners who held very particular ideas about what was appropriate and what was true. Certainly, all Tillamook discourse about the world embodied their shared lore, values, agendas, and assumptions (Sherzer 1987). But tale-telling, among the most routinized and public discourse of the Tillamook, gives us a view of some of that culture's most fundamental values and assumptions. Not only did the epic tales of the Tillamook embody their culturally situated view of the world, but they also served to shape their worldview actively. Thus, despite the significance and talents of early twentieth-century Tillamook orators such as Clara Pearson, the content of the South Wind tale that we present here is largely the product of the Tillamook, as a people, interacting verbally, rather than the product of lone orators. The tales make reference to information not likely known or salient to Pearson and other Tillamook narrators of the twentieth century on the basis of firsthand knowledge—the location of particular wild foods or hazards, appropriate relations among people of differing rank, the look of a certain rock as seen from an offshore canoe. These things nonetheless appeared in their tales, persisting voices from past peoples to whom this information was vital.

The South Wind epic cycle tells us much about how the Tillamook collectively viewed their environment, providing descriptions of the landscape's genesis and illuminating those features the Tillamook recognized as important among the potentially infinite range of environmental phenomena (see Deur 1996). Transformer tales stand out among oral traditions with explicit environmental themes. They describe the process by which the landscape is shaped to fit the whims of a Trickster-Transformer, who is—by definition—both extremely powerful and extremely mischievous. Indeed, it is quite difficult to appreciate the complexities of a Transformer tale without a familiarity with the Transformer's creations, on the land and in the culture of his origin. Despite the familiarity of early anthropologists with Tillamook cultural practices and the Tillamook South Wind tales, there was much that these people (all educated urbanites, most originally hailing from the East Coast) did not understand about the tales, and that was lost when the tales were extracted from their cultural and environmental contexts. A wealth of information, of cues and of plot devices invoking the common social and environmental ground of the Tillamook, were inextricably tied to Tillamook terrain, revealing the Tillamook sense of place and knowledge of places.

In the winter the south winds blow hard across the lands of the Tillamook. Climatologists have their own explanations for why this is so: through this season, low pressure systems sit in the Pacific Ocean, sending massive winter storms spinning counterclockwise, tracking eastward and colliding with Oregon's rugged outer coast. In winter, south winds seldom cease. During storms, hurricane-force winds are commonplace; the surf goes wild. Rainfall is measured in feet. On the oceanfront, rains will fall horizontally and adults may struggle to stand. However, these are warm storms for such northerly latitudes; they assure that coastal frosts are rare. South winds and relative winter warmth seldom ceased through the winter season historically, passing only when high-pressure systems appear over the ocean, bringing east winds, north winds, clear skies, and, often, ice.

In many respects, the Tillamook South Wind is a classic Trickster-Transformer. But South Wind has his own, distinctive personality; like Raven to the north or Coyote to the east, South Wind is, in part, a personification of his namesake. "South Wind traveled in the winter," the Tillamook would say, "It was always stormy then." In the South Wind tales, the Tillamook never explicitly state that South Wind and the meteorological south wind were two sides of the same character; they probably never had to. Like the south winds that blow across the coast in winter, South Wind travels from the indistinct southern edges to the indistinct northern edges of the Tillamook world. He topples trees, breaks their branches, crashes through their crowns. South Wind creates ocean surf so that, on bad days, "no skiff, no small boat of any kind will be able to travel on it." He makes pacts with Ocean, saying "I will destroy things for you, so that you can possess them . . . When I travel you will be angry and drift things and drown things." He gets East Wind to stop singing so that the weather will warm, the ice will melt, and the Tillamook people can find berries, fish, and game. In one episode (not included here) he fights Ice with mild, wet weather, and melts Ice's wives, Snow and Hail.

These tales were told in winter, when the awesome south winds dominate the lived-in world and constantly rework the land and the sea. They were told in winter-dark longhouses, as south winds rattled the roofboards, howled at the door, caused smoke to back up and fill the room. They were told as south winds toppled nearby trees, and the surf churned into an unnavigable froth, tearing at the shoreline, overturning ocean-going canoes. To the Tillamook people, the telling of South Wind's epic tale would have been, by necessity, intimately interwoven with the experienced winter environment as a larger part of the Tillamook winter ceremonials. For the Tillamook, gathered in extended-family households for the winter, the South Wind tale served as a partial explanation for these environmental phenomena, a metaphorical way of knowing, a story told to children that would place a human face, comical and familiar, on the roar beyond the door.

Situated as they were, on the rugged and exposed outer coast, the Tillamook experienced some of the Salish-speaking world's most turbulent weather. It is not particularly surprising, then, that the Tillamook Transformer would manifest this ominous force; in a Lévi-Straussian vein, south winds occupied the top of the food chain among all other environmental forces in the Tillamook lands, save possibly Ocean, "the chief of chiefs." South Winds have perpetually traversed and transformed the Tillamook world in winter. It is appropriate, then, that South Wind, the Tillamook "everlasting man," would walk the land and shape the land, ushering them from their remote Myth Age to their lived-in world. He was at once man and meteorological phenomenon: "The whole world was South Wind's house!"

As an explanation of how the world came to be, the South Wind epic is replete with references to the physical landscape, and allows one to tentatively grasp an undeniably Tillamook environmental gestalt. A Tillamook ordering of space is revealed: as South Wind progresses into the sea world, the sky world, or the deep, inland forest, the beings he encounters become increasingly supernatural, increasingly powerful and mythologized. As South Wind travels farther from the core of the Tillamook world—the villages on the protected waters of Nehalem and Tillamook Bays—the terrain grows increasingly fictionalized, exhibiting less ground truth, while the people he meets, on the whole, grow more alien and often more dangerous. Tillamook civilization was at the core, wrapped in successive layers of lesser-known terrain, greater wildness, and cosmological chaos.

Yet the ground truth of the South Wind epic cycle is impressive, particularly in those parts that address the traditional territories of the Tillamook. One can walk the trails and beaches where South Wind traveled and recognize his handiwork: sand spits, round rocks, cascades, sea stacks. Almost every point in the tales where South Wind encounters humans correlates with a known former settlement site (Collins 1953; Seaburg and Miller 1990). No doubt, the characteristics of each of the people encountered by South Wind may have served as commentaries on or markers of the actual people who dwelt there, though this knowledge is largely lost to us today. The trails South Wind walked are documented contact period pathways, used for winter travel by the Tillamook, and later by arriving white settlers (Dicken 1978). As a winter traveler, South Wind traveled by trail or on the most calm, protected, interior waters. In the summertime, the Tillamook would have traveled South Wind's route by canoe, circumventing steep headlands, but the winter ocean, driven by south winds, was commonly too treacherous for canoes. For South Wind, as with the Tillamook generally, winter was the time of travel by trails.

Based on what we know of the telling of such tales, the original South Wind epic cycle would have been told over the course of hours, or even over several consecutive winter nights. What we present here is only a fragment of the original, the high points of the South Wind tale. In the fragmentary story cycle we have in our possession, the sites mentioned are seldom more than five miles apart, even in the most sparsely inhabited portion of the Tillamook territory. In the densely inhabited shorelines of the Tillamook world, mentioned sites are rarely a mile apart. Almost all places mentioned are connected by a continuous line of sight. It is conceivable, indeed it is probable, that in its original tellings the South Wind epic would have followed the entire coastline of the Tillamook world. Orators likely invoked a consecutive line of visible landmarks, giving a line-of-sight narrative, talking the coastline, starting as far south as Siletz and progressing at least as far north as the Columbia River's northern shores. (Perhaps, as part of the world-renewal rites of the winter ceremonies, this was not so much talking the coastline as symbolically remaking the coastline.) These tales would have been told to children, and likely taught rote, line by line. The tales would have taught them to navigate the terrain, to locate its resources, to avoid its threats, to recall the epic origins of its place names. One might also suspect that, when walking the land, the Tillamook were being "stalked with stories" (Basso 1984). There was nowhere they could travel in their own land that did not have a story attached—nowhere that did not invoke an event from myth-time, provide an explanation of the landscape's genesis, and give an implicit or explicit moral lesson. The physical landscape did not consist of inert matter, but was full of life and power—a collage of mnemonics, places with their own supernatural genesis and their own stories, that both informed the Tillamook and guided their behavior as they traversed the land.

The environmental cues in the South Wind tale often seem subtle but would have been readily apparent to Tillamook listeners. As South Wind leaves the protected, muddy bays of the Tillamook world, entering its exposed and rocky northern frontier between Neahkahnie Mountain and Tillamook Head, his transition is marked not by explicit mentions of such a transition but by the presence of strange and dangerous women, and by his use of rocks and sea-shells endemic to the outer coast as weapons. As he heads inland, the plants he uses reflect actual environmental gradients, and when he returns to the coast, his arrival is marked not by an explicit statement to the effect that South

Wind was again at the ocean but through a passing mention to his gathering ocean crabs for food. To underscore certain points, South Wind is shown causing plants and animals to appear out of time and out of place. Like the meteorological south wind, he changes the weather in winter so that berries grow and stored fish grows mildew. Here, his involvement in the return of berries and game, told during the dead of winter, would have spoken to the world-renewal functions of the winter ceremonials. Like the actual south wind that, for example, carried downed redwood trees north up the coast from California, providing the Tillamook with huge logs for specialized canoes, South Wind brings things from long distances away to suit his whims or save him from imminent danger. Particularly when in trouble, South Wind calls on remote but powerful plants and animals. Almost drowning with his penis stuck fast, he calls to various grasses to cut him loose; when they fail, he calls to the uniquely strong but geographically distant "mountain grass" to cut him loose. When small Woodpecker cannot peck away the rock where he is trapped, he must call for Flicker (or Yellowhammer), a much larger bird that retires inland from the ocean coast during the hard winds of the winter months.[1] These were big requests South Wind was making and served, to Tillamook listeners, to underscore the urgency of South Wind's plight. Still, such summonses were not outside of the power of South Wind or the south winds.

In addition to illuminating the Tillamook understanding of their landscapes, the South Wind tale also provides a glimpse into how the Tillamook viewed their neighbors and how they conceptually ordered other tribes and their territories. The Clatskanie of the Nehalem River headwaters consistently are depicted as somewhat mysterious, alien, potential trespassers from deep in the woods. The Yaquina make occasional appearances within Tillamook tales, but seem to be depicted as culturally similar, familiar, and largely unremarkable. Still, from the Tillamook perspective, not all tribes could be dismissed so easily, and not all places were created equal. Their wealthy and powerful neighbors and kin to the north, the Clatsop and Chinook, lived in places of plentitude, central to regional trade networks, and containing spectacular quantities of such coveted resources as Chinook salmon and wapato. Descriptions of the Clatsop and Chinook land in the South Wind tales are remarkably detailed; it is a land where the Tillamook possessed kin ties, where they sometimes lived, where they visited often, for trade, group resource harvests, marriages, and other social events. Most Tillamook, by contrast, lived on the fringes, peripheral to trade networks and lacking resources on a Columbia River scale. Among the Tillamook this could be blamed, in part, on that Trickster South

Wind, who found the Tillamook harvesting Chinook salmon and wapato on their land, but took these things away on a whim. The Clatsop and Chinook had such things, but South Wind left the Tillamook with poor replacements, such as sculpins and bulrushes. This repeating theme in Tillamook oral traditions may have been an expression of envy, a self-deprecating joke, or an in-group taunt passed between Tillamook and their Chinookan kin; regardless, it demonstrated that the Tillamook acknowledged their relative resource poverty. This suggests, like the Trickster-Transformer tales of other tribes, that the Tillamook sensed they were not entirely in control of their own fate.

As a being who *did* have certain controls over the fate of humankind, South Wind was capricious and mischievous. He had the power to turn mortals into rocks and the will to do so. His momentary desires for food or sex left permanent imprints upon the land and lives of the Tillamook. His actions might have explained the genesis of landmarks or customs, but the Tillamook did not presume to attribute the emergence of many of these things to any logical motive, just South Wind's capricious whims. They knew that animals are shaped and distributed to fit South Wind's moods; in one place he leaves salmon, in another he flattens them into flounders, in another he makes them into sculpins and sturgeon. He takes away the cockles' oil and insists that there be only one cockle per shell. From his hunter adversaries he makes wolves or panthers. Every time the Tillamook went to fish or hunt they would have to respond to these events, going to the places where South Wind created desirable animals or avoiding those places he cursed with a paucity of game.

As the creator of many food plants and animals and a personification of winter scarcity, South Wind is obsessed with food and with eating, and is often depicted as being near starvation. Sometimes he appears to feign starvation so that he will be pitied and fed. South Wind, a resolutely masculine character, concerns himself with defining and shaping those parts of the world of interest to men, such as the character and distribution of fish and game animals. In contrast, his female equivalents of the Tillamook transformation era, Wild Woman (who was similar to the Dzonokwa character of the Kwakiutl and the čínəkʷa [basketwoman] character of the Salishan Klallam) and the Younger Wild Women (sometimes depicted as South Wind's daughters) direct more attention to women's concerns, such as the character and uses of plants. In the patrilocal and patrilineal world of the Tillamook, South Wind is a more powerful modifier of culture, landscape, and regional climate; however, in their possession of strong spirit powers, as well as their propensity for lasciviousness and bungling gluttony, South Wind and the Wild Women are equals. It is perhaps telling that one of the few tales that brings together these characters is, in fact, the story of the creation of humankind (not included here).

Not only does South Wind transform the land and its inhabitants, he can also transform himself and his excrement. When trapped in tight spaces, he can disassemble and reassemble himself. He can sever his penis, transform it into dogs or digging sticks, and then reattach it when it has served him. (Such risqué subjects were translated into Latin by Boas [1898: 140–41, 145], as was then the tradition.) At the conclusion of the epic cycle, he turns himself into a rock. Like Coyote in other Native American oral traditions, South Wind's scat often serves as his advisor; when he wishes information or help he defecates and consults this scat. Sometimes he transforms it into helpers, especially for tricks played on other people. Elsewhere, in the dead of winter, he turns his scat into fresh leaves and berries out of season.

Both hero and antihero, he teaches moral lessons by negative example. He finds mischievous ways to coerce women into sex: he turns his penis into a digging stick and encourages a woman to inspect and polish it. Later, he becomes an abandoned baby, and gropes his sympathetic caretaker. He disguises himself as a medicine doctor to gain access to a young girl, and later fondles the female flicker. This behavior gets him into trouble; he is nearly drowned, or nearly copulates with Stinkbugs. In most cases, it is apparent that he is violating Tillamook moral codes, and people protest with varying degrees of vehemence. Even as South Wind violates Tillamook codes of conduct, he is keenly aware of etiquette and gender roles, and instructs the listener on how these things are to be done in the future when human beings occupy this coast.

South Wind does not always teach by negative example. He sometimes punishes malicious or greedy people, turning them to stone. And, in the tradition of his fellow Transformers, Raven and Coyote, South Wind sees to it that the people of the world have access to food and water. He thwarts the greedy ambitions or neglectful gluttony of powerful beings who hoard the world's food and water. Within a classic "box of daylight" motif,[2] he assures listeners that nobody will monopolize these things: "no one person." His flawed, and sometimes awkwardly dualistic, character is redeemed by providing these essential resources to less powerful mortals, and he serves as a moral example of the redistributive generosity that coastal peoples expected of their elite.

At the conclusion of many episodes, South Wind is prone to declarative statements, creating natural laws and social mores, commenting negatively, after the fact, on the actions of himself and the creatures he meets as he travels through the world: only women will be paid for sex, no one will be killed or eaten on a particular beach, one must wait before preparing and eating freshly caught fish, men shall not have babies, no animal will swallow people. From the chaos of myth-time he creates a moral universe, where the behavior of humans, animals, supernatural beings, and environmental phenomena were shaped by his fiat, as if they were guided by the same indivisible and inexorable body of supernatural laws. To make the environmental and cultural dimensions of this moral universe understandable to a broad, contemporary audience, we have provided many endnotes (beginning on p. 49) in the present telling of the South Wind epic tale.

South Wind fixed the world to be as it is now. You can walk the land and see where he both walked and shaped the land before you. Concluding his epic journey, South Wind declared "When I get through fixing things, I am going back to the south . . . where my home is." But every year, from the south, his presence is felt in the Tillamook world, though the Tillamook people are now very few, and although some have heard stories of Coyote, they almost never utter the name Asə?ayáhaɬ, South Wind the Trickster, South Wind the Transformer. "For all time" he will tumble across his creations, topple trees, and work with Ocean to tear at the land. "For all time" the south winds will blow across the Tillamook world.

South Wind's Journeys

South Wind traveled in the winter.[3] It was always stormy then. He had many different kinds of headbands. He would say to himself, *I'll put on my headband to run on the trees. I'll walk just on the limbs.* That's the time the limbs break off the trees and fall down. And sometimes he'd say, *Well, I'll wear this different headband. I'll break off the tops of the trees.* With another headband he would break off whole trees, just like they were chopped down. Very rarely he'd start out, saying, *Well, I guess this time I'll wear the headband in which I pull trees up by the roots, roots and all.*

On the ocean beach he'd always see a pretty girl. She'd sit by the waves, close on the beach. He was always trying to catch her, but just as he almost touched her she'd disappear. Oooohhh, he'd think, he'd like to catch her. Even after he'd seen her many times, the same one, he didn't know what kind of girl she was. After a while, Bluejay asked him,[4] "Well, you still want to catch that girl?"

"Yes, Auntie," he said, "would you tell me how?" She told him, "When you see her, if you want to catch her keep your eyes on her, don't blink or anything, just have your eyes on her till you grab her with your hand, then it will be all right. You will have caught her. Do you know what she is?" "No!" he replied. Bluejay said, "She's that Ocean's daughter. That Ocean, he's a king, he's the chief of all the chiefs. She's his daughter."[5]

South Wind had often destroyed things for Ocean to have. So the next time he found her, he did what Bluejay had told him and he caught hold of her. He took her home, he took her south. He made her his wife. That girl, she didn't like it there. "Oh, I never had a home like this!" she said. "My bed at home is soft, like a feather bed, I didn't sleep on a hard bed at home." South Wind had a wooden bed. After a while he told her, "Do you want me to take you home to your father? We'll go and stay with your father a while."[6] She was tickled to death. Yes! She wanted to go home. He took her home.

Oh, he saw many different things there. His father-in-law had everything! All kinds of things were his pets. Those whales, and all sorts of ugly animals were his pets. Then they talked together. South Wind said, "Well, we'll work together for all time. I'll destroy things for you, so you'll have them, and you do your part. When I travel, you get mad, drift things and drown things, and that way we'll work together forever." Then he took his wife home again to the south. Then she took her own things from her father's place because she had to stay with South Wind.

———[7] South Wind already had another wife. She was continually getting mad and jealous. *I'll leave, I'm not going to live with him no more. I'm going to leave.* She'd go in the night, and travel and travel for all she was worth. She'd think, *Well, I'm far away now.* He'd get up in the morning and his first wife was gone. He'd look in the far corner of the room and there she'd be, with her stuff scattered around and her bed made there. She couldn't go far enough to get out of South Wind's house.[8]

Always she'd think, *Now I've gone a long way.* She'd get so mad. *He owns the whole world, the whole world is South Wind's house!*

———Once South Wind was traveling, making and naming places. He came from the south. He lived far up the country, in the country of the salmon.[9]

He reached Neskowin in the wintertime.[10] It was cold. He came to a house where he saw people lying around the fire. He asked them, "What is the matter? Are you sick?" "No," they replied, "we are starving. The East Wind[11] wants to kill us. The river, the sea and the beach are frozen over, and we cannot get any food." Then he said, "Can't you make the wind stop, so that you may obtain food?" Then he went out of the house and down to the river, which was completely frozen over. It was so slippery that he was hardly able to stand on the ice. He didn't like it too cold. He said, *Up this way it's already spring*. He said, *Why is it so cold in the springtime?* He went up Neskowin Creek to meet the East Wind and conquer him. While he went on, mucus flew out of his nose and froze at once because it was so cold. When he came near the house of East Wind, he picked up some ice, broke it into pieces, and threw it in the river, saying, *Henceforth it will not be as cold as it is now. Winter shall be a little cold, but not very much so. You shall become shiners.*[12] The ice turned into shiners. Every piece became a shiner and swam down the river. Oh, he saw them in the waves that came up on the sand, so he picked up the shiners and put them in his soft rush bag. He talked to them, and he said "Oh, you must cook very quickly because if it takes too long you might melt because you're made out of ice."

He reached a house. He went in and left his soft rush bag outside. "Oh, I forgot," he said, "I've already found many shiners." This one old person said, "Oh," he said, "you talk so queerly."[13] South Wind said, "Really, there are shiners in my bag." This woman went out (to look). She found there really were shiners. She cooked some. Soon the shiners were done and they ate.

——Then he went on to another house in Nestucca. He heard somebody singing. He said, "Who is singing?" They said, "East Wind is singing." He said, "Indeed, I'm going there." He went. He got to East Wind's house. He sat down far from the fire and whistled. His whole face was covered with frozen mucus. His whole body was trembling with cold. They said, "Sit by the fire." "Oh, no—I feel so warm I cannot go near the fire," he said, "I am perspiring," and he told East Wind that he came from a house where they were drying shiners. This old woman, "Oh," she said, "You talk funny, this is wintertime." East Wind said, "Don't say so. It is winter now. There will be no shiners for a long time to come." "Oh, no," said South Wind. "This is springtime. I picked up lots of shiners down on the beach. I left my bag out by the door there. You go get it," he said to the old woman, "and bring it in. I put shiners in it."

The old woman went out, brought it in, and sure enough there were fish in that bag. She fixed some. She cooked them on long stakes standing before the fire. They got toasted nice and brown. He told her, "They don't take long to get done, they get brown awful quick." And sure enough they got done awful quick, and she gave some to everybody. And the women went to the beach, then, and picked up lots of them. There was plenty because there was so much ice.

East Wind was singing, and as long as he sings it's wintertime. So South Wind said to him, "Now, my friend, stop. Don't sing again for a long time." He said, "Now it's spring." So East Wind stopped blowing, the ice began to melt, and the people had plenty of food. Up to that time it had been winter all through the year, but South Wind had made summer and winter alternate.

——Then he left. He went back to the people he had helped. "Go out and catch shiners, and when you have enough tell your wives to pick berries. And you may hunt elk and deer." Then they rose and did as he had told them, and they lived happy lives.

——Then South Wind moved on toward the north. He arrived at Netarts. There he gathered clams and mussels.[14] He made a fire and roasted them. When he opened them he found that there were two animals in each shell. He began to eat, and found very soon that he had enough. He grew very angry and said, *There shall be only one fleshy part in each cockle shell in the future.*

——He got to Tillamook Bay, near Bay Ocean. He couldn't figure out how to get across, because north of Bay City he saw a creek where an adolescent girl was bathing.[15] He thought, *Ohh, that's a nice looking girl. I wish I could get to her*. He said, *Oh, I want to copulate with her*. His penis grew incredibly long, and he carried it in his arms. He waded as far out as he could wade.[16] Then he threw his penis across toward the girl many times. Finally it reached into her. Soon this girl grew cold, for she, too, was standing in the water. After a bit he couldn't get it out. The tide came in and they both nearly drowned, fastened there.

Then he called on sharp grass and sent it down to cut him loose. Then he called on three-cornered grass. He called tideland grass, and reeds, all the grasses. Each one drifted down and cut his penis in a different place. He suffered dreadfully. He grew angry. "Oh—you're bad. You didn't cut my penis. You didn't cut my penis!" Nothing could get him loose. Then he called mountain grass.[17] He said, "Come here. Oh, mountain grass, drift down and cut me. I'm nearly drowning and freezing to death." Then mountain grass drifted down and cut it off. South Wind was left with only a piece of his penis. Part of it stayed in the girl, and the rest, which was all cut up, he left lying to form the sandbar. The cuts made the bumps (hilly places) in the sandbar. He said, *In the future there will be nothing but sand there. Tillamook Bay will have just a small mouth from now on. Shot-huckleberry bushes and salal bushes will grow and there will be much berry picking.*[18] And that is how the bay became nearly closed. It used to be wide open before South Wind came.

——Then he traveled. He came to the Tillamook River, which was full of salmon who were clapping their hands (fins). He took one of them, threw it ashore, stepped on it, and flattened it. It became a flounder, and ever since that time flounders have been plentiful in the Tillamook River, while there have been few salmon.[19]

——He went upstream.[20] Then he waded across it near its headwaters, as he had no canoe and was unable to cross it where it was deep. He met a number of women who were digging roots. He asked, "What are you doing there?" They replied, "We are digging roots." He said, "I do not like that." He took the roots away and sent them to Clatsop, and ever since that time there have been no roots at Tillamook, while at Clatsop they are very plentiful. He descended to the beach and said, "Henceforth you shall gather clams at ebb tide. When the water rises you shall carry them home, and you shall quarrel about them." It happened as he said. He gave the women the Tillamook language. He said, *This river has too wide a mouth*. He put quantities of sand there.[21]

——Finally, he reached the Kilchis River, which was full of salmon.[22] He thought, *I am hungry, I will catch some salmon*. He caught one and fastened it in a split stick and roasted it over the fire. While it was roasting, he lay down and covered his eyes with his left hand and patted his breast with his right hand, humming a song. When he looked up he found the salmon dancing to his song. Then he lay down again, patted his breast, covered his eyes, and continued to sing. When he looked up the salmon was gone. Then he got angry and thought, *How foolishly I have behaved! I am very hungry and have nothing to eat*.[23]

——He went up toward Kilchis Point. Pretty soon he caught up with an old woman carrying a big pack. "Oh," he said, "Where are you going, Auntie?" She said, "I'm going to Kilchis Point where my grandchild is awful sick. I'm going to see her." The old woman sat down. She opened her pack. She took out a lot of cooked camas and gave him some. "Sit down and eat," she said. South Wind ate, and ohhhh, he liked them. Then the old woman said, "Now I'm going to Kilchis Point." The old woman went on.

Then South Wind said, *Oh, I haven't had enough [to eat]. I'll put a spell on this old woman so she'll just walk and walk, but she won't be able to get any farther*. The old woman couldn't go any farther. Then South Wind went around her. He got ahead of her and made himself look different. He took out his penis[24] and cut it in three parts and made dogs of the parts. One dog he named Head, another Middle, and one Stub. Then he approached from another side with his dogs. As soon as he came near, the dogs wanted to creep under her clothes. The old woman again put down her pack. She gave him camas. South Wind said to his "dogs," "I want her camas." So the dogs begged for camas. The old woman was suspicious, and said, "I never saw a dog that ate camas." He said, "Well, my dogs do!" She gave all the dogs some. They ate. Then the old woman went on. Then he went in the opposite direction. He wanted to keep meeting her.

The old woman began to think, *Ain't that funny? Why is it I walk and walk and can't get anywhere?* Soon South Wind went back again and met the old woman again. She thought, *This man looks almost the same as the first one I met. I wonder if that isn't South Wind because he seems tricky.* He said to her, "Auntie, where are you going?" She said, "I'm going to visit my grandchild." Then South Wind said, "Hu! hu!, ha! ha!" The old woman said, "Oh, indeed, nephew, I see you're a doctor?" "Yes," he said, "Yes." "Ah, you must go right up there and doctor my grandchild." He said, "Indeed, maybe." This old woman thought, *Ah, perhaps now it's South Wind.* She thought, *I'll tell him not to eat this camas.* She said, "Far off, at a place where there is no wind you may open this camas pack and sit down there and eat them." He said, "Fine." The old woman went on.

South Wind took the bundle and looked for a place where there was no wind, he wanted to eat them right away.[25] He found a place, sat down under dense bushes and opened the pack. Oh, bumblebees flew out and stung his face. He was almost blinded. They stung him all over his body! *Oh, she put a trick over on me!* South Wind thought, *I hope she can't get any farther! Now I'm going to follow her.* So he caught up with her. He didn't bother to go around this time, he just caught her and killed her. He turned her into a rock. She is that rock right there at Bay City. He kicked the rock. He said, "You'll lay right here. You'll be a rock. You'll be an awful rough rock. In the time to come they will look at you. When people want to sharpen their knives they will come here and sharpen them on you." He made her something like a grindstone.[26]

He took her pack and he ate and ate. After he had plenty of the camas he threw the remainder clear to Grande Ronde. He threw some toward Tillamook. He threw some toward the Wilson River. He threw some to the Kilchis River. He threw the rest to Bay City and way over to Onion Peak at Nehalem. There was a great amount of it. He said of each place, *That will be a big camas field, they'll always grow there.*[27] He went down the river and destroyed all the camas roots he found on his way.

——Then South Wind went on. He himself went to Kilchis Point. He had learned about the sick girl from the old woman with the camas. He arrived at a place where an old woman lived alone. He said, "I understand there's sickness in that next house." She said, "Yes, there's a young girl there. She's my grandchild and she's awful sick. They have doctored and doctored her and they can't tell what's wrong with her." He said, "Oh, yes, I can tell there's sickness there. I can see it from outside here in the yard. But don't tell anyone I'm a doctor." She said, "Oh, no, I won't tell anybody."

Pretty soon she ran over to the other house. "Oh, there's a doctor in my house. Go get him." They told her, "You send him over here." She came back and said, "Oh, they want you to come over, they want you to look at my grandchild." Ohhh, he was tickled, that's just what he wanted. He went, he saw her, he knew that girl. That's the girl who had the end of his penis in her, that's what was making her sick.

He said, "I understand there's sickness in this house." These people said, "This girl is sick. Can you really doctor her?" He said, "Fine." He told the people, "I don't want anybody around. All the young people, everybody but these two old women should go outside. Only these two old women will help me sing." South Wind sang. Everyone had gone outside except the two old women. They were blind. They stayed to help him sing. He said to them, "If I mention in my song anything about 'splicing them together,' take tanned elk hides and throw them over me." They sang and pounded with their sticks.[28] Then he spliced his penis onto the piece still inside the girl. He doctored this girl. "I hear something queer," this one old woman said, "What can he be doing with our grandchild?" (The girl was making a noise during copulation.) "Oh," the other one hit her. "So. Can't anyone here sing along that way? You get these [sexually charged] ideas because you did such things when you yourself were young! Go ahead with your singing so the girl will get well." Then soon South Wind finished. He had spliced his penis back together and pulled it out. He went out. The girl said, "Ohhh, catch him! Don't let him get away! That was something awfully good he has. He did something wonderful!" The old blind women chased him. These old women grabbed hold of his penis. Then they realized what he had been doing to that girl. They couldn't hold onto it. One of them said, "It is slick!" Then they called the other people to catch him, but he ran outside and got away. The girl sent them after him with tanned elk hide. She wanted him to have it. Outside there they caught up with him, they gave him the elk skins as payment for doctoring. He laughed. He said, "No, I don't want to be paid! In the future they won't pay a man when he does that, they'll only pay women for intercourse." Then he laughed and ran away. The girl was well then.

——Then South Wind went on. He hung around Bay City a lot. He was hungry. He stopped at one house. When South Wind arrived this woman roasted cockles (clams), and South Wind ate. Then he got enough cockles.[29] They were very oily. He said, *Oh, why is there oil in the clams?* He poured out the oil. He said, *Clams should never have oil. In the spring the clams will be lean. There will be nothing but water*, he thought.

——Then he went on. He came to another house. He took off his penis and made it look just like a clam digger made of hard spruce wood.[30] It looked just like that. He stood it outside by the door and went in. He said to the woman, "Oh, I just remembered the clam digger that I found over there. I picked up a fine digging stick. It's brand new." He said, "It's no good to me, I have no use for it. If you want it, you take it."

The woman went out. Indeed it was brand new. She took the digging stick. South Wind said, "Rub it. Oh, it's nice and smooth." The woman felt along it. Indeed, it was smooth. "Keep on rubbing it!" he said, and she did. As she rubbed, it turned more and more into flesh and skin. Soon South Wind burst out laughing. The skin on the stick moved. Then she saw that it was no digging stick, it was South Wind's penis. She threw it in the fire, but South Wind grabbed it out and immediately had it on again. He laughed, "Ha, ha! It's a fine thing when a woman will play with the penis of a stranger the first time he comes to her house!" Then he went on. He said, "I'm going."

——South Wind went downstream. Right by Bay City he found a whale, a fresh whale, on the beach.[31] (Whales never come into this bay any more.) South Wind didn't know what to do. He thought, *Oh, I've got no knife. How can I cut up this whale? Oh, I know what I'll do. I'll go see Flintnose, he's living at Hobsonville, and that Copperman lives right here at Bay City by the Point.[32] If I can get those two to fighting, Flintnose will get his face chipped off, and that will make a knife for me, and then I'll tell them to quit fighting.*

He came to Copperman first. He said, "Ha." He said, "Look here. That fellow from across the way, Flintnose, speaks very ill of you. He says he'll beat you. He says he'll hit your face and it'll be bent into all different shapes." Copperman said, "What's the matter now? We've lived here forever, and he never spoke angrily to me. He's been my friend. I wonder what's wrong with him." South Wind said, "Oh, I tell you Flintnose is pretty sore at you!"

Then South Wind went back. He reached Flintnose. He said, "Look here, that man who lives on the other point speaks evil of you. He says he'll hit your face and it'll chip off." "Ha!" Flintnose said, "He hasn't ever talked angrily to me before." South Wind said, "Well, that's what he told me. He said he was going to give you a beating." Flintnose said, "All right. If he wants to, we'll fight. Tell him to come and we'll fight. Tell him to come halfway, and I'll go to meet him."

South Wind went back to Copperman. He said, "He said to come halfway and fight." Copperman said, "Well, if I have to do it, I have to do it." South Wind ran back to Flintnose and said, "Well, Copperman's coming."

Then Copperman went to Flintnose, and they fought. And, ohhh! Great pieces of flint, big ones and little ones, fell. South Wind ran and picked them up. He picked out three good flint knives. Pretty soon South Wind said, "Ha! Now stop fighting." He said, "There's a whale lying right over here on the beach. Come on and cut it up." He went out to cut the blubber of the whale. They said to each other, "Oh, it was just South Wind that got us in trouble. He just made it all up to get himself a knife. Well, anyhow, we're friends," they said. They found out that South Wind was a troublemaker.

——He traveled on north of Bay City. He met an old woman who carried a basket of camas. He asked, "Where are you going?" She replied, "I am carrying this camas to the old men in those houses." South Wind replied, "That is good, they are just now carving a whale." Then the old woman ran down to the shore as fast as she could, sharpening her knife. She wanted to have some of the whale meat, too.

——Then he went on here toward Garibaldi. He sat down on a rock near a river. Soon he saw a canoe coming down the river. There were three people in it, a man and his wife and a young girl. Then he thought, *Ohhh, I see a young maiden, and I'd like to have her. What can I do to get her? Oh, I'll make myself into a baby on a cradle board.* So he made himself into a baby in a cradle.[33] He waded out and lay down on a rock. So then he cried and cried.

Those people saw him. "Oh," they said, "That's a deserted baby on that rock! Someone must have tipped [their boat] over. How did the baby get there on the rock? We'd better pick up the baby and save him." The baby cried. They took him, and whenever the woman or her husband held him, the baby cried. No matter in whatever position they held him he kept on bawling. His arms were tied on the cradle board. After a while the woman unwrapped the baby from the cradle board and let his arms free. She gave him to the daughter.

Then she handed him to the daughter to see if she could keep him quiet.

He was still, then. That was what he wanted. Then he played with her ce-dar-bark skirt. The daughter said, "Oh, he's feeling around a lot for a young baby!" Her mother said, "You leave him alone so he'll be quiet." Soon he felt inside her skirt.

This maiden said, "Why does this baby reach around under my dress?" Her mother said, "Come now, leave him alone so he won't cry." Then the baby put his hand underneath her dress and felt of her vulva. Then this maiden said, "Oh, this baby is bad!" and she threw the cradle into the water. It didn't even touch the water, but flew to the opposite bank of the river. Then South Wind was himself again and laughed, "Ha, ha, ha! Well, a young girl's parts are just like an old woman's. They're pretty soft!" Ohhh, that girl was angry and ashamed. They all said, "He's bad. It's South Wind himself, indeed." He put down the cradle and left it.

——Then after a while he went ashore below the old Garibaldi.[34] Soon he saw two women with black hair talking together confidentially. One of these women said, "South Wind has come. Let's go tease him. We'll tell him we'll screw him, then we'll put a spell on him so he'll be impotent." So they sang to him, "South Wind, come over here, and lie with us." But he could read their minds, so he said, "No, I know you, you're no good. I won't have anything to do with you." He said, "You stink." These women said, "He's found us out." They were Stinkbugs. Those bugs are no good.[35]

——Then he went a little farther on; there he made a fool of himself in-deed! He saw two girls. Ohhh, they were so pretty, with red hair and light complexions.[36] They just took his eye. South Wind said, *Ohh, gee, they're good looking! I'm going to tackle them.* He went and talked to them and they made love to him. Both of them got hold of him. Now those girls lived in the water. They didn't do it on purpose but pretty soon they took him into the water. Oh, South Wind was cold. After a while he couldn't stand it. Some-times they liked to take him under the water. He nearly drowned! He fought against them, but there were two of them and they were much stronger than he was. He begged, "Turn me loose! I want to go to shore." After a while they turned him loose.

——Then he went ashore at Barview.[37] He walked down the beach where the rocks are. Ohhh, he was very cold but the sun was shining. He sat down on the sand. He thought, *Oh, that nice sunshine! I'll sun myself. Oh, I wish a high bluff would come on this side of me to shield me from the wind.*[38] He looked, there was a bluff on that side of him. *Ohh, I wish a rock would come on this side so I'd be in a cove.* Pretty soon he looked and there's rocks there; he's in a cove all right.[39] South Wind grew warm. He lay down there and went to sleep. Oh, I don't know how long he slept. When he woke up, ohhh—he was sweating. He opened his eyes, everything was dark. He didn't know what to make of it. He felt around all over and—ohhh!—he was all locked in the rocks, rocks all around him. He cried, *How am I going to get out?* He thought, *I'll have to call a bird with a bill that will pick and pick, maybe it can pick a hole. I want Woodpecker to peck a hole in this rock.* Little Woodpecker came, she pecked and pecked and couldn't do very much. "Oh," he said, "I wish to be turned loose. Make a hole in this rock." Then Woodpecker broke her bill so she flew away. Then he called Flicker. He said, "Auntie, come here. Make a hole in this rock. I'm in awful shape!"[40] Then Flicker came. She said, "Yes, I'll make a hole in the rock." Pretty soon Flicker had made a big hole. Now he could see daylight. Ohh, she must be big! She made a big hole! South Wind looked up where she was pecking overhead; she was a woman! He could see her legs. He reached up and felt of her legs. Flicker got mad. She said, "Ah, you're bad! I thought you really wanted me to dig you out." Flicker flew away. "Ohhh, come back, Auntie! I made a mistake!" South Wind called. She wouldn't come back. She'd pick no more. After a while he gave up trying to get her back.

Then he thought, *Well, I guess I'll pull myself apart.* He took off his arm and tore off his leg. He threw them out. Even though his eyes wouldn't take any room, he pulled them out and threw them out. He also pulled off his head. He threw it out. Then somehow that body crawled out. Then he put on his arm, his leg, and his head. But he couldn't find his eyes. They were gone. Seagull and Raven liked his eyes, and they had eaten them. He was blind then. He felt his way. He thought, *I'll have to follow the bank all the way, it's all I can do.* Then South Wind found some snowberries, and he put two of them in his eye sockets so it would look like he had eyes.[41]

He went on, feeling his way. Pretty soon he felt the side of a house. He thought, *Well, I'll keep feeling till I find the door.* The person who owned the house, Bald Eagle, spoke from the roof: "There's South Wind. Why is he measuring my house?" "Oh," he said, "my friend, it's only because I understand your house is very big. I've heard about this house for a long ways. I wanted to see just how big. It's sure a fine big house!"[42] What are you doing up on the roof?" Bald Eagle said, "Oh, I sit up here and look over the ocean. I can see out to the middle of the ocean.[43] Come on. Climb on top of the roof." South Wind climbed up there and sat down. Bald Eagle said, "I can see all over, I can see everything." South Wind asked, "Ha, partner! Can you look *clear across* the ocean?" Bald Eagle said, "No, I can't see that far." South Wind said, "I can see clear across. I can see people traveling on the other side. I can see women with big wooden bowls of berries. Can't you see them?" Bald Eagle said, "No, I can't see that far. Ohh, you beat me."

South Wind said, "Well, I'll tell you, if you want to try my eyes I'll take them off and you can try them on, and I'll put on yours and then I'll know just how far you can see." He said, "Now you won't be able to see with my eyes right at first." South Wind took Bald Eagle's eyes and put them on himself and gave the snowberry eyes to Bald Eagle. Then South Wind quickly rolled off the house. He came down and ran away. Bald Eagle went to speak to him and he was gone. So Bald Eagle called to the people, "Follow him! He must be a blind person and he's run off with my eyes. His are not eyes, they're just berries!" They followed him, but South Wind wished they couldn't run fast and they couldn't catch him.

Then Bald Eagle landed. After a while he heard Snail up on the bank. The snails had a voice like Eagle. Bald Eagle heard them talking. Snails had very good eyes but they couldn't travel fast. Bald Eagle felt his way there, and he found Snail. He tore off Snail's eyes and put them on. They were good sharp eyes. Bald Eagle also took his voice, saying, "Snail, you will be nothing, no eyes, no voice." Then Bald Eagle was all right again. The voice eagles have now was once Snail's.

——South Wind went on his way up the coast toward Rockaway. He was carrying a quiver filled with arrows. Whenever he desired to amuse himself, he took the arrows out of his quiver, broke them to pieces, and threw them down. At once they were transformed into men who began to sing and dance. On the following morning, when he opened his quiver, they all resumed the shape of arrows and jumped into the quiver.

——He went *all* over, way up streams and down to the ocean, all over. He arrived at Fishery Point.[44] He made little round rocks for playthings. You can pick them up there to this day. They look like half of a hard-boiled egg, cut in two with the yolk removed. They're white like that.[45]

——He went on to Nehalem. He went to a house there. No grown persons were there, just a lot of children. He said, "Where are your folks, your parents?" The children answered him in Clatsop (a Lower Chinookan language). "Oh," he said, "Nehalem is too close to Tillamook to be speaking Clatsop." Then he grabbed one of them and rubbed his mouth. Pretty soon they all spoke Tillamook. They said, "Our mothers went to dig wild potatoes [wapato]." "No!" he said, "There's no wapato at Nehalem. They are digging straw-roots."[46] Then the children said, "Our fathers are seining for Columbia River Chinook salmon." When the men came back, ohhh, they brought canoes loaded with fish. They threw them ashore. They were indeed Columbia River salmon. *Oh, no!* South Wind thought, *There are no Columbia River salmon around here.* He went up to the salmon and stepped on them and flattened them. He said, *You'll be nothing but flounder. You'll be bullheads. There aren't going to be any Columbia River fish around here.* Then some of those fish he turned into sturgeon. *There will be flounder and sturgeon, but no Columbia River fish here.*[47]

——Then he went on up the Nehalem River. He thought, *Well, now, I'll make some falls.* Still he heard the ocean. It was a big place. *Oh,* he said, *this is too close. I'll go far upstream.* He went far upstream. He made falls there. Then he said, *That far, then, the fish will go. They'll reach here.*[48]

——Then he came back to the beach again. He arrived at Fishery Point. Well, they didn't get mad at him there, so he stayed on there at Nehalem for a time. After a while he got ready to leave. He said, "Now I'm going on, I'm going on along the coast. You people set me across, I'll go around on that Neahkahnie Mountain." A person there said, "No, no! You don't want to go that way on shore. There aren't any people who ever go that way. There are four places where there are dangerous things, they look like ordinary women but they're cannibals. They kill and eat people." "But really," South Wind said, "I'll go on the land." The person said, "You must only go in a canoe. If you go too close to shore you'll be grabbed and killed by the Ogresses who live there." But he said, "No, I'm going on the shore." They begged him not to, but finally they set him across.[49]

——Then South Wind went on. He walked along the ocean beach. On the sandspit at Nehalem he gathered striped shells with a hole in the middle.[50] He picked them up until he had quite a few, then he rolled up a string and strung the shells on it and tied those strings around his knees. When he walked—ohhh! those shells rattled!

He had them on, he went, and he saw a little house with smoke coming out. *Maybe that bad woman lives there. Well, I'm going anyway.* That woman, she talked just like anyone. "Hello, Nephew!" she said. "Ah," he said, "Auntie, I've come visiting."

Then South Wind sat down. Every once in a while he moved his leg to make the shells rattle. And the old woman said, "Oh! Ohh! Ohh! Ohh! I like that sound! Ohh, that sounds nice! I'd very much like to be that way, too, with legs like yours." South Wind said, "Yes. Do you know how I did it? I fixed them that way myself." The old person (the First Ogress) said, "I want to be fixed that way myself. What did you do to yourself? Can you fix me that way, too?" He said, "Well, I hunted up a good flat rock, and another rock I could hold good in my hand, and I laid my knee on the flat one and hit it all around with the round one. That's why my knees rattle when I move them. Both my knees are fixed that way." "Ohh! I want my knees fixed that way!" she said. And South Wind told her, "All right. You hunt up a rock, a flat one, and one that you can hold good in your hands, and I'll fix your knees for you. You'll be that way, too."

The old woman went looking for rocks. She brought them. "Well," South Wind said, "Close your eyes and put your leg on this flat rock. We'll fix your knee." This old woman, "Yes," she said, "all right." Pretty soon, the old woman said, "Uuuuu! I don't like it! I don't like it! I'm scared." South Wind said, "All right. If you don't want me to, I won't fix your knees that way." The old woman said, "Oh, I really do want it. I'd like to be like that, too. I want my knees to rattle that way. You fix them." South Wind said, "Very well, but it works better if you keep your eyes shut." So she shut her eyes, and he hit her on the knee so hard it just killed her. He kept on hitting and mashing her all over. The old woman died.[51] After a while he set her house on fire and burned it up, and she was all burned up. And he thought, *Now no one will be killed or eaten on this beach. There's going to be a trail on this mountain.*[52]

——Then South Wind went on. He climbed to the foot of the trail, and he saw boys playing with a toy boat down on the beach. He thought, *There must be no such thing as kids playing in the ocean.* Then he built a fire and heated large, round rocks. They grew hot and he threw them in the ocean from Neahkanie Mountain. Then the ocean boiled. He made breakers. He thought, *So in the time to come, only in the summertime, when it's a good day, will the water be smooth. On bad days that ocean will boil and there will be breakers. No skiff, no small boat of any kind will be able to travel on it then. Children will no longer play out in the ocean.* Today one can see those round rocks up on that mountain where he built his fire. They're all red where they were burned.[53]

——He went on. He got to Short Sand Beach and came downhill. He heard an old woman bawling. "Oh, my poor old sister, she's all smashed up by a rock. She's smashed, all her bones and all by a rock. She's burned up and everything." South Wind got kind of afraid. *Maybe she got wise to me.*

Well, I'll wait. After a while he went in the house. "Hello," she said, "Oh, my Nephew!" "Hello, Auntie," he said.

Then he sat down and moved his knees and those shells rattled. And my goodness! That old woman got crazy over the same thing. The old woman said, "Oh! I'd very much like to be like that." He said, "I fixed myself this way." He said, "If you like, go get some rocks and I'll make you this way." The old woman said, "Fine." She got some rocks and came back. He said, "Close your eyes." The old woman said, "I'm afraid." He said, "Oh, no." This old woman said, "Oh, really, I do want to be like that." He mashed her leg. Then the old woman (the Second Ogress) died. He killed her in the same way. It was all the same way again. He burned her house, too. This was near the foot of Neahkanie Mountain. He thought, *No more, no such thing here, nobody will be killed and eaten.* (He didn't get a meal off them, he'd always kill them first.) He thought, *Way later on there won't be any Ogresses living here. People traveling here won't be killed in the future.*

———Then South Wind went on again. He found another woman, a *real person.* He stayed there at Arch Cape with this woman for the year. He liked to stay with her. He lived with her. (Her name was Year Around.)

He asked her, "What are you doing with so many baskets? You're all alone and each basket is full of dried fish."[54] She told him, "Each basket counts for one month." But she had twenty baskets. He said "Twenty baskets for one year? No! That's too long a year, that can't be!" "Yes!" she said. So every time she'd go out, he'd take ashes in his hand and throw them on a basket of dry fish and then they'd look gray. When the woman picked up her fish she said, "Ain't that funny? Why is there mildew on my fish? My fish spoil too quick." South Wind said, "It's almost summer." Then the woman said, "No, you always talk that way. It's too soon, it ain't summer yet."

When they'd go to bed, he'd go to work and get hold of the strings of her cedar-bark skirt and break them off here and there. And, "Oh!" she said, "Why then, here's my skirt wearing out before spring. It's never done that way before." South Wind said, "Well, it's getting summer. You ought to know that. I'm going out and peel some cedar bark for you." "Oh," she said, "it's wintertime, you can't get any cedar bark." He said, "Well, you wait! I'm going to get it for you." Then he went.

Well, he went and he found a cedar tree, and he knew it was wintertime yet. So he took off his penis, and he talked to that tree and he said, "This year it's going to shift early." Then South Wind hit the cedar tree with his penis and said, "Your bark will come loose, Cedar. Now! Come on, you shift early! It's springtime." So pretty soon he took his knife and cut bark, and he got off all he wanted and made a bundle of it.[55]

Then there were no leaves on the bushes (because it was not yet spring), so South Wind sat down and defecated. Then South Wind finished. He took his own feces and threw it on the salmonberry bushes. He said, "You'll be berries," and there was all kinds of leaves and salmonberries. Then South Wind went and picked them. He fixed evergreen ferns and put the salmonberries on them,[56] and he made another bundle. Then he packed the cedar bark on his shoulders, and he laid the bundle of salmonberries on top. Then he went back home. He got there and he left his bundles outside by the door. He came inside. "Oh, see," he said, "I'm just sweating from too hot a day." This old woman said, "Oh, where do you get that stuff? It ain't hot today." "Yes, it is hot. Oh, yes. I got your cedar bark and yes, I got you some salmonberries."[57] He said, "Go out and bring in the bundle of bark and the bag of berries." She didn't say any more. She went out and got the bundles. She brought them in and said, "Oh! Salmonberries!" She put them in a wooden bowl and pretty soon they ate them. "Well," he told her, "You know this is summertime. You've got to throw those dried salmon away, they're all mildewed." So she threw them away.

He said, "Now one year has got to be twelve months, no more twenty-month years."[58] "All right," she said. He had gotten the best of her. "It must be like that." Then he said, "I'm going." After he got her the new skirt to make and got her to believe that way, he left her. (Guess he didn't care about her that much.)

——Then South Wind went. Soon he grew sleepy. He lay down on the beach to sleep. He slept. He was found by five hunters, who tied up his hair and fastened ugly things to his head. After a time South Wind woke up. *Oh, it's too hot. I'm thirsty.* He went to the creek right there to drink. He leaned over to drink. He saw a frightening animal in the water (it was his own reflection). *Well my goodness! What's that funny thing?* He got afraid of it and said, *Oh, I'm not going to drink right here.* He went farther up the creek. He leaned over to drink. Again he saw a monster, and again he was afraid.[59] *What kind of thing is that in the water? Animal or something?* He thought it was the image of some enemy who wanted to kill him and ran away. He ran a whole day, until he was too tired to run any longer. Then he touched his head and discovered what had happened. *Oh!* he said, *am I frightened at myself? Who may have done that to me?* But he was not quite sure he had been frightened by his own reflection. He went to the creek and shook his head to see if the image shook its head, too. Whenever he moved, that thing moved. Again he felt of his head. It was, indeed, his own hair! It was tied up in knots. Someone had made all knots in his hair. The thing in the water did the same thing. *Oh, that is my reflection!* he said. Then he drank and went back down to the beach. *Somebody must have made knots in my hair while I was sleeping.* He saw tracks on the beach. They were the footprints of five men.[60] He said to himself, *Well, whoever you are, I hope you won't go far. I wish that you get sleepy and lie down on the sand to sleep.*

Then South Wind walked and walked. He followed these tracks in the sand. Pretty soon the tracks turned off toward the bank. He saw them sleeping, all of them. They were men on a hunting trip whom he had put to sleep. They each had a panther-hide bag where they kept their bows and arrows. He went up to them and took their panther-hide quivers and fixed them so they couldn't wake up. He pulled their ears long and tied up their hair. He emptied the quivers and put the bags over each of their heads. Then he walked off a ways and he woke them up. "Hey! Wake up! Wake up and turn into panthers!" he said. They all stood up. "Run off in the woods, you're panthers!" When they woke up they were all so frightened at seeing their own images that they ran up the mountains into the woods,[61] they were panthers, poor fellows. "You'll not make fun of me anymore," he said. "You'll be panthers now." He took their bows and arrows and went on.

——South Wind went on. Next he found a person with a dog. He asked him, "Where do you come from?" This person spoke Clatskanie. South Wind didn't understand him. He said, "In the future, they won't talk Clatskanie traveling down this side to Ocean Beach." He said, "You'll be nothing but a rock. Many mussels will grow on you. And your dog will also be a rock."[62]

——He went on. He saw a youth. This youth was kind of playing. South Wind didn't like it. He said, "You'll be a rock and later on they'll call it Walk Funny."[63]

——He went on and before he got to Cannon Beach he found a house with two old women (the Third and Fourth Ogresses) and a young girl, the last of them. *How will I get the best of them? I'll sing, "Oh, that power of mine, he told me I have to go without eating for two years if I am to continue living."*[64] He went around on the beach, singing and singing. One old woman heard him. She said, "Why! That is our nephew! He can't go that long without eating. I'm so sorry for him. Let's go take him in." They went and got him. They said, "You come in the house, Nephew." They fixed a place for him, they put matting on a place for him to lie down. And he sang steadily for five days and five nights.[65] He did this just to tire them out. He did it on purpose like that.

He said, "I'd like to have it, my power told me to have pitchwood and put it all around on the house, and fine dry grass to be put all around with the pitchwood. That's the way my power said to do it."[66] One old woman said, "During the day I travel all over in the woods, and I pass by lots of pitchwood. I surely can get that for you." The second old woman said, "I pass lots of fine dry grass during the day, I run across lots of it. I can get you that." So next day they left to get those things for him. After they were gone he went to sleep, so he'd have a good rest before they got back. When they came home, he was awake again, singing. The girl had been out in the creek all day bathing, because it was within the ten days after her first menstruation, her first monthly purification ritual.

When they brought him the pitchwood and grass, he said, "Oh, that's fine! That's the right kind. I'm going to be better now, I'll just sing now and then and not all the time." So after a while, about midnight, he went to sleep, and the old women went to sleep, and the young girl was still out at the creek, she was staying out all night. South Wind was not really asleep. After a while, when he was pretty sure they were sound asleep, he got up and walked around, and he fixed that house: from the roof he made it solid rock from the floor up. All around he made it that way. Then he lit the pitchwood that had been placed around, and he went outside. He turned the door into solid rock so they couldn't get out.

Ohhh! It got too hot for those old women and they woke up. They said, "Ohh! Our house caught fire! Ohh! we must take care of our nephew!" They looked for him, but he was gone. They wanted to break the door down, but they couldn't do it, it was solid rock. Pretty soon they burned to death.[67] Then he left. He hunted the young girl, then. He found her at the creek. He kicked her, and turned her into a rock. Now they were all done away with. And he said, *No more! No such thing here, no one will be killed and eaten.*

——Then South Wind went on. He walked quite a ways. He looked along the beach. Near the bank he saw a teeny little boy lying there, only it looked more like a grown person than a baby. It had its arm over its eyes, asleep. He went over and looked, *Oh, ain't he cute? What's he doing here all alone with no grown person? I think I'll destroy him. I'll trample on him.* South Wind hit the boy. His arm stuck fast.[68] He did it again and the other hand also stayed there. Then next he stepped on him. His foot stuck there. South Wind pondered. He thought, *Why?* Then South Wind thought, *I'll go lay down on him there. I'll roll on him and crush him and smother him.* He bent over, started to fall down, but South Wind got stuck. He couldn't move and he got afraid. He began to tremble all over, just like he couldn't help himself. The boy slept on quietly.

When South Wind was tired out by his attempts to kill the boy, the little man moved his arm from his eyes and woke up. He turned around and suddenly became a very strong man. "Who is bothering me around here when I'm sleeping?" the little person said in a rough voice. "It's just me," said South Wind, trembling all over. "What are you doing here?" the little person said. "It's just me," South Wind said, scared to death, "what are you trying to do to me, you who are a grandchild of mine?"

The youth said, "Don't call me that. Name my real name." South Wind said, "Yes, your name is kind of like Single Arrow." "Oh, no," he said. "That's only my hired man." He said, "Hurry up and name me." South Wind said, "Yes. You're Twin Arrow." "No, that's only my hired man," he said. "Come on. Name me." South Wind said, "Yes, you're Third Arrow." This boy said, "No, that's my hired man, too. Hurry and name me." South Wind said, "Oh, yes! Fourth Arrow." The boy said, "No, that's my hired man. That's not my name."

Finally, South Wind said, "Yes. You're Double-Bladed Knife. You're Xeha.[69] That's your name." The boy said, "Now that you've named me, I'll have to take you with me to my home to be my slave. You've got to go with me up in the sky. I live up there."[70] Then he took him. This boy, Xeha, said, "Don't open your eyes or you will fall." South Wind obeyed. He couldn't help himself, he had to go. Double-Bladed Knife took him with his eyes closed. He said, "If you open your eyes I can't help but drop you."

He got to the sky with him and South Wind stayed with Xeha, or Double-Bladed Knife. Then South Wind said, "Oh, I'm hungry." Double-Bladed Knife said, "I have no food. I don't eat food. If you're hungry, go to that lake.[71] I've got wives, but they don't live with me. They live there in that lake. Don't think anything is strange. Don't think foolish things. Just think about 'Poor me! I'm so hungry!' Finally they'll give you food. They are my own wives. But if you make fun of me in your thinking, or wonder what you're doing there, they won't give you anything. They'll just laugh at you." Then South Wind went to the edge of the lake, and he sat down. He waited a long time. He just couldn't help it, pretty soon he thought, *Why am I looking for a meal at a lake? How foolish I am. There's no food. Who's going to give me anything to eat?* The lake bubbled up. He saw bubbles in the water, that was all he saw, just bubbles where they were laughing at him. He sat there for a long time. Then he got tired and he went back to his little man.

Double-Bladed Knife said, "Did they feed you?" He said, "No, there was no food." He said, "The lake bubbled." Double-Bladed Knife said, "They made fun of you. You were probably thinking it was queer. They were laughing at you." South Wind answered, "Well, I thought, 'What am I doing, sitting here by this lake?'" He said, "Didn't I tell you not to think those things? What did the water look like?" South Wind said, "Oh, just bubbles, lots of bubbles." Double-Bladed Knife said, "Well, they're laughing at you, making fun of you. You can't go back until tomorrow. Now tomorrow you go again." Oh, South Wind was hungry, starving to death. "Well," Double-Bladed Knife said, "you can go tomorrow, but don't think anything funny, just think about yourself. If anything floats up in a wooden bowl, eat it and put the dish back on the water. And anything you can't eat, don't pack it back over here. You're bound to eat it all up."

Next day South Wind went again. He was very hungry. Double-Bladed Knife said again, "Now you go. When you're fed, when you empty the dish put it back on the water. When you've had enough, don't bring any food back." Then he obeyed. He sat down again and thought of nothing. He didn't wonder at it. Soon a dish came up on top of the water. It came to him and landed right where he sat. He picked it up. Oh, he got those wild potatoes (wapato), they're cooked. He took them and ate. He ate them up. He put the dish on top of the water. It went away and then it sank. Then another one came up and landed where he sat. Oh, there was dry Columbia River salmon on it. He grabbed it and ate it. Then again he ate it up, and he put the plate back and it sank. Then another one appeared with mashed sun-dried salmon. It came to him. He took it and ate it. Again when he had enough he put back the plate and it sank. Soon another appeared. It came to South Wind. He grabbed it, too. Oh, it was camas. Ohhh, he liked them—camas. (You remember, to be sure to get enough, he once cut up his penis and turned it into three dogs!) He ate them all and put the dish back.[72] He got full. Double-Bladed Knife had said to leave when he was full, lest they give him more. South Wind got up. He said then, "I'll leave you, my nieces." He thanked them in his mind as he went home.

He went back. He got back to Double-Bladed Knife, who said to him, "Did they feed you today?" He said, "Oh, yes. They fed me lots." "Well, every day you go there and don't think anything wrong and they'll feed you."

Well, after a while he got foolish, though he had been warned already.

Double-Bladed Knife had said, "Never go near that lake at night. It doesn't look like a lake at night. It's a house, all lit up, all kinds of yelling and drumming. I myself, even I am afraid of my wives. They're bad monsters, those wives of mine. They are more powerful than me. Even me, I don't dare to go there at night. For your own good don't go there." At night South Wind went out. Oh, many people were singing and yelling. Then he came back in.

At night South Wind would hear so much excitement he would go outside and listen. And after a while it just ached his heart, he wanted to go there so bad. Finally, he sneaked out and went there. He went close. There was no lake there at all. Then he looked into a house. Oh, he saw Double-Bladed Knife's wives, beautiful women, pretty young ladies and many young men— the hired men. They all did tricks. They were gambling and playing different games. They were dancing and singing and having a fine time. It was like broad daylight in the house. There was a real moon there in the house. And a great big bullfrog sat there. And this bullfrog, after the singing and excitement, swallowed the moon.[73] It grew dark. Then after a while she'd spit out that moon. Then it would be like daylight, and they'd dance again. South Wind noticed that when Frog swallowed the moon everything was dark and everything was quite still then. After a while he thought, *I wonder what they're doing when everything is dark? And I wonder what they're doing when everything is still?* Then South Wind went back.

He got back there and his grandchild, Xeha, said to him, "Never go into that lake." Again it grew light. Then he went for food. They gave him food. At night he went again. And all of them were singing. They were doing all sorts of tricks. Then he thought, *Well, I guess I'll hunt me a big long rock. I'll find out what they're doing!* He picked up a rock and went in. Things ceased. Frog had swallowed the moon again. Well, he sneaked in, he took this rock, he hit Frog right on the back of her neck that way. He knocked her senseless, that Frog. She spit it out, that Moon. Well, for goodness sake! All those women and all those hired men, they're all screwing, that's what they're doing. When it got dark, the men made a grab for the women. South Wind got mad then. He said, *That grandchild of mine, his wives are all no good.* Oh, he didn't like it.[74]

He went back to Double-Bladed Knife. Double-Bladed Knife knew what he had been up to. "Oh," he said, "that's no good. I don't like it. It pretty surely means death for you. What did you do that for? Why did you go? Those women are Ogresses. Oh, I'll have to give you up to them, but you can beat them if you do just what I say." He told him, "I'll fix you up, I'll dress you so you'll be warm, and you must never look up. Hang your head down, don't look up. You sit here on this platform but don't look up. They're going to holler at you, those wives of mine and those hired men, they'll holler at you. They'll tell you this way, 'Hey! South Wind! If you don't look up that platform's got a spring and you'll be bounced way far away.' Whatever they say, don't look up! Don't do it! You just sit there and after a while they'll get tired and give it up and you will have beat them. Finally, if you look up, you'll be thrown far away." Double-Bladed Knife had to give him this trial, or he might be punished himself.

Then he fixed South Wind. He put him there on that platform. He said, "If they can't beat you, then I'll bring you back down home where I got you." Then these women started in hollering at him, they called him all his names, they said "South Wind!" They said, "Hey, Sanəč'aw',[75] look up! You'll get thrown off if you don't look up. Hey! you are going to fall off there, and oh, you'll be a long ways off. You're going to tip over, oh you'll be thrown far off. Hey! Look up! Hi there, South Wind, look up or you'll get thrown off. If you don't look up pretty soon you'll sure get damaged. Oh, come on! Look up!" No, he wouldn't look up.

After a while their power made him look up. He got thrown off. Awaaay, he was gone! Now South Wind was no more. He flew far away, nobody knows how far, even Double-Bladed Knife couldn't find him.

Then Double-Bladed Knife said to his two boys, "When you two go out playing take your bow and arrow and play all over. And if you find a large old man, that's your grandfather. Your mothers, they destroyed him. If you should find him, if he's alive, bring him home, you boys, bring him back." The children played with bows and arrows, shooting birds. Then they heard this old man crying. They listened. "Yes, a person is crying." They went there and they found him, and—ohhh—he was just skin and bones, he had had nothing to eat for so long. They said, "He must be our grandfather." He spoke to them, "Who are you children?" They said, "Our father said our grandfather was thrown far off from a platform, because our mothers were mad at him and wanted to punish him. Our father told us to bring that old man home." South Wind said, "It's me, grandchildren, it's me!" Then they packed him back with them (they had power); they brought him home to their father. Indeed he was just bones.

"Oh," Double-Bladed Knife said, "didn't I tell you not to look up? Oh, I have nothing to eat, I can't feed you, and you don't dare to go to the lake, they wouldn't give you anything." South Wind was all skin and bones. He saw a little bag with oil in it hanging on the wall. He pointed to it. He said, "What's that? It's oil, isn't it?" "Yes," said Double-Bladed Knife, "but it is no good for you." South Wind thought, *I wonder what it's for?* He said, "Oh, my mouth is dry! I want that oil to put on my lip. Just put a little bit on my lip, I need some kind of oil on my lip." Double-Bladed Knife said, "No, it's a bad thing." He said, "It's not good for anybody. No, you can't have it." South Wind said, "Just a little bit to put on my lip." He was bound to have some. Double-Bladed Knife said, "Oh, he's a nuisance." He took a quill feather and dipped it in the oil. He painted it on his lip. South Wind sucked his lips; he liked it; he swallowed the oil. Then South Wind's belly commenced to swell, swell, swell, swell. He was all blown up, oh, he was ready to burst. Double-Bladed Knife said, "Didn't I tell you? You see! It's no good for you."

Now South Wind decided to get rid of the swelling. Double-Bladed Knife couldn't help him, so he went out and defecated. Then there came out all kinds of bad animals—lizards, snakes, poison-no-good animals. They all crawled back into the lake.[76] Pretty soon the swelling went down, he was all right. Then he went back in the house. Double-Bladed Knife knew he couldn't keep him because there was nothing for him to eat. So he said, "Well, you've been here with me quite a while. Now I'll take you down. I'll set you down there where I picked you up." Then he took him back where he had found him and put him there.

——South Wind went walking along once more. Ohhh! he was hungry! He went over Tillamook Head and down to Seaside. That far he went.[77] There he saw Wild Chicken (Grouse) with lots of young ones.[78] He said to her, "Where are you going?" "Oh, I'm moving around; I'm going another place," she said. After a while he was so hungry, *Oh, I'm going to kill those young chicks*, he thought. He got a couple of them. The oldest, biggest one squealed. The hen turned around, "Ohhh! He's killing my children!" And she flew away. South Wind thought, *Oh, I miss that mother hen. I'd have more to eat if she were here.* He grabbed at one, the biggest of the grouse chicks. The big chick opened her eyes. She flew away. He couldn't get her. Then South Wind built a fire. He roasted the little grouse and ate. He didn't get enough. Then he went on again.

——After a while he saw a house. He went in. He visited a man and his son. This man had no wife. He wore a belt of two live snakes. South Wind wanted that belt, it just took his eye. "Oh, say, my friend," he said, "let me wear your belt for a while." The man said, "Oh, no." He said, "My belt is really pretty powerful. No, that belt is not made for anyone else to wear. I'm afraid it would harm you, it's just for me." South Wind said, "Ohhh, I'd like to have it just a little while!" That person took off the belt and put it on South Wind. Then he was satisfied.[79]

In a little while it commenced hurting him, those snakes were eating into his flesh and nearly squeezing him to death. He couldn't get the belt off. Soon South Wind said, "Oh, I'm very sick." The man said, "Didn't I tell you? There's no one fit to wear them. It's my belt."

The man took the belt off him. Then South Wind thought, *Ohh, I'm going to get even with him.* He went outside and he defecated. He said to his feces, "Let's you be a Lucky Bird. Let's hear you talk like one." At first, she didn't do it right. "Now talk like a Lucky Bird. Let's hear you talk right this time."[80] Then she talked to suit him, so South Wind said, "If this person comes out, tell him to keep climbing up higher. I'm going to tell him to come catch you. You go on up the tree and keep going up all the time. Don't fly away, you stay on the tree!" He went back inside. He said, "Say, I saw a Lucky Bird out in that tree!"

The man and his son went out with bow and arrow and tried to shoot that Bird. The son went up in the tree, looking for the Bird. They tried to shoot at the Bird with bow and arrow. South Wind kept saying, "The Bird is higher up in the tree." The boy said, "Indeed, I heard my grandfather say the Bird is higher up." The Bird kept going up the tree, and that tree kept growing taller till after a while it got clear up to the sky. That Bird went clear up to the sky. South Wind had told the Bird, "When he gets clear up to the sky, when he has followed you all the way, let him shoot you." Finally, the tree was stretching and this person arrived in the sky. He shot the Lucky Bird, and ohhh! It was no Bird, it was just feces! Oh, he was angry. He came back down. He thought, *I didn't force him to put on that belt of mine, what did he want to play a trick on me for? Now South Wind has played a bad trick on me. But I'll get even on him. I hope I find a whale on the beach.*

The man found a whale, and he spoke to the whale. He said, "When South Wind attempts to pack you ashore, you take him away out across the ocean with you and don't pay any attention to anything he tells you, just keep him out in the ocean." He then said to South Wind, "I want you to pack this whale." South Wind said, "Yes." He packed it. He was carrying the whale. Pretty soon he walked along, he tried to walk toward the house. He couldn't walk that way. Something seemed to pull his feet toward the beach, and pretty soon he found himself in the water.

Then the whale took South Wind way out in the ocean. Ohhh! He was cold! He'd try fooling the whale. Then he said, "Oh, you take me ashore. Oh, there were many sardines in by the rocks, they're plentiful in near the bank!" Ohh, this whale wouldn't obey. Again he said, "Oh, there are many sardines on the rock." South Wind was so cold. After he had been out there for months, finally then, indeed, the whale went in near land and South Wind thought, *Oh, this whale will soon spout*. South Wind got away from him then, he jumped ashore. He crawled up on the bank, and he was pretty weak.[81]

——From there he made it by beach to Fort Stevens. He met people.[82] This one man was tall and slim; he was Snake, that man, but he looked like a person. He was a fisherman. South Wind became friendly with him. The man asked, "Do you want to stay with me?" South Wind said, "Yes, I'm pretty hungry." The man told him, "Tomorrow we'll seine for fish." He said, "I make nets myself." South Wind said, "I'll help you." This Snake said, "Good." Snake made his nets from the fiber from some weed. He'd put it in his mouth and it foamed. Pretty soon he'd take it out and there was his net.

Then South Wind and Snake went out fishing. South Wind helped him catch some fish. They got back. They were hungry. South Wind brought the fish into the house. Then they cleaned them and roasted them. They ate.

Next day they went fishing again. They got no fish. Next day they went fishing. They got no fish. And every day, no fish! They ate all the fish they had caught, and they didn't have anything to eat any more. They wondered why. Snake didn't know what to do, but South Wind said, "What's the matter?" He went out and defecated again. Again he spoke to his feces. He asked her, "Would you tell me why there are no fish?" She answered, "Well, when you got those fish you cleaned them and ate them right away. You don't want to do that. Now, tomorrow when you go fishing again, if you catch fish, bring them ashore and cover them up with green branches and leaves. Let them stay like that till afternoon, then you can clean them and cook them. Then we'll eat. Then you must burn up its bones and its skin and anything that's left of the fish. Then put out the fire and build a different fire. Then it will be all right. And every day you'll have plenty of fish." The feces said, "When you wash your hands, don't throw the washing water outdoors. Throw it there at the edge among the ashes." South Wind said, "Now is that all?" The feces said, "Yes. That's all."

Then South Wind went back in. He told the news to the Snake. He said, "Tomorrow we'll go fishing again." He said, "You mustn't eat." Then again next day they caught fish. He said, "We'll bring them ashore. We won't clean them." They only covered them up, just as she (his feces) had instructed.

Finally in the afternoon, South Wind said, "Now we'll clean them. We'll cook and eat. We'll wash our hands and throw the water beside the fire on the ashes. We'll burn all the skin, bones, and the remains of the fish. We'll put out the fire and build a fresh fire." Then after a while South Wind got tired of staying in one place. He said, "Well, partner, I have to leave you. Now I'll go." Oh, Snake felt sorry, he said, "Oh, I wish you'd stay with me." South Wind said, "Maybe I'll see you again."

——He rose and went down to Clatsop, where he found salmon.[83] He caught one and threw it ashore. It flopped its tail. He transfixed it with a stick, but it still flopped its tail. Then he took some sand, put it on its eyes and face, and thus killed it. He said, *When my children come to be grown up they shall kill salmon in the same way by putting sand on their eyes*. So the Clatsop kill the salmon by putting sand on their eyes.[84] Then he made a large fire, intending to roast his salmon. After having eaten, he wanted to cross the Columbia River.

——Then he went upstream, up the Columbia River. He saw a man wading across right at Peril Rock. South Wind asked, "What are you going to do?" The man said, "I'm going to wade across. We have just one shallow place here where we wade across." South Wind said, "Ahhh—There must be no more wading across the Columbia River. It is going to be too deep." He said, "There, you turn into a rock." The man turned into a rock. (I've seen it there, right in the water.)[85] Some people point out that rock as South Wind turned into stone. But he himself traveled on.

——Again, South Wind went on. Well, somehow he got a canoe and he went on upriver. South Wind didn't believe what they told him. They said, "Don't you go across over there or a Monster will swallow you." There was a big animal living there in the water and he would open his mouth and suck in those canoes. South Wind tried. South Wind waded and he tried to paddle. He got swallowed—the water sucked his canoe under. He wasn't sorry, maybe he was a little cranky. He found lots of canoes inside, and some people down there inside the Monster.[86] Some were dead, they had starved to death, they'd been there for so long. South Wind got worried and thought, *What can I do? Oh, I hope those Fire Drill Carriers get foolish and get swallowed, the ones who always carry fire drills*.[87]

Pretty soon some Fire Drill Carriers were swallowed. These people felt around and felt around, and they felt around on him. South Wind got mad, he yelled, "What are you doing? What are you feeling around for?" These people felt around. They laughed at him and said, "What are you doing here,

South Wind? Why, did you get foolish and get swallowed?" They said to him, "Get up, South Wind. You can help. We'll build a fire." (And that's his wish. He's sure cute, he is.) Oh, he was pretty weak, he'd been going without food for several days. South Wind said, "Oh, is that you? Are you those firemaking people?" These people said, "Now we'll make a fire." "Yes, come on! We'll make a fire." Oh, South Wind got freshened up, he got up and helped.

Soon they built a fire. They split up canoes for firewood. They built a fire in the animal's stomach. They looked around, they built their fire right on the animal's heart. All sorts of beautiful canoes were inside, and that's what they built the fire with, with those canoes. Oh, many of the people were dead. They picked up the people who were alive yet, and they put them in the best canoe, with good paddles. And they picked out a good canoe for themselves and South Wind. Then there was a big fire there, of the canoes.

Pretty soon that animal began to suffer. Then the Monster said, "Ohhh! My heart is burning!" He was a big chief, and he said to his slaves, "Pack water for me! My heart feels like it's burning. I've got to drink water." Sure, it was burning, all right. He drank water and drank water. These people built many fires inside the Monster. They picked out the best boats. The people sat in them. They sat in the boats. Finally the Monster burst. All the people came out in their boats. South Wind came out also. That's how he lived in an animal's stomach one time. He spoke, "Well, from this time on, no animal shall swallow people. When people travel here, this river will be free and nothing will harm them. No animal will swallow them."

——He went on. He kept on going up the Columbia. Finally, he left his canoe and walked along.[88] Next South Wind took sick. He thought, *Why now? Oh, I'm sick.* South Wind stopped and camped. He didn't know who did it or how he got that way, but he got in the family way (became pregnant). He didn't know how it happened, but he knew what was wrong, and he began to have labor pains all by himself. Ohhh, he suffered, suffered, suffered. He nearly died, because as you know there's no place for a baby to come out. He don't know how to figure it out. After a while South Wind looked for a wild cherry tree and found it. The bark is like rubber, it's tough and stretches, and is peeled off around the trunk. He took the bark off it and he said, *I'll have to put this around my penis so it'll stretch. That's the only way I can do it, otherwise my penis will burst.*[89] He wrapped the bark around his penis. Then South Wind gave birth to a child. It was a girl. After that baby's born, South Wind thought, and said, *Well, men won't give birth. In the future only women will. Men aren't built to have babies.*

After a while he got ashamed of that baby. He said, *Oh, I'm not going to have this baby to carry around. I'll kill her. Now I'll go and bury it, this child*. Then he buried it. South Wind cried. He felt bad about it, and he didn't like to do it, but ohh, it is so disgraceful for a man to have a baby.

He walked on feeling awful bad, he was crying. He came to where some young men with feathers in their hair were laughing and making lots of noise, having a good time. He said, "I'm crying and you're laughing and having fun. You heard me crying and yet you're having a good time. You're going to stand right there. You shall be rocks." And he turned them into rocks. Five of them, there were. And you can see those rocks, with trees growing out of their tops. That's from the feathers that stood up in their hair.[90]

He walked on. A little farther on—my goodness!—he heard a baby crying. He found the same one, his own child. And there she was, just ahead of him. She was a little bigger already. She's grown like a weed. He hated it. *Oh, I can't have it, no! People will laugh at me*. Oh, he hated it. He killed her again. He picked her up and buried her again.

Again he went on, and he bawled and bawled. He found a child crying. He walked on, there she was. He found that it was the same one, his own baby. She was a little bigger, she was growing all the time. *Oh, ain't that a shame? That's my baby but I can't have it!* He did the same thing. He didn't like it. He killed her again, he buried her. He put limbs over her grave. He went on, crying. *Oh, she's going to beat me, she has more power than I have*.

He went on, and there she was again. She was crying. She's a pretty good-sized child, now. He said, *Oh, it didn't die, and now it's big*. He thought, *Oh, I'm not going to kill her*.[91] (Of course, he's got feelings for her.) He picked her up, he talked to her. He said, "You're my child, I'm your mother, but I can't pack you around, I'm traveling. I'll put you up here on the highest mountain, up on Mount St. Helens. You'll live there, that will be your place. When I get through fixing things, I'm going back to the south. That's where my home is, there in a cave. That's where I'll live. When our children get too mean, when there are too many people being mean here, you'll be powerful for this world. You'll stand up on your mountain and raise your hand like this (palm outward). And if you'll say just one word, I'll see you from the south, and I'll answer you with one word. And our words will go to meet each other, and everywhere as they go all kinds of sickness will happen. And those sicknesses will meet, and people will die off."[92]

"All right," she said, "I'll do that." Then he picked her up and put her there, and South Wind cried. Then he went on, and he didn't cry anymore because she's alive, now. He didn't name her, she's called South Wind's Daughter. Some place along the Columbia where he sat and cried there's a rusty, striped rock and they call it That's-His-Tears.[93]

——He turned around, and came along back downriver on the Washington side. He came down, didn't do much on the way down. He got to Ileac. He stayed there a while camping.

——Then South Wind came on down. South Wind made mashed dry fish. It is possible this occurred on the south side of the Columbia River, since this mashed dry fish was the product for which the Clatsop people were named.

——Then South Wind went to Fort Canby. He stayed there. South Wind went after crabs.[94]

——Then he moved on. He went to Bay Center (Washington). South Wind was hungry. He didn't know *how* he could get something to eat.[95] He said, "I think I'll make a fish trap, catch fish maybe." He built it and he built a fire. He went out, but there were no fish. Then he defecated. He put his feces there by the trap. He said to her, "Look here now! You'll stay here on watch." He said, "Should a fish jump into my trap call out to me and tell me." Then South Wind went back to his fire. He lay down.

Then his feces called out. She said, "A fish, a fish!" He went down but it was nothing but a leaf. He was angry at her. He said, "Why are you fooling me? Only call out to me if a fish comes to my trap." Then again his feces called, and again she said, "A fish!" South Wind went down. A little piece of wood was caught in the trap. South Wind was angry. He kicked his feces. He got her all over his feet. He said, "Now you'll call only for a real fish." Then he went back to his fire. Soon his feces called out again, saying "A fish!" He went down. It was only a spruce limb. Then he was angry. South Wind took the spruce limb and clubbed her with it. He said, "I told you that you were to call me only for a fish." She was of a mind not to call him at all. But after a long time she yelled out, "A fish!" Then South Wind went down. He saw a small female salmon, and he took it. He didn't beat the feces. Then he went back and cleaned it. He didn't eat the eggs. He only broiled the fish and ate it. It was rich and fat. South Wind didn't have enough to eat. Oh, he needed more fish.

Then he thought, *Well, I'm all alone. I think I'll make a person from the eggs. I'll turn those salmon eggs into twin girls.* Then South Wind looked at them. They were pretty little girls. He said, "You are my daughters." He said, "I am your father." (They were fish, so he wasn't ashamed of them.) He doubled back south to the Columbia River. He said, "Now we'll go far up the river." Now he had to have a canoe to take them on farther along the river. To the girls he said, "You two will steer the canoe." He put those girls, one to steer, one to sit in the middle. Then they went upriver. South Wind sat on the bow. He said, "You children will do the paddling, I'm not going to paddle." So they did. But they would make the canoe go this way and that and wobble it around, and he said, "Why is the boat going crooked? Don't do that! *You* paddle straight, and *you* steer straight!" But every time he turned his head they would do the same thing.

Then South Wind got mad. He said, "Why, why do my two wives steer the boat crookedly?" Those girls said, "Say! It sounded as though he said we were married to him. Let's steer the boat crooked again and see if that's what he said." They steered crooked, and again he said, "Why do you steer crooked, my wives? Oh, my two wives can't make the boat go straight." He did it to hurt them, you see, they thought he was really their father. He turned away again. The girls said to each other, "Oh, really! He called us his wives." They said, "Let's leave him. He's no good." They left. He didn't know it.

That canoe was a long and narrow one. They call this river Knot River, because the canoe going crooked made the river so crooked. And the fish are all small there because South Wind caught nothing but a small little fish.

South Wind said, "You're steering the boat crooked again." Then South Wind turned around. Nobody's steering and nobody's paddling. There was nobody there. His children were gone. Oh, he was sorry. He called. He said, "You're my Daughters. Come back. Oh, poor me. Come back to Dad! What did you want to leave me for?" They wouldn't come back. They kept on going. Then South Wind went on all by himself.

——These girls went on and they found an old woman taking care of a baby.[96] This old woman was blind. She was taking care of her grandson while her daughter was gone digging roots. Those girls took the baby. They fixed rotten wood to look like a baby.[97] They put it in the cradle. That cradle was hanging, and the old woman kept swinging it back and forth. These girls went far. They took the baby away with them. (They must have had an idea who that baby is.) They took him. That old woman was swinging that rotten wood.

After a while she thought, *Well, those girls, they're gone. That's funny that baby hasn't said a word or cried or anything.* Finally then, this old woman got up and felt in that cradle, felt for the baby and discovered it was only wood. *Oh,* she said, *That's what I thought. Those girls are South Wind's daughters, they're tricky, they're bad girls.* The old woman cried. She can't do anything, she can't go any place, she's blind. Finally her daughter came back. She asked, "Mother, what are you crying about?" She told her daughter, "South Wind's daughters came here. They stole the baby and put rotten wood in the cradle."

The woman said, "I'll follow those children of South Wind." Then she went on. She put a lake in front of them. Then South Wind's children got across. Then she put up a big mountain, with many trees. Oh, South Wind's children went on. They went through the mountain. Then she put down a big river. Nevertheless they got across. Oh, they were powerful.[98] They got the best of her. She gave it up and went back home. Ohh, she cried and cried. Now her mother became very ill from weeping and after a while she died. The lake was dried up. This woman's mother was the lake. The woman herself got blind from crying and crying, day after day. Ohh, it's awful.

When that woman got home after she gave up chasing South Wind's daughters, she took the bedding from the baby's cradle. It had been urinated on. This woman washed the baby's bedding. She talked to that urine water and said, "You're going to be another baby like my baby."[99] And from this dirty water she made another baby boy. She raised that boy. When he got bigger, the child went fishing in the lake. He caught frogs, water lizards, poison lizards, water dogs, all kinds of bad things, and he ate them raw. He'd catch a pollywog and eat it alive, and all the Monsters. Soon the boy got to be ugly. He had no legs and his belly got bigger and bigger, he's perfectly round, and black. Oh, he was just shining black.

——The women went on to far places, perhaps over the mountains. They are known as the Younger Wild Women.

Those two girls, the Younger Wild Women, went. They got to a cave and they made their home there in that cave. They took that boy and they raised him. When he got to be a young man they married him, both of them. That was what they stole him for. After a while they raised children by him. They never allowed him to do anything. They'd go get things to eat. They'd go away every day and come home way late in the evening. He would stay home and take care of those children.

Everybody knew about that baby being stolen. Soon Ice said,[100] "Ah, I guess I'll go look for South Wind's children." He said, "They stole the baby. I'll go and look for them." Ice had a strong power. He could turn things into anything he wanted. He went in a canoe. After a while he got to a cave (where the kidnapped boy lived with South Wind's daughters as his wives). *I'm going to look around here, I believe it's such a place where they'd stay.*

The boy came to the door. He was a young man and had lots of children. Ice said, "Oh, do you live here?" The young fellow said, "Oh, why did you come here? I don't want you to stay here. My wives are powerful. If they catch you they'll kill you."

Ice said, "You've got to come with me, you come along with me. I'm looking for you." The boy said, "No, I can't. I'm frightened. My wives are bad things." He said, "I can't do anything. These are my children, poor little things. I can't leave my wives on account of my children." Ice talked to him, he said, "Really, I'll take you along. Your mother is blind from crying." This boy said, "Oh, now, you'd better go. They'll see it wherever you had your hand and wherever you sat." Ice said, "That's all right." He said, "Oh, come along. You've *got* to come." Well, after a while Ice talked to him so much, the boy said, "Yes, fine—I'll go with you." He got ready.

The children cried and cried. Some of his children cried so much they spit blood out of their mouths. Some cried so much they had blood streaming from their eyes. Oh, he felt bad, too. He'd been making his children lots of little toys. Some looked like men, some were wolves, those playthings he'd carved for them. *Oh*, he thought, *I can't leave my children to be this way. I'll turn them into something else, I'll change them into fish.* So he turned them into little fish. Some were sturgeon. Then he put his children in the water. He took all his children's toys, and he put them all around their heads and he said, "They will be bones around your heads. After a while, when people catch fish they'll find these little bones around their heads." (And one does find them on sturgeon; they look like different kinds of animals.)[101] Then he put those fish into the water. He left. He went with Ice. He said, "All right, it'll all burn down, even the rocks will be cracked up."[102] They all cracked.

——Then South Wind's children (the two Younger Wild Women) got home. Oh, the boy was gone. They had no husband. Then they said, "Ohhh, we can't find our husband." They said, "All right, we'll go into the water. We'll turn into fish."

——Then Ice took him along—he's tricky, too. Close by there was a town. Ice talked to the young man. He said to him, "Do you want to get married? You should have a real woman, not like those two wives. They were too powerful, they were liable to get mad at you and kill you." Ice said, "There is a town. I guess I'll call a young girl." The young man said nothing. When they got to this town, Ice hollered, he said, "Oh, anybody wants to, come down to the canoe. There is a good-looking man with me."[103] Then he told the young man, "The one who can reach the canoe, that's the woman you'll marry." After a while this maiden came down. Ice did the talking. Of course, he put a spell on her, I suppose. He kept saying, "Pee, pee, pee!" And that young girl was so attracted to that fellow, she got kind of funny, and she peed on herself before she could reach the boat. Ice said, "You go back now, you're disgraced. You go on in the house, you're disgraced." (Ice was a bad old man, but he was comical, too. He just couldn't leave anything alone, he had to have his nose into everything.) She went back into the house. Ice said, "Now we'll go on."

Then they found another town where Ice lived with his own daughter. Ice's daughter came out toward the canoe, and he talked the same way to her. Again he called to the maiden, "Come here. Here is a good-looking man." He said, "Come on down. If you reach this canoe, you'll marry this man." Then he said, "Pee, pee, pee!" His daughter also couldn't reach the boat. She also peed on herself. He told her to go back in the house. She was ashamed and ran back.

Again he said, "Now we'll go on again." Then they reached another town. Again Ice hollered. He said, "Come on, maiden. There is a handsome man in my boat." The maiden came down. She urinated and ran back. Ice said, "Now we'll go."

They moved to another town. Again Ice called. He told the maiden to come out. "Come here." Soon she came out, "Mmm mmm mmm." Frog hopped out. (That's a frog, but she's a person.) She hopped around, she came, and he said, "Pee, pee, pee!" But no! Frog wouldn't do that, she wouldn't pee on herself. She reached the canoe, she climbed in and sat down beside the young man.[104] Oh, he didn't like it. After a while he said, "I can't take anyone, except if she be beautiful." He didn't like her—she wasn't cute-looking or anything.[105] Frog said, "You can't find another woman like me. You are going back home to your mother. Your mother is blind from crying, your grandmother is dead, and your little brother is ugly. He grew a funny shape. He's been eating monsters. That's what made him ugly, and he's all black. If you accept me, I'll make him better. I'll make your mother see again."

She said, "Look at me, I may not be beautiful, but I'm pretty smart. I can do 'most anything, and I can make 'most anything. See what else I can do." She took some deer hide and put it in her mouth. After a while she pulled it out. It was soft and white, like perfect chamois skin.[106] She said, "See that? See what I can do?" The young man looked. Frog said, "If you accept me, I'll fix your mother's eyes, I'll bring your grandmother to life, I'll fix your brother and he'll be far better looking than you are." She told him that way.

This man said, "Good. All right. I'll do that." They went on back to the young man's home.

——Ice left them and went back to his own home.

——The young man and his wife, Frog, got home. His mother didn't know him because she was blind. And that lake was all dried up, that was his grandmother, the lake. First Frog fixed the mother. She rubbed her face so she could see. Ohh, she saw her son then! And then Frog brought the grandmother to life and made her able to see, too.

His little brother was ugly. You could hardly see his feet. Then Frog got hold of the little brother. She took him by his feet and turned him upside down and shook him. All the Monsters came out of his mouth—the poison lizards, water lizards, and pollywogs he had been eating came out and went back into the lake. She fixed the child. He was better. Then she rubbed him down until he was nice and slim and good looking. She polished him until he was so bright he just made everything hot. You couldn't look at him, he was so bright. The limbs of trees split open, they were so hot, and people couldn't stand it, they had to stay in the water to keep from burning up. The ground was all dried up and rocks were cracked open, they popped, everything was just burning up.

The older brother said, *Oh, this won't do. If a baby is born in the summertime it can't live. It'll die if it's this way, it's too hot.* The older one (the son returned from being kidnapped) said, *It's not right for my little brother to live down here.* He said, "My young brother, I'm going to put you way high up in the sky. You'll travel in the daytime. Then I'll live close by. I'll be Moon in the nighttime." Did you ever notice the spot on the full moon? That's Frog, that's Moon's wife.

——South Wind made all the rocks, rivers, and cascades while traveling all over the world. Finally, he returned to the country of the salmon where he came from.

——South Wind went back south then.[107] He went to visit this misshapen old man. South Wind said, "Come visit me, my friend, and bring feathers, coal, and ashes, also clay and blankets. Then you will meet many Monsters along the way. When you meet one, you must put clay on him, and stick feathers and coal on him and throw ashes on him." Later this man went to see South Wind. Oh, on the way he met many Monsters. He got hold of a Monster in the dark and put feathers on it. He also put coal on the Monster, and ashes and clay.[108] Finally, then, there were no more Monsters. Soon it was lighter. This person could see and here soon it got to be day. Then he came to South Wind's house. South Wind was happy. He said, "My friend has come." Then South Wind went to get a whale and cut up the meat. He said, "Eat, since I, myself, brought the whale some time ago." Then this person ate the whale.

Finally, South Wind said, "Do you want fish? If you'd like to have some, go hook one." This person said, "Yes, I like to eat fish." This person hooked one. South Wind said, "Take one of your blankets. Spread it and clean the fish there." This person really did so on his blanket. South Wind said, "Now burn that blanket—put it in the fire." This person did so to his blanket. Then he roasted the fish and ate them. Then South Wind said, "This evening many people will visit me for fun. They'll come to see you."

Soon it was evening. They heard a noise. South Wind said, "Now they're coming." They came in, one by one. Each went and stood, and then another one came in and stood up. Then they reached around the house. Then South Wind said, "Look over there. That's your blanket he's wearing. You thought you burned it, but he's wearing it." Then they sang and they danced. Ohhh, they danced. Finally it was midnight. Then how they went![109] This man grew tired. Finally he said, "I'll go away. I'll leave you, my friend." Then he went away.

He reached home and brought the news. Occasionally, after a long time, again this person would say, *I think I'll go visiting*, and he went to visit South Wind several times. Each time he brought all sorts of things. Then when he got there, South Wind said, "Oh, you've come again." Always this person said, "It's long enough since I saw you. So I had to come again." South Wind fed him whale again. Again he said, "You want fish. Go hook it. Clean it on your blanket and burn it." This person did that way. Again in the evening they danced. Again people came. This man saw his blanket. They were wearing it. They danced long. Finally it was midnight, and they went away.[110]

Finally this person said, "If I should die, I'll never come again." South Wind said, "Yes, yes, fine." South Wind told this person, "When you get home, tell the people that if they mistreat my children, then I say my own daughter will send sickness.[111] If my children are mistreated they come back and tell me." Then this person went to Yaquina. He told everything.

Then a young man went and told the news, also at Nestucca. Then also one young man from there brought it here to Tillamook. A youth told it, and then at Nehalem. Also one youth went to Fort Stephens to tell them.[112]

——South Wind went back down the coast toward his home in the south. He came to a place called NtsEa'nixil on the Siletz River. People say he transformed himself, his wife, and his child into rocks, which are seen up to this day. The head of the man and the breasts of the woman are easily recognized. He is standing between the two other rocks. His life returned to the country of the salmon, of which he is the master.[113]

Notes

Terry Thompson's research on Tillamook has been supported by the National Science Foundation and the National Endowment for the Humanities. Douglas Deur's research on Tillamook has been supported by the Oregon Council for the Humanities.

1. "Yellowhammer" is an East Coast local term, but the West Coast subspecies does not have the yellow feathers.

2. The "Box of Daylight" story is a widespread Trickster/Transformer tale on the Northwest Coast. In the various retellings of this story, Raven saves humankind from perpetual thirst and darkness brought about by a miserly chief who keeps the sun, the moon, and often the world's water or food in boxes in his house. Taking on the form of a grandchild of the chief, Raven opens each of the boxes in turn, releasing the sun, the moon, and the world's water so that these essential things may be shared by all people. Parallel stories are commonplace among Amerindian groups, though the specific beings and withheld objects vary between regional tellings.

3. South Wind or Everlasting Man was in addition called *tkahyal*, "our grandfather," and Sunnutchul, an untranslated pet name given to him by the powerful sky being, Double-Bladed Knife (E. D. Jacobs 1959:123).

4. The Steller's jay (*Cyanocitta stelleri*), locally called "Bluejay," was an important figure in Tillamook mythology, a female messenger who brings valuable information to frustrated characters, or warnings to travelers in imminent peril.

5. Among the peoples of the coast, such a "king" did not have titular powers, but would simply be the highest-ranking and most wealthy chief among all villages.

6. It was customary to take a new bride back to visit her family early in the marriage.

7. Each time South Wind journeys on, it will be with a new paragraph, which will be introduced with a long line: ——.

8. In other Northwest stories it is revealed that his wife is Louse, who is very small and did not travel very fast.

9. A mythical place, which was probably conceptualized as being up the Siletz or Yaquina rivers.

10. A village at the mouth of Neskowin Creek where it flows into the ocean at the present town of Neskowin.

11. The East Wind blows from the mountains in cold weather, but not usually in the spring.

12. Probably a reference to the shiner perch (*Cymatogaster aggregata*), a widespread small fish of shallow bays. These fish tend to aggregate in schools and are easily fished with scoop nets and other devices.

13. Since shiners did not appear before spring, this was a strange thing to say.

14. Netarts Bay is an ecological anomaly along the Tillamook coastline, a large, protected bay that lacks a major tributary river. As such, it is unusually saline, and was, at the time of European contact, noted for its abundant shellfish, particularly native oysters (*Ostrea lurida*). The bay was briefly called Oyster Bay by early settlers for this reason, but the Tillamook village name, Netarts, persisted. Clams and the bay mussel (*Mytilus edulis*) are also common in the bay. While clams

and mussels can still be found there, the native oyster is now gone, a victim of overharvesting, diminished water quality, and introduced parasites. With the mention of mussels—which thrive with greater salinity than is found in some other bays in the Tillamook area—this passage probably invoked this difference in shellfish between bays to Tillamook listeners.

15. Although Clara Pearson vaguely describes the creek as being somewhere north of the town of Bay City (which is east of Bay Ocean), the actual sandspit points due north. Directly north of the sandspit, near Barview, Smith Creek drains into the bay. Smith Creek is a large stream, suitable for such bathing, and it may have been the creek in which the girl bathed in earlier tellings of the *South Wind* epic.

16. According to legend, he can increase the length of his penis at will.

17. The exact identity of these grasses is uncertain, and the same grasses may not have always been involved in the Tillamook retellings of the *South Wind* tale. Still, the grasses listed would have been known to the Tillamook as sharp and durable grasses: "sharp grass" and "tideland grass" may both have been sedges of the genus *Carex*, including the stout and sharp-edged slough sedge (*Carex obnupta*), the Lyngbei's sedge (*Carex lyngbeii*), or both; three-cornered grass was probably the American bulrush (*Scirpus americanus*), and the reed was likely the sturdy "common reed" (*Pragmites australis*). All were used in Tillamook basketry. The "mountain grass" to which South Wind finally appeals is *Xerophyllum tenax*, a very tough grass from high elevations. So prized was this grass for use in basketry that coastal peoples traded or traveled long distances into the mountains to collect it; so sharp was this grass that Tillamook women historically wore leather finger stalls to avoid cutting their fingers when splitting the grass for basket weaving (Crawford 1983:53). To the Tillamook listener, South Wind's progression of appeals, from locally abundant basket grasses to more valuable, stronger, and more geographically remote "mountain grass" would have served to underscore the urgency of South Wind's plight.

18. There are stories throughout the Northwest about sprinkles of menstrual blood becoming berries. The implication probably is that the girl was a virgin. "Shot-huckleberry" is a reference to the evergreen huckleberry (*Vaccinium ovatum*)—the small, dark-blue to black berries presumably looked like buckshot to early explorers, and the term for these berries in Chinook Jargon was *pow ollallie*, or "shot berry." The term "shot berry" was commonly used by early Euro-American settlers and tribal members alike. The hills on the sandspit are still visible and consist of small dune areas stabilized by scrub vegetation, including salal (*Gaultheria shallon*) and huckleberry. Both of these berries, salal in particular, were of importance to the Tillamook diet. Most of the bays along the Oregon coast are almost enclosed by long peninsulas of this type.

19. Although salmon were found in the Tillamook River, they may not have been present in quantities that justified intensive fishing at this site. Unlike most of the rivers that drain into Tillamook Bay, the Tillamook River is a short river, slow moving, with a very low altitudinal gradient. As such, it is a relatively poor salmon stream but has many flounder and other fish that can tolerate such sluggish waters.

20. Up the Tillamook River.

21. Probably a reference to the sandbars at the place where the Trask and Tillamook rivers converge as they enter Tillamook Bay.

22. A long river that tumbles through the high mountains east of Tillamook, the Kilchis River (named for the contact-period Tillamook chief, Kilchis) has long held a reputation as an excellent salmon fishing river.

23. Several Northwest area stories include a portion about Coyote going to sleep while his fish cooked. Another trickster comes along, eats the fish, and smears grease on Coyote's mouth. Coyote wakes, tastes the grease, and wonders why he is still hungry.

24. Termed *Membrum virile* by Boas (1898c:141).

25. In a place with no wind, South Wind may have been less powerful, and less able to defend himself.

26. This is the rock outcrop at Sandstone Point, which, as the name suggests, is made of coarse sandstone. Sandstone net sinkers and other tools likely made from this sandstone outcrop have been found around Tillamook Bay. The claim that people sharpened their knives on the coarse stone there is entirely plausible.

27. Some say that he destroyed the rest of the camas root that was in her pack. Camas (*Camassia quamash* and *Camassia leichtlinii*) were important parts of the Tillamook diet, and were, according to the field notes of Elizabeth Derr Jacobs (1933 ms.), the most important root in the diet of the Tillamook prior to European contact. Camas was largely dependent on Tillamook land management—most notably the use of fire—to survive in clearings in the dense coastal forest. As the tale suggests, its distribution is very "patchy." Despite South Wind's claim that they "will always grow there," camas has almost entirely disappeared from the ocean coast, as the Tillamooks ceased burning and introduced livestock occupied those clearings that were not promptly overgrown by young forest. Deur (1999) has suggested that camas was not truly native to much of the Tillamook territory at the time of contact and was essentially a "cultivated plant" in the spruce-hemlock zone; populations of camas were likely introduced or maintained through the active trade in this plant, a trade reflected in the portage of camas mentioned in this episode of the South Wind epic tale. The mention of South Wind distributing camas to parts of the Tillamook territory might reflect some cultural memory of a human role in the introduction or maintenance of camas.

28. It was usual for old women to sing and pound their sticks for a shaman during a curing ceremony.

29. The heart cockle (*Clinocardium nuttallii*) is similar in appearance to other clams, but has a deeply ridged shell. Cockles are abundant in the soft sediments and calm waters of bays throughout the Tillamook territory, and have been a popular food source for the inhabitants of these bays, past and present.

30. The sturdy wood of the Sitka spruce (*Picea sitchensis*) was often used for the construction of digging sticks, though the distinctly hard wood of the western yew (*Taxus brevifolia*) was preferred when available.

31. References to beached whales are common in Tillamook folklore. When whales were beached it was a major event, attracting Tillamook people from many villages who butchered, divided, and processed these animals' blubber. It was this type of gathering that drew William Clark and other members of the Corps of Discovery to Nehalem-Tillamook territory near present-day Cannon Beach, Oregon, in January of 1806. Historic Tillamook made references to their ancestors hunting whales when speaking with ethnographers; this appears to have been attempted through harpooning, canoe ramming, shamanistic intervention, or some combination.

32. Copper and flint were two of the most coveted mineral resources of the Tillamook.

33. This was on the Miami River, which meets Tillamook Bay between Hobsonville Point and Garibaldi. The small river is navigable a short distance upstream, a fact reflected in the river's name (*mi-mie*, a Chinook Jargon term, meaning "downstream"). Infants were commonly strapped to a

wooden cradle board, often shaped like a small canoe. If infants were from elite families, their cradle boards had an additional, smaller board attached at one end, pressed against the child's head and bound to encourage the flattening of the head.

34. A village on the bay shore, a short distance west of the mouth of the Miami River, near the modern town of Garibaldi.

35. Probably of the genus *Acrosternum*, these bugs were of no practical use to the Tillamook. True to their name, they stink.

36. Ethnographic consultants noted that reddish hair and light complexions were considered evidence of great beauty among the Tillamook. These traits appear to have existed prior to regular European contact, and it is unclear whether they reflect outside genetic influences.

37. Barview is a community on the north shore of Tillamook Bay, where it meets the ocean.

38. At this point, Clara Pearson noted, "Whenever he wished something it always happened. It was magic power" (E. D. Jacobs 1933 ms.).

39. This steep bluff is still visible at Barview, as is this cove surrounded by small offshore rocks. These rocks are of significance in other Tillamook tales, and are elsewhere depicted as supernatural beings turned to stone.

40. "Little woodpecker" was one of the two small woodpeckers of the genus *Picoides* found locally, either the downy woodpecker (*Picoides pubescens*) or the slightly larger hairy woodpecker (*Picoides villosus*). Ultimately, South Wind is forced to call the larger woodpecker, the red-shafted flicker ("Yellowhammer") (*Colaptes auratus*), underscoring the urgency of his situation.

41. Versions of this story are known throughout the Pacific Northwest. The eyes are usually the first part of a carcass eaten by gulls and ravens. The common snowberry bush (*Symphoricarpus albus*) produces berries that are vaguely eyelike, white, with a small black dot on the terminal end. Snowberries were described as the food of dead people in the oral traditions of many coastal peoples.

42. The large house would have indicated Bald Eagle's wealth and high status, and its size would have been deserving of such scrutiny and admiration. The bald eagle (*Haliaeetus leucocephalus*) was formerly very common in the Tillamook territory, particularly around bays and salmon-bearing streams; eagle populations declined abruptly after white settlement, but their numbers have increased in recent years.

43. Eagle was noted for his ability to see far.

44. Fishery Point is located directly across from the large village site of Nehalem. It would have been the most prominent landmark in the immediate vicinity of this village, and it is therefore not surprising that so many events in Tillamook folklore occur there.

45. There are many unusually round, egglike rocks at this site, polished smooth by the passing of sediment-laden tidewaters. Certain round rocks were a traditional part of a shaman's equipment among some Oregon tribes, while other round rocks were used as playthings by the Tillamook.

46. Possibly the seacoast bulrush (*Scirpus maritimus*) "*swahalh q'eigi's* . . . grow on water, look like natural weeds, but you eat them raw" (E. D. Jacobs 1933). It is less likely that this is a reference to the roots of eelgrass (*Zostera marina*). Both of these plants have roots that grow partially or wholly submerged, like wapato, and would have made an environmentally suitable, but far less desirable, replacement for wapato, and a starvation food by some tribes' standards.

47. The mention of "Columbia River salmon" or Chinook salmon (*Oncorhynchus tsawytscha*) and wapato (*Sagittaria latifolia*) here is telling. The Clatsop and Chinook peoples of the lower

Columbia River, living to the north of the Tillamook, were among the wealthiest tribes of the entire coast. Not only were the Clatsop and Chinook blessed with excellent access to trade routes between the coast and the interior, but they also had unlimited access to the most coveted foods of the coast, most notably the Chinook salmon (which had relatively small runs in Tillamook territory) and wapato (almost entirely absent in Tillamook territory). The fish South Wind left in place of Chinook salmon are edible, but a poor substitute for the abundant and tasty salmon. They include "bullheads," a generic local term for a number of sculpins, all considered "junk fish" by contemporary fisherfolk and thrown back when caught. The sculpin mentioned here is probably the Pacific staghorn sculpin (*Leptocottus armatus*), while the flounder is likely the starry flounder (*Platichthys stellatus*), and the sturgeon is of the genus *Acipenser*. Most of these fish were abundant in Nehalem Bay, and remains of all but the sturgeon were identified in the excavation of the village site at Nehalem (Minor 1991:62–65).

48. These falls are roughly ten miles upstream from the village of Nehalem, on the Nehalem River. Actually a series of cataracts rather than a falls, this was an important salmon fishing site for the Tillamook. Fish do regularly progress beyond the falls (a fact almost certainly known to the Tillamook), but the falls appear to be the most inland site at which the Tillamook exploited fish with any regularity. "They'll reach here," therefore, was more a statement of the *salient* distribution of salmon from the Tillamook perspective, rather than a statement of the overall geographical distribution of the salmon. Large social gatherings used to accompany the fish harvest at this site and some tribal descendants have continued to visit the site through the twentieth century (Deur 2005).

49. Reportedly, the people of Nehalem traditionally ferried people (who were traveling by foot) by canoe across the Nehalem River between Nehalem village and Fishery Point. This is apparently what is meant by "they set him across." Many early historical accounts mention residents of the Nehalem Bay village ferrying non-Indian travelers across Nehalem Bay at this point by canoe.

50. This took place on the beach just south of Manzanita. The shells were those of the keyhole limpet (*Diodora aspera*), a species of the open ocean, common on the ocean beach there, but rare inside the protected bay. Some people called them "squaw cap" and others call them "Chinese hats."

51. The mention of rocks as South Wind's weapon of choice, along with the appearance of limpet shells (the shell of a creature that occupies only the rocky outer coast), would have marked South Wind's transition from the protected, densely populated bays of the Tillamook world to the Tillamook's rocky northern territories.

52. The trail over Neahkanie Mountain was a very important one, connecting the lands of the northern Tillamook world with the densely populated bays of the Tillamook core during the wintertime. Its route is now largely overridden by Highway 101, though parts of the original trail still persist as maintained trails through Oswald West State Park.

53. The place where South Wind created heavy surf is still visible. In local lore, a hollowed-out area on the side of the hill is the place from which he scooped the stones, and the site is littered with large round rocks. From this cliff-side site, dramatic surf can be seen below, rolling, bubbling, and crashing. The red on the rocks mentioned in the tale, in fact, appears to have been caused by fire. The Tillamook extensively burned the vegetation on the slopes here, in order to aid in the growth of desired plants and to attract game. During the late nineteenth and early twentieth centuries, non-Indians continued this practice to maintain forage for cattle and sheep.

54. The Tillamook commonly stored such food in watertight baskets, placed on shelves or in rafters within the longhouse.

55. The western red cedar (*Thuja plicata*) was an important source of wood and bark to the Tillamook, as it was along the entire coast. The thin but strong bark of this cedar was peeled in the warmer months when the sap was running, as the tale suggests; this bark was pounded into a soft, cottony consistency, and used to make waterproof clothing or ceremonial regalia, for example.

56. Salmonberries (*Rubus spectabilis*), the watery, orange-colored cousins of the blackberry, were a common and important food among the Tillamook, becoming ripe in late spring or early summer. "Evergreen ferns" or sword ferns (*Polystichum munitum*) are common throughout the Tillamook area—they were used to wrap stored foods, or to line food containers and racks. Clara Pearson said, "The ferns would keep the berries fresh until they were packed back home" (E. D. Jacobs 1933 ms.).

57. This was always a sign of spring.

58. Clara Pearson possibly converted the year to twelve months for the benefit of her English-speaking listeners. Elsewhere (E. D. Jacobs 1933–34 ms.), she noted that the Tillamook recognized seven distinct segments of the year, based upon the foods gathered during each period: salmonberry sprouts (April), salmonberries (May–June), salal berries (June–August), Chinook salmon (late August–September), silver salmon (October), chum salmon (November), and steelhead (December–April).

59. This was possibly Fall Creek, near Hug Point.

60. Some say it was four men, some that it was five cougars, some that they turned into wolves, others say they became panthers. Both cougar and wolf are large predatory animals; only wolves tend to travel in groups as described here. Both wolves and cougars were found on this coast. Wolves are now extinct in this area, but cougars are still encountered on rare occasion in the mountains directly behind this beach. The animals were identified as "panthers," but cougar is the usual term in this region.

61. Steep, densely forested mountains rise from these beaches, rising to over 3,000 feet in height at Onion Peak, only a short distance inland.

62. Probably the mussel-covered rocks at Silver Point, at the southern end of Tolovana Park, south of Cannon Beach. One is quite facelike, and the other is a large rock with a long "tail" segment. The Clatskanie were a very small tribe inhabiting the headwaters of the Nehalem River and are poorly represented in the ethnographic literature. Their Athabaskan language probably seemed quite alien to the Tillamook, as would have their culture. Sharing the resources of the Nehalem River, there may also have been some mild animosity between these tribes, and possibly some interest among the Tillamook in geographically "containing" the interior Clatskanie, who had successfully established fishing rights on Chinookan lands on the Columbia River prior to European contact.

63. Likely an unnamed rock on the beach in central Tolovana Park, facelike, facing westward and slanting eastward.

64. A person had to carry out the commands of his spirit power. Other persons always obliged and aided in every possible way during a spirit power visitation.

65. Events surrounding persons in Tillamook folklore tend to occur in patterns of five for males and four for females.

66. Pitchwood torches were a common source of light, and were used extensively during shamanistic rites and winter ceremonies. They were commonly made from the wood and sap of the locally abundant Sitka spruce (*Picea sitchensis*); where available, torches of the Douglas fir (*Pseudotsuga menzeisii*) were preferred.

67. These rocks are probably Haystack Rock and the Needles, just south of downtown Cannon Beach. In other tellings of the tale, the women became rocks (the Needles) outside of the house during the fire, while Haystack Rock appears to be the house itself.

68. This boy was the legendary character Pitch Boy. Everything sticks to him. In another Tillamook version of this story, South Wind raises his arm to hit the boy and it stays raised and won't move; the same happens with his legs, then his whole body. He is immobilized and helpless, but not stuck to the boy. [For another version, see "The Story of Mink and Miss Pitch" in this volume.—Eds.]

69. That was the boy's Spirit Power. Double-bladed knives were weapons, used in hand-to-hand combat, though they also served ceremonial functions. They ordinarily consisted of two blades, hafted to either end of a handle, pointing in opposite directions. One blade was usually long and large, while the other was much smaller, and each was used differently in battle. Such knives were found along much of the Northwest coast. Elsewhere on this coast, double-bladed knives were often decorated to look like mythic humans or animals, with a face etched in the smaller blade, so that the small blade had the appearance of a head, the handle had the appearance of a long, narrow neck (or torso), and the long blade had the appearance of a torso (or long legs). As such, they may have been objects conceptualized as being in some manner convertible to supernatural beings, such as the character Double-Bladed Knife. This character may have been a manifestation of Thunder or Thunderbird.

70. This would have been a great hardship for the powerful South Wind, but the specter of capture and enslavement by outside tribes was a threat known by all tribes of this coast. This passage suggests that Double-Bladed Knife had no kinship relations with South Wind and was probably a being of some power and social standing.

71. While the topography of this episode of the South Wind tale seems heavily fictionalized, the scene may have been situated on the cliffs north of Cannon Beach, in what is today Ecola State Park. This is the only site for many miles in any direction at which one would have found a lake (now eliminated by twentieth-century landslides). Also, villages on these cliffs were situated at such high elevations as to warrant awe from Tillamook informants speaking to twentieth-century ethnographers, and this site fits within South Wind's south-to-north progression.

72. These delicacies being presented to South Wind were all common in the Clatsop and Chinook lands just over the horizon, but comparatively rare within the Tillamook territories to the south.

73. Probably a manifestation of the large western toad (*Bufo boreas*). There are many stories in the Amerindian Northwest about the relationship between Moon and Frog (or Toad). [There is a Spokane tale where Toad affixes herself to a handsome man's face and he decides to be the Moon; one can see the Toad's skin on the moon today. See also William R. Seaburg's contribution to this volume.—Eds.]

74. This may have upset South Wind not only because of the wives' promiscuity but also because of the violation of customs regarding sexual relations between people of differing social rank.

75. This was South Wind's sky name, probably used here to stress the seriousness of the situation.

76. Nearer the end of this epic, the child made from urine-soaked bedding grows up eating the bad animals from a lake, and grows very ugly. Frog repairs him by shaking him upside down, and the animals tumble out and crawl back into the lake.

77. At this point, South Wind had crossed out of the territories primarily occupied by the Nehalem-Tillamook into those of the neighboring Clatsop. This may explain why the narrator under-

scored that he had actually gone *that* far. The Seaside area, nonetheless, was an area of joint Clatsop and Nehalem-Tillamook use and occupation since the time of first European contact. William Clark noted a combined settlement of Clatsops and Nehalem-Tillamooks on January 7, 1806: "the Salt makers had made a neet Close Camp, Convenient to wood Salt water and the fresh water of the Clat sop [Necanicum] river . . . Situated near 4 houses of Clatsops and Killamox, who they informed me had been verry kind and attentive to them" (in Moulton 1990). Nehalem-Tillamook elder and Hobsonville resident, Ellen Center (n.d.), recalled in the 1930s that, "Lots of times I heard the old people speak of the Necanicum River. That was a place where the Clatsop and Nehalem—all people around here—would come together to hunt and fish. The wives would get berries. They were friends, great friends, always visiting, playing games." Nehalem-Tillamook interviewees, speaking with Melville and Elizabeth Jacobs in the early 1930s, reported that the Nehalem and Clatsop often gathered to spearfish at Seaside, while women picked berries in the vicinity of the fishing stations (Jacobs 1933–34: folder 106:7(2):10, 13; 106:8:23).

78. Called "Wild Chicken" in the original English narrative, this is a type of grouse, probably the ruffed grouse (*Bonasa umbellus*), a locally common and prized, somewhat chickenlike, game bird of the forest understory.

79. These events were probably situated at or near the Necanicum estuary. The motif of two snakes, or double-headed serpents, is common throughout North American and East Asian folklore, and such creatures regularly pose challenges to the culture heroes depicted in Northwest Coast oral traditions.

80. South Wind's feces is always spoken of as a female. The "Lucky Bird" was probably a swift or swallow; these birds were fast moving and difficult to catch. When caught, they were considered a source of great luck among many peoples of the coast. [See also the (Interior) Thompson story of Nx̣ík'smtm in this volume.—Eds.]

81. The South Wind tale as told here appears to intersect with versions of South Wind tales told by proximate groups, such as the Clatsop, with whom the Nehalem-Tillamook had strong ties. The Clatsop, whose territory is being described in this part of the tale, have recounted a South Wind tale that brings together South Wind, a whale, and Thunderbird—possibly the "Double-Bladed Knife" being mentioned earlier in the tale presented here. The Clatsop, Chinook, Chehalis, and possibly others indicate that South Wind goes inland to Saddle Mountain, east of Seaside, and participates in the creation of the ancestors of the tribes of the region. Some contemporary Nehalem-Tillamook descendants accept this story as their own creation story as well. As told in Anglicized form by Swan (1857:203–4), based on the accounts of Chinooks,

> Toölux (or the South Wind), while traveling to the north, met an old woman named Quoots-hooi, who was an ogress and a giantess. He asked her for food, when she gave him a net, telling him that she had nothing to eat, and he must go and try to catch some fish. He accordingly dragged the net, and succeeded in catching a grampus, or, as the Indians called it, "a little whale." This he was about to cut with his knife when the old woman cried out to him to take a sharp shell, and not to cut the fish crossways, but split it down the back. He, without giving heed to what she said, cut the fish across the side and was about to take off a piece of blubber, but the fish immediately changed into an immense bird, that when flying completely obscured the sun, and the noise made by its wings shook the earth. This bird, which they called Hahness, then flew away to the north, and lit on the top of the Saddleback Mountain, near the Columbia River. [South Wind] and the old woman then journeys north in search of

Hahness, and one day, while Quoots-hooi was engaged in picking berries on the side of the mountain, she found the nest of the thunder-bird, full of eggs, which she commenced breaking and eating, and from these mankind were produced.

82. A site near the mouth of the Columbia River, close to the ocean beach. Before the construction of Fort Stevens there was a large village on the beach that is mentioned frequently in the historical literature and was a popular place for intertribal gatherings. Clara Pearson noted that the Clatsops, Chinooks, Tillamooks, and other tribes "used to go there and have a big time and all go but 'the fort got that!'" (Harrington n.d.: 386). This episode of the South Wind epic, with its references to friendly and casual interactions between unaffiliated creatures, seems to invoke this quality of the site. The use of fish nets at this site, described in the tale, also reflects historical fact.

83. The term "Clatsop" has been geographically ambiguous in historical accounts. Clatsop here appears to refer to the village on the south side of the Columbia River estuary, not far from the river's mouth at present-day Fort Stevens. A highly productive fishing village, this community produced an abundance of pulverized dried salmon, the product for which the "Clatsop" people were named. The name of this village was ultimately applied to all Chinookan-speaking peoples occupying the river from Tongue Point west, and from the south bank of the Columbia to Tillamook Head, in what is today southern Clatsop County, Oregon. It is unclear what cultural and linguistic differences existed between the Clatsop and the Chinook proper; by all accounts, such differences appear to have been minor. Many of those differences appear to reflect degrees of intermarriage and cultural confluence with their neighbors; the Clatsops exhibited extensive connections with the Nehalem Tillamook at contact, in addition to the Chinook, while the Chinook possessed strong connections to Lower Chehalis groups and to other Chinookan-speaking groups up the Columbia River.

84. The mention of the Clatsop throwing sand in the salmon's eyes may reflect the practice, sometimes noted among lower Chinook peoples, of wading into the tidewater and churning up water (and presumably the sandy floor of the bay) to scare fish into basketlike fish weirs along the shoreline.

85. This is probably Pillar Rock, located at the first narrow point one encounters in the Columbia River when traveling upstream from the estuary, roughly twenty miles from the ocean.

86. [A similar story occurs in Moses-Columbian, and it is widespread on the Plateau (M. Dale Kinkade, personal communication). There is a Sêliš (Flathead) story where Coyote similarly is swallowed by a monster, and discovers other people there; Coyote engineers their escape.—Eds.]

87. Fire starting is difficult on this soggy coastline. Individuals would carry fire drills with dry tinder and sometimes individually wrapped coals, carried in clam shells or other small containers.

88. Beyond the tidal waters, the strong, winter river currents would have made rowing almost impossible for one man.

89. This was the wild cherry or "bitter cherry" (*Prunus emarginata*). Durable, peeled strips of reddish bark from this tree stretch, but do not easily break. This property would have allowed South Wind's penis to stretch considerably without bursting. The Tillamook and other peoples of this coast commonly used strips of this bark for many things, particularly for hafting together a tool consisting of separate pieces, such as the point and shaft of a harpoon. This tree is uncommon on the outer coast, and its use here may be a means of underscoring South Wind's interior location at this point, and his access to the plentiful resources of the Chinook lands.

90. There are several pillars of rock of this sort on the Columbia. As Clara Pearson noted (E. D. Jacobs 1933 ms.), these small islands may still be seen along the Columbia River—they may be the rocks in the vicinity of Three Tree Point, in Washington.

91. Note the four times that the [female] child appeared.

92. The mountain that one sees directly from this vantage point on the Columbia River is Mount St. Helens. This passage's ominous tone was either a product or a prophecy of the contact period. The arrival of the earliest white settlements was accompanied by a period of intensive volcanic activity on Mount St. Helens. Between 1831 and 1857, this mountain experienced some nine recorded minor eruptions from its conical top. From the Tillamook view, these eruptions may have been associated with the actions of South Wind's daughter, and her standing with palms outward may be a reference to the appearance of these small, skyward eruptions of steam, ash, and smoke. During this same period, the diseases brought by non-Indians (smallpox, as well as measles, malaria, and dysentery) decimated the Tillamook, the Clatsop, the Chinook, and many other tribes of the area. At the beginning of the 1830s, though they were already suffering from such diseases, these tribes still occupied a number of traditional villages along the coast; by the late 1850s, they had been reduced to a few small, consolidated villages of epidemic survivors (see Boyd 1990).

93. There are several locations along the lower Columbia River at which exposed groundwater-seeps on exposed cliffs cause a red staining, usually associated with oxidized iron in the groundwater, and sometimes by reddish orange algae.

94. Fort Canby is located right at the mouth of the Columbia River, on the north shore, on the rocks of Cape Disappointment. The waters in the immediate vicinity of the Fort Canby site are still reputed to have plentiful Dungeness crab (*Cancer magister*). To the Tillamook, the gathering of marine crabs at this site may have denoted South Wind's return to the ocean and hunger for seafoods after returning from the interior, fresh waters of the Columbia.

95. This ignorance of how to acquire food may reflect the fact that South Wind was in a foreign place. Bay Center marks the northernmost spot that can be clearly identified in the South Wind epic, and also, incidentally, marks the likely northernmost extent of the Chinook lands, where they abut those of the Lower Chehalis. As the northernmost extent of South Wind's journey, the tale may have been marking this territorial divide. A multitribal community emerged at Bay Center in the nineteenth century, made up principally of Chinooks, as well as descendants of the Lower Chehalis, the Clatsops, the Tillamooks, and other tribes. Franz Boas and other researchers visited this community in the course of research on Chinook and Clatsop cultures. The residents of Garibaldi maintained personal and kinship ties with this community through the mid-twentieth century and its provenience would have been known and important to tribal members at the time these tales were recorded (Deur 2005).

96. South Wind's travel stops for a while here, and others take up the story.

97. Rotten wood is a common inert material in Tillamook tales, often used as decoys to trick old women. [This episode is similar to an Interior story about Grizzly woman and the four Bear cubs. See Egesdal and Thompson (1994:325); also see Kinkade's Upper Chehalis story, "The Kidnapping of Moon" in this volume.—Eds.]

98. From this point in the South Wind tale until he returns south, the described landscape seems to lack reference to exact geographical locations. [Other Salishan tribes use different obstacles, depending on the terrain where they live. For example, on the prairies they use wide expanses of grassland. See Kinkade's "The Kidnapping of Moon" in this volume for another version of this episode. Also note that the traditional fourth obstacle was omitted.—Eds.]

99. This is similar to the story about Snot Boy (or Mucus Boy) told among the Tillamook and many other groups in the Northwest.

100. Another culture hero of the Tillamook, Ice knew everything and had great power. He was also a Transformer. He often appears to be in conflict with South Wind, reflecting in part the meteorological reality of winter weather on the north coast, which historically alternated between mild south winds with rain and periods of intense cold associated with north winds.

101. At this point in the story, Clara Pearson brought in to show to E. Jacobs three different shapes she had used as dolls as a child: bones from the back of a sturgeon's head, around its mouth, and the top fin along the back (E. D. Jacobs 1933). [Also see Compton et al. 1994.—Eds.]

102. This was probably intended as the story of the destruction of the place where the two Younger Wild Women had lived with the stolen boy. The cracking of hot rocks would have been well understood by Tillamook listeners, who witnessed cracking rocks whenever they heated stones for cooking.

103. A loud proclamation made while standing in a near-shore canoe was a common means of arranging or announcing social events to a village in which one did not live.

104. Note that Frog was the fourth maiden.

105. There are many kinds of frogs on the coast, of diverse appearance.

106. It was very useful to have an industrious wife who could cure hides well. Frog seems to be providing a moral lesson about youthful, masculine superficiality; she is not at all beautiful, but she is an extremely valuable wife. This is similar to other frog-marriage motifs found worldwide, such as frog-prince tales.

107. The implication is that he had finished his work as Transformer/Trickster and had come home to settle down.

108. This evidently disabled the Monsters.

109. The really exciting dancing often only began at midnight.

110. There were probably five trips made in the original tale.

111. Recall the daughter who was born to South Wind who kept coming back to life and who South Wind finally put up the Columbia River on Mount St. Helens.

112. Note the significance of the five young men going to tell the news.

113. Another person called the people represented by the three rocks "Tk'a," the first man, his wife, and his child. Tk'a knew all the thoughts and plans of men, and for this reason they must refrain from bad thoughts. When they give away or waste berries, Tk'a feels annoyed, and sends a dry year in which berries are scarce (Boas 1898c:145n1). This is probably Coyote Rock, a rock pillar in the Siletz River, a short distance upstream from Siletz Bay. The name "Coyote" may reflect this rock's continued folkloric significance as South Wind's final physical manifestation, even after the Siletz River became the site of the multitribal Siletz Reservation. Within this Reservation, linguistic and cultural common denominators of several western Oregon tribes became the foundation of the culturally hybrid Siletz Tribe with Chinook Jargon becoming the primary language here and at the Grande Ronde Reservation, for a short time (see Zenk 1988). "Coyote," South Wind's more widely known equivalent outside of the Tillamook world, was the intersubjective Trickster-Transformer among these people during the historical period. The English name "Coyote" may have been attached to places and events once attributed to South Wind by the Tillamook. The Yaquina tell that South Wind transformed himself into a dead tree at Yaquina Bay, and that his life returned from there to the salmon country. The Alsea and Yaquina, when passing this tree, shot an arrow at it. It was quite full of arrows.

A Bluejay Cycle
Traditional Quinault Stories

Told by Bob Pope

Edited by Dell Hymes

The English version of this series of Bluejay stories is a manuscript in the Library of the American Philosophical Society, taken down in 1898 by Livingston Farrand with the assistance of W. S. Kahnweiler. Cycles of adventures of a single hero focus usually on a Trickster-Transformer, such as Raven in British Columbia and Alaska, and Coyote along the Columbia River. Among the Quinault of the Washington coast at least one narrator, Bob Pope (Toshiu), knew, perhaps created, a long cycle around Bluejay.[1] The cycle expresses an interest in Bluejay that is both unmatched and unusual.

The cycle begins with a sequence of nine episodes, with Bluejay as bungling host. Lacking food, he goes to someone who can provide and is fed. He then invites his host to become his guest, but fails. Throughout, his wife is long-suffering, foreseeing what will happen. And in the end, Bluejay's own child dies.

There are other sequences of bungling host visits in the region, sharing some of the same benevolent hosts, but this is the longest, the most varied, and the only one integrated into sequences to follow. It is the death of the child at the end of host episodes that prompts the next part.

In part 2, Bluejay and wife travel, with failure in their attempts to punish others for mocking their sorrow, and encounter Xwo:n Xwo:n: (commonly Xwoneh in the manuscript), a Trickster-Transformer known for a cycle of his own among the Salish peoples of southwestern Washington. When Bluejay comes to certain kinds of adventure, in part 3, he indeed is no longer the protagonist. Such adventures fall to his companion, Xwoneh. And the next set of adventures (part 4) have Bluejay, not in charge, but a servant. Only at the beginning and the end, visiting the land of the dead (part 5), is Bluejay the central protagonist. It is as if Sancho Panza had an epic beginning and ending with adventures of his own, but with Don Quixote intervening in between.

All this suggests a personal concern with Bluejay, recognizing him as a character with limitations, not one to be cast as a Transformer, but with a value of his own. In this role he exhibits something essential about the nature of life at the beginning and of death at the end. The world is intended as providential, what beings need as food is a gift, but they must recognize the limitations of their own natures.

The selection presented here gives the preface, the first and last of the visits between hosts, and all of parts 2 and 3. The preface shows something of the conception of the story; the two incidents from part 1 show the character of that major section; part 2 restores details of incidents rather changed in the published version; and part 3 presents material not published at all, but merely summarized. "Bluejay left his wife at Wreck Creek and went on south with xwo:n xwo:n:, and had many adventures" (Farrand 1902:92).

A footnote remarks: "A number of stories of xwo:n xwo:n:, all of a gross character, were interpolated here; but, as they were obviously borrowed from southern sources, they have been omitted." Some of the southern sources must have originally borrowed them as well, since they were widespread, and there is no reason to doubt that the Quinault told them under compulsion.

The published version of these stories (Farrand 1902) rewords the original into conventional English, and adds a variety of details. The rewording changes the English enough to imply a different pattern of relations. The original, so far as studied, almost always shows relations of three and five among verses and stanzas, but sometimes two and four. We cannot be certain that the manuscript has every word spoken by Bob Pope. If the transcriber already had editorial revision in mind, he may have let an occasional article or pronoun go in the press of transcription. I have supplied some of those, in parentheses, but restored the original wording, such as "grub" instead of "food," and I have trusted the original punctuation, which shows several astonishing runs of predicate phrases, often as many as seven.

It is worth mentioning that Bob Pope himself inscribed his Indian name at the end of the cycle: "This ends Toshiu's story of Blue Jay."

A Bluejay Cycle
Part One: The Adventures of Bluejay

PREFACE |

People used to live on Quinault River from (the) mountains
    clear down to the mouth.
All the birds and animals were people then.
Bluejay lived near the upper end.
The last man up the river.

Had a large family of children.
They were out of food,
for he didn't hunt or fish,
just *cultus* [worthless] sat around [doing nothing].

Just before daylight he said to his wife,
  "We will go to the Magpie,
    our next neighbor,
      and see if we can get some grub."
So he started down
  and came to Magpie's
    and he was there alone.
Bluejay looked around the house,
  but there was nothing there.

Pretty soon Magpie made a fire
  and heated some rocks,
    and put the pot by the fire
      and threw in the rocks,
        and water began to boil.

Magpie undid his hair
  and took out one salmon egg,
    and threw it in,
      soon the pot was full of salmon eggs.

Bluejay got to work,
  and ate and ate
    until he could hardly move,
      but still there was lots left
        and he didn't know what to do with the rest.

Then he got ready to go back
  and started to take the whole pot.

Bluejay told his wife to go out first
  and she did.
Then she heard Bluejay say to Magpie,

"You come up to my house tomorrow
        and you shall have a feast."

Bluejay went out
        and came to the canoe,
                and his wife scolded him for inviting Magpie
                        when they had no grub.

And Bluejay excused himself,
        saying that he was just thanking his cousin,
                and wanted to have him visit him.

Night came;
        and next morning,
                just before daylight,
                        Bluejay made a big fire
                                and went out,
                                        and soon came back wet,
                                                for he had been bathing.
Then he lay down by the fire,
        and then went out
                and sat on the roof,
                        and thought hard,
                                tapping his foot all the while.

Soon he said
        "Magpie is coming up (the) river,
                I can tell him by his hat."
Then his wife scolded him again.

Magpie came in (the) house,
        and Bluejay was happy,
                and took the pot he brought from Magpie's,
                        and heated some rocks,
                                and took one egg he had brought from Magpie's,
                                        and put it in his hair.
He was going to do just what Magpie had done.

When the water was boiling,
    he fingered around in his hair
        and found the egg
            and threw it in the pot
                and stirred and stirred the water
                    until it was cold
                        but nothing came.

Then he gave up
    and sat still.
Magpie just sat
    and Bluejay could give him nothing.

Magpie grew tired at last,
    and took Bluejay's rocks
        and heated them again,
            and put them in the pot
                and took one egg from his hair,
                  threw it in,
                    and in a few minutes the pot was full.

He left this there for Bluejay,
    and went home.

II. HAIR-SEAL |

Next morning early he said to (his) wife,
    "Wake up
        and we will go clear down to (the) mouth of (the) river,
            to Hair-seal,
                and get grub."

So they came down
    and went in (the) house of Hair-seal
        and he had five children.
And Hair-seal built (a) fire,
    and sent (his) wife and children to bathe in (the) river,
        and told them
            when done
                to go and lie on that island

and they did.
And the youngest was on the end.

Hair-seal watched
and when he saw them lying on (the) island
he took his stone hammer,
and went out,
and Bluejay watched.

Hair-seal went over
and hit the youngest on the forehead
and killed him.
And told the rest to go in (the) water
and they did,
and when they came up
there were still five children.

Then Hair-seal took it up
to pack home,
but it was so fat
he had (a) hard time.

Finally he came in
and the children came home
and he put the seal on the fire
to burn the hair off.

Then he dressed his meat
and it was covered with fat
and Bluejay watched it all.

Then he boiled the meat,
and gave some to Bluejay
and Bluejay ate so much fat
that he lay back
and could not move.

His wife was scared

for she felt sure
        Bluejay was going to try the same trick.

(Bluejay had done the same as usual
    and asked Hair-seal to come up next day.)

Bluejay's wife cried most of the way up.
Finally they came home.

Next morning (Bluejay) did as usual.
[He] hollered from (the) roof
    it was Hair-seal.

Jui (his wife) got mad
    and scolded Bluejay.

Hair-seal and (his) family came in.

Bluejay made (a) big fire,
    told (his) children
        "Go swim
           and then lie on the point of that sandbar,
             and keep your eyes closed."

He watched,
    and when they were on the bar
        then (he) went over
           and took his hammer
             and hit the youngest on the forehead
               and broke in his head.

Then he told the others,
    "Dive down, quick, quick, quick!"

But the others were so scared
    they could not get under water,
        and they lay there crying,
           and there were only four children

and Jui was nearly crazy with grief over her youngest boy
and mad with Bluejay,
and there was hell to pay all around.

Then Hair-seal told his boys to bathe
then lie on the sandbar
and they did
and Hair-seal clubbed one
and the four jumped in (the) river
and came out five as before.
And they packed the hair-seal into the house for Bluejay,
and Hair-seal went back.

Now they were full of grief for the child,
and they cut their hair,
all except one tuft on top.

Part Two: Bluejay & His Wife Travel

I. Squirrel and Black Diver Mock Bluejay |
After this they never went anywhere any more
and someone told him
the Squirrel and some other fellow (Black Diver)
were making fun of Bluejay
because he had killed his child

So Bluejay said to his wife
"We will go down
and tie those fellows up
and bring them home here."

So they went
and before they reached the house
they heard the men laughing and making fun of Bluejay
and came over
and they kicked the wall.

Bluejay said,
"Is it so you are mocking me

because I killed my child?"
And they said,
    "Yes, it's so
        see what you got on your head
           for doing it."
(They meant the crest which was left after they cut their hair.)

They went in
    took them by the arms
        and dragged them out.
And threw them in the canoe
    and tied their hands and feet and bodies
        and started up—
But every time these fellows moved
    the ropes broke.

ii. Diver Escapes |

After this he asked them
    "What kind of rope is the best
        to hold men like you?"

Diver said,
    "Weeds are the best."
And Bluejay said,
    "I know where there are some weeds
        in that slough over there—
           let's go."

So they went
    and got long weeds
        and tied their hands and feet
           and the men lay there grunting and crying
         and Bluejay said
           "Serves you right—
               If you hadn't made fun of me,
                  I wouldn't have done this to you."

Had got about half way
    when Diver jumped up

and dove under (the) water
and Bluejay poked his pole in (the) mud after him
and said,
"Now I've got you."
But Diver came up on the other side of (the) river
and poked fun at Bluejay
and went ashore.

iii. SQUIRREL ESCAPES |

Now Bluejay had only Squirrel left

Went further up
and asked Squirrel
where there would be a good place to put a man like him.

And Squirrel answered,
but so low that only Jui could hear.

Jui told Bluejay
he said the best place would be a brush pile along the shore,
and to go close to the bank—

So they came close to some brush hanging over the bank
and Squirrel jumped up
and ran ashore
and laughed
poked fun at Bluejay.

And now the latter had no one.

II. XWONEH & SNAIL |

So when they got home,
they thought
they would have to leave there
and live somewhere else.
They felt so badly over the dead child.

They started downriver
and came to (a) beach
and saw quite a crowd on (the) beach

and came up to see what was going on
and he found Xwoneh Xwoneh and Snail competing.

And Snail said,
"I can see the smoke of the village out there over the ocean."
Xwoneh said,
"I can beat you.
I can see that woman packing wood."

Snail had come up from Wreck Creek to get a wife,
the Crow,
who was a fine girl but blind.
Snail took the crow back
and she gave a name to every little place between here and Wreck
Creek.

Now Snail had not believed Xwoneh,
and said,
"Now let's trade for a few minutes.
I would like to see how good your eyes are."

So Xwoneh said all right
and took out his eyes
and gave them to Snail
and Snail looked with Xwoneh's eyes
but could see nothing.
They were ordinary *cultus* [worthless] eyes.
But Xwoneh with Snail's eyes could see the smoke
as plain as possible.

So they traded back
and then they all went back south
and Bluejay along.

III. SNAIL & CROW |

And as they went along,
the Crow sang
and every time she finished the song,
she would say,
"How far are we now?"

And Snail would tell her
      and she would give the place a name
            and it was that way all the way down to Wreck Creek.

When they got down home,
      Snail took one of his eyes
           and gave it to his wife,
                 so they had one eye apiece.

And Snail's wife used to go out digging clams every morning
      and every night she used to say
            "It looks funny to see us each with only one eye.
            One of us ought to have the pair."
And at last Snail gave his other eye to the Crow
      and then she had two
           and Snail had none.
And he had to stay inside
      and could not go out
           for he was blind.

Crow was white in those days
      but she got burned
           and since then has been black.

She used to go out after clams.
And she told Snail
      to go and get wood
           and he felt around to get wood
               and found the house post
                   and cut it down for a tree
                      and the house fell in on the fire
                     and burned up
                        and her white dress was there
                          and it got burned black.

Crow saw him
      when she saw the smoke
           [and came hurrying home]

but she was too late.
It was already burned.

Part Three. Xwoneh and Bluejay Travel

I. Xwoneh and Raven's Daughter |

Xwoneh and Waswas [Bluejay] went on further south—
    got below Joe Creek
        and saw Whippoorwills digging clams.

Xwoneh took his tool
    and turned it into Chinook salmon
        and put it in a lagoon
            and its back was sticking up.

The women started to club him
    but Xwoneh said,
        "Don't club him,
            don't club him,
                it will spoil him."

But he picked out (the) best-looking girl
    and said,
        "You go and sit on him—"

And she did
    and (the) salmon disappeared under her
        and Xwoneh said to (the) other women,
    "Now you see if you hadn't made motions with (the) stick
        you would have got him."

Then they all went home.
Bluejay went with the women.
Xwoneh traveled back and forth out on the beach—

Next morning Xwoneh came to (the) village
    and Bluejay said to Xwoneh
        that nicest girl in (the) village,
            Raven's daughter,
                who had sat on (the) salmon,

was very sick and nearly dead.

Bluejay went back
    and told people
        Xwoneh was there
            and he was (a) good Tamanawas man [shaman].
And Raven sent Bluejay
    to ask
        if he was (a) good doctor.

And Bluejay came to Xwoneh
    and asked him
        and he laughed
            and said,
                "Yes, I can cure any kind of sickness,"

And Xwoneh came
    and there was this girl squealing
        and her belly swelled big.
And Xwoneh sang his doctor song
    but said
    he would have to have the girl and himself closed off from the rest
        and then he knew he could cure her.

So they put a mat around them.

And Raven's wife was just outside the mat screen.

Xwoneh stopped singing
    and they suspected something
      and Raven peeked in
        and Xwoneh was right on (the) girl's belly
          and Raven had no club.

While he was looking for a club—
    Xwoneh got his tool fastened on
        and as he went out

wiped it through Raven's wife's mouth
and through (the) girl's mouth
and now she was cured
and all his people were happy.[2]

Xwoneh and Bluejay went on still farther south.
Every little ways they came to camps
    where people were digging clams.
And they were invited into every camp to eat clams.
So they were so full
    they could eat no more
        and would sometimes just sit down
            and look at the clams.
Xwoneh felt badly
    for he wished to eat more
        and he wished and wished.

Went into a small creek this side of Copalis
    and saw a man working on a canoe
        but he could see no chips or shavings.
Soon he saw that this man's penis was eating all the chips.
He thought
    Now I will trade tools with this man
    and then I can eat clams all I want
    if I have that penis to help me.

So at last Xwoneh said,
    "Cousin, don't you think it would be a good plan to trade tools?
    I would like yours.
        I have been asked everywhere
            to eat clams
                and I would like to have help."

The man said,
    "I am afraid it will be lots of trouble for you
    for it is very hoggish—
    You can see how he eats everything I can chop out here."
Finally, however, he agreed

and said to his tool,
        "Now don't be hoggish at first,
           but you may be
                after he gets further on."

After his trade
      he came back to places where they were digging clams
           in order to have a good time with his tool.
When he came to the first camp
      the women were just coming in with clams
           and they gave him lots
                and he finished them all.

When he got halfway through that camp
      the tool began to get hungry
           and ate shells and all.

Before he ended that camp
      he could not get one clam—
           his tool ate them all
                and sometimes he nearly bit Xwoneh's hand off
                    it was so hungry.

Went on to (the) next camp
      and could not get one clam
           (his) tool ate them all.
Whenever it touched his arms or leg
      it bit a piece off.
He could not walk around
      for when the tool swung
           and touched his leg
              it bit him
                so he just sat still.

Now he thought,
     Now I will go back to that man
       and get my own back.

He went a little ways
    and his legs were nearly gone
        for the penis ate him so.
So he had to hold him in his hands
    while he walked.

Finally he came to where (the) man was making canoes
    and then was cutting piles of chips there then.
And Xwoneh said to the man,
    "I want my own tool back—
    This fellow of yours is too much trouble."

The man answered,
    "I told you so."
So they exchanged
    for the man used his to eat chips
        and Xwoneh had his own tool.

III. Xwoneh as Sea Otter |

And they started on again
    and came to (the) mouth of (the) Copalis River
        and saw a little girl playing on (the) beach near her cabin.

Xwoneh came
    and asked her
        "How many people living there,"
        and (the) girl said,
          "Why just my mother and I."

Then Xwoneh wondered what to do.
Finally turned himself into (a) sea otter.
And before this, he told the girl
    to tell her mother
        there was a sea otter lying there
           and to come out with a basket with a hole in the bottom.

She went home
    but (the) mother didn't come
        for she thought it was Xwoneh.

And (the) girl came
    and told Xwoneh
        and he was angry
           and said,
                "You will get to be just like your mother
                if you don't look out.
                Go tell her to come out."

At last the woman came with her basket
    and saw a big sea otter lying there.
She came
    and put (the) sea otter crossways in her basket
        but (the) otter said,
            "No, that isn't (the) right way to pack (a) sea otter.
                You want to have the tail sticking out
                    through the hole in the bottom."

Then she did so
    and as she walked
        the tail began to flop down
            and curl up
                and finally went right into her vagina.

And as soon as he had crammed her
    he turned into Xwoneh
        and ran away
            laughing,
                said,
                "You mustn't think that was a sea otter.
                It was Xwoneh
                and I am he."

Notes

1. The neighboring Quileute, unrelated to the surrounding Salishan groups, also consider Bluejay as Bungler-Trickster.—Eds.

2. The last stanza presupposes that part of Xwoneh's tool was cut off when the women clubbed it as salmon.

Fly

A Southern Lushootseed Epic

Told by Annie Daniels and by Peter Heck

Retold by Jay Miller

This retelling of the Fly epic is based on the 1952 version recorded by Annie Daniels at Puyallup for Leon Metcalf (Hilbert 1985:33–41) and the 1927 "The Young Man Who Was Stolen by Lion" told in English by Peter Heck, then the Shaker Bishop at Chehalis, to Thelma Adamson (1934:83–87).

The epic also has debts to the Klallam Mucus or Snot Boy epic in which many sons and a daughter disappeared and the collected mucus of their mother became another son,[1] named Smun, who grew up to kill the monster Cougar (Mountain Lion) who had clawed out the brothers' hearts. Smun took the hearts from Cougar's stomach and put each back into the appropriate brother's chest to revive them all. The oldest one was dead longest and needed the help of spit or medicine to revive fully. The two-faced child of Smun's sister and Cougar warned whenever his uncles visited and so contributed to their murders. After the mother and child were rescued, this two-faced boy told Smun, "Shoot my Hand!" and called him all kinds of names until he got to "snot," and then Smun shot an arrow chain into the sky and disappeared. Some say he went to the moon (Gunther 1925:125–31).

Fly

In the early days of the world, Flytown hosted a gathering. Many people came. A man heard about it and decided to go. He floated on the river and paddled with his hands. Along the way, he met the Changer, who told him to carve paddles and a canoe out of cedar. But when the man picked up a piece of wood, it fought back. So the Changer used his mind to deaden the wood so people could use it. That was how woodworking began. At Flytown, the man worked in the woods, hollowing out his canoe during the day and attending the gathering during the evening.

Another person who came for the gathering was a girl who had just had a baby. She and the baby were supposed to stay secluded for several days, but she came to Flytown instead. She hid the baby in the brush near the town and went off to watch the dancing through cracks in the plank walls of the houses. In time she forgot about her baby, who would wake up and cry until it fell asleep again.

The man working on the canoe heard the baby crying off and on for several days. Finally he looked for and found the baby. He went home and told his wife, who pretended to be pregnant for a day. The man built a birthing hut for her, brought the baby there, and the woman pretended to have the baby. In five[2] days he grew into a boy, and his father made a bow and arrows for him.

The couple already had an older girl, who resented her new brother. While he was trying out his new bow, she teased him. "Bet you can't hit me! You never could hit me!" The boy ignored her for as long as he could. After five times, however, he shot at her hand and hit it. The girl screamed, again and again, "I was shot by the discard claimed by my parents." When their mother heard this, she said, "My daughter is all mouth," and ran into the woods to calm the situation.

But the boy ran far away, flung himself onto the ground, and cried his eyes out. The searchers never found him. After a long time, the boy got up and went on.

Eventually he met Cougar Woman, who decided to raise the boy until she could marry him. She tried to feed him some of her big red berries, but the boy knew that these were lizards. Instead, Crane Woman, who lived with Cougar, went out and got salmon fry for the boy to eat. He liked those.

After a time, Cougar got possessive of the boy and he decided to run away. Crane helped him by saying that Cougar could only be safely shot from the front, because she kept her head down and looked backward when she walked. The boy shot Cougar to slow her down and ran off. Cougar then turned on Crane, who was ready. Crane had made wings for herself and, as she flew off, she shot and killed Cougar.

As the boy walked along, he heard a woman singing in the distance. When he got near her, she stopped singing and refused to continue. Her sister appeared and joined the boy in urging her to continue. After five times, the woman began to sing the words "Summoning Heat" and the world caught fire.

The boy fled from the flames and looked for a refuge. He ran to Rock and asked for help. Rock said, "I snap and pop, sending off sharp pieces. You would not be safe." He ran to Water, who warned him, "I boil and you will be cooked. You would not be safe." He ran to Road, who said, "I will burn on both sides and roast all in my path. You would not be safe." He ran to Fir Tree who said, "I only burn on the very bottom. If you climb up into my branches, you will be safe." So that is what the boy did.

He climbed up into the fir tree, but the flames got closer. For safety, he grafted his bow and arrows to the top of the tree and used them to climb up into the Sky. Then he reached down and retrieved his bow and arrows to take along.

In the Sky was a big grassy meadow, where the boy wandered until he found a path and followed it. First light began as he walked along. He saw movement ahead and stepped off the trail. A Grey Elk went by. Soon after, five Grey Dogs passed. Then came a Grey Man. The man stopped and called the boy over. They talked. The man said he was Dawn. He had five daughters up the trail. The boy should go to his home for food and marry the girls. Then Dawn went on and the boy resumed his trek.

He walked all day before he saw movement ahead. He stepped off the trail while a gaunt man who looked like a walking skeleton went by. Soon after, five Dark Dogs passed. Then came a Dark Man, who called the boy over. They talked. The man said he was Dusk. He also had five daughters. The boy should go to his home for food and wives. Then Dusk went on, and the boy went in the opposite direction.

He came to a fork in the trail. The right side was dark and grassy, but the left side was dimly lighted and paved with dry cedar bark. The boy took the dim side by mistake. Dawn, who had his own light, went by the dark trail, while Dusk used the lighted one. Thus, the boy got to the home of the daughters of Dusk. The youngest and smartest one knew when he got there.

His first impression was not favorable. The girls were smelly, dark, and had big noses. They welcomed him and rubbed him over with oil from human corpses. This changed his senses, and he liked the four girls and married them. They tried to feed him human flesh, but he dug up nearby roots and ate those instead. He threw away the flesh when they were not looking.

The oldest (fifth) daughter stayed in a coffinlike box. During the day, while her four sisters were out getting food, the boy (now a man and husband) and oldest sister visited. One afternoon, a man came to the door. He was called Split Foot. The oldest sister took the visitor away and the boy did not see him again.

That night, Dawn came home and asked if the boy had arrived, but his daughters never saw him. So he sent his daughters to get him from Dusk's daughters. When the Dawn girls arrived, they demanded the boy, but the

Dusk girls refused to give him up. The girls fought, while the boy peeked through a hole in the wall. The eldest Dusk daughter used a human leg as a club, and the boy saw that it was the leg of Split Foot. He also noted that Dawn's daughters were bright and beautiful.

The Dusk daughters drove off the Dawn daughters, but the boy had made up his mind. Five days later, he explained that he needed to stretch his legs and was going for a walk. Once he was out of sight, he ran back down the trail and turned into the dark fork. In no time, he was at the house of Dawn. Four sisters greeted him. They washed him and dressed him. They fed him elk meat. He was very happy.

One day he went for a swim and returned to the house looking for a comb. He looked into a basket hanging from the wall and found the youngest, smartest, and most beautiful daughter. He took to his bed, he was so stunned. That night when Dawn came home and asked why the boy was abed, the other girls explained that he had found the youngest daughter. Dawn roused the man and told him to marry the girl in the basket. He was delighted.

One day, as they sat in the sun while his wife was grooming his hair, the man poked a hole into the ground. He looked down and saw Flytown. He saw that his natural mother now had a younger son. He became very homesick and again took to his bed.

When Dawn came home, the youngest daughter explained why her husband was not feeling well. Dawn told her to go to their grandmother and ask her to take them to earth. This grandmother was Spider, who agreed.

Dawn gave the couple many gifts, including a goat wool blanket, dentalia, roots, meat, and fragrant oils. They took these into a basket, and Spider lowered them down. In this way, many treasures came to earth.[3]

The couple landed near the spring where the town came for water. They waited. Soon the younger brother arrived. He was blind, potbellied, and awkward. The man called him over, but the boy did not believe him at first. Dawn's daughter brushed the boy's body and he became slim and handsome. Then his brother blew into his eyes and he could see. His brother also patted his head so his hair grew in thick and lustrous.

The couple told the boy to go to his mother and say that her older son had returned safely. She should clean the house so that her new daughter-in-law from the Sky could live with them in a fresh and purified environment.

When the boy got to his mother, however, she did not believe him and scolded him severely. She too was blind, but she refused to touch her son and learn the changes to his body. The boy went back and was made older, slimmer, and more handsome. Five times he returned to his mother and was scolded. But the last time, she touched his body and believed. She too came to the spring, and she too was given sight, thick hair, and a nice figure. Then she cleaned the house thoroughly. The couple moved in.

Because the natural mother had abandoned and lost her first baby, she had been shunned by her relatives and friends. Eventually, Bluejay had claimed her and her younger son as slaves. Bluejay had been off when the couple came to earth and improved their relatives.

Bluejay arrived back home and crouched on the eaves of the house, calling to the younger boy, "Wipe me off! Wipe me!" The younger brother realized that he was now free and looked at his brother, who nodded slowly. It was time for revenge. So the boy reached into the fire and grabbed a burning stick. He shoved it into the place that Bluejay wanted him to wipe. Bluejay screamed and flew off, realizing that he was no longer in charge. But he too would have his revenge.

In time, the Dawn wife became pregnant. Because she was at Flytown, she gave birth to twin boys joined at the back. For this reason, flies are sometimes stuck together today. In five days these Siamese twins grew into boys. Their father made them bows and arrows. He set up targets at each end of the house so the boys could stand in the middle and shoot in opposite directions. Everyone enjoyed this game.

Bluejay came to watch. Five times the twins passed in front of him. The last time he jumped up and cut them apart. They fell down dead. Bluejay said that twins would always be born separated from then on.

The twins' mother, Dawn's youngest daughter, was grief stricken. Her children were dead. She brooded for a short time and then decided to revenge herself on Flytown. She took a sharpened stick and stabbed everyone there, killing them. From each hole, flies emerged. Ever since, flies have hovered around wounds.

The couple called to Grandmother Spider to pull them back into the Sky, and she did so. But they left all their treasures, foods, and gifts on earth for good people to use in the future.

And so, the world became more like it is today because of the deeds of these people. In addition, this epic teaches that the easiest path is not always the best one to take.

Notes

1. See the Tillamook saga, "South Wind's Journeys," for an episode where the mother loses an infant son and in her sorrow makes a new baby from the urine washed from the stolen baby's cradle blankets.—Eds.

2. The pattern number for this tale seems to be five.—Eds.

3. The motif of Grandmother Spider lowering a hero from the Skyworld back to Earth occurs elsewhere in Salish. See the Thompson River Salish Nx̣ík'smtm story in this volume.—Eds.

The Pentlatch Myth Corpus

Edited by M. Dale Kinkade

Very few texts are known from Pentlatch. The language became extinct in
the early 1940s, but virtually the only mythological or linguistic data on the
language in existence are these few texts (all myths) and some vocabulary that
Franz Boas collected while he was in Comox, British Columbia, from November 12 through December 3, 1886, his first year on the Northwest Coast
(Rohner 1969:58–69). He recorded only six myths in Pentlatch; most of these
are very short and fragmentary, and they may reflect the moribund state of the
language even at that date. The speakers from whom Boas collected material
were already part of the Island Comox community. These six texts were never
published, but Boas did publish three texts in German in 1892 (republished in
his better known *Indianische Sagen* of 1895), and he refers to a fourth (giving only the name of a man who killed his wife, and referring readers to the
Comox version of the story; the Comox version is not given either, but gives
only the name of a youngest brother, and refers further to a Nootka version).
Two of the three German myths correspond to two of the Pentlatch-language
texts. The other does not (nor does the one referred to by title only), and it is
unclear how this text was obtained. It is likely that Boas had to do his work
on Pentlatch via Chinook Jargon, and used German glosses for vocabulary
and translations for texts, but the details of his working methods in the field
are unknown, and the manuscript of *Indianische Sagen* and notes for it are not
among his papers at the American Philosophical Library in Philadelphia or in
the National Anthropological Archives in Washington DC.

Boas never provided smooth translations of the texts he collected in Pentlatch, with the exception of "The Thunderbird," although all are given rough
interlinear glosses in both German and (later) English. His German version of
"The Flood" is considerably longer than the Pentlatch version, has a different
title, and must have been told independently; without the German version, it is
difficult to make sense of the Pentlatch version. His *Indianische Sagen* does,
however, include Comox versions of the remaining Pentlatch-language texts,

and these help considerably in making sense of these other Pentlatch stories, especially "Raven and His Sisters," which has special problems because of its very abbreviated rendition.

Because the Pentlatch myth corpus is so very small, and mostly unpublished (with only the three texts published in Boas 1892 and 1895, and my English translations of both the Pentlatch and German versions of "The Thunderbird" in Kinkade 1992b), all nine of the texts are given here. My translations of the Pentlatch texts are given first, followed by my translations of the three texts in German. The order in both cases is that of the original Pentlatch manuscripts (Boas 1896) and the German publications (Boas 1892, 1895). They are all arranged in verse format, such as that used in Kinkade 1992b (see there for my rationale for using this format). For the most part, each line here corresponds to a sentence in Pentlatch as set off by Boas by the use of periods. Other features of the verse structure used here are based on semantic content; not enough is known about Pentlatch grammar to use that as a guide. There is indeed an introductory particle, which I have consistently translated *then*, but it does not seem to correspond in any way with the narrative structure, as such particles often do in other Salish languages.

My translations of the Pentlatch-language texts are based on Boas's German and English glosses, then checked against the Pentlatch. The latter was only a rough guide, because the grammatical structure of Pentlatch is yet to be figured out, and vocabulary glosses are often uncertain. Where possible, the Pentlatch vocabulary and grammar were compared with neighboring Sechelt and Comox-Sliammon to assist in understanding the Pentlatch, but this is only partially helpful. Finally, the translations were checked against Comox versions of cognate texts in *Indianische Sagen* to determine the correct sequence of events and identification of characters in some of the myths. I have occasionally added information in brackets to clarify sentences or situations. Names of characters have been transliterated from Boas's 1886 transcription into what I believe is fairly close to a modern phonemic transcription.

A few comments on some of the texts will help the reader understand them, since their shortness often results in a very elliptical narrative. Speakers of the language would have been familiar with the stories already, so they would have known what was omitted by the narrator. Others, however, need assistance.

1. Pitch: The name of the character Pitch is a completely different word from the term for the substance pitch found in the last half of

this little story; it is not unusual for a myth character to have a name that is distinctive in this way. The name of the character appears to be a diminutive form, and the root is cognate with other Salishan words for "excrement" (appropriate, since pitch is a substance excreted by trees). There is a Comox version of this story in *Indianische Sagen*, but only its first part corresponds to the first half of this Pentlatch myth; the second parts are completely different. The Pentlatch version explains why some trees (the identification of which is not entirely clear, due to Boas's unfamiliarity with the trees of the area and some tree names that do not always correspond one to one between German and English) have pitch, but Red Cedar does not.

2. "Beaver and Frogs" corresponds reasonably well to one of the Comox texts in *Indianische Sagen*, although the latter has some of the women turn into frogs at the end of the story, and others into snakes.

3. "The Flood" is preceded by a sentence in Pentlatch that Boas did not translate. It is probably not part of the story, and may be a response to a question from Boas about the origin of the Pentlatch people. All that I can identify in this sentence is a word meaning "he knows" and one meaning "Pentlatch." The German version of this story (text 7) is given a title consisting of the names of the two men who were the ancestors of the Pentlatch people, and who are the protagonists of the story. They are not mentioned in the Pentlatch version until the story is half finished, and then the names are given, but not identified specifically with any action. The Pentlatch version would be very difficult to understand without the German version.

4. Boas alternatively entitles this story "Shining Boy" and "Tlaiq" [ƛáyq], suggesting that the latter is the Pentlatch name of Shining Boy. That this is not the case is clear from the Comox version of the story; ƛáyq is the father of the Yənisáq girls, and not a major character in either version. In the Comox myth, ƛáyq lives in the sky, and Shining Boy and his brother live on the earth and are sons of Good Weather. It is curious that this Pentlatch myth refers to only three daughters; the Comox version has four, and it is clear from other evidence that four is the pattern number in Pentlatch.

5. This and the German version of "The Thunderbird" are given just as

in Kinkade (1992), except that I have replaced "boat" with "canoe" and removed the act and scene designations (instead of providing them for the other texts).

6. "Raven and His Sisters" is the most difficult of the Pentlatch texts to translate because of all the information that has been left out. The story itself is familiar, and there is a Comox version in *Indian-ische Sagen*, without which it is impossible to know who is doing what much of the time in Pentlatch. The fourth and fifth lines may be a false start, since Raven does not go to the shore until after his excrement has shouted (to frighten the sisters into hiding in the forest because enemies are supposedly approaching). The last three lines may be completely mistranslated here. The antepenultimate line is in quotation marks in Pentlatch, but not in the German or English glosses, which say "he has . . . ed the sisters."

7. "Kʷayímən and Híqtən" is the title given to the German version of "The Flood" (text 3).

8. "The Eight Brothers" is the only story that has no cognate version among the Comox texts in *Indianische Sagen*, nor is there a Pentlatch-language version of this story.

9. "The Jealous Man": After a reference to a Comox text in *Indian-ische Sagen* (which in turn is not given, but refers further to a Nootka text), Boas writes only "The name of the man who killed his wife is xʷakʷxʷɔ́kʷlač."

10. "The Thunderbird" is the German version of text 5.

The Pentlatch Myth Corpus

1. Pitch (Smamənáč)
   Pitch goes fishing.
       Then the sun rises.

   His People call,
       "Paddle on both sides of the canoe, Pitch!
           Paddle on both sides of the canoe, Pitch!"

   He doesn't manage to reach the shore,
       and he melts.

   Then the Fir tree goes to the shore
       and takes pitch.

Then the Spruce tree goes to the shore,
    and takes pitch.

Then the Douglas Fir tree goes to the shore,
    and takes pitch.

Then the Cedar tree goes to the shore.
    And there is already nothing there.
      It's all gone.

2. Beaver and Frogs[1]
The Frog Women go along with the Snakes.

Beaver comes.
    He goes to take a woman.
      He finds a woman.

Then he wants to sleep with her,
    and she pushes him away.
      Then he wants to sleep with her,
        and she pushes him away again.

"Stop!"

Beaver goes back to his house.
He comes back to his grandmother's house.

Then his grandmother cries.
    She cries,
      she cries,
        then she cries.

He and his grandmother keep crying.
    They keep crying,

    and it rains,
      it rains,
        (and) it rains.

The river rises.
　　It rises,
　　　　it rises,
　　　　　　the river rises higher.
　　　　　　　　Then the river rises higher.

　　It rises over the trunks of fallen trees.
　　　　Then it rises over the trunks of fallen trees.

And Frog goes further.
　　Frog climbs up on top.

　　Beaver comes along.
　　　　Then Beaver takes a stick.
　　　　　　Then he picks her up by the inside of her upper leg.

　　　　"Truly, you are a beautiful woman, Frog,"
　　　　　　says Beaver.

3. The Flood
　　Then he twists a rope [of cedar withes].
　　　　The sea runs dry.
　　　　　　He knows that God is angry.

　　　　He twists the rope intended as an anchor.
　　　　　　He knows that God is angry.

　　　　　　He finishes twisting.
　　　　　　　　The sea dries up.

　　　　　　The men are hungry,
　　　　　　and they send their wives.
　　　　　　"Go grab the fish!
　　　　　　Go grab the food!"
　　　　　　They get a full basket of fish.

Then the water comes back.
　　It comes back.
　　　　The sea rises,
　　　　　　then floods the land.

The Pentlatch Myth Corpus | 89

It isn't long,
                    and it reaches the treetops.
                                        It isn't long,
                                                            and it reaches the mountains.

Then the first [ancestor] ties boards over canoes.
[They are] Híq[t]ən and Kʷayímən.

Then he goes to anchor himself to the top of the
                    mountain.
Ten days,
twelve,
the sea is high.

It runs dry.
          It runs dry quickly.

                    Then all the people are torn away in the current.
                    Some want to tie fast [to his rope],
                    others want to give him a daughter.

And they are pushed back.
The chief holds [it] tightly.
The people are torn away.

The land becomes dry.
          The land dries up.
                    And he builds a house on the land.

                    The land is dry,
                    and a whale [remained] on the dry land.

4. Shining Boy or x̌áyq

A young man goes shooting from a canoe.
          The young man comes to the middle of the water.
                    Then he shoots upward.
                              The arrow hits the mark.

Then he takes another
      and shoots it again.
            He hits it,
                  then he hits it.
                        then he hits it again.

He takes another,
      then he hits it.
            His arrows are all gone

He seizes his arrows.
    Then he shakes his arrows.
        And they become a rope.
            He shakes it,
                and it does not fall down.

Then he says to his younger brother:
    "Don't cry!"

    Then he goes up.
        And then he disappears above.

The boy goes home.
    He reaches his house.
        All his people cry.
            And the boy goes up onto the roof.

———

He gets to the sky.
    Then he walks along the trail.
      Then he sees smoke from his grandmother Squid.
        Then he asks his grandmother to give him some of her pitch.
          Then his grandmother gives him some of her pitch.

He walks on.
    Then he reaches the Ducks.
        They are all blind.
           They are chewing on roots.

Then one gives one to him.
　　　　She gives it,
　　　　　　　　and he takes it.
　　　　　　　　　　　　He takes the root.

　　　　She gives him another,
　　　　　　　　and he takes it again.

　　　　　　　　That is the end (of that).

The Ducks laugh.

　　　　Then he sprinkles water on them
　　　　　　then they begin to see,
　　　　　　　　and they fly away.

Only one remains;
　　　　he has stepped on her blanket.

　　　　Then she says:
　　　　　　"Go further on the trail.
　　　　　　　　You will get to a lake.
　　　　　　　　　　Stay sitting there.

　　　　　　They will sing
　　　　　　　　when they come to wash themselves.

　　　　　　　Do not give your hand
　　　　　　　　when the eldest offers you hers.
　　　　　　　　　　And do not give your hand
　　　　　　　　　　　　when the second one offers hers.
　　　　　　　　　　　　　　Give your hand to the youngest one.

　　　　　　　She has teeth in her vagina;
　　　　　　　　likewise the second one has teeth in hers.
　　　　　　　　　　Only the youngest one does not have teeth
　　　　　　　　　　　　there.

Give your hand only to the youngest one
when she offers you her hand."

——

They go to their house together.
"My father, he is truly a good one.
I have found a young man.
He is outside.
It will be good if he sits in the canoe at the deer hunt."

Yənisáq[2] goes to offer herself;
he does not take her hand.

The second one goes.
The young man does not take her (hand).

And the youngest one goes.
And he takes her;
they go inside.
She throws him down before the fire.

Yənisáq eats.
Then she gives him the gills.
She throws him the gills.
And the young man does not swallow them.
The young man has a big belly.

Again, the second one gives him some,
and he does not swallow them.

The youngest one gives him some,
and he swallows them.

It gets dark.
Then Yənisáq goes to sleep.
She sleeps.

The young man takes off his robe
the robe of his grandmother.

Then he goes to lie down with the youngest one.
He shines beautifully.
He lies down.

He says:
"Do not do as your sisters do
when they give me fish bones.
Prepare it well
when you give me food."

He shines inside the house.

It becomes daylight.
He puts his grandmother's robe back on.
He goes and sits before the fire.

They eat again.
Yənisáq gives him some fish bones.
He doesn't swallow them.

Again, the second one gives him some.

The youngest one prepares his food well.
She goes and sets it before him,
and he eats it.

It becomes night again.
He goes to lie down again.
He shines beautifully.

It becomes day.
They fetch the things for the deer hunt.
They put them in the canoe.

Yənisáq goes to bring the young man down.
The young man remains sitting.

The second one goes,

and he remains sitting.

The youngest one goes.
She puts her hand near,
he takes her hand.
She brings him to the shore.
She takes him into the canoe.

———

They paddle.
They come to land,
and the young man stays in the canoe.
They go into the woods to shoot deer.
And the young man stays in the canoe.

They come to the shore from the deer hunt.
The young man is out on the water.
The young man is beautiful.
He has thrown off his robe.
He shines just like the sun.

ƛáyq says:
"I will give you my oldest daughter."
The young man does not want her.
The young man shakes himself.
He goes further out on the water.

ƛáyq says again:
"I will give you my second daughter."
The young man shakes himself.
He goes further out on the water.

Again ƛáyq says:
"I will give you my youngest daughter."
The young man shakes himself.
Then he goes ashore.

He gets in the canoe,
ƛáyq goes into the canoe.

He goes into the house.
>> The young man shines.

Then Yənisáq gets out.
> She goes inside,
>> and fixes her bed nicely.

> Next, the second one gets out.

>> The youngest one does not make her bed.
>> She knows
>>> that he will come to her in the night.
>>> He goes in.
>>>> He goes directly to the youngest one.

5. The Thunderbird
> He goes to bathe in the lake.
>> He bathes for many days.
>> The young man becomes handsome.

> Then he goes to the mountain.
> It isn't long
>> and he sees the house.

> He stands at the door.
>> He is called in by the woman.
>> He goes inside.

>> "It will be good for you
>>> to hide yourself in the corner."

> He is not hidden long
> when there is a noise.

> He comes inside.
>> He asks his wife,
>>> "Human odor!"

"It is true!
            A person is inside."

He takes off his clothes.
        He takes off his belt.
                He hangs his robe over the drying pole.

———

The man stays inside for one summer.
        All his People (summer)dance.

        And he carries him away.
                He is on the other side.

Then all the People know.
        Then the People launch the canoe.
                They go to the other side.

        All his People go over.
                They go ashore
                        and they see nothing.
                                They only hear his call.
                                        "Hoo, hoo, hoo!"

The People go ashore.
        The men go ashore.
                Then they surround him.

        And they do not see
                how he goes into the canoe.
                        They only hear
                                how he calls in the bow [of the canoe].

The People paddle.
        They come home.
                They sweep the house.
                        All the men are inside.

They do not see
. where he sits.
They only hear
how he calls
"Hoo, hoo, hoo".

6. Raven and His Sisters
Raven goes to get food.
He sends his sisters to pick berries.
Then he loads the canoe to bring the food.

He goes to the shore at a point of land.
"You go ashore, Snail!"

He defecates.
"You shout
when we come to the point of land!"
He comes to the point of land,
and it shouts,
"Hoo, hoo, hoo!"

Then Raven goes to the shore.
He calls his sister by name.
"You go ashore, Snail!"
She goes ashore,
(and) hides on the beach.

_____

Then he swallows everything in the canoe.
Raven eats it.
Everything that was in the canoe is all gone.
He smears his whole body with berries.

Then his sisters come.
Raven lies there [as if] wounded all over.

The sisters come down.
The sisters weep.
"He has stolen from his sisters."

"Be quiet, Snail!
I am beginning to be sick all over."

7. Kʷayímən and Híqtən
A long, long time ago
two men, Kʷayímən and Híqtən, came down from the sky.
They were the founding ancestors of the Pentlatch.

One time the sea retreated far out from the shore,

and the women went far out
and filled their baskets with fish.

For a long time the sea bed remained dry.
But Híqtən feared
that the water would later rise all that much higher.
He therefore made a long rope of cedar withes
and tied four canoes together.

Finally the water really streamed back
and began to flood the shore.

Then he tied the rope to a large boulder at the mouth
of the Pentlatch River,
fastened the other end to the canoes,
and the two chiefly families drifted about on the rafts.

The other People asked Híqtən:
"Oh, let us tie our canoes fast to your rope.
We will also give you our daughters as wives."
However, Híqtən did not allow it,
but pushed them away with poles.

When the water now ran out again,
they found their homes alone again,
while all the others were scattered throughout the wide
world.

A whale remained lying near Pentlatch Lake up on the mountain.
The water solidified him,
and he could not leave there.
He can still be seen thus today,
and therefore the glacier in the Pentlatch Valley is called Whale.

8. The Eight Brothers

Eight brothers went out to hunt mountain goats.
When it became evening,
they built a fire
and lay down to sleep.

On the next morning
they saw some goats high up on the mountain.
Then they washed themselves,
ate their breakfast,
took bows and arrows,
and chased the goats.

The oldest of the brothers spoke:
"Let me shoot the goats.
We will meet again at that place at the foot of the
mountain."

The brothers agreed,
and the oldest climbed up the mountain.

But on the way he found fern roots,
ate them,
and thought nothing more of the mountain goats.

In the meantime, the brothers went to the agreed-upon place,
and were already looking forward to the goat fat.
But when the other brought nothing but the paltry fern roots,
they became angry,
and were ashamed of their brother.

They took his robe away from him

and tied him naked to a tree,
　　　　where he was to starve to death.

They left,
　　and when they arrived back home,
　　　　they said:
　　　　　　"Our oldest brother fell down the mountain
　　　　　　　　and is lying there dead."

But all the animals came by to help the abandoned one.

　　　　And an old woman,
　　　　　　who knew what the brothers had done,
　　　　　　　　put some fat in a small mussel shell,
　　　　　　　　　　and went to the place where the young man
　　　　　　　　　　was tied up.

　　　　When she had smeared him with the fat,
　　　　　　the ropes became loose,
　　　　　　　　and she untied him completely.

　　　　　　Then he went,
　　　　　　　　caught many mountain goats,
　　　　　　　　　　and returned safely to his wife.

9. The Jealous Man
　(no text) "The name of the man who killed his wife is xʷakʷxʷɔ́kʷlač"
　(Boas 1892).

10. The Thunderbird
　Two brothers went into the woods
　　and stayed hidden there for a month.
　　　　Every day they bathed in a lake
　　　　　　and then washed themselves with spruce[3] boughs,
　　　　　　　　until they had become completely cleansed
　　　　　　　　　　and had no more human smell about them.

Then they climbed up onto the mountain Kwlénas
  and there found the house of the thunder god Wálxwm.

They stepped inside the door
  and saw a woman sitting in the house.
      She invited them to come in,
and told them
  that her husband and his brother had flown out.

      Before they returned
        she hid the visitors in a corner of the house.

It wasn't long,
  before they came flying in
    and set down in front of the house.
      It sounded as if a tree was being blown down by a storm.

When they came into the house,
  they at once smelled the visitors
    and asked the woman
      where she had hidden them.

  She called them forth.

Then the Thunderbirds took off their belts,
  which gleamed like fire
    and were made of Aihos[4] skin,
      they hung up their feather cloaks
        and took on human form.

Toward the end of the summer the Pentlatch tribe celebrated a feast.
  Then the Thunderbirds came flying
    and brought back the young men,
      whom they had given the names Xwúmt'iq and Qápnats.

  The dancers heard
    how they called,
      "hoo, hoo, hoo, hoo."

Then they tied two boats together,
  laid boards across them
    and went out
      to look for them.

But they couldn't see anyone,
  although they reached the place
    where the voice came from.
      Suddenly they heard
        how something settled on the high
          prow of the boat,
            but still couldn't see anything.

Then they returned to the village,
  cleansed the house,
    and now Xwúmt'iq came in,
      danced with the Thunderbird mask
        and sang.

He was the founder of the Xwúmt'iq family.

His daughter was called Sixsíxawit.

His descendants can see the thunderbird,
  and, when there is a bad thunderstorm,
    they are able to persuade him [Thunderbird]
      to return to his house.

Notes

1. In a Thompson River Salish narrative told by Annie York, Frog Woman rejects Beaver, and he retaliates with a rain power song that causes a flood. Beaver's song also shows definite Coast Salish origins (see Egesdal 1992:53–54). Also see the Nooksack story "Beaver and Mouse" in this volume.—Eds.

2. Literally, Toothed Vagina.

3. The German here says *Fichtenzweigen*, which would probably usually be translated as "spruce boughs." The ethnographic literature, however, suggests that other trees were used for this cleansing purpose, but which one specifically (if a single variety was indeed used) is unclear. Barnett (1955:95) mentions cedar and hemlock; Kennedy and Bouchard (1983:47) mention cedar. Fir is also sometimes cited.

4. The Aihos was a mythical double-headed monster (i.e., with a head on each end), usually translated as a snake or serpent. It was considered very powerful, and it could turn people to stone. It is better known by its Kwak'wala name Sisiutl.

Basket Ogress Stories

Ch'eni, the Giant Woman Who Stole Crying Children
A Traditional Lummi Story

Told by Aloysius Charles

Edited by Richard Demers and Bill James

This story about Ch'eni (čəní),[1] the giant woman who stole crybabies, was told by Aloysius Charles in July 1972. The telling was spontaneous and fluent. It was recorded in Lummi by Richard Demers. The original recording was played back for Mr. Charles, who then translated and discussed the story. His translation and discussion were recorded on a second tape recorder by Elizabeth Bowman. Mr. Charles's translation appears in this volume.

It is impossible to understand fully the complete cultural import of a story such as this. We do know that children had to be warned about the danger of being lost in the woods. The forests around the waters of Puget Sound were extremely dense, and even if one was only a few feet into the woods, it was possible to become disoriented and lost. The Lummi word for "door" and "road" or "path" is the same, reflecting how a passageway through the woods is typically closed and not open. So the story of Ch'eni would reinforce the admonition for children not to venture too far into the forest where they could easily be lost.

A few points of interpretation by Mr. Charles will make the story clearer. He explained that the snake at the bottom of the basket intimidated the children so they would not move or cry out. He also explained that the pitch was used to seal the eyes shut on some of the children so they could not escape.

The story of Ch'eni exists in various forms, with each Lummi family telling slightly different versions. Barbara Efrat has collected the same story in the Sooke language on Vancouver Island. Sooke and Lummi are very closely related members of the Northern Straits dialect continuum.

This story also highlights the Lummis' cultural view that certain animals' physical characteristics are a consequence of changes effected by a being referred to as "The Transformer." A modern louse is the transformed Ch'eni, for instance, and flocking birds are the lice from her hair.

Ch'eni

I am going to tell a story and it is an old one that I will tell. This story was told to children—it is "her story." Her name is Ch'eni, and she came from way back in the woods. She would emerge from the woods when it started to get dark, and she came looking for children who were crying.

She had a big basket. If the children were crying she would come into their house. She held a piece of smoked salmon, and would say to the crying child,

"Here—take this! It is good to eat."

Then she would grab the crying child and put him in her basket. She then went to the next house and she did the same thing again to the next crybaby. She put him in her basket.

There was a big snake at the bottom of the basket—a BIG SNAKE.

And she moved on and continued her trip to the next house. And she did the same thing to the crybaby there.

"Take this. It is good to eat."

Then she would grab the child's hand and put him in her basket.

Then she would sling the basket up on her back. It was a big basket. A BIG BASKET.

And she kept moving along. She was still doing this until the basket was full of children who had been crying.

But one of the children was a little older, and the Ts'uXaelech (čux̣éləč)[2] ("giant woman") knew that he was coming up next.

So she took pitch and she heated it.

And she came up to him.

She said, "Take it. Eat it."

She grabbed him, put him in the basket and walked on. As she was walking along, on her way home, she walked under a tree. The older boy grabbed ahold of the growth above and got away. The Ts'uXaelech did not know that the boy did this.

She finally arrived at her house. A big fire was inside—a BIG FIRE. She was preparing to bake the children. She was going to roast the children for food. The fire was getting big. A little girl said to the other children:

"When the Ts'uXaelech is ready to cook, you watch and wait for when she comes out dancing. When she gets right here, we'll push her, burn her up (and pointing to the ground) when she gets right here."

The children got ready, and so when the Ts'uXaelech came in dancing they pushed her into the fire and she started to burn. The air was full of flying lice from the Ts'uXaelech.

This really happened and it is that way today. When you're out walking, and when you see a louse, you see the transformed Ts'uXaelech. And a flock of birds are the transformed former lice.

Notes

1. The name of the giant woman is written in the orthography in use by the Lummi Nation in 1996, followed here by the phonetic version. —Eds.

2. Ch'eni is also referred to as Ts'uXaelech (čux̣éləč) from this point in the story.

The Basket Ogress, Slapu?
Two Traditional Klallam Stories

Told by Martha Charles John

Edited by Steven M. Egesdal

I have selected these two Klallam stories because they contain the same motifs as in a well-known Thompson River Salish traditional legend about the Bear Cub Transformers.[1]

In the first story, Trickster Mink ferries Klallam's Basket Ogress, Slapu?, in his canoe, having arranged with Crab to bite her and cause her to fall into the sea and drown.

In the Thompson version, Grizzly Woman, no less an evil ogress, is ferried across a river by the Bear Cubs' powerful Grandfather, and is forced to sit on a hole in the middle of the canoe. The ferryman has arranged for Sturgeon (and other animals) to disembowel her through a hole from beneath the canoe.

In the second Klallam story below, Chipmunk teases Slapu?, and she scratches his back, giving him his characteristic stripes. Chipmunk plays the same role in the Thompson analogue.

These Klallam stories also are significant because some scholars have theorized that the Bear Cub Transformer motifs in Thompson River Salish narratives originated on the coast and moved into the interior (see Teit 1898:11). That Coast Salish Basket Ogress has the same role as Grizzly Woman in the Thompson River Salish stories lends support to that theory.

Both Klallam stories were told by Martha Charles John to Laurence C. Thompson, in April 1969, at Port Gamble, Washington. In July 1983, I worked on the analysis and translation of these two stories with several of the last native speakers of Klallam: Tom Charles, then of Becher Bay, Vancouver Island, British Columbia, and Adeline Smith and Bea Charles of Elwha, Washington.

Little Mink and Slapu?

Little Mink was the child of Mink.

He was out looking for crabs.

He was out looking for crabs, and he caught one.

He was paddling around looking, and Slapuʔ came down to the beach.
Slapuʔ said to him:

> "I want to go with you, little fella.
> I want to go with you."

Little Mink said to Slapuʔ:

> "Oh, all right."

He landed on the shore. He told her:

> "Get in. Sit right in the middle."

Slapuʔ got aboard, and she sat in the middle of his dugout canoe.
Little Crab was walking there, the one Little Mink had caught.
Little Mink paddled out.
He went way out in deep water, toward Sequim Bay.
When he got out into deep water, he said something to Crab.
Crab bit Slapuʔ on her ass.
Crab went after her. Crab was going after Slapuʔ.
When she moved, he moved.
She kept on moving away, until she came to the stern of the canoe.
She fell into the water, and she bubbled.
She sank bubbling, way down deep. Slapuʔ was bubbling.
Slapuʔ is still bubbling down there in Sequim Bay.[2]

Chipmunk and Slapuʔ

Chipmunk was up in a tree.
He was lonely for his Granny. He sang:

> "I wish my Granny would come."

Chipmunk was at the door. Chipmunk sang something.
He sang a song for his grandmother.

> $x^w \partial c$ ' $x^w \partial c$ ' $x^w \partial c$ '[3]
> $x^w \partial c$ ' $x^w \partial c$ ' $x^w \partial c$ '

Slapuʔ showed up, walking by.
Chipmunk sang his song again.
So Slapuʔ came over.
Chipmunk was gathering something there (perhaps acorns).[4]
[Chipmunk had something that Slapuʔ wanted.]
Slapuʔ got there.

Chipmunk threw that stuff.
Slapuʔ lunged for it, but she couldn't get it.

She thought that it was Chipmunk jumping.
Chipmunk sang again:

> x^wəc' x^wəc' x^wəc'
> x^wəc' x^wəc' x^wəc' x^wəc' x^wəc'

Chipmunk gathered up something. He threw them.
Slapuʔ grabbed for them, but she missed again.
Chipmunk sang once more.

> x^wəc' x^wəc' x^wəc'

Then Chipmunk jumped from the tree.
Slapuʔ grabbed for him.
He was going into his hollowed-out log.
He was going into his log.
Chipmunk must have gotten scratched.
That's why Chipmunk's back is scratched.

Notes

1. See Egesdal and M. T. Thompson 1994.
2. Klallam elders Adeline Smith and Bea Charles explained that in Sequim Bay there is a whirlpool or bubbling spring.
3. Song, sung by Tom Charles and presumed to be Chinook Jargon, sung twice.
4. Tom Charles did not recognize what Chipmunk said as a Klallam word. He presumed that it was Chinook Jargon, but he suggested that it was "acorns." Martha John told L. C. Thompson (personal communication) that she always told the Boy Scouts that it was acorns when she performed the narrative for them, because she suspected their parents would not want her to tell them it actually was chipmunk turds.

Qálqaliɬ, the Basket Ogress
A Traditional Squamish Story

Told by Louis Miranda

Edited by Aert H. Kuipers

The Squamish once lived around Howe Sound and along the banks of the lower Squamish River and Cheakamus Creek in southern British Columbia. More recently they spread to the shores of English Bay, False Creek, and Burrard Inlet as far as Seymour Creek on the northern bank, and Coal Harbour on the southern bank (Hill-Tout 1900:473–75; Barnett 1938:140). The language was close to extinction when I recorded this story, and only a few older people living in the Vancouver, British Columbia, area spoke it.

In a longer English version presented by Hill-Tout (1900:546ff),[1] the story is in more elaborate English, although not necessarily better representing the original story. In that version, the children were swimming and playing in the shallow water on the beach. The young carver, T'it'kiʔctn, was sitting on the beach with his back to the others making arrows so that he did not see the Basket Ogress (Qálqaliɬ) approaching. He was older and bigger, and he would probably have otherwise escaped. Hill-Tout also describes the Ogress's basket as one made from woven snakes.

T'it'kiʔctn had warned the others to screw up their eyes very tight so the pitch would not seal their eyes, but some of the smaller children forgot and so found their eyes sealed tight. After disposing of the Ogress, T'it'kiʔctn found some grease and oil in her house and rubbed the pitch off their eyes. The children collected the ashes from the fire and T'it'kiʔctn blew on them and scattered them. The ashes turned into the little birds known locally as snowbirds.

An interlinear, grammatically analyzed version of this story was published in my grammar and dictionary of Squamish (Kuipers 1967:219–29). Most of the material on which that book was based was collected from 1951 to 1954, while I was on the faculty of the University of British Columbia.[2]

I returned to Vancouver in the fall of 1956 for a short period, when I had the good fortune to engage the services of Mr. Louis Miranda of Mission Indian Reserve. Mr. Miranda was of great assistance in checking and clearing up a number of difficult grammatical points, and he was also able to dictate stories that in turn provided more material for the grammar and dictionary. Translations and a rapid analysis of these stories were made while I was working with Mr. Miranda. His alert and tireless assistance yielded much, both in material and in insight.

The recordings were made in the following way: Mr. Miranda would tell the story in Squamish without interruption, and I would write it down as he went along. The story was then read back to him sentence by sentence, and he would repeat the sentences slowly in the same form, with occasional changes or additions.

Qálqaliɫ, the Basket Ogress

In the old days they used to warn the children to be careful,
not to accept anything from anyone they didn't know.

The children were at home, and they were crying.
A big woman came in, carrying a large basket on her back.
The children didn't know that it was Qálqaliɫ.
Then Qálqaliɫ said,
    "What is the matter with you, children?"

Qálqaliɫ had some cedar bark with her.
Then she fooled the children.
Qálqaliɫ said,
    "There you are, kiddies, take this dried salmon!"
Then she held it out to them, and the children reached for it.
Then Qálqaliɫ caught them by the hands,
and she threw the children in the basket, T'it'ki?ctn among them.

Now this T'it'ki?ctn was an excellent carver.
Then Qálqaliɫ went up (the mountain),
carrying on her back her basket with the children in it,
T'it'ki?ctn among them.

Then T'it'ki?ctn cut the basket until he had made a hole in it big enough
    to push through his comrades.
When the children dropped (to the ground) they made a thumping noise.

Now Qálqaliɫ asked,
        "What's that, T'it'kiʔctn?"
(He answered,)
        "Nothing, Granny, those are your heels thumping."
T'it'kiʔctn freed many of his comrades,
only the bigger children were left in the basket.

Then Qálqaliɫ reached her house.
Qálqaliɫ put down her basket and took out the children, one after the
    other;
only a few of them were left.

Then Qálqaliɫ prepared some pitch to seal up the eyes of the children.
Then T'it'kiʔctn told his comrades,
        "Squeeze your eyes very tightly shut,
        then they won't be so tightly sealed up."
Then Qálqaliɫ had her pitch ready, and she sealed up the eyes of the
    children.

Then she went and painted herself, and then Qálqaliɫ danced.
Then T'it'kiʔctn said,
        "Come a little closer, Granny, doing your dance!"
She consented and came dancing closer by.

In the meantime the fire had become quite big.
She came in front of the children.
Then they pushed her into the fire.
Then her hair was set ablaze.
Then Qálqaliɫ's lice flew away.
(Those are the swarms of birds you see flying around.)

Then Qálqaliɫ hollered,
        "Come and help me, T'it'kiʔctn."
Now T'it'kiʔctn had the fire tongs in his hand.
Then he said,
        "I am helping you, Granny!"
But in the meantime he was pushing her deep into the fire.

Then T'it'kiʔctn took his comrades down
and got them all (safely) home.

Notes

1. This was reprinted in Maud 1978:93–95.

2. The Canadian Social Science Research Council, through the good offices of Professor Harry Hawthorn of the University of British Columbia, defrayed my expenses for travel and informant fees.

Why Things Are the Way They Are

The Transformer and the Blind Old Man

A Traditional Sooke Story

Told by Cecilia Joe

Edited by Barbara S. Efrat

This tale was chosen as typical of those about the Transformer, explaining why things exist the way they are. It relates the story of why the different fish are found at different depths. It also typifies the notion of caring for the elderly and the good or helpless (the blind old man).

The story was told by the late Cecilia Joe, on the Esquimalt Reserve, Victoria, British Columbia, in February 1964. It was told first in Sooke, then translated into English. Mrs. Joe was my principal consultant during the collection of material on the Sooke dialect of Northern Straits Salish.[1] She was born in 1890 on Vashon Island in Puget Sound. Coming from a family with ties to Salish areas in the state of Washington and to the Nootka region to the northwest of Victoria, Mrs. Joe could also speak Klallam (across the Strait from Victoria), and she understood Nitinat, a Nootkan language on the west coast of Vancouver Island. Her retention of the Sooke language was excellent, and her skill was acknowledged by others on the Sooke Reserve.

Although her formal education reached only to the fourth grade at the Kuper Island Residential School, she proved a very interesting consultant due to her own linguistic curiosity. She spent most of her adult life on the Esquimalt Reserve where Songish (also a dialect of Northern Straits Salish) is spoken and where her husband was chief.

The Transformer and the Blind Old Man

It is told that there was a poor old man. He was sitting down outside. There was nothing for him to eat. He could do nothing to get his food.

Someone was passing by. It must have been x̣éʔiʔs, the Transformer. The poor old man was asked: "Indeed, what's the matter with you?"

"Ohhh, I am poor! I cannot see. There is nothing for me to eat. I cannot go to get my food."

"Ohhh, your blanket is good! Let's exchange!" the person said. That must have been the Transformer.

The Transformer took the old man's blanket. The Transformer put his own blanket on the old man. "Ohhh, you look good wearing my blanket. To finish, I am going to arrange it so you'll get your food."

The Transformer broke off the fringe of his blanket. But not much. He said to him: "Your food will be the small fish. They show up close to shore. They come in on the waves." He let the fringe go, but he did not throw it in right away. (That's the way people are with anything they do; they lift it up four times,[2] and then they let it go.) The herring and smelts came ashore right away with the waves.

He took the bigger fringes, and it was done the same way. "These will be bigger fish, way out in the deep. There will be plenty in your land." He took the little bigger fringe of his blanket and threw it in. And again he did it the same way. That's why halibut and cod are known only in these places. They are not so plentiful everywhere else, when one is searching for them.

That's what the Transformer did. That's how it is—another story of the Indian people.

Notes

1. This research was supported by both the National Museum of Canada and by the National Science Foundation of the United States. An interlinear grammatical analysis of the story was included in Efrat 1969.

2. Four is the Sooke ritual number. —Eds.

The Seal

A Traditional Sliammon-Comox Story

Told by Mary George

Edited by Honoré Watanabe

The Sliammon people live in the area about 120 kilometers (75 miles) north of Vancouver, facing the Georgia Straits, in the vicinity of present-day Powell River, British Columbia. The area abounds in natural resources. The sea offers many kinds of fish (different kinds of salmon, herring, red snapper, and cod), and shellfish (horse clams, littleneck clams, butter clams, cockles, mussels, etc.). On land, plants and game are plentiful. The Sliammon people had, and continue to have, a tremendous respect for their natural surroundings. Such an attitude toward their environment can be observed in the following story.

In linguistic terms, the language spoken by the Sliammon people is often referred to as the Mainland dialect of Comox, or Mainland Comox. Comox is actually the name of (and the language spoken by) the native people who live on Vancouver island, across the Georgia Straits from the area where the Sliammon people live. The languages spoken by the Comox people and that of the Sliammon people are classified as two dialects of the same language. "Comox" has been used as the cover term for the language in linguistics literature. The dialect on the mainland is spoken by three groups: Sliammon, Klahoose, and Homalco. No systematic study has been carried out on the possible dialectal differences among the speech of these three groups, but the differences seem to be very slight. There is no cover term for the language (or the dialect) spoken by these groups, and thus the somewhat odd term "Mainland Comox."

The following story is a popular tale told among the Sliammon people. It is interesting that this story is not a myth or legend (that is, it's not about a time when "the world was created" or when "people were animals"), but rather it is remembered and told as something that actually happened in the past. The cave at Tuqwanen (tuqʷanən; present-day Theodosia Inlet) where the people find the man in this story is an actual location.

All traditional Sliammon stories have been passed on orally. This characteristic gives storytellers some freedom to add their own flavor and "twist" to the stories. Thus, there are some stories with versions that differ slightly in detail. There seems to be no "authentic" version of a story; therefore, all versions are authentic. The particular version recorded here was narrated by a Sliammon elder, Mrs. Mary George. Different people remember details of this story differently from others. For example, another elder remembers the seal that appears in the beginning of the story as being harpooned instead of being clubbed (as it is in the following version). People all seem to agree, however, that the basic plot of the story is the same, and they enjoy recounting the different details that each of them has heard from their parents or grandparents.

In order to appreciate the story, especially its beginning, one needs to understand how the Sliammon people traditionally hunted seals. Storytellers do not provide such information, because it is assumed to be common knowledge among the People.

Sealing was carried out by a pair of men in one canoe. When they found a seal, they approached it quietly. When the seal was within striking distance, they harpooned or clubbed it. The seal killed, or severely wounded, in this way sinks quickly beneath the surface. Immediately, one of the men, holding one end of a rope, dives for the seal. He must capture it before it sinks too deep and tie the rope around it. The other man remaining in the canoe then pulls the seal on board. The one who dives for seals, therefore, must be able to hold his breath long enough, as well as be quick enough in the water, to catch the seal before it sinks beyond his reach. Such a sealing method is no longer practiced; however, there are many members of the Sliammon community who remember diving for seals in this way.

In addition to the basic plot and the cultural background of the story, there is another aspect upon which everyone seems to agree; that is, the story sounds beautiful in its native language but sounds awful in English translation. Unfortunately, then, what follows does not do justice either to the story or to the Sliammon language.

It goes without saying that in translation from one language to another subtle nuances are often lost; however, this is more so the case when the two languages are as radically different as Sliammon and English. A word in Sliammon consists of a root (the core) usually followed by a number of suffixes, and such a word is often semantically equivalent to a whole sentence in English. In the following story, for example, where a man (dips and) turns his hand around in the water, in the original Sliammon this is expressed in one word that is composed of a root followed by five suffixes. A more literal translation of that one word would be "he-turns-hand-in-relation-to-it."

I have refrained from adding to the translation, so that what follows is more or less a word-for-word translation from the original Sliammon. Lines are grouped into what may be called paragraphs. As can be seen in the first few paragraphs, there are many repetitions of the same line. In addition, lines are frequently introduced with "then" or "and then." These traits seem to be characteristic of storytelling in Sliammon. They appear somewhat odd in a written English translation, but give a certain rhythm reflecting the Sliammon—again, a beautiful trait that is inevitably lost when the story is written down—let alone in translation.

I thank the Sliammon people for allowing me to have the chance to touch their lives through their rich and precious traditions. I would especially like to thank Mrs. Mary George for telling me this story and helping me in its transcription and translation. My gratitude also goes to Mrs. Elsie Paul for her help in the translation and explanation of the story.

The Seal Story
I will tell a story about seals.

One man was taken by seals.

He went looking for a seal.
 He took his weapon.
  He took it.
  Then clubbed its head.

And then, he killed it.
 It sank.
 The seal sank.

The seal didn't come up.
Then, its blood showed up.

He dove for the seal down below.
 The man dove.
 This man was strong.
 The man was strong.
 He dove for it.

He didn't come up.
His partners were waiting and waiting and waiting. . . .
    They waited for him to come up.

Nothing.
Nothing came up.

The two canoes gathered.
    There were two men on the other canoe.
This man was by himself.
    He was waiting in the canoe from which the man dove.

Nothing came up.
The rest of his partners were worried.

They went and told the people at Grace Harbor.
    That's the name of the place where the people were.
    They went and told the people.

The people all came.
    They paddled to where the point was.
    They came and saw.

They asked the one waiting if he came up.
    "No. He didn't come up," said the one waiting.

They were there . . . all in a circle.
    As if they were all praying.
They asked God why they took that man away.

One person said, "I will do it this way."
    He took water,
    And then, turned his hand around in the water.
    And then, held his hands around his mouth.
    And then, hollered to the depths.

There was no answer.
    Nothing.

The people all went around in a circle.
    And then, they were all praying.
    They asked God.
    Why he was taken.
    Why he was taken.

The people felt really sad.
They all stayed and waited for him.
They searched for him close by at the shallows.
    He might have drifted away.
    He might have become out of breath.
They all went and searched the shallows,
    and then the ocean.

Nothing.
    They saw nothing.

One person always stayed waiting where the man dove.
    The rest of the people went home.
    They went home.
There was always one person waiting there for the man to come up.
    People took turns to wait for him where he dove.
    The rest of the people went home.

Next morning, they looked for him again.
    Nothing.

He must have been taken.
    He must have been taken by the seals.
    One elder said.

"Our relative must have been taken away by the seals.
    We probably will not see him."

They went looking for him again.
People saw that, at one place,
The seals were all in a circle.

He was in the middle.
      The man who was taken was in the middle.
      He was in the middle.

They wouldn't let him go to see the people.
The people called to the man,
      "Come.
      Why are you like that?
      Why did you leave us?"
      They said to him.
The seals went in front of him.

The people went into the narrows.
      Tuqwanen is the name.
      (They always went into the inlet.)

They saw a big cave in the narrows.
The man was there facing this way.

There were seals surfacing beside him.
      The people went toward him.
      They wanted to take him.

      "Come here," they said.
      "Why did you do that to us?
      Why did you leave us?"

      "Come here," they said.
      "Come and tell us what you're doing."

No.
The seals, lots of seals blocked them.
They were blocking.

The people all felt very badly.
They all went to Tuqwanen,
      where the people lived.
There they always did everything.

They gathered food.
They burned[1] his food for him.
And then, they came and poured the food where he was.
They made everything.
Barbecued fish,
Smoke-dried fish.
They came and poured them where he was.

They always used to see him where the cave Is.
They used to see that man there.

And then, everybody felt badly.
They wanted to forget.
They used to see him come up.
And then, they recognized that it was him.

Then, his body began to change.
He was just like a seal.

They tried to talk to him.
Then, he just looked around.
Then, he dove again.
He dove like a seal.

The people, the first people, remembered him for a long time.
Not now.

The present-day people would now know,
and respect what happened to the first people.
And what happened to the man who was taken away by the seals.

They named that man Tih'exwthut (tihʔəxʷθut).
That man was very strong.
That's why they call him Tih'exwthut.
He was strong.
That's what the first people said.
That's why they call the seal Tih'exwthut.

They told us that Tih'exwthut will take you
    when you go jigging, fishing, or clam digging.
My grandfather always warned us.
    Tih'exwthut will take you.
That's what we were told.
    We were told that when we went rowing and jigging.
    We used to see seals.

My grandfather really respected seals.
    He never, never made fun of them.

You always see seals.
    If you see them, you appreciate them.
    Talk nicely to them.

Don't give him bad words.
    You appreciate seals.

When my grandfather would take a seal,
    he wanted to eat it,
he never said anything. He did it by himself,
    he went and killed it.

The seal is from our relative.
    That's what he said.

He went out gently.
    He did not say that he was going to kill a seal.

He would bring it home.
Then, he would put it gently down.
    He talked to the seal first.
    And then, he cooked it.
    He cooked it before we ate it.

They are a part of us.
That's why we really respect seals today.
    Don't make fun of the seals.

Do not.
Don't make fun of them.

That's why there are a lot of seals today.
Seals are our people.

That's the story of the seals.

Notes

My research on the Sliammon language has been supported at various times by the Japanese Ministry of Education, Science and Culture (International Scientific Research Program), the Jacobs Research Fund, and the Phillips Fund of the American Philosophical Society.

1. In most Northwest groups it was traditional to burn food and invite the ghosts of deceased members of the group to partake. —Eds.

How Kingfisher Got the Red under Her Wings

A Traditional Klallam Story

Told by Amy Allen

Edited by Steven M. Egesdal

This short, traditional Klallam story was told by the late Amy Allen of James-town, Washington, to Leon Metcalf in July 1953. No more about the telling is known. Thirty years later, in July 1983, Steve Egesdal worked on a translation of that story, with a few of the last native speakers of Klallam: Tom Charles, then of Becher Bay, Vancouver Island, British Columbia, and Bea Charles and Adeline Smith, both of Elwha, Washington. The plot of the story is straight-forward. Kingfisher cheats on her husband, Great Blue Heron. She pretends to be sick, while he gathers food for her. Cuckolded Heron eventually discov-ers unfaithful Kingfisher in flagrante delicto, and he punishes her. Kingfisher wears her badge of shame today, a patch of red plumage under her wings where Heron stabbed her.

Some comments on the story's avian dramatis personae may be helpful. The Klallam aboriginally were keenly aware of animals' habits in their envi-ronment, and perhaps especially those of surrounding birdlife. Such aware-ness would have been presupposed cultural knowledge serving as a contextual backdrop for this story. The male and female belted kingfisher (*Megaceryle alcyon*) show different coloring and marking. The male kingfisher is bluish gray above, with white underparts and a bluish gray breast band. The female kingfisher is similar, but she has a rufous band below the bluish gray one. This story concerns the mythic origin of that red band in the female's plumage. The great blue heron (*Ardea herodias*) is an imposing creature (four feet tall and a seven-foot wingspan), with a daggerlike beak. The connection between his beak and the stabbing of Kingfisher in the story is transparent. A heron's wingbeats are slow and appear labored; it hunts by standing still in shallow water, waiting for prey to come within striking distance. One can imagine how Heron's apparently slow flight and patient manner of hunting gave Kingfisher ample time for her adulterous dallying.

Both characters can be characterized generally as waterbirds, which perhaps supplies a superficial basis for their mythic marriage. A deeper understanding of their traits reveals important behavioral differences. Herons build nests in trees, often in colonies; kingfishers construct no nest. Herons usually are silent; kingfishers often give a harsh rattling call, on the wing or perched. The two birds also fly and hunt quite differently. Kingfishers fish by diving while in flight, or by hovering and then plunging; herons stand still or stalk methodically. Kingfishers fly with quick and deep wing beats, paced irregularly. That differs from how herons fly, as mentioned above. The erratic (and unfaithful) Kingfisher is married to the steady (and lumbering cuckold) Heron. The story may reflect the natural outcome of the unnatural pairing of these two birds. More specifically, it also may reflect that the nestless female kingfisher was considered as lacking a domestic nature.

There is an Upper Chehalis version of this story (Adamson 1934:41), and a Skokomish [Lushootseed] one (Adamson 1934:369). Elmendorf (June 1961:103) also presents a Twana version titled "Helldiver and Crane," which he indicates has Klallam origins.

How Kingfisher Got the Red under Her Wings

All right, I'll tell you folks how it was that Kingfisher got red patches underneath her wings.

Her husband was Great Blue Heron.
She pretended that she was really sick.
Blue Heron—poor soul—went looking for something to feed his sick wife.
She meanwhile did it with another man. She screwed another man.
When she figured Heron was about to arrive home, she blew into the fire to ashen her face.
That way Heron would think she was really sick.
And so Heron believed that his wife was really sick, because of her pale face.

Heron went out again, to gather food for his sick wife.
She did the same thing. As soon as Heron left, another man came in.
She did it with another man.
Poor Blue Heron. He believed that his wife was sick.
It wasn't very long though, and Blue Heron got suspicious.

He went out for a little while, and he came back.

He caught his wife in the act. He stabbed her.
That's why Kingfisher has red underneath her feathers.
It's where Heron stabbed her, when he caught her with another man.

When you see the Kingfisher flying, you see that red under her wings.
And it's the same today.

Tribal Legends
Traditional Stories of the Cowlitz

Told by Roy Wilson

Edited by Judith Irwin

Because of extensive intermarriage, a Cowlitz storyteller could have learned Salish tales when young, but be speaking Sahaptin as an adult among the Upper Cowlitz. In the 1920s two ethnographers, Dr. Thelma Adamson and Dr. Melville Jacobs, recorded Cowlitz legends from both Salish and Sahaptin speakers. Both scholars also made notes about their informants' languages. The Melville Jacobs Collection, bequeathed to the University of Washington, includes sound recordings in addition to written accounts.

Not surprisingly, variant versions of a myth were given by different narrators. Roy Wilson offers here a different version of a myth from that in Thelma Adamson's collection (Adamson 1934:213). Both accounts explain how Mosquito ceased to be a dangerous being.

Most legends come from a much earlier time, when animals and other natural phenomena were people. In *Takhoma, Lawelatla, and Patu*, for example, Roy Wilson speaks of how Creator, not wanting to destroy the great Chief Takhoma and his two wives, turns them into mountains.

Roy Wilson is a former chairman of the Cowlitz Indian Tribe. He remembers these five Cowlitz tribal legends being told to him when he was young.

The Flood Story

Once, in the long ago time, the Great-Chief-of-the-Above told the tribal Holy Man to tell the people that a great flood was coming. The men were instructed to look for the largest cedar tree that they could find and cut it down. They were to make the largest canoe they had ever seen. It was to be the largest canoe that they could possibly make. Some of the women were to go to their basket trees and gather enough cedar bark to make the biggest and longest rope they had ever seen. The other women were to prepare much food: smoked salmon, dried berries, and many other foods.

The men finished building the great canoe. The women placed all of the food they had prepared in the canoe. The men took the rope the women had made and attached one end to the canoe and the other end to a very large rock near the edge of the river.

It began to rain, and they placed all of the children in the great canoe. They then put one of their finest young braves and a young woman of sixteen summers in the canoe to watch over and care for the children.

The rain continued to fall and the river overflowed its banks. The canoe began to float on the floodwaters. Soon the lower hills were covered with water. Finally, only Lawelatla (Mount St. Helens) could be seen. In time even she disappeared under the waters of the flood. The canoe tugged on the long rope the women had made, which was attached to the large rock far below.

One day, one of the children cried, "Look, there is another canoe!" They all could see a tiny speck in the distance. The thought of seeing other people made them feel very good. The next day the other canoe seemed to be a little bit closer. At least it was a tiny bit larger, but the following day they realized that it was not a canoe. It was Lawelatla coming back into view.

When the waters finally receded, the canoe rested on the banks of what is known today as the Cowlitz River. And the children in that canoe became the ancestors of today's Cowlitz Indian people.

Takhoma, Lawelatla, and Patu
Once in the long ago time there was a great chief. His name was Takhoma, and he had two wives, Lawelatla and Patu. They were doing some things that the Creator did not like, and they would not heed his warnings. He had to punish them, but he did not want to destroy them because they were such great people. They should remain as a lesson to everyone, forever. So, he changed them into great mountains. Today we know Takhoma as Mount Rainier, Lawelatla as Mount St. Helens, and Patu as Mount Adams.

Mount St. Helens and Mount Rainier Eruptions
Once in the long ago time Coyote was going up the Seqiku, the Toutle River, and he heard a great rumbling. He perked up his ear and realized that it was Lawelatla. She was very angry. Soon he heard another great rumbling coming from another direction, and he realized that it was Takhoma, who was also very angry. They were having a husband and wife argument, and he was in between them. Soon he saw Lawelatla blow her top and knock off the head of Takhoma.

The Seatco

Spirit Lake was always a bad place. My ancestors feared going there because that was where the evil spirits of the departed bad Indians went. These evil spirits were known as the Seatco. If you should get too close to the lake, you may hear strange sounds or see strange things because these evil spirits could change themselves into any form they wanted to. You might hear sounds of things that were not really there, or you might see things that were not really there.

There are many of these stories. One of the favorites told when I was young was about a hunter whose family was hungry, and he was determined to bring home some food for them. He saw an elk, but it was always a little too far in front for him to shoot his arrow at it. He knew that it was leading him closer and closer to the lake, and he was afraid. But his family was hungry and he continued to follow the elk. The elk led him to the shore of the lake and then walked out into the lake and disappeared. The hunter walked around to the other side of the lake looking for where the elk might have come out of the water, but he found nothing.

When he returned, he could still see the tracks of the elk where it entered the water. Suddenly, a long arm reached out of the lake and dragged the hunter into the lake. It was the elk, and yet today you can still see the elk and the hunter in the mists above the water of the lake.

Mosquito

Once in the long ago time Mosquito was a very dangerous person. He would attack people and kill them by drinking their blood. One day he was paddling his canoe up the river, and as he was passing a village, the people who saw him called out to him, inviting him to come and eat with them. They did not recognize who he really was. He called back, asking them what they had for dinner, and they answered, "Rabbit stew." He answered, "Oh, no, that will burn me," and he quickly paddled on.

He passed another village and refused their invitation. He passed a third village and they also invited him to dinner, but when they told him they were having duck stew, he became very angry and would not even answer them, and he paddled very fast to get away from there.

He was passing another village,[1] and the men there recognized who he really was. They called out to him, inviting him to dinner. When he asked what they were having, they answered, "Blood soup." He was very excited, and quickly accepted.

As he was paddling his canoe toward the shore, this large group of men quickly cut themselves and drained some of their blood into a large bowl. When he arrived they fed him first. They gave him bowl after bowl until he was so big and fat he could not move. Then they killed the dangerous one. He called back to them, begging to be allowed to come back, but they said they would only allow him to come back if he agreed to be a very small being who did not have the power to kill them, but instead be only a pest. And that is how we know Mosquito today.

Notes

1. Four is the Cowlitz pattern number. —Eds.

Trickster Stories

Coyote and Buffalo
A Traditional Spokane Story

Told by Margaret Sherwood
Edited by Steven M. Egesdal

Coyote is the culture hero of the Spokane, as he is more generally for other Plateau peoples. Indeed, the genre of traditional stories (*sqʷllúm'l*) commonly is called "Coyote stories" in English. For Coyote, however, the term "culture hero" means something different from what a Euro-American audience might expect. Coyote (spílye?) is both hero and heel, trickster and dupe, often playing both roles in the same tale.[1] The present story illustrates that characteristic paradox clearly. It contains two episodes, one in which Coyote plays the champion, and another in which he plays the chump.

The tale opens in an expected manner, with the quintessentially itinerant Coyote walking along. He is frightened by a dust cloud following him, which he tries to elude in vain. That dust cloud turns out to be a pitiful buffalo. Coyote's powers instruct him and help him to befriend the buffalo. Coyote takes the buffalo's tattered horns, and having attached them to his own head, he then battles four buffalo pursuing the first buffalo. He fatally gores three of them, and scares off the fourth. The surviving fourth buffalo runs home and tells kith and kin of Coyote's prowess.

The tale then changes course, with Coyote's change in course. He goes to the buffalo village. Their chief offers him a buffalo bride—or buffalo bribe—for Coyote's agreement to leave and leave them be. Coyote agrees and heads homeward with his wife-to-be. She, being a buffalo, stops repeatedly to graze. He, being a coyote, must wait and watch, growing hungrier with each stop. He finally loses patience with her feeding and his lack thereof, and he kills her. He butchers her, fillets her flesh, and places it on a smoking rack.

Just as the meat is cooked to perfection, he needs to defecate. When he squats nearby to do so, his hemorrhoids slip out and become fixed in the ground. He cannot stand up. As he is trapped in that delicate position, birds, kindred coyotes, and all manner of beasts come and eat up his bride-turned-feast. When the last bone is picked clean, his hemorrhoids let go. Coyote rushes to his smoking rack, finding nothing but his disappointed hunger. He decides to return to the village for another bride. He wails about the loss of his beloved wife, but the chief is not fooled. The chief knows all. Coyote's slaughtered wife reappears in the lodge. The chief scolds Coyote and sends him on his way empty-handed, ending the tale.

To understand the tale requires some knowledge of the Spokane cosmology, wherein an important duality prevails: man lives in two worlds. One is material, oriented toward mankind; the other is spiritual, accessed through animalkind. Animals are in touch with, and move between, the two worlds. That sensitivity allows certain animals to foretell events, such as weather, death, or the arrival of a guest. They can see into the spirit world, their special domain. They can guide man into it. Through animals, man can obtain a vision into that other world; through them, he finds his spirit power (*sumés*). Before man, animals lived alone in that otherworldly dimension—the *qʷllúm't* era. Coyote tamed that world, readying and righting it for man.

In this tale, the ostensibly animal dramatis personae reflect traits of both worlds. Centaur-like, they are neither man nor horse, but both. Coyote smokes a pipe with the bullied Buffalo. The pipe is a product of the People world. Coyote then uses buffalo horns to kill the Buffalo bulls. The horns are a part of the Animal world. Coyote uses a bow and arrow to kill his Buffalo bride; he butchers her and smokes her on a rack: tools of the People world. They marry, as People. But she grazes, as an Animal. The tale interweaves and moves between the two worlds.

At first blush, the tale seems to be a simple, humorous story. Coyote comically fits buffalo horns on his head and defeats several Buffalo bulls. He absurdly barbecues his Buffalo bride, and once undone by his hemorrhoids, he seeks another in vain. The tale may reflect more than such playful humor. Noted anthropologist and Amerindian folklorist Melville Jacobs thought that traditional stories acted as a psychological safety valve for these cultures; pent-up societal anxieties could be vented cathartically and safely within the humorous context of such stories (Jacobs 1959). A Flathead elder once explained that anything one needed to know about life was in Coyote stories. Thompson River Salish (Nɬeʔképmx) elders echoed that belief. Those insights perhaps permit the following speculation on the tale's deeper meanings.

The overriding theme of the story perhaps concerns the adverse consequences for misuse of power. Coyote's powers allow him to befriend a pitiful Buffalo and conquer four bullying Buffalo. That prowess and conquest, in turn, bring Coyote fame and a trophy wife. But Coyote then acts foolishly. He chooses to have his Buffalo bride for dinner over having her for his mate.

To understand what happens next requires some knowledge of Coyote's powers. Coyote keeps his powers in his rectum. Coyote summons them when in trouble, and they come out.[2] They appear as four scat balls. That manifestation is quite fitting, given that Coyote's (scatological) behavior often epitomizes anal expressiveness. Coyote's powers are anally expressed.

Coyote's hemorrhoids punish him, by preventing him from enjoying the fruits of his ignominious labor. The hemorrhoids originate where Coyote keeps his powers. Coyote's powers effected the hemorrhoidal humbling. Although that rectal and causal relationship is not made explicit, a knowledgeable Spokane audience likely would have drawn that transparent connection. In short, the theme is that the proper use of the power brings a reward; the improper use takes it away. And even the culture hero cannot escape that karmic justice.

Coyote's encounter with the Buffalo also might reflect something about the Spokane's encounter with novel, if not hostile, Plains culture. Interestingly, in this tale Coyote travels to the land of the Buffalo, very far from his home territory. The Plains tribes were Buffalo People.[3] The Spokane shifted from strict Plateau culture toward certain elements of Plains culture with the advent of the horse. Plains culture centered largely on the buffalo. Plateau culture centered largely on salmon. Indeed, one of Coyote's most important exploits as Plateau culture hero was to release the salmon for mankind.[4] As fishing may have given some ground to hunting buffalo, perhaps not all elements of buffalo culture fit naturally. In the tale below, Coyote as Spokane culture hero takes a tattered set of horns from a pitiful Buffalo and fits them on himself. The image is an awkward one, perhaps reflecting some discomfort or conflict about the Spokane's adopting "things buffalo," that is, Plains culture.

The other four buffalo may represent (at some level) Plains tribes with whom the Spokanes may have had to vie for hunting territory. (Four also is the pattern number for Spokane.) The description of the battle between Coyote and the Buffalo is graphically violent—stomachs gored open and guts splattered out. It imitates the gore too realistically to have originated purely as fantasy. Maybe the tattered horns symbolized a tribe (e.g., Shoshone) beaten by other Plains tribes (e.g., Blackfeet) and forced to retreat near(er) Spokane territory. Perhaps the tattered horns represent a relatively late access to Plains buffalo herds. That Coyote ultimately kills his Buffalo wife somewhere beyond Spokane territory also may have "explained" mythically why there were no buffalo in Spokane territory.

The tale also shows a misogynistic theme. Coyote does not relate to his wife's grazing habit—her means of sustenance. He kills her, for dinner. Bluebeard with a cannibalistic twist. Why so? Perhaps it reflects a fundamental antagonism between the roles of women and men in traditional Spokane culture: female "grazers" versus male "hunters." Spokane women were like the Buffalo bride, in that they spent much of their time gathering and preparing plant foods, especially roots (camas and bitterroot, among others) and berries. Spokane men, conversely, hunted game and fished. Indeed, Coyote's traditionally mythic wife Mole (pl'yahál'qs) characteristically is portrayed as digging and storing roots.

Margaret Sherwood told this tale to the author in the summer of 1979, in the Spokane language. She later translated the story into English. Normally, traditional stories were told only in the winter, that is, between the one year's first snowfall and the next year's first thunderstorm. Failure to abide by that rule risked early cold weather or a storm, and possibly worse sanctions. One common saying warns that telling Coyote stories out of season means snakes will come and crawl on you.[5] Mrs. Sherwood nonetheless felt comfortable telling this and other traditional tales in July, although she joked that we might be seeing some cold weather because of it.

Margaret Sherwood was an excellent teacher of Spokane. She worked for several years with Barry Carlson (University of Victoria), a highly respected Amerindian scholar and the foremost (non-Native) expert on the Spokane language. Mrs. Sherwood was a patient and tireless teacher, with a wonderful sense of humor and kind heart. Unfortunately, her delightful laughter could not be translated in the tale below.

Coyote and Buffalo

This tale is about Coyote and Buffalo.

Coyote traveled along. He noticed a dust cloud approaching him, from where he had come. He kept an eye on it. He saw something black coming. He looked back again.

It's still coming.

That thing took Coyote's route exactly. He thought:

Hey. Maybe it's tracking me.

He looped off the road and then got back on. He went on from there, checking back behind.

That thing followed the same course. He realized:

It's been tracking me. It's been chasing me.

He took off running. He glanced back. That black thing also ran. It was Buffalo approaching.

Coyote ran as fast as he could, but Buffalo still closed in on him. Buffalo was just about upon him, when Coyote thought:

> *What should I do? What should I do?*
> *Oh, yes. I have powers. I'll use them.*

He said: "Help me! Help me!

> Buffalo is just about upon me. He is chasing me."

They told him:

> "Here's a pipe. When he arrives, put that pipe in his ⊔⊔⊔⊔⊔⊔
> When you smoke, he'll stop. Then give that pipe to him."

Then Coyote lighted the pipe. They told him:

> "Don't run away. He'll stop."

Sure enough, Buffalo came to him and stopped. Coyote stuck the pipe in his mouth, and Buffalo smoked. Then they sat. Buffalo told Coyote:

> "I'm pitiful. Just look at my horns! I hardly have any horns left.
> Four buffalo have driven me from my home territory.
> Whenever I show my face, they attack me and beat me.
> Now I just wander around. I'm pitiful."

Coyote told him:

> "Give me your horns. I'll use them."

Buffalo gave him the horns. Coyote fastened the horns on himself. Buffalo told him:

> "Those others probably are already near."

Coyote said:

> "I'll look around for them. When they come, I'll engage them."

Coyote stayed there. Not too long and those four buffalo showed up. They approached Coyote and then stopped, facing him.

One of them rushed him—charged him. Coyote stood still. He did not run away.

That one Buffalo said:

> "What's going on here? He doesn't run away.
> Whenever one of us charged him, he used to run away.
> But now he stands his ground. What's going on here?"

Coyote stood still. Right when that Buffalo reached him, Coyote bellygored him.

His stomach tore apart, and his guts splattered out. He dropped dead.
Another one came at Coyote. He met the same end. Coyote rent his belly
wide open. He dispatched him.

When Coyote had killed three of those Buffalo, that last one thought:

> *I'm not going to attack. I couldn't live through it either.*

He turned tail and left.

Coyote went from that place, toward where those Buffalo had come
from.

That only remaining Buffalo left and returned home. He said:

> "He killed my brothers. I'm the sole survivor.
>
> That Buffalo came upon us, and he killed my brothers."

Coyote arrived and went to the chief's house. The chief told him:

> "You're gifted. Of all the people, you're the most talented.
>
> I'll tell you what, if you go back, I'll give you a wife."

Coyote said:

> "Fine. I'll go back."

Then the chief gave Coyote a Buffalo for a bride. Coyote accepted, because his home territory was far away from where he was given his wife-
to-be, and he only had borrowed horns. Then they left, he and his acquired wife.

They went on a ways, and his wife-to-be stopped to graze. She grazed.
Coyote could not graze, so he just had to wait for her.

They stopped again and again. She grazed again and again. Coyote grew
tired of that.

> *Ah! She's really a nuisance. I'm already really hungry.*
> *I think I'll kill her.*

No sooner had he thought that, and she knew his intentions.

He killed her with a shot from his bow. He slew his woman-to-be.

He skinned her. He butchered her. He made a rack for smoking meat.

He cut strips for dry meat. He placed all of them up on the smoking
rack.

He made a fire underneath. He smoked that meat.

> That meat was perfect. Just as it was done, he felt the urge to def-
> ecate.

He walked off nearby, not far from where he was smoking meat.

He squatted, and out slipped his hemorrhoids. They stuck fast into the
ground.

He tried to stand up again, but his hemorrhoids gripped the dirt.

In vain he tried to get up. But no, his hemorrhoids were fixed in the earth.

Then a flock of birds gathered at the smoking rack.

Magpies, blue jays, and other birds gathered there. All kinds of birds. They ate that dry meat. Then his kindred coyotes came. All kinds of animals.

They devoured the dry meat. They finished it all off.

Just when they had finished, he struggled to rise again.

Before when he tried, he could not stand. This time though, just when they had finished off the dry meat, he tried and managed to get up. He went there. He said:

It's already all gone. It's finished off.

There was nothing left. They had eaten, until they had gobbled up all of the dry meat.

And he was so hungry. He wandered about for awhile. He had nothing to eat. He thought:

I know. I'll go back to that Chief.

Maybe he'll give me another bride.

He set out again. He got to that Chief's house again and cried:

> "Whatever could have happened to my wife.
>
> We never even made it home before she died.
>
> Whatever could have happened. Oh—I am heartsick with grief."

He opened his eyes. Then he saw her sitting in the back of the lodge, that woman he had killed. The Chief told Coyote:

> "I know very well what you did. She is all you'll get.
>
> I won't be giving you anything else. Now be on your way.
>
> The only reason I gave you anything in the first place
>
> was because I pitied you. I have nothing more for you.
>
> Now go! Be off!"

Coyote exited the lodge and was on his way. That is the end.

Notes

1. Looking to the Northwest Coast mythology for comparison, Coyote seemingly combines traits of the Transformer with tricksters such as Mink or Raven or South Wind. (There were no coyotes on the Coast.)

2. Coyote calls for his powers (or "partners," "helpers") with stylized speech, uniquely Coyotese: p̓s p̓s p̓s p̓s. The action is described as p̓isp̓sm, analyzed as the onomatopoeic root √p̓is, reduplicated, followed by middle suffix -m: p̓is·/p̓s-m. With that invocation, Coyote's powers

slip from his bowels. Reichard (1947:17) similarly explains: "Coyote had helpers which could predict his behavior. When he came to an impasse, he could summon them. None of my informants could (or would?) tell me exactly what these helpers were. They always said, 'That's a Coyote-word.' The Thompson (and other Salish tribes) attribute special powers to Coyote's excrement." Teit (1937:173n3) adds: "Coyote's use of his excrements for advice occurs frequently in tales of the Salishan tribes. It was one of the magical powers given to Coyote by Chief[.]"

3. James Teit's (1917b:76) Okanagan version of this tale begins: "Coyote was traveling about, and went northward from the Salish to the Blackfoot country." That version makes explicit what is implicit in the Spokane version: Coyote ventured into (enemy) Plains territory.

4. See the Moses-Columbia story, "Coyote Releases Salmon," in this volume. —Eds.

5. n̓e kʷ qʷllúm̓t, n̓e m čtyéʔšmncs t č'ewíleʔ. "If you tell traditional stories [out of season], then snakes will crawl on you."

Coyote and the Goblin
A Traditional Shuswap Story

Told by Lilly Harry

Edited by Aert H. Kuipers

This story was told by Lilly Harry of Dog Creek, British Columbia, after the publication of Kuipers 1989. It is a continuation of Text 6 in the above book, which contains four texts produced by her.

Lilly Harry was one of the most knowledgeable speakers of Shuswap I have met. Mrs. Mary Palmantier, also of Dog Creek, assisted in transcribing the material. Both Lilly and Mary have passed away since then.

Mrs. Harry ended that earlier story by saying she didn't know what happened to Coyote afterward. She told the story again, years later, with some differences in the details only, and then, unprompted, after thinking a moment, continued with the following story.

Recapitulation of the earlier story: Two sisters go berry picking. Coyote wants the younger one for his wife and gets her pregnant. They go to the girl's parents, who don't want Coyote for a son-in-law.

Coyote and the Goblin

So Coyote took the woman, he left taking her along, he took his child.

A goblin ate his child, ate his wife, and then he was about to get to Coyote himself. Coyote said, *What am I going to do? He's left me for the last to eat.* He said to Whistler, "Come on, brother, help me! What shall I do with that goblin when he comes (to me) to eat me?"

Whistler told him, "Shoot him, kill him! You must eat him and lick up every bit of him, there must not be a drop of blood left when you kill him. You must eat all of him!"

The goblin went by and Coyote got ready to kill him. He was shot by Coyote and fell down. (He must have bled, of course.) Coyote licked it (blood) up and ate the goblin. He licked up his blood, not a drop was left.

He left. He said, *Now I go away from here, I won't stay here.* He left, crossed the river, came to his wife's relatives and told them, "My child was killed, my wife was killed. I was left for the last. I killed the goblin (and) I licked up every bit of him, not a drop is left."

An old man told him, "He'll come after you. He'll get to you. You can't kill those goblins, he'll get to you." Then the old man said to his folks, "Pack up so we can leave and go away from here. He will come after Coyote."

Coyote said, *My canoe wasn't checked. On my canoe there may be blood of the goblin, there his blood may have dripped.* He remembered now. Apparently he hadn't seen some blood that had dripped on his canoe.

Then he (the goblin) got to him. Where the blood had dripped he had recovered, and left from there having become a louse. He got to Coyote and Coyote was killed. You see, smart as Coyote is, all the same he was killed by the goblin. He had become a louse. When he left from where his blood had dripped, he left from there as a louse, until he reached Coyote. Coyote didn't suspect anything until he was killed and eaten. He (the goblin) sat there with a big belly. He had become big bellied.

You could see that he was sitting there as Coyote, but big bellied that he was! Then from there he (Coyote) arose again and went away. The goblin must be powerful. He was big bellied because he had killed two people, that's why he was big bellied, and yet he had been small, like that (showing).

The Place of Coyote
Two Traditional San Poil (Colville-Okanagan) Stories

Told by Bob Covington and William Burke

Edited by Dell Hymes

These stories both show a continuing respect for the figure of Coyote as Transformer as well as Trickster. The second adds a being superior to him. The texts were dictated to the anthropologist Verne Ray during his work between 1928 and 1931 with the San Poil people on the Colville reservation in northeastern Washington (see Ray 1933). They were told by men on whom he evidently relied for much of what he learned (see Ray 1932).

The older, Bob Covington, was respected and intelligent, fluent in both San Poil and English; he interpreted stories told by an older shaman, John Tom, who spoke no English. Covington died in July, 1930, at about sixty-five years of age. William Burke was about forty-five in that year, considered something of an adventurer, and also an interpreter, and talented raconteur. Both of these accounts were spoken in English, for Ray did not attempt to transcribe stories in San Poil.

Ray notes of Covington that "he used much profanity for the purpose of emphasizing significant points." Any profanity in what follows was edited out of the published record, if indeed it was written down. That indication of what Covington treated as significant is lacking here. Through noticing the patterning of what was said, however, expressions of time that start sentences, parallel ending points at the end of passages, and the ways in which sequences may use pattern numbers of a tradition, we can trace the shape that Covington, and Burke, gave to what they said, and so visualize something of their artistry and intentions.

Covington's account of Coyote's motives and accomplishments would be accepted by many, though not all, for evaluations of Coyote could differ. Its geographical scope, from the mouth of the Columbia (Astoria) to Kettle Falls, far up the river, reflects an element of unity among the many languages and communities of that river: again and again Coyote starts near its mouth and keeps traveling east along it.

The account, Ray remarks (1933:131), was given in narrative style. It has five parts, no doubt because five is the principal pattern number of the San Poil. As often happens in such a sequence, the third step is an intermediate outcome, echoing and qualifying the first. (Relations of three go with relations of five.) In brief,

(1) in the beginning Coyote was a man, helping people
(2) his relation with his partner, Fox
(3) his motives and accomplishments (as in 1)
(4) his trips and their stories
(5) in the end he was just a coyote.

Within the sections, except the last, the number of sentences is four or two, a counterpoint that reflects a pattern also salient among Salish speakers.

Here are Mr. Covington's words.

Coyote

In the beginning,
 a long time ago,
  Coyote was a man.
He went about helping the people.
He was interested in their fortunes,
 and he did a great deal to make life better on earth.
It is hard to tell
 what a miserable place the world would be now
  if Coyote hadn't changed things as he did.

Fox was Coyote's friend and advisor.
Whenever Coyote was in trouble,
 he called Fox to help him,
  and usually he did.
Coyote nearly always took the credit, though.
He would say,
 "Oh, yes, I knew all the time."

Coyote was sometimes tricky and sometimes foolish.
Most of what he did was for the best, though.

He made several trips up the Columbia river,
 usually starting from Astoria.

Many things happened on these trips
    and there are lots of stories about them.

On the last trip,
    when he reached Kettle Falls,
        he was just an ordinary animal,
            coyote.

Coyote Encounters God

Many Native thinkers found ways to link Christianity with Native tradition. A frequent assumption was that what tradition said that Coyote, or another Transformer, had done needed to be done. The question became who did what. Among the Upper Chehalis, Pike Ben and his wife identified the Transformer with Jesus, and told of Jesus himself doing mythological deeds. Among the San Poil, Okanagan, and Thompson there were accounts of a creator, often called Old One, and his varied relations with Coyote. They often involved a contest in moving mountains.

William Burke told such a story (Ray 1933:160–62). Coyote meets three dangerous beings, Grizzly Bear, Ice, and Steelhead Trout. He overcomes and transforms each of them in turn, pronouncing what each will be like so as not to harm the Indian people who are to come. In a second part, he has to discover who is ultimately in charge.

Going on, Coyote meets a man he does not know. Their encounter comes around three times to Coyote's claiming, with some apparent reason, to be older brother, that is, senior and superior (I). The stranger then shows the truth of the matter (II). Coyote ponders, God proposes a division of labor, and that is how it is decided (III).

Each of the three parts has three parts. Within them the elements shown flush left (verses) are mostly pairs, but sometimes triplets.

Who Is to Be Older Brother?

Coyote went on.   I. |
    He was going along.
He met a man.   i. |
    He didn't know him.
The man said,

"Hello, my younger brother."
"No," Coyote said,
  "I'm not your younger brother;
  I'm your older brother."

Then the two of them argued for a while.   ii. |
Finally the man said,
  "You make that mountain move over there—
  then I'll believe you."

The man gave Coyote strength to do it.
Coyote moved the mountain.

"Now move it back," the man said.
Coyote moved it back.
"You see," Coyote said,
  "I can do anything you ask;
  I'm the older."

Then the man said,   iii. |
  "Now move the island up the river."
Coyote moved it.
"See," Coyote said,
  "I'm your older brother."

               II. |

"Now move the mountain again," the man said.

Coyote tried,
  but he couldn't.
He tried several times.

Then the man told him to move the island back.
Coyote couldn't do it.

Then the man moved the island back.
He said,
  "You see, I'm the older.
  I'm God.

I'm the ruler on earth and in heaven."

III. |

Coyote thought,
    I'm talking to a great man.
        He "drew his horns in."
God said,
    "You be the smart man here on earth;
        you take care of things here.
    I'll be the smart man in heaven;
        I'll rule there and look after everything."
So they decided at last
    that God was the older
        and Coyote was the younger.

Nx̣ík'smtm and Other Episodes of a Traditional Nɬeʔképmx Coyote Narrative

Told by Hilda Austin and Millie Michell

Edited by Steven M. Egesdal

The Nɬeʔképmx (Thompson River Salish) have a phrase to describe an elo-quently performed traditional narrative (*sptékʷɬ*): *nx̣aʔxén̓i kn*. It means some-thing like "my ears have been sweetened." That aptly captures the following translation of overlapping episodes of the same narrative told by Hilda Austin and her younger sister Millie Michell, augmented by another version by Julia Kilroy and interpretive comments by Louis Phillips.

This Nɬeʔképmx traditional narrative begins with Coyote, as Trickster, sending his son on a wild goose chase in the Skyworld so that Coyote can seduce his son's wives. Coyote tricks his son into climbing after some young birds nested in a tree that expands ever skyward, which ultimately takes him to, and abandons him in, the Skyworld. Coyote peers magically each time his son is about to grasp the false nest and decoy fledglings (actually made of Coyote's excrement). Hence the name of the story, Nx̣ík'smtm, the Peered-at-One, referring to and identifying Coyote's beguiled son as the focal character. The motif of a hero going to the Skyworld is familiar throughout the North-west aboriginal America generally and throughout Salishan more specifically (see Reichard 1947:77–88).[1]

After some adventures in the Skyworld, Nx̣ík'smtm is helped by Spider and his Wife to return to earth in a large covered basket. Nx̣ík'smtm then sets out to get revenge on his father. Nx̣ík'smtm magically draws all of the game away from his people's hunting grounds, and they begin to starve. Nx̣ík'smtm feeds them with game he has shot, but he leaves a special cache for his father to retrieve in the woods. That "prize," like the bird nest prize his father sent him to fetch, is fixed to a booby-trapped packstrap—symmetrically karmic justice. Coyote fetches the dressed-out game. While he carries it across a log bridge spanning rapids, the packstrap breaks; unbalanced Coyote is thrown into the raging waters below, and he drowns.

That Nx̣ík'smtm episode introduces a longer Coyote story. Duped and drowned Coyote turns himself into a plank, pulled from the river by four maidens. They use the plank as a serving dish (dishes were made of wood), allowing transmuted Coyote to gobble up all food they unsuspectingly place thereon. Once they discover his trick, they throw the plank into the fire; Coyote changes into a baby, whom they rescue and then raise until he abuses them, sexually and otherwise. Coyote closes that episode by releasing salmon and some pests kept by the maidens.

This overall narrative ends with Coyote taking advantage of the youngest of another group of maiden sisters. Coyote lures her into the river, and then he sends his elongated penis to enter her. The swift current against his penis pulls her in, threatening to drown her. Her sisters cut his penis with a special kind of grass, but Coyote's tip is left inside her. She becomes very sick and none of the medicine men can cure her. Coyote then disguises himself as an itinerant medicine man from the Plains, in an attempt to reclaim his tip. Coyote "doctors" the girl in a sweathouse, but his trick is discovered while the two are in flagrante delicto. After a hurried coitus interruptus—or *coyotus interruptus*—he is chased away, smiling, by the People. Of interest in Austin's version, the maidens are Okanagan (and speak that language in the story); for Michell's version, the maidens are Lillooet. Teit (1898:27–28; 105nn66–69) helps to resolve that anomaly: Coyote visited both the Lillooet and Okanagan (Similkameen) maidens, among others, attempting to trick each group in the same way.[2]

I recorded Austin's performance of Nⱥíksmtm in June 1981, and "Coyote and the Young (Okanagan) Maidens" in May 1983. I also recorded Michell's performance of Nⱥíksmtm in May 1983. Those performances took place in Austin's log home near Lytton, British Columbia. Lytton, in Austin's words, is "the center of the universe, because the two Changers [Nqʼʷəqʼʷilehíʔt and Qʷíqʷⱥqʷəⱥt] once met there." Austin also helped to translate and analyze Kilroy's version of Nⱥíksmtm in June 1983. Phillips and other Nɬeʔképmx elders (Annie York, Mabel Joe, among others) offered interpretive comments, insights, and refinements concerning the Nⱥíksmtm episode and other related Coyote episodes during the summers of 1981 to 1983 and winter of 1982.

Phillips and Austin retraced the travels of Nⱥíksmtm with the author by car in July 1981;[3] they indicated and named the places that attest to the truth of that narrative, including the place near Lytton where Nⱥíksmtm landed from the Skyworld, the ridge trail he climbed toward Botanie Mountain seeking his faithful wife, the point where his baby boy called back to him, and where his father Coyote fell off the bridge beyond Botanie Lake, among others. Those place names and the events in the story have a critical reflexive relationship:

the events explain the shape and appearance of the modern environment, and those physical signs and landmarks conversely authenticate the mythic events.

Teit (1898:21–29; 1912a:205–6, 296–300, 301–3) and Hill-Tout (1899:551–61) published detailed versions of Nx̌íksmtm and its following episodes of the longer Coyote narrative presented below. More recently, Darwin Hanna and Mamie Henry, both Nɬeʔképmx, have published versions of Nx̌íksmtm (including one by Michell), with other episodes of the related Coyote narrative told by other Nɬeʔképmx elders (including Phillips and Annie York) (1995:23–43).

Nx̌íksmtm and Other Episodes of a Traditional Nɬeʔképmx Coyote Narrative

All right, then. I'll tell you about Coyote.
This is a Coyote legend, the one about Nx̌íksmtm (Peered-at-One).

Coyote was there. He had a son.
His son stayed with him, until he was old enough to marry.
Young Coyote took a wife. It wasn't long, and he had a son.
A little while later Young Coyote married again. He had two wives.[4]

His father was there, Coyote. He lusted after his daughters-in-law.
He really wanted them. He thought:
>   *Oh, they should be mine.*
He thought hard about how to trick his son, so he could steal his wives.
He puzzled on that a long time. An idea finally came to him.
>   *I'll deceive him with my peer-magic. I'll maroon him up*
>   *in the Skyworld.*
He saw a tree standing nearby, a big one, just the right size.
He hustled up that tree, and once on top, he defecated.
He concentrated on his scat, and instantly it became a bird's nest.[5]
He wedged it in the crook of the uppermost branches.
He sought his child and told him:
>   "Hey, there are some beautiful birds up there, sitting at the
>   top of that tree.
>   Flicker fledglings, I think. Perfect toys for your baby boy.
>   Go fetch 'em. Climb up after 'em.
>   Grab 'em, break their necks, and toss 'em down to me."

Young Coyote replied:
>"Where?"

Coyote urged him:
>"Up there. Really fabulous birds. Just sitting there.
>Waiting to be snatched."

Coyote kept coaxing him like that, until Young Coyote agreed to scale that tree.
He went after those birds.[6] The prospect of those fledglings induced him to climb.

>Young Coyote climbed that tree.

He almost reached the nest, and Coyote used his peer-magic on him.[7]
He peered at his son, and instantly the nest shot skyward.
The tree stretched, moving the nest just beyond his son's grasp.
Young Coyote was almost there again. Coyote called from below:
>"You just about have 'em. You just about have 'em.
>Keep going. Keep going."

Young Coyote climbed farther. He just about had them in his grasp.
But Coyote thought about it, and immediately the nest moved away.
The tree grew longer and longer, while Coyote kept encouraging his son from below.
>"You just about have 'em. Be strong! Be strong!
>You've almost reached 'em."

Coyote did that to his child, until he disappeared, until he was lost from sight.
(When Young Coyote finally grasped that nest and birds,
>it was nothing more than Coyote's excrement.)

>Young Coyote—Nx̣íksmtm—arrived up there, reaching the peak,

wherever the top of this side of the sky is.[8]
And he pierced through that layer, too. Into that far-off place beyond, the Skyworld.[9]
As soon as Nx̣íksmtm touched foot in the Skyworld, Coyote made the tree return (to the ground), leaving his son on the other side of the sky.
>Coyote was there below, desiring his son's wives.

He tried to seduce the one with a child. Not a chance. She got angry at him.
But the one without a child, she became Coyote's wife.

The faithful wife wept and wailed, and her child did the same.[10]

Meanwhile, Nx̣ík̓smtm traveled in the Skyworld. He walked around. He kept on walking. Farther and farther.
There were some wood filings—a sign of people living nearby. He said:
> *I must be nearing someone's house.*
> *I must be nearing someone's house.*
He kept on his way. He arrived at a cellar house.[11] He took a look in there.
Nothing but combs. Everywhere. Combs and more combs, all the way around.
He climbed down the ladder and inspected them. He said:
> *I'm going to take a comb.*
He took one. He just started up the ladder, and all of the combs smothered him.
> "Oh, all right. Stop doing that to me!
> Oh, I'll put your friend back there. I'll put him back."
He returned that stolen comb to its resting place,
and immediately the other combs returned to their places, as well.
He hurried up out of there, muttering:
> "Goodbye then!"

He left from there and walked around, traveling quite a ways.[12]
He noticed wood chips strewn about again.
He also spotted a fire, smoking in the distance.
He headed for it. He made a beeline for that smoke, until he got there.
He looked and saw two old women sitting there. Two blind biddies, chattering away.

One was hammering something into fine meal, which she then poured into the other's palms. Then the second one hammered, and she poured that pulverized stuff into the other's hands. They took turns doing that. They traded off hammering and pouring.
Nx̣ík̓smtm sat there, watching them. One of them said:
> "Hey, friend. Here is my powder."
He snuck his hands over the palms of the one receiving the powder.
One blind woman poured the powder, while the other waited with readied hands.

But he intercepted it.

> "So, where is it?"

She said. And the other replied:

> "Huh? You got it already."

The other answered:

> "I didn't get anything."

Then the other one hammered. She told her companion:

> "Here it is, friend. Here is my powder."

Nx̣íksmtm did that again with his hands. She poured it into his palms instead.

The other blind woman still had her hands outstretched, groping for the powder.

> "Where is it?"

The first one said:

> "Huh? You got it already."

The second answered:

> "I didn't get anything."

The first one replied:

> "You got it."

Then they quarreled. As they were arguing, one chirped in their odd speech:[13]

> "What smells? Do you smell it?"

The other one said:

> "Yes. I smell it. Hmm. It smells like Nx̣íksmtm's
> smegma."[14]

Nx̣íksmtm heard that and felt greatly insulted.

He grabbed one of them, broke her arms, and threw her. He told her:

> "You'll be Ruffed Grouse. People are going to snare your
> descendants."

Then he threw the other one.

> "You'll be Franklin Grouse."

He muttered:

> *Oh, let that be their fate. [To hell with them!]*

And he sped away from there.

He traveled around again. He saw some smoke again. He went straight for it.

He headed for the smoke. He arrived at a cellar house. He took a look inside.

This time it was an elderly married couple. A man and woman. Spider and his Wife.

They were making rope, twisting really fine strands of hemp.

It was like they already knew, those elders.

They knew how his father had treated him. They summoned him:

>"Come in, dear child! Come in! Come in!
>
>We're busy making rope. We already know what you did.
>
>We know what was done to you. Come in, then! Come in!"

He went there. His grandmother cooked for him. She gave him something to eat.

He ate and ate. She fed him until he could eat no more.

Spider told him:

>"We know what was done to you. How it came about that you got here to us.
>
>You must be really lonesome for your wife and child."

Nλíksmtm said:

>"Yes. I am heartsick. Look at my wife and child.
>
>There's no one to take care of them for me.
>
>There's no one to help them. My wife will go hungry.
>
>My child will go hungry. There's no one to look after my son for me."

Spider and his Wife told him:

>"All right. Now you need to cleanse yourself and prepare yourself spiritually.
>
>Every day you'll bathe, at dawn and at dusk. And then you'll gather hemp."

He said:

>"All right."

Spider's Wife told him:

>"Listen up. I'm going to show you your child and wife."

They did something with a rock, slid it aside to reveal the Earth below.

He saw the People below.

>"Look! That's your wife. She's carrying her child."

His other wife was there, too. She was with his father, Coyote.

>"You see, that's why we're making all this rope. We're going to lower you.
>
>But first, you need to ready yourself spiritually.
>
>Every day, at the first of the morning's four dawns,

that time of greatest power, you'll bathe.

And with the coming of twilight, you'll bathe."

That young man did that, as he was told, for a long, long time.

Until he had attained great spiritual powers.

Then he went on a hunt. He hunted game.

The old couple then took his killings and made dried meat.

That young man was bathing. He said:

Oh, I'm going to make some hemp.

He plucked four of his pubic hairs.

He threw those strands around him, front, back, and to each side.

Hemp sprouted everywhere. It grew all about, lush and tall.

He finished bathing.

He picked some hemp to bring to his grandmother and grandfather.

There was so much hemp, enough for a whole armful.

He hugged a bunch of it, and took it back to the old couple. He said:

"Hey, I got to a place where there's hemp. Here it is.

I don't know if it's the same kind as you're using."

They told him:

"Say, that's it. It must be very good where you got to."

He said:

"Yes. There's really a lot where I bathe. Plenty."

They told him:

"Good. Good. Again! Do it again!

We'll need a lot of that. Lots."

Right away Nx̣íksmtm was off again. He went to gather more.

He brought it back to his grandmother and grandfather.

The old man took it. He hammered it. He hammered where he had peeled it.

He stripped the outer layer from the inner one. He peeled and peeled.

Then he went over and handed the fiber to his wife.

That woman pressed it straight, softening it with a sharp deer bone awl.

She pressed it straight, over and over. She pressed it, like she was whittling it.

Once she finished pressing it, she twisted the strands into rope.

She twisted those strands in twine, rolling them on her thigh.
The old man meanwhile kept at his task, hammering the hemp and wringing the fiber.
They were there, working on that a long time.
Nx̌íksmtm brought them a lot of hemp.
He also hunted game, and they made dried meat.

His grandmother continued to twist the fiber into rope.
She kept winding up what she had twisted into rope.
She wound it all up, until it was a huge ball.
They thought it was big enough for the descent. Then they said:
> "All right, that's plenty of rope. It's long enough for
> the descent.
> You're going home now. You're finally going home."

They had a special craft for the descent.
It was a certain kind of cedar-root basket,
round, tightly woven, with a lid.
It was called a *st'úk*^{w}.[15]

They were going to have Nx̌íksmtm sit in there, and then lower it, attached to the rope.
They just thought about it, and all that food turned into four small pieces.
The mounds of dried meat, deer kidney fat, everything.
They transformed it into four small pieces, which they stowed on board the basket craft. They said:
> "All right, everything's ready. Time for you to go back."
His grandmother said to him:
> "All right, I'll give you flight instructions.
> We're going to put you on board that basket craft.
> Then we'll lower you by rope. Don't open eyes!
> You'll drop and stop, bumping into the clouds.
> Roll yourself four times, to shake free, and you fall
> through that layer.
> You'll drop and stop again, bumping into the treetops.
> Roll yourself four times, until you fall through.
> You'll drop and stop once more, bumping into the grass.

Roll yourself four times, until you fall through.

You'll drop and stop one last time, touching down
on the ground.

That time when you roll yourself four times, you won't
fall any farther.

Don't open your eyes until you hear Crow. Crow will call:
'ʔeʔ ʔeʔ ʔeʔ ʔeʔ.'

When you hear him caw, then you can open your eyes.

When you get out of the basket, run back and forth
with it four times.

Then let it go. We'll know that you've touched down.

We'll feel that movement and reel it back up."

Nx̣íksmtm said:

"Oh, all right. I understand."

They took ahold of him.

They sat him down in the basket craft and closed the hatch.

They fastened the rope to it.

The man and woman sat next to each other,

so they could work together to lower the rope.

They extended the rope arm over arm, in rhythm with their chant:

"Lower away! Lower away!"

They lowered him, until he stopped. It was the fog layer.

He shook until he dropped through. He kept on falling, until he stopped
again.

Right away he said,

Hey, I must have got there already.

But he had stopped only two times. He opened his eyes.

As soon as he opened his eyes, he was back in the Skyworld with Spider
and his Wife.

She was mad and scolded him:

"I told you not to open your eyes, until you heard Crow.

Only then can you open your eyes.

If you do it your way, you'll never get home."

He said:

"Oh, all right. I was just teasing you."

They put him back on board. They lowered the rope.

He bumped into the fog. He stopped, rolled four times, and dropped.

He bumped into the trees. He stopped, rolled four times, and dropped.
He bumped into the grass. He stopped, rolled four times, and dropped.
He touched down on the ground. He stopped, rolled four times, but did not drop.
As he was rolling himself, he heard Crow:

> "ɁeɁ ɁeɁ ɁeɁ ɁeɁ."

He said:

> *Oh. That's the signal. I'm down. I'm there.*[16]

He opened his eyes. He sat up. He loosened the hatch. He got out.

The basket was full to the brim with food and provisions.
Dried meat and dried salmon. He unloaded his cache. He refastened the lid.
He ran back and forth with the basket four times, and then let go of it.
Away it went. He stood and watched it fly out of sight, back to Spider and his Wife.

He departed from that place. He went to his family's settlement.
But it was still. No one was there but some old folks.
He asked one of them where the People had gone. One of them told him:

> "They left for Botanie Mountain. They left us here."

Nx̣íksmtm told them:

> "I'm going after them. I'm going after the People."

That old person told him:

> "Go after them. Go after them. Catch up to the People."

Nx̣íksmtm left there, setting out after the People.
He crossed the Thompson River. That place is called He Followed the Ridge Up.
He climbed up there and got to the place called They Looked Back.

His wife was lagging behind the main group. She packed her baby on her back.
Her only companions were a pitiful lot, Weevils. All she did was weep and wail.
Nonstop crying. The well-off and able-bodied had gone on ahead.
His wife struggled along with those other stragglers, the Weevils who accompanied her.

His wife was traveling along, when suddenly her child peeped:
> "Papa. Papa."

The baby was facing back from where they had come.
> "Papa. Papa."

She scolded him:
> "Oh, you and your 'papa papa.' Your father is lost.
> Gone.
> We don't know what happened to him.
> It's anyone's guess where he lies, dead and buried.
> And you keep on with your 'papa papa.'"

They went on. Not too far, and the child looked back. He peeped:
> "Papa. Papa."

She got mad at him and spanked him. But part of her thought:
> *Maybe it's true.*

She looked back. She didn't see him.
> "Your father is not here. But you keep calling 'papa
> papa.'"

She stood there. She looked back.
Her husband blew on her face, with a magical breath.
Then she saw him.
> "Hey, you got here."

Then he sat down. He hugged his child and wife. He gave them food.
He also fed her companions (the Weevils) with some of his provisions
from Spider and his Wife.
He told his wife:
> "When you get to Botanie Mountain,
> set up your lodge away from the other People.
> Build it from branches and dried needles.
> Don't set up camp near them. Stay far off.
> Don't mix up with other People."

He also told her:
> "However you've been crying and carrying on,
> keep doing that the same way. Act as if nothing's
> changed."

His wife agreed.

She and her child climbed up. They got to the top of Botanie Mountain.
The People were building their lodges there.

She set up her lodge away from the others, away from where her father-in-law Coyote was camped.

Clark's Nutcracker squawked:

> "What's the matter with our in-law?
> She's camping away from us! She's camping away from us!
> I wonder what's happened. I wonder what's happened."

But it was as if nobody listened to him. It was like he was by himself talking.

He was a medicine man. He knew that Nx̣íksmtm already had returned.

The woman also followed Nx̣íksmtm's other instructions.
She also tried to cry and carry on as she had been doing,
but her feigned tears and weeping weren't quite the same.
Somehow the People knew that Nx̣íksmtm was back. They commented:

> "That woman doesn't act the same. She used to wail. Now she only whimpers.
> He must have come back to her. She must have seen her man again."

And that thought made them envious.

Nx̣íksmtm then used his powers to drive all the game into one special area, away from where the People tried to hunt.
No matter what, where, or when the People hunted, they could find no game.
They began to starve. They still did not shoot anything.
They did not even see a deer. Nothing.
Nx̣íksmtm had gathered all the game into a secret place.
That is how he would get even with his father.

Then Nx̣íksmtm rejoined his wife at the camp.
He gave his son some dried salmon. A piece of dried salmon.
The boy was hungry. He gobbled it up.
He hardly chewed it and swallowed it.
It got stuck in his throat. He choked on it.

Clark's Nutcracker squawked:

> "Oh—she's choking. Our in-law is choking. I wonder what happened.
> Our in-law is choking. Let's go look!"

They ran over. They looked. But it was the boy choking.
He dislodged that piece of dried salmon. They took it.
They looked at it. They said:
>"Oh—it's dried salmon. He was choking on dried salmon."

The woman said nothing. She just stood there until the People left.
They camped overnight. Early the next morning, Nx̣íksmtm said:
>"All right, I'm going hunting."

He went hunting where all the deer were. Nx̣íksmtm shot scores of deer.
He brought back the dressed game, to give to his friends. He called his friends:
>"Come on! Come on! Take some meat! Roast it! Eat hearty!"

But he did not call his father. He only called his friends.
His friends came and took the deer meat. They roasted it. They ate it.

The next morning, Nx̣íksmtm went hunting again.
He shot a deer, but this time he did not bring any meat home.
He dressed it out, but left it there.
He gathered some entrails and fashioned them into a packstrap.
Then he conjured on that packstrap, and it turned really fine,
as if it were made of mountain sheep wool.

He went home. He got to his father and told him:
>"I shot some deer over there. I left a deer's back there
>for you.
>It's all ready to pack, even tied to a packstrap.
>Go pack it out, then you'll have quite a
>meal."

His father was all excited to fetch that cache. He thought:
>*Oh—my dear son is going to be good to me.*

Nx̣íksmtm then thought:
>*That creek—that creek.*

It was a big creek like the Stein River. Nx̣íksmtm concentrated on that creek.
It was like he felled a tree across that creek, in the very path where his father was going to cross.
His father went on his way. He got to that deer.
He was astonished at the sight of it.
>*Wow!*

And the packstrap was made of mountain sheep wool, too.

He picked up the game and carried it off. He just started, a little ways.
He didn't get too far, and the packstrap broke.

> *Damn! My dear boy's packstrap. I broke it.*

He picked it up. He managed to tie it back together.

He got to where he was going to cross the creek, on that fallen log bridge.
He was walking across that log. He got right to the middle of it.
Nȼíḱsmtm was there watching.
He used his mental powers, and that packstrap broke.
The sudden snap spun Coyote around, and he fell into the water.

The creek swept him away. Coyote floated away.
The rapids swallowed him up and carried him off.
He was swept up in the current. Gone. Vanished downstream. His child got even with him.

Coyote continued to float to that place called Coyote's Intestines.
All that floating had worn his hide bare, right on through to his guts.
His intestines came undone, and they unraveled like a rope unwinds.
The old people called that place Intestines. That's Coyote's Intestines.

He came to that place and floated on, until he flowed into the Thompson River.
He floated still farther, to where the Thompson River ends at the Fraser.
Some women had a fish weir there. Four women were trapping fish.
The salmon could not swim by. Those women captured them really well.
Nothing could get past.

Coyote floated until he bumped into that fish weir.
He changed himself into a wide wooden plank, like a splinter off a large log.
A good-sized piece. He transformed himself, as he entered that fish weir.
The women went to gather the fish, to cook for dinner. They said:

> "Hey. Look at that plank floating there. That'll make a fine serving dish."

They grabbed that plank. They barbecued some salmon.
They placed it on that plank, and sat down for dinner.

But before anyone could get a bite, the meal vanished.

> Hey. What's going on here?

They didn't bother to do anything about it.

They just barbecued some more salmon and placed it on the plank.

The same thing happened again. They said:

> "Hey. That thing's going to make us go hungry. I wonder what it is."

They took it and hurled it into the fire. It was about to burn and suddenly it screamed:

> "Ouch. Ouch. Ouch. Ouch."

One of them shouted:

> "Quick, grab it! Someone grab it."

They grabbed it. They said:

> "It's a boy. A boy. Oh, goodie. We can have him do chores for us.
> He'll be our little helper."

Then they took a trip to dig roots.

His elder sisters were traveling along, and one of them asked:

> "What are we going to do with him?"

Another responded:

> "Oh, we'll make him a swing for his cradle board."

They made him a swing for his cradle board. They were digging roots.

Coyote was there, swinging in his cradle board. He grew so fast. He got tall.

They were there for a while, and one of his older sisters commented:

> "Hey. Look how strong our little brother is.
> We might as well take him along. He can come with us."

That was Coyote's idea for her to recommend that. He thought it, and she said it:

> "We'll take him. We'll carry him."

The others consented:

> "All right."

The eldest sister carried him on her back. They hiked along in a straight line.

Coyote slipped down on her back.

Slowly, little by little. He kept slipping down.

Then he copulated with her from behind.

She threw him down and screamed:

"Ah! Filthy brat!"

The others asked:

"Why did you do that to your little brother?"

She answered:

"You carry him! I don't want him. I'm done carrying him. He's obscene."

Then the second eldest sister carried him. He did the same thing.

He did that to all his sisters, violating one after the other.

Even the youngest.

After that excursion, they agreed:

"We won't take him along anymore."

His sisters kept four large storage baskets there.

Each basket imprisoned a different pest: Wind, Bees, Flies, and Fog.

His sisters had locked those four things away in those baskets.

They told their little brother:

"All right, you're going to stay home. Don't you dare touch any of these baskets. Don't take the covers off!"

He said:

"Oh. All right. Fine. I won't do that."

His elder sisters left. He said:

Oh, I'm going to go home. I'll head home.

He knew his sisters were far off.

He knew that they had gotten to where they usually dug roots.

He took the cover off the first basket, holding the Wind.

Immediately, it was windy. He then pulled the lids off the other baskets.

Out came the Bees, Flies, and Fog.[17]

As his sisters went along, they sensed what he had done.

Oh, he took the tops off the baskets!

They took off running for home. They arrived there.

He was crossing the river on their fish weir. He got to the other side.

His elder sisters arrived back.

They tried to recapture those pests, without success.

They dashed all over gathering what Coyote let loose. It was no use.

They were blown by the Wind and surrounded by the Fog.

They couldn't catch those things. They were furious.

Coyote stood on the other side of the river. He pulled on their fish weir.

It snapped apart. The salmon escaped.

Coyote then bid his sisters farewell,
who'd yet to discover another surprise he'd left with each of them:
>"All right. If my child is male, take care of it for me.
>
>But if it is female, abandon it in the fork of a tree."

After that, Coyote left them and headed for home.
He traveled, naming fishing spots along the way.

Coyote was walking along.
He saw Okanagan maidens across the river, bathing.
There were four of them, sisters. He lusted after them.
>*Oh, I'm going to have one of them for my wife.*

He sat down there a long time. He thought about his penis.
He made it grow really long.
He wound it up and wrapped it in a pack on his back.
The Coyote called out to those women, in Okanagan:
>"Hey, you there. Yes, you. Do you want some
>
>*soxʷsoxʷíkn̓?*"

That was Coyote's pet name for his penis.[18] The eldest sister answered:
>"We don't want any of that soxʷsoxʷíkn̓.
>
>We crave the back of the neck of a mountain sheep."

Coyote stood over there, and the youngest called out:
>"I want some. I want some."

Her sisters got mad at her.
>"What are you saying!"

Coyote told her:
>"All right. Wade in a bit. So the water is above your navel.
>
>I'll throw it to you. Get ready!"

She waded into the water, just past her belly button.
He cast his penis toward her.
It slipped right inside her, like an arrow hitting a target's bull's-eye.
Then she started to scream.
The water pushing against the length of his penis began to draw her into deep water.
She was bobbing up and down in the water, about to drown.
Her sisters held her up and scolded her:
>"Look at the mess you've got us into. We're really upset with you.

We warned you, and still you wanted that."

They pulled and pulled on his penis. But it wouldn't come out of their little sister.

They pounded on it with a rock. But it had no effect.

One of them ran for their grandfather's knife.

She took that knife and tried to cut through his penis.

But all it did was bounce off. Then he said:

> "Cut me with cut grass. It's the only thing that can cut that."

They asked:

> "What did he say?"

He repeated himself:

> "Cut grass. Cut grass."

He even told them where it grew.

One of them ran to get some cut grass.

She found it, gathered it, and ran back to them.

She took a blade of it and just barely touched his skin.

Immediately it was severed, as if sliced by a razor.

Coyote reeled it in.

The women took their younger sister from the water. She was half-dead.

They told her:

> "Look, we warned you. You just wouldn't listen. See what happens?"

They took her home. They got to their lodge. She fell ill.

Her parents hired an Indian doctor.

He worked his medicine on her, but it didn't take.

She got sicker and sicker.

They hired all sorts of Indian doctors.

But their daughter didn't get better.

She was beyond cure. One of the People said:

> "That's all of the Indian doctors there are."

Meanwhile, Coyote headed toward their settlement.

He knew about the girl's sickness.

He made his clothes really fine.

Plains Indian style, with a feather headdress and buckskin.

He got to their houses, and one of them said:

> "Hey, here comes somebody. Look at him. He's wearing

really fine clothes.

He must be an important Indian doctor. We'll hire him.
Let's engage him."

They tried to talk to him, but it was as though he couldn't hear.

To them, he was mumbling nonsense:

"ču? ču? ču? ču?. ču? ču? ču? ču?."

Coyote just made up that language to fool them. Then the People called
Mole.

She had had husbands from countless lands.

She spoke many languages. They told her:

"You're the one we need. You've been married to men
from all over.

Maybe you can catch something of what he's saying."

Mole talked to Coyote in several languages.

It was no use. He kept on with his gibberish:

"ču? ču? ču? ču?. ču? ču? ču? ču?."

She told him:

"The woman is sick. Really sick. All the Indian doctors
have tried to cure her.

Now you're going to try. You're going to doctor her."

Coyote chanted in some obscure, foreign tongue:

"ču? ču? ču? ču?. Sweathouse, sweathouse,
sweathouse. I'll blow. I'll blow."

Mole understood him this time:

"He says he'll doctor in a sweathouse. Go prepare it!"

They ran. They readied the sweathouse.

They covered that place up with blankets.

He got there. The woman was lying in there, about ready to die.

Coyote sat in there. He doctored. He was singing in there.

"t'u? t'u? t'u?. t'u? t'u? t'u?."

He was moving up and down. Up and down. The People said:

"What's going on?"

The woman was screaming. They removed the covering.

He got the tip of his penis back, that had detached in that woman.

He kept on copulating after it reconnected.

The People attacked him. They struck him.

He managed to escape.

His clothes were lying there. They fought over them.
But what remained was no longer a fine buckskin robe.
All of those things disintegrated, into excrement and pubic hair.
Coyote ran off. He got to the top of a hill and shouted:
> "If my child is female, put her in the fork of a tree.
> If my child is a male, then take care of it for me."
The woman was sitting up, already cured.
She went to her elder sisters. Her sisters asked her:
> "He managed to cure you?"
She answered:
> "Yes. It was really good.
> There's nothing really quite like what he did to me,
> When he laid on me, it tingled all over. My whole body tingled.
> I felt it all over. It was extremely pleasurable.
> There's nothing quite as good, as what Coyote did to me."
She told her sisters:
> "Don't tell on me. Don't tell on me. Don't repeat what I told you."
They promised her:
> "We won't tattle on you."
Coyote was on his way from there. That is the end of the legend.

Notes

1. Reichard (1947:80) reports that "[t]his myth has a wide distributution" among aboriginal peoples of the American Northwest.

2. The Okanagan have a similar story of Coyote's encounter with a group of maidens, where he has an elongated penis and he asks them if they would like some "salmon backbone" (Boas 1917:67–71). Coyote uses the same term for "salmon backbone," (soxʷ)soxʷlíkn, in the Okanagan and Nłeʔképmx versions. Egesdal (1992:41–43) examines the bilingual aspects of this episode of the Coyote narrative. Hilda Austin apparently consolidated two episodes into one, where the Okanagan maidens accept Coyote's offer for salmon. Teit (1898:28; 1912b:297) explains that the Okanagan maidens actually rejected Coyote's inquiry, and hence there were no salmon in that country. The Okanagan version is in accord with Teit's Nłeʔképmx versions (Boas 1917:68–69). A version of this extended tale is also included in the Coastal Oregon Tillamook Salish epic, "South Wind's Journeys" in this volume.

3. Annie York also pointed out to L. C. and M. T. Thompson (personal communication) the ridge on the way up Botanie Mountain that is said to be his family. The ridge looks like a row of people walking uphill.

4. Nx̣íksmtm's wives were birds, one dark complexioned and the other fair. They might have

been Loon and Swan, respectively, whose plumage would be consistent with such complexions. In the Coeur d'Alene version of this myth, the wives were Tern and Black Swan (Reichard 1947:77). Hilda Austin later identified Nx̌ík'smtm's faithful wife as sx̌íq, "Mud Duck," a bird with dark plumage. The more favorable role of the more favored dark complexioned wife might reflect ethnocentrically a contrast between faithful (dark-skinned) native versus fickle (fair-skinned) whiteman.

5. Louis Phillips said that the nest was made of pubic hair. Coyote's media of choice for fabricating false articles were his excrement and pubic hair, sometimes combined.

6. For Hilda Austin, the birds were goslings; for Millie Michell, flickers. Hill-Tout (1899:553) has eaglets, as does Teit (1912a:205). Reichard (1947:77) shows eaglets in the Coeur d'Alene version. Tillamook refers to "Lucky Bird" (see the story "South Wind's Journeys" in this volume).

7. Annie York described Coyote's action as a kind of winking. Teit (1898:104n43) described the action as "lifting the eyelids." In the Coeur d'Alene version of the same tale, Coyote arches his eyebrows (Reichard 1947:77). In any case, Coyote did something with his eyes to cause the tree to extend ever skyward. English "peer" is used here to capture Coyote's action and expression with his eyes.

8. After Coyote succeeds in sending Young Coyote to the Skyworld, Young Coyote becomes Nx̌íksmtm.

9. In the Thompson organization of the universe, there were three worlds: the Sky World, the Earth, and the Underground World. The Sky as people see it from the Earth is the ground of the Sky World (see Teit 1898:103n44).

10. The dark-skinned wife (Mud Duck) was faithful; the fair-skinned wife (Swan) was fickle.

11. It was very cold in the Skyworld, like a perpetual winter. Teit (1898:22) explains that there was "a steady cold wind blowing" there, and Hill-Tout (1899:553) adds that "he feels cold, for he has no clothes on." That climate would explain why the dwellings were cellar or pit houses, the traditional winter abodes of the Nɬeʔképmx.

12. In other versions, Nx̌íksmtm went to other cellar houses and had three other similar encounters attempting to steal items therein. Overall, the four episodes included cellar houses containing combs, baskets, mats, and awls. Those additions would be consistent with the pattern number of four in Nɬeʔkepmx traditional stories.

13. Teit (1898:103n48) explains that some versions have Coyote putting his penis in one of the old ladies' hands.

14. Hilda Austin and Millie Michell used different words for smegma. Austin used nčq̓ʷmə́čək̓; Michell used nčq̓ʷméy̓stn. Both agreed that Michell's word probably was foreign, perhaps Shuswap. (Austin and Michell both spoke Okanagan; Austin also spoke Lillooet. Both had heard Shuswap when they were growing up.)

15. Hilda Austin used the term st'úk̓ʷ (or its diminutive st'út'k̓ʷ); Millie Michell and Louie Phillips used the term sx̌úk̓ʷ. Historically, Proto-Salish *t' became x̌ in Nɬeʔképmx. Austin's word likely reflects an archaism.

16. There used to be a stone where Nx̌íksmtm landed near Lytton, British Columbia. It was moved by the railroad in the twentieth century. Hill-Tout (1899:556n1) notes that "[t]he old Indians point to a stone near a creek which they believe is the stone mentioned in the story." Teit (1898:104n57) also discusses that rock, sacred because Spider had said that the place where Nx̌íksmtm first landed would be the center of the Earth.

17. The release of the Bees and Flies contemporaneously with the salmon, explains why blowflies, sandflies, wasps, and the like are prevalent during salmon season (see Teit 1898:104n65).

18. Teit (1898:27; 1912a:297) reports that Coyote offered the maidens he encountered "the backbone of the humpback salmon." Hill-Tout (1899:560) similarly writes that the maidens Coyote encounters ask for the "back of salmon." In the Okanagan version of this same tale, Coyote asks the maidens if they wanted "salmon backbone" (Boas 1917:71n2). The term *soxʷsoxʷíkn̓* was not known nor recognized by any of the many Nɬeʔképmx elders I consulted. It also allows no etymological analysis in Nɬeʔképmx or Okanagan-Colville, except that the suffix *=ikn* means "back."

Coyote Releases Salmon

A Traditional Moses-Columbian Story

Told by George Nanamkin

Edited by M. Dale Kinkade

This Moses-Columbian story is one of five recorded on August 20, 1965, from George Nanamkin of Nespelem, Washington. Mr. Nanamkin worked as interpreter for the Colville Confederated Tribes; he spoke at least Moses-Columbian and English, and probably one or two other languages of the region. He recorded these stories for me in English only, but declined to tell them in Moses-Columbian; I have no other data from Mr. Nanamkin. The story presented here is just as he told it, except that I have eliminated a few false starts and his occasional pause (heard as "uh . . .").[1]

Most people who identify themselves as Moses-Columbian live today on the Colville Indian Reservation in north-central Washington. Most are of mixed ancestry, partly because several linguistic and political groups were placed on this reservation, and partly because the Moses-Columbia had frequently married outside their group (particularly with Yakimas, Colvilles, and Spokanes). The Moses-Columbian people were frequently bilingual or multilingual, and those who still speak the language tend to know Colville-Okanagan as well as their own language. As of the mid-1990s there were only forty or fifty speakers remaining.

The Moses-Columbian people lived originally along the Columbia River from Priest Rapids to just south of the mouth of the Methow River, and along its tributaries (particularly the Wenatchee and Entiat rivers), along the lower shores of Lake Chelan, and at the mouths of various creeks. Three dialects can be recognized, although the precise differences (apart from a few vocabulary and grammatical items) can no longer be determined: that of the Moses band to the south, the Wenatchee River band along the Wenatchee River (and probably including those along the Entiat River), and the Chelan band. Nearly all moved to the Colville Reservation with Chief Moses, the major leader of the southern band, after 1892. Most members of this group today refer to themselves as Moses, although a few prefer to be called Chelans or Wenatchees. However, all agree on the self-designation nxaʔámxəxʷ (literally, "local people" or "the people here") and their language as nxaʔamxcín (literally, "language of the local people").

The Moses-Columbian people caught fish (especially salmon) in the rivers and lakes of the area, hunted in the mountains adjacent to their rivers, and gathered berries and roots, making annual summer trips to the Big Bend country to the east of the Columbia River for camas, bitterroots, and other produce. A few followed these traditions until recently, and most still hunt and fish and gather berries in the mountains. Descriptions of their culture can be found in Teit (1928) and Ray (1936, 1939).

This story of Coyote releasing salmon is a very popular myth throughout the Plateau and along the Columbia River, and it can be elaborated in many ways. Each group that told this story would localize it to their own territory, as is done here. This is a fairly full version, beginning with Coyote's lustful nature toward his own kin, his punishment for this, his releasing of the salmon, and his subsequent distribution of them in various rivers and streams. Throughout the story, Coyote's foolish and often improper deeds play an important role, but are balanced with his good deeds. This is typical behavior for Coyote throughout western North America, and Coyote stories are extremely popular throughout this area. Numerous Coyote stories, including versions of this one, can be found in such collections as Boas (1917) and Jacobs (1929, 1934, 1937). The only published Moses-Columbian texts are Kinkade (1978), and a few in English included in Yanan (1971). No major collection of Moses-Columbian myths or tales exists in either the native language or in English, although there are four or five small, but unpublished, collections of tape recordings.

The title of the story is my own. As is usual among the Moses-Columbia, stories are not given specific titles, but the content of the story is usually indicated in the first sentence. The arrangement here is fairly arbitrary, but I have tried to use a format that more or less follows that promoted and exemplified by Dell Hymes (particularly as found in D. Hymes 1981 and V. Hymes 1987). Because the story was told in English only, whatever markers of divisions into sections (that is, discourse particles and conjunctions) are unavailable. However, Mr. Nanamkin's use of intonation patterns, pauses at the ends of clauses, and of introductory conjunctions (particularly "and," "an'," and "'n") make it easy to punctuate the text and to break it up into lines. Other groupings are based on the fact that the pattern number in Moses-Columbian is five (like that of the Sahaptins and Chinook to the south). For this reason, I have quite arbitrarily tried to arrange sections into groups of five or into groups of three or seven (which have been found to correlate with groupings of five in other languages). These arbitrary groupings are based primarily on narrative content, such as when characters change, when a new adventure begins, or when new travel is indicated. Alternative arrangements of the text are certainly possible.

Coyote Releases Salmon

I. Coyote Is Duped and Gets Lost |

This is a story of a Coyote.

This story of your Coyote that I'm gonna tell about had a family.
He had five sons.
And each one of his sons were married.
An' they all lived together as one big family.

Coyote was married to a mole.

And as this story goes on,
Coyote would look at his wife,
an' she was beginnin' to get old.

And deep down in his heart, he would envy his son's wives,
they were young and good looking.

An' he thought up some way that he would destroy his sons,
then he would have one of his daughter-in-laws [*sic*] for his
wife.

And it seems to me that the youngest son of Coyote knew what his
father was thinkin'
and what he wanted to do.

So, he made up his mind that he would destroy his father,
rather than have his father kill his brothers and himself,
that he would destroy his father.

So one day he went out hunting way back out in the mountains,
and he killed a deer.

And he came back,
an' told his father,
"I killed a deer,
an' I want you to go after it."

An' he showed 'em just where the deer was, quite a ways.
He had [t]o go through mountains 'n streams.

And Coyote says,
"All right, I'll go."

An' his son gave him a piece of
rope to pack this deer.
Course he didn't tell his father
what this rope was.
But this rope was just made over
of deer intestines.
He had fixed it so it looked like rope,
but it was a deer intestine.

Coyote started out,
'n he walked, an' walked, 'n walked,
'n finally he come to the place.

And he started packin' this deer,
'n got ready to go home.
Just about that time it started to rain,
and all of that was prearranged anyway.
An' so it started to rain,
an' it rained, 'n rained, 'n rained real hard.

And Coyote, he started goin' home with this deer.

First creek he come to,
he had to wade this creek.

And the next one he come to,
he made it,

but it was gettin' pretty deep.

       An' the third stream he come to,
       he couldn't cross.
       He did try to cross,
       but the river was too . . .
       by that time it was quite a stream . . . quite a river.

            And this river took him downstream.

II. Coyote Releases Salmon |

As he went downstream,
he caught ahold of a log or somethin',
an' he hang on this log,
an' he floated downstream.

       He floated down until he hit the Columbia River,
       which was a big river then.
       And he floated down.
       Down the middle part of the stream.

          An' as he floated down,
          he begin to think what he was gonna do.
          He knew that there was a falls downstream there around
              The Dalles,
          an' it was a mighty falls.

             And the salmon couldn't go beyond this falls
             because the falls were so high that the salmon
                    couldn't go past this falls.

             An' Coyote would know—
             he knew about this falls.

An' as he got near the falls,
he turned himself into a baby.

       And . . . as he got near the falls he started to crying.

And there were five sisters that used to watch this falls,
and they lived there all the time.

And they heard this baby cryin',
so they ran out,
and went out there,
'n got him—got Coyote,
an' brought 'im back to their home.

And they thought,
"Ohhh, I wonder what happened to their
folksts—to his folkts.
Ohhh, the poor thing!
I guess we better keep 'im."
So they kept 'im.

And of these five sisters,
the youngest sister knew right then what
    was goin' on.
She knew that Coyote was not a baby,
but was a grown person turned into a baby.
But she never said nothin'.
She never said nothin' to her sisters.

An' as the days went by,
they kept pamperin' 'im,
'n he was quite a baby.
They kept babyin' him,
'n fed 'im,
an' took care of 'im.

And Coyote—
every time these women would leave,
well, he would turn into Coyote,
into himself.

An' he figured just what he would do.
He wanted the salmon to go upstream.

So he thought this to himself,
Well, I'll prepare myself,
and so that I could be protected when I's doin' my work.

> For then and there he would go up north,
> and he would pick up the horns of moose that were
>   dropped,
> and he would bring 'em back.
> An' he fixed himself an armor of moose horns.
> An' he kept that up
> until he was satisfied that this armor would
>   protect 'im.

>> So the beginning of a new day,
>> he started in real early
>> as the young ladies left 'im,
>> and he started in to dig channels in these
>>   falls.
>> An' he worked as hard as he could
>> an' as fast as he could.

An' [in] the early afternoon,
as these women were diggin' camas,
their digger broke.

> And this one sister said,
> "Well, there's somethin' wrong at home.
> Let's hurry back."
> So they hurried back.

>> An' after they got back to their home,
>> they saw Coyote.
>> He was diggin' 'n workin'.

>>> And they went up and try to stop 'im,
>>> they got sticks 'n hit 'im,
>>> but he was pretty well protected,
>>> so he kept on aworkin'.

Finally, he got what he wanted to do,
an' then he broke up this falls.

>   And as he broke up this falls to where he thought that it would do,
>   and as he started up the stream,
>   the salmon followed him.

>>   The salmon run over these falls that he had uh . . .
>>   the channels that he had made in these falls was enough
>>   for the salmon to go upstream.

>>>   An' as he went upstream,
>>>   the salmon followed 'im.

>>>>   An' they went for days 'n days 'n days.
>>>>   IIIa. COYOTE CATCHES SALMON |

Finally, one day he was so hungry.
What he could look downstream,
an' see those salmon goin' along there with 'im.
He thought that he would try somethin'.

>   So he went up in the shale rocks,
>   an' he said,
>   "Salmon, salmon!
>   Jump out of the water!"

>>   An' as he said this,
>>   the salmon jumped out of the water
>>   'n landed by his feet.

>>>   But there was no way
>>>   that he could stop the salmon from goin' back into
>>>>   the river,
>>>   because as they jumped back up an' down,
>>>   it finally slipped back into the river.

>>>   And he didn't have nothin' yet again.

So then asked his sisters,
that was always of help to him,

    an' she said,
    "You have done wrong,
    because when you make that salmon jump on that shale rock,
    there's no way that you can get it,
    because everything is slick.

        The salmon is slick,
        an' as he jumps up an' down,
        there's no way that you can stop it.

            But the next time,
            you go an' make the salmon jump.
            Pick out a sandy beach."

So he done that.
He went up,
an' they come to a nice sandy beach,
an' he said,
"Salmon, salmon!
Jump out of the water!"

    An' as he said "jump out of the water,"
    the salmon jumped out,
    'n land at his feet.

        And it wasn't very long that he killed a salmon,
        an' he started a fire
        'n he started cookin' the salmon.

            IIIb. Coyote and the Wolf Brothers Trick Each Other |

An' as he was cookin' the salmon,
along come five of the Wolf brothers.
And they were from Moses Lake country.

    An' they looked over
    an' they saw Coyote cookin' this salmon,

an' they were hungry too,

> so they put Coyote to sleep.
> Coyote felt drowsy,
> 'n he laid back,
> 'n he went to sleep.

An' as he slept,
these five brothers—the Wolf brothers—came down,
an' et [h]is salmon.

> An' with the five brothers
> there was a Fox,
> which was the brother of Coyote.
> But the Fox et too with the Wolf,

>> and when they got through eatin' that salmon,
>> they took the fat from the salmon,
>> an' rubbed Coyote's mouth,
>> and rubbed his hands,
>> an' then they left 'im.

Then pretty soon Coyote woke up,
an' he says,
Whoopie!
What is the matter with me?
I'm still hungry.

> An' he put his hands up to his mouth,
> an' he says,
> *Well! Looks like I've been eatin'.*
> *But I am still hungry!*

>> 'n he looked at his hands,
>> 'n they was all greasy,
>> and he wondered what was wrong.

So he finally decided to ask his sisters.

So he asked his sisters.
He says,
"What happened?"

And his sisters told him,
"Well, you had visitors.
There were five Wolves and a Fox come to visit you.
And they et all your salmon.
And they left you.
And they went back to Moses Lake —
that's where they live."

And Coyote, he says,
"I will get even with 'em."

So he started out to Moses Lake.
An' as he left,
an' started to Moses Lake,
well, his salmon just stopped, right there,
an' they just stayed.
And he traveled overland until he come to Moses Lake.

And he peeked over,
an' he saw these five Wolves.

They were cookin' duck eggs and goose eggs,
and they used a barbecue method.
They dug a hole,
an' then they had rocks in these hole,
'n then they put their eggs in there,
an' then after eggs cooked,
they would dig it up 'n eat it.

And then Coyote watched 'em,
an' he made 'em go to sleep too.
And these five Wolfs,
they felt drowsy,
and they laid back
an' went to sleep.

An' as they slept,
Coyote came in there,
an' dug up this pit,
et aaall the eggs he could eat,
and he destroyed the other eggs,

an' he disfigured the Wolfs—
made 'em ugly . . .
An the Fox, he painted 'im with the eggs,
stretched his ears 'n made 'em long,
'n made his nose long 'n slender.

An' as he got through,
he left 'em,
an' he went back.

IV. Coyote Gets Wives |

Went back down to the river where his salmon were.
From there, he started up the river.
And as he went along,
the salmon followed 'im.

And the first place he came to was Leavenworth.
That was one of the best fisheries we've had in this part of the
    country.

He proposed to a Chief there.
And this Chief told 'im,
"Yes, I have a daughter,
and she is old enough to marry,
so you can marry her."
And this young lady and Coyote were married,
'n they lived there loong time.

And as he lived there,
he made a lot of things that was of interest.
One was a slide for the children.
He made a slide there of rock.
Another one was a rock that the men used to try to pack.

Many things he done for this tribe,
because he became a member of that tribe.

An' then him an' his wife had a baby daughter.

And as the years went by,
this young lady begin to grow up.
And she grew up,
and after fifteen, sixteen, seventeen years
she became a nice-lookin' young girl.

And Coyote,
he was always schemin' an' thinkin'.
He look at his daughter, you know,
and she was a fine young lady.

An' he thinks this to himself,
Somebody will come along,
an' marry her.

And so one day he thought to himself,
Well, I am gonna change myself,
and I will have her for my wife.

So he went upstream an' changed himself,
and he came down in a canoe.

And as he got near this village,
he got out and walked in to the village,
an' he was a fine young man.

Well, in the meantime he had changed himself
to this nice-lookin' young man.
'n he'd talk a different language.
He talked,
an' nobody would understan' 'im.
Only the Mouse could understan' 'im,
and she acted as his interpreter.

Coyote said,
"I have come down,
an' I will propose that you give me this young
lady,"
an' he pointed at her,
"that you give me this young lady for my wife."

Of course, there was just a mother then,
and she didn't know what to do,
so she says,
"Yes, you can have her for your wife."
So, Coyote and his daughter lived as man
an' wife for many years.

Then in the meantime, Prairie Chickens knew what was goin' on.
So one day they made up their mind
that they would reveal Coyote of what he was.

So they put on a dance,
'n they started dancin'.
An' they danced all over the village,
'n then they come to where Coyote was,
an' he try to stop 'em,
'n they wouldn't stop.

Finally, they said that this first man,
or whoever he was,
was nothin' but a coyote.

And his daughter was there
an' she heard it.

So, she was so ashamed of herself,
that she got up
an' ran down to this stream where the fishery is,
'n she jumped in.

And as she jumped in,
she turned into stone.

And she was always there.

> An' that became one of the best fishing places,
> because as she sit in this stream,
> it would cause an eddy.
> And the salmon would come upstream in this swift
>> water.
> They would rest behind this rock,
> and the Indians would catch 'em with hooks or
> whatever they used.

V. Coyote Distributes Salmon |

So there we were,
'n Coyote left,
and he went upstream.

Then wherever he stopped,
he would always propose to the Chief for a daughter.

> First place he came to was Chelan.
> Was quite a village there at Chelan.
> An' he went up to the chief of the tribe,
> an' he asked the chief for his daughter.

>> Chief looked at 'im,
>> 'n told 'im,
>> "No, I couldn't do that.
>> You're an old man.
>> My daughter is young,
>> and I don't think I'd want to give my daughter up to an old
>>> man."

>>> So, Coyote says,
>>> "All right, if that's the way you feel,
>>> I will go on.
>>> But before I go,
>>> I'm goin' change the course of the river."

>>> So, he built a big . . .

he stopped their [*sic*] . . .
river,
'n caused it to be falls,
and the salmon couldn't go upstream
because they couldn't go up the stream
because they would come to the falls,
'n that's 's far as they would go.

And Coyote went upstream.

And this story really has no ending.
It goes on an' on an' on.
The other stories would pick it up.

He went on up to the Okanagan Falls,
made it a nice fishery there,
up to Kettle Falls,
he made a nice fishery, Kettle Falls,
up to Spokane Falls.

Of course, that is another story.
As I said,
this story goes on an' on,
and really has no ending.

As Coyote went north,
then these northern tribes would pick it up,
an' their stories were just a little bit
different from ours,
but that is another story altogether.

Notes

1. Brackets are used to indicate elided material that needs to be replaced for greater clarity.

Skunk

A Traditional Colville Story

Told by Charles Quintasket

Edited by Dell Hymes

Stories in which Skunk's musk sac is lost and regained are popular in the Plateau and Columbia River area. This story was told in English by Charles Quintasket to Jay Miller, and first published (in prose paragraphs) in Miller's edition of *Coyote Stories* by Mr. Quintasket's sister, Christine Quintasket, better known by her pen name, Mourning Dove.

Mr. Quintasket makes use of modern references and colloquial expressions, bringing the story at the end into the visible here and now. He shows the continued vitality such a tradition can have. Through the courtesy of Miller, Mr. Quintasket has seen this presentation. His comment was, "There's a lot of craft in that." I hope he meant reflection of his own.

Skunk

I. PREFACE |

An old woman had two granddaughters,
    Chipmunk and Rock Squirrel.
They all lived together.
The girls had a boyfriend.
He was Fisher.

II. SKUNK GETS THE GIRLS |

One day they heard the ominous sound of Skunk coming:
    Phuw, Phuw, Phuw, Phuw, Phuw.
He kept breaking wind.
They could hear him coming.

The old woman hid the girls
    in the place they used for emergencies like this.
He came there
    and looked around.

He said,
> "Where are the girls?"

The woman concocted some story
> about why they weren't there,
> > maybe they were off berry picking.

He did not believe her.
Skunk was the most dangerous man in the Animal Kingdom.
Nobody messed with him.
When he started looking around for the girls,
> the woman stayed away.

Skunk found the girls.
He found them by golly.
He said,
> "Come with me girls,"
> > and they took off.

They went on like that.

Nightfall overtook them
> and they found shelter in a cave.

He slept between the girls.

III. Fisher Gets Them Back |

Meanwhile, Fisher came over to see his girlfriends.
The grandmother tearfully told him what had happened.
The great Skunk had taken the girls with him.

Fisher went after them.
He followed the scent
> and caught up with them at the cave.

Skunk was sound asleep.
Snoring and blasting.
Fisher whispered
> "*tsmps*"
> > to get the girls' attention.

They were pretty desperate,
> hoping that he would follow after them.

He motioned for them to come out.
Easy and quiet, they got out.
One at a time.
They got loose
and came out to him.

Of course, Fisher was a medicine man, too.
He had powers of his own.
He made the cave close in on Skunk

He and the girls took off.
If he had left well enough alone,
there would not have been any further story.
But Fisher wanted to crush that guy.

IV. Skunk Gets Out, Ravens Get His Ahso, He Gets It Back |
All at once, the ceiling was like to close in on Skunk.

He thought the girls were snuggling up to him.
He said in Skunkese, through his nose,
"Get over.
Move over.
You must love me too well."

Finally, just when he was going to be crushed to a pulp,
he smartened out,
Hell, this cave is going to crush me.
He tried to zip out,
but it was too late.
He got as far as the entrance,
but it was only a small hole.

He said,
Gee, how am I going to get out?
He decided that the only way
was to take himself apart.
He took off his legs,
his head,
his shoulders,

his hips,
       and, last of all, his rear end.

He was especially careful with his *ahso*.   ii. |
That was his atomic bomb.
He held on to that.
It was his most precious part.
It made him what he was
    and made everyone else fearful.
He could not lose it.
Then he would be nobody.
Most carefully, he started to stick it through the hole,
    but then he heard Ravens,
        so he would pull it back.
He could not let the Ravens have it.

The cave was still closing up,
    but more slowly.
Skunk had to decide what to do.
The rest of him was already outside
    and needed to be protected from the Ravens.

By gosh, he was getting pretty desperate.
He had to take a chance.
He thought
    that if he would leap out
        and put himself together,
           he could sit down
               and protect his valuable end.

He called out threateningly,
    "I'll sit on that atomic bomb
        so Raven can't get it."
That was his plan.
He had to do it.

He got ready,
    threw out the ahso,
        and got himself together.
But he was not quick enough.
A Raven had swooped down
    and taken his rear end.
The Ravens flew back to the village
    and everyone began to play with Skunk's asset.

Skunk did not feel right   iii. |
    and felt himself all over.
When he got to the back,
    he realized that something was missing.
He saw the Ravens fly off with it.
He followed them.

Finally, after a long search,
    he found a bunch of kids using his ahso as a hoop.
They were rolling it in the dark
    and watching it flash.
Phuw. Phuw. Phuw. Phuw. Phuw.
That's the flash.
It was something to watch.

Skunk had to figure a way of getting his asset back.
Now, how am I going to do it?
He thought out a scheme.

He waited
    until the kids rolled the hoop back.
Then he ran alongside it
    and when it fell over,
        he sat on it.

As soon as he sat down,
    all systems were go.
He was recharged.

He used his dog-gone power.
He turned the dangerous end of himself onto the crowd.
He just mowed them down.
Yeah, they all fell down.

V. Skunk Wins Out |

Now he was ready to start tracking Fisher and the girls.
He finally caught up with them
>   just this side of where the town of Colville, Washington, is now.
They call that place,
>   "blasted in front of the face."

There is a little spring there,
>   right at the bottom of the cliff.
Skunk was looking down
>   when he saw them.
He started blasting at them.
Nothing happened.

He tried again and again.
Finally, he looked up
>   and saw them up on the cliff.
Heck, he was shooting at their reflections.

Now he tried shooting at them,   ii. |
>   but he fell short.
He was almost out of ammunition.

He started chewing grass
>   and recouped.
He was ready,
>   acting like a darned machine gun.
All of them missed,
>   except for a tiny spray that just touched Fisher's toe.
Down he came.
Tumbling down and dead.

Skunk got those girls by saying,
        "You guys are next if you don't come down."
They did not like him,
        but they did not want to die either.
So, down they came.
They must have married on the spot.
Skunk ended up in Wonderland.

It is funny, you know
There are still three stony figures on that cliff,
        above that spring,
                across the road from where the Drive-In is now.
When you are going east toward Colville,
                you can now see those stone columns,
        but coming west along the road,
                they are plain as day.
You can see their outline against the cliff.
Of course the big one is Fisher.
Chipmunk and Rock Squirrel are the little ones.
They are still there to this day,
        proving this story.

The Seal and the Raven
A Sechelt Raven Story

Told by Charlie Roberts and/or Jack Isidore

Edited by Ralph Maud

The Sechelt may be the most southern tribe to have had a strong connection with the raven as an omen and as a subject for storytelling. The raven is a prophet of doom: "When they see him sitting on the branch of a tree, ruffling his feathers and croaking dismally, they believe that someone among them will shortly die." So reported Charles Hill-Tout in 1904 in the *Journal of the Royal Anthropological Institute*, where the following story can be found. The role of Raven as an omen of death becomes even more pertinent if you are a seal.

The story begins as if it were to have been the "Bungling Host" theme; but here the melting of oil from the seal's flippers just serves to remind Raven how tasty seal meat is. His voraciousness simply takes over; Raven becomes an automaton of greed, therefore funny.

It is in the ending that this story differs from an episode of the Raven cycle that might be heard farther north. The Salish Transformers come on the scene to punish Raven with metamorphosis.

The Seal and the Raven

Raven, who lived in one part of the country, had a sister named Seal, who lived with her large family in another part. One day Raven determined to visit his sister; so taking his canoe he set out. Upon his arrival, Seal set about preparing a meal for him. She did this by roasting her hands before the fire and catching the oil from them as it dropped into a dish. When Raven had satisfied his appetite, he told her that he desired to adopt and take home with him one of her children. "Very good," replied Seal, "you shall have my youngest daughter."

In a little while Raven set out for his home, taking his youngest niece with him. When they were about halfway there, Raven asked his niece if she were not thirsty. She, replying in the affirmative, he pulled ashore. She got out and stooped over to drink. As she was stooping, Raven struck her on the head and killed her. He then placed the dead body in the canoe and made straight for home. When he arrived, he held a feast and devoured the body of his niece.

In like manner, he got possession of all his nieces, twelve in number, and devoured them in the same way.

When all his nieces had thus been disposed of, he made up his mind to kill and devour his sister Seal; but she is too clever for him. When he attempted to kill her, she jumped into the water and got away. Thus defeated in purpose, he has perforce to return home empty-handed.

His many crimes and wickednesses shortly after so incensed the Sky God, Qeqals, that, to punish him, he turned both him and his many wives into stone.

Sun and Moon Are Brothers

A Traditional Quinault Story

Told by Bob Pope, interpreted by Harry Shale

Edited by William R. Seaburg

Ronald L. Olson's Quinault fieldwork was conducted during three month-long field trips in "the spring of 1925 and the winters of 1925–26 and 1926–27" (Olson 1936:3). "Sun and Moon Are Brothers," published here for the first time, was told by Bob Pope and recorded (with pen and paper) during the evening hours of January 15, 1926. Although Bob Pope told the story in the Quinault language, Olson did not make a phonetic transcription. Instead, he recorded in longhand the English translation by Harry Shale, one of Olson's Quinault interpreters. Bob Pope, according to Olson, was "over ninety" years of age and "spoke no English." His knowledge of Quinault culture was both reliable and extensive, indeed "all that could be desired" (Olson 1936:3).

The narrative texts in Olson's field notes are often thematically related to the ethnographic notes in which they are embedded. This can be seen in the case of "Sun and Moon Are Brothers." Olson began his January 15 session by eliciting information about the Quinault "calendar," including Quinault terms for the various seasons and beliefs about eclipses. Eclipses are explained by reference to a large animal, Upper Fisher, "who tries to bite the sun or moon. (He got up there at the time of the Star Husband episode)." Although the "people were afraid and would shoot, holler and make all the noise they could to scare that Fisher away"—"There is a lady frog (*wagí*) up there who helps the most and really saves the moon" (Olson 1926).

After transcribing "Sun and Moon Are Brothers," Olson recorded a short narrative about encounters with a wealth-giving frog. The consultant remarked, "That is the frog that married the moon." This embedding of myths and tales within the ethnographic notes suggests that Olson was not eliciting particular texts but was writing them down as they occurred naturally in the course of the fieldwork session.

Nearly thirty years earlier Bob Pope had been Livingston Farrand's main consultant during Farrand's brief fieldwork with the Quinault in the summer of 1898. Most of the stories published in Farrand's (1902) *Traditions of the*

Quinault Indians were from Pope. According to Olson, Harry Shale also acted as one of Farrand's interpreters. Although "Sun and Moon Are Brothers" was recorded in English translation by Farrand (1898), he chose not to publish it or any of the other Xwoni Xwoni texts, noting that they were "all of a gross character" and "as they were obviously borrowed from southern sources, they have been omitted" (Farrand 1902:92). The sometimes "obscene" and erotic nature of the adventures of the Trickster-Transformer Xwoni Xwoni may have been the primary reason Farrand decided not to publish them.

The plot structure of Farrand's version is nearly identical to Olson's; there are, though, differences in stylistic details. In Farrand's text, Pope adheres to the culturally expected five-pattern repetition of certain events; he does not do so in the Olson text. For example, in Farrand, Xwoni Xwoni makes and destroys five successive watchmen before the sixth truthfully announces the arrival of a Chinook salmon in his trap. In Olson, the second and last watchman correctly announces the salmon's presence. Similarly, the Farrand version chronicles the five nights Xwoni Xwoni awaits the transformation of milt into two young girls; the Olson text skips the intervening four days. It is unclear whether Pope, Shale, or Olson is responsible for this stylistic change. The Olson version, on the one hand, does not account for the origin of Moon's brother; Farrand's text, on the other hand, explains: "Now the old pheasant when she got home had taken the piss from the child's cradle and squeezed it all out and made a boy from it and this man was that child" (Farrand 1898). In the Farrand story, the Harpoon boys feed two of the biggest fish from each day's catch to their grandmother Fire; in Olson, they feed her only one salmon. There are other similar differences in descriptive detail between the two renditions.

It is my impression that Olson was adhering more closely to the interpreter's English translation than was Farrand. Olson himself (1936:3) felt that Farrand "failed to give verbatim renditions." Unfortunately, Olson did not indicate how he worked with Pope and Shale, how the translation proceeded, whether phrase by phrase or perhaps in larger "chunks" of text. We cannot be certain that every word or phrase is a verbatim record of the interpreter's English. I believe Olson's voice occasionally overrides Shale's.

Cognate and partially cognate texts from the Upper Chehalis, Cowlitz, Humptulips, Puyallup, and Skokomish have been recorded by Thelma Adamson (1934). Melville Jacobs (1934) transcribed a Cowlitz/Upper Cowlitz version. Franz Boas transcribed a Lower Chehalis version in 1927. M. Dale Kinkade (this volume) notes additional parallels from southwest Washington State.[1]

My rendition of "Sun and Moon Are Brothers" is based primarily on Olson's original field notebook transcription (Olson 1926) and secondarily on a manuscript version, presumably typed by Olson (ca. 1927). I have kept my editorial intrusions to a minimum. Those portions of the text enclosed within parentheses are so enclosed in the notebook transcription. It is unclear whether they represent Pope's, Shale's, or Olson's parenthetical comments. My paragraphing sometimes differs from that indicated in Olson (ca. 1927). The title is mine; neither Olson nor Farrand noted a title for this text.

Olson published a short autobiographical sketch of Bob Pope (1936:182–83). For ethnographic background on Quinault culture see Olson (1936), Hajda (1990), and Capoeman (1990). For information about the life and career of Ronald L. Olson, see Stewart (1980) and Drucker (1981).

Sun and Moon Are Brothers

There was one time a person named Xwoni Xwoni who made a fish trap out of little round poles. Xwoni Xwoni was a man who could do miracles. When he had it finished, he defecated, made it [feces] into a man and put life in it, and then said to his feces, "When I have caught a Chinook salmon (and none other) you holler to me." And he laid by the fire and laid by the fire until he was nearly asleep, when he heard that person say, "Xwoni Xwoni, Xwoni Xwoni, Chinook salmon, Chinook salmon," and Xwoni Xwoni ran as fast as he could. But when he got out there he found only a rotten log in the trap. And he began to kick his watchman. He told him, "I told you to call me only when I catch a Chinook salmon." And then he killed him.

Then he made a second man in the same way and advised him the same way. And again Xwoni Xwoni went and laid by the fire until he was sound asleep, when he heard, "Xwoni Xwoni, Xwoni Xwoni, you've got a Chinook in your trap." And when he got out there close he could see the fish splashing, and oh! how his heart cheered up! This time it was a big male Chinook salmon and he was satisfied and took his trap out.

And he went and dressed the fish and saved the milt for a purpose. He put it across from his bed on the other side and wrapped it up nicely with a blanket. And when he had it all wrapped up he said, "Now I am going to lay you there all wrapped up nice for five days." On the morning of the fifth day he was awakened by these two (halves), whispering that he had wrapped nicely. And he heard them laughing and their voices sounded like women laughing. And he got up just before daybreak and he said to them, "Get up, get up and go and bathe." And they got up and it was two young women. They got through bathing and came in. They were just as pretty as can be. And he told them, "I am your father—you are my daughters."

These girls began to run around here and there, here and there. And pretty soon Xwoni Xwoni got sick and wasn't able to get up. He didn't have strength enough to raise himself from his bed. And he told these two girls, "Now if I pass away don't bury me in the ground. Put me about four feet off the ground on a [rack ?], [shaped] like [this:] #. And after you bury me and whenever you feel like crying, don't cry in the house but come near the grave so you can hear your little brother crying. He will be right under my grave."

And then it wasn't long until he passed away and the girls took his advice and buried him the way he wished. And in a day or two the girls were right near the grave when they heard a little boy crying. And they went over and found a nice little boy right there and they took him home. They took good care of the little brother, bathed him twice a day—and you could almost see him grow.

It wasn't long until he was quite a size of a boy, this little brother (supposed to be). And this little boy slept with the oldest sister. And it wasn't long before little Xwoni Xwoni was thrown on the ground. (He had been feeling around and the older sister woke up.) Then the younger sister got angry at the older sister because she saw him on the floor; the older one had thrown him down. And the older sister didn't tell the younger one why she had thrown him out. She thought, *I'm just going to let the little boy sleep with you and you will find out the next night*. So the night came and she told her younger sister, "Now you let the boy sleep with you." And it wasn't long after they were asleep when down comes the little boy again—he got tossed out of the bed onto the floor.

Then things went on that way. The boy was growing up fast and they made him a bow and arrow. And the little boy was gone nearly all day getting some little game. And they suspicioned him when he was gone, and they said, "I think that's Xwoni Xwoni. Let's go over to his grave and see." And they went over and looked in and there wasn't a thing there. Then they found out it was Xwoni Xwoni. And then they were well satisfied that it was Xwoni Xwoni when they saw he had disappeared. And so they got ready and were going to run away.

And when Xwoni Xwoni came back the girls were gone. Then they cut across the country and went and went and went and by and by reached a stream. They peeked through the brush and saw quite a number of people fishing steelhead, it being wintertime. And one lone fellow in a canoe would spear at a salmon and miss, would spear at a salmon and miss. And he got so sore that he said, *Miss, miss; maybe Miss(es) Xwoni Xwoni are watching.* And they were watching and he didn't know it. (His name was xē ́ēsᴇᴋ.)

And there were a couple of bright-looking young fellows and every time they would spear they would bring in a fish and never miss. And they took a liking to these two boys. "We will notify them." One said, "You take the one in the stern and I will take the one in the bow." Then they hollered at the boys and the boys paddled towards them and permitted them to come in the canoe. And they took them down to their house and took them in. The older boy had his bed on one side and the younger one on the other. Then they took the girls and did to them as they wished.

When they first got in they took dry wood and built a big fire and then from their catch selected the largest fish and threw the whole fish right in the fire. And every time they would go out fishing they would bring in quite a large catch and every time would select an extra large fish and throw it in the fire. Things went on and the older brother told his wife, "Now whenever that fire dies down, don't bother it at all but leave it as it is when we leave the house—just as we leave it."

And after the boys had gone the girls whispered between themselves, "I wonder why they won't permit us to touch the fire?" Now the boys hadn't given the reason for not permitting it. So the girls said, "Now let's build the fire." So they took a stick and pushed it this way and that and tried to rebuild it. But the fire kept just as it was and kept on dying out.

And the boys came in. And this fire was the boys' grandmother, and the girls had been poking her eyes and her mouth and everywhere. And that extra fish was what they were feeding her. But this time they didn't do it because she was near death. And soon the fire went out. She died. And when that night came they told their wives, "We, I and my brother, are Harpoon— you call that *k!lăkă ́n*—that is me and my brother." (In the early days this harpoon that we use was those two boys and their grandmother was the Fire and these girls didn't know.) And then that night the four slept and both girls were awakened at the same time. They heard something rattle and they felt and their husbands had turned into Harpoons.

Bright and early they got ready. They were going to make another trip— due east they were going to go this time. They went quite a ways and they reached a small house. They heard a noise and they peeked in and saw an old lady that was blind. There she was rocking a little baby—a boy—in a cradle. The baby looked good to them, and the oldest took it out of the cradle and put it next to her breast under her blanket and covered it that way. She thought it was a very pretty baby.

And they took a piece of wood, put it in the baby's wrappings, and advised the old lady, "Now don't disturb the baby because he will be asleep for a long time." They took the baby and started to run. And the old lady wondered why the baby didn't cry. So she felt around and felt around and discovered it was wood. Now the mother of this baby was making a noise right back of the house. The old lady began to holler and to say, "Come on, come on. Misses Xwoni Xwoni ran away with your baby." And she came in the house and found her baby was gone. And that mother was Pheasant—that was also at one time a person. And she was out there drumming while the girls were running away with her baby.

And she got hold of her mother and carried her along and started to chase the girls. They went quite a ways, quite a ways and then they saw the two girls going. She had almost overtaken them. And she got close to the Xwoni Xwoni girls and then mother Pheasant dropped her mother down and it formed a lake ahead that came up to the waist of the girls. Yet they were making headway. Once more she overtook them and again she dropped her mother down. But there wasn't much water there that time. Then they gave up and started back. (The old lady's name was Flood Lake.)

And the girls got to the place where they planned to go. And the boy grew and grew until he became a good-sized boy. You could almost see him growing. Then he became a young man and he began to realize things. The girls sang songs and from the words they used he was able to see that, and he said, *Oh, these girls have captured me and taken me from somewhere.* He learned that his mother was Pheasant and that his father was a log—that hurt him worse than a slap, and he began to think what he was going to do. Then he thought to himself, *Now I am going to leave these girls. I am going to build me a good-sized canoe, then I can go wherever I want to.* So he began making one and in a short time had one to suit.

So he jumped into his canoe and down the stream he went—down, down until he reached quite a large village bright and early. And he anchored outside. And the People came out and then rushed right back and said, each one did, "There is a man anchored out in front in a canoe and I never in my life saw such a pretty young man as in that canoe." Then the single women dressed in their best, painted themselves, and went out to try and make a match with this young man. Many pretty young ones of sixteen or seventeen went out, and most of them were not able to contain themselves. But so much did they wish for him that they urinated a little—not being able to control it. This was because he was Sun and is bright to look at.

And Bluejay pointed out Miss Frog—she looked terrible with all her spots—and said, "See Miss Frog—maybe it's her that will fall in love with that young man." But Miss Frog didn't answer a word. And Miss Frog was the last one to come out—(none of the ladies missed the chance). She washed her face, combed her hair, took her paint and painted [paint?], and then went out. And she grabbed her little box of belongings and her little bucket about the same size. And when Bluejay saw her he pointed at her and said, "Piddle, piddle." But it wasn't her that urinated but Bluejay who did it instead. He fell backwards and pissed a little. Then Miss Frog walked right on, went out to the canoe and sat down. Then they started downstream in their canoe.

And they came on down to a young man who was fishing by the bank and who swallowed everything that he caught; no matter what, he swallowed it whole. And as they came down they (i.e., Moon [and Miss Frog]) saw that this fisherman was pretty and looked like he [Moon] himself did. Yet he was swallowing lizards and everything. So he pulled in his canoe nearby and began to question him. But the man would not answer at all but only averted his face (put down his head). Finally, he said, "Well, I will tell you. They tell me that my brother was kidnapped by the Xwoni Xwoni girls." Then the man with Frog said to himself, *Well, this must be my brother then.* Then he answered and said, "I am the young man that the Xwoni Xwoni girls ran away with and I am your brother."

And this young man was eating everything and so much that his belly was puffed out hugely. So this young man said to Frog, "You better have mercy on my brother. See if you can cure him or help him." And she answered, "Yes, I can. I can do a lot toward curing him." And she took him by the leg and turned him upside down and shook him so that he threw up all those reptiles and lizards that he had swallowed. And some that he had recently eaten were still alive. (In those days there were a lot of those things.) And after she had done that he was of normal shape again and he started to jump around and to feel good.

So the oldest one (Frog's intended) said before daylight, "I am going to turn myself so that I will be recognized as a sun and people will call me Sun." Then Sun came up but he didn't have it regulated right. He was too hot. As soon as he came up the streams started to boil and the rocks began to burst. And most of the People were killed with the heat. So he said to his younger brother, "We don't want to kill all the People with heat. Perhaps you wouldn't be quite so hot as I. It wouldn't be right to kill all the People with heat." So they changed off, and the younger one became the Sun and the older one became the Moon. Then Frog and the older brother were married. And often at full moon you can see that blue mark around it. And she is holding her box of belongings and her bucket.

Notes

1. Also see the Tillamook epic "South Wind's Journeys" in this volume for several matching themes. —Eds.

Coyote and the Birds
A Traditional Coeur d'Alene Story

Told by Margaret Stensgar

Edited by Ivy G. Doak and Margaret Stensgar

Coeur d'Alene is a Southern Interior Salish language spoken by only a handful of elders on or near the Coeur d'Alene Reservation in northern Idaho.
Margaret Stensgar is the talented storyteller who provided the tale presented
here.[1] This mythological story is an integral part of the Coeur d'Alene oral
tradition.

Mrs. Stensgar refers to this story as a "fairy tale," one of her Grandpa Joseph's repertoire of traditional stories. Mrs. Stensgar told me this story a number of times, this version in 1986 at the request of her grandson, Joseph Reno
Stensgar, who called it the story of "Coyote and the Birds." Gladys Reichard
recorded a similar tale in the 1930s, labeled "Coyote Loses His Eyes" (Reichard 1947).[2] Mrs. Stensgar told the story first in English, then in Coeur d'Alene.
What follows is the transcription of the English version, which I chose in order
to include a brief interaction between teller and audience. The Coeur d'Alene
and English versions are essentially identical except for this interaction.

Coyote and the Birds

Reno:

Tell Coyote and the Birds.

Margaret:

Ah, Coyote. It's a short story, too.

Coyote thought oh, it's such a beautiful day! I am going to
take a walk. So Coyote goes out there, he starts trotting along, you know,
so happy and . . .

Waggedy-tail
Waggedy-tail
Waggedy-tail
Waggedy-tail . . .

His tail is wagging while he's walking.

Reno:

   wɛʔ wɛʔ wiʔšups

Margaret:

   Yeah, in Indian they say:

   wɛʔ wɛʔ wiʔšups

   wɛʔ wɛʔ wiʔšups

So that would be waggedy-tail, waggedy-tail. That's Coyote.

Finally he stopped. He looked up. Oh those birds are sure having a lot of fun. He watched them as they were playing around there. They take their eyes out and throw it up in the air. And you know and pretty soon the birds would go there and their eyes would drop back in their eye sockets.

Golly, he says, *that looks like fun!* Like I say, Coyote will try anything that he sees, you know, he always wants to.

So Coyote says, *that looks like fun*. I'm going to try that. So Coyote says, all right. He takes his eyes out and he throws it way up in the air. And Coyote there, he was standing there, then the birds come around and they ate it, ate his eyes out.

And Coyote then . . . he lost his eyes!

So Coyote started going, and he'd bump into something and, *Ouch! My head!* And he'd go along, and he'd bump into things, you know.

Then finally an old lady come along and says, "Coyote, what's wrong with you?"

"Well, I . . . I cannot see! And I don't know where I'm going! I can't see anything!"

"Well, how did you get blind?"

"I was watching the birds throwing their eyes up in the air then get back into their eyes, so I thought I'd try it. I lost my eyes."

"Coyote, you're crazy, trying to do those things." She says, "All right, I'll tell you. I'll give you this, what I have in my hand."

Of course Coyote cannot see, but it's tallow.

She gave it to Coyote, told him, "You hold it in your right hand and you hang onto it and you go down to the river."

"Well, how will I get down to the river? I can't see."

"As you go along, you ask the trees, and the trees will tell you what they are. When it comes to the willows and all that, you know you're getting close."

"All right."

"So, when you get there then you . . . you walk as far as you can out into the river, then you turn. Then you take that, what you have in your hand, and you throw it over your left shoulder as far as you can. And you say, 'Get my eyes back.' You'll be able to see again."

"All right. (I'll) try that."

She says, "But one thing I'm going to tell you, Coyote, don't you ever, ever look back to see what you threw. Don't look back."

And Coyote says, "All right, I will."

So, "All right."

So Coyote thanked that lady, so Coyote started going along. "Ouch! I hurt my head! Oh, that hurts! What tree are you?"

"I'm Yellow Pine."

And he'd go along and "Ouch!" into another tree, then, "What tree are you?"

Coyote's getting all kinds of bumps from hitting the trees.

Then a bull pine or whatever . . . it went on like that.

Finally, he had come to the willows. Coyote says, "What willow are you?" Well, then it would say what kind of willow it was. Well, it's getting closer to that lake or river. Finally it come to red willows; well, he was getting there now.

So Coyote starts wading in the water. He went as far as he could. Then he turns around. And he takes that tallow that he had in his hand the old lady had given him. He threw it back as far as he could. Then all right. So he says, when he threw it back, "I want my eyesights back." Boy, everything was clear: he could see!

Oh boy, I can see! I can see! Really, I can see! Good to get my eyesights back!

But that darned little Coyote, anyway, what he's told, he never does. He started walking away . . . and it started bothering him, *I wonder, what did I throw back there?* And he was told not to look back.

But it kept bothering him. *I wonder what it is that I threw back there.* Finally [it] got the best of him, and Coyote turned around to look back.

He went blind again.

Notes

1. Margaret Stensgar passed away in April 1996 and so did not see a final version of this paper. The story is hers; any errors are mine. —IGD.

2. There are several versions of this story in this volume. —Eds.

The Border Monsters

A Story about Salishan People from a Bordering Group

Told by Hal George

Edited by J. V. (Jay) Powell and Luke J. Powell

Coauthor Luke Powell grew up in a family committed to anthropological field-work. From toddler to teenager, he spent summers on the Kwakwaka'wakw (Kwakiutl), Gitksan, and, especially the Quileute reservations with grammas and grampas telling him the old stories. When the call for Salish cultural nar-ratives for inclusion in this volume came, Luke said, "How about the story of the origin of the Sol Duc hotsprings. That's a Quileute story about a Clal-lam monster." So, we dug out the field notes and transcriptions and wrote it together. Hal George loved to tell stories to children. The fact that his tellings were tape-recorded and later transcribed did not impact them as examples of traditional stories, appropriately told in their social context. Luke and his fa-ther, Jay Powell, later collaborated on the preparation of this text.

This is not, as far as we have been able to determine, a Salish story. It is a cultural narrative of the Quileute, a non-Salish neighbor group of the Salishan Elwha (Southern Klallam). As such, it presents an outsider's view of an aspect of Salish history and ethnogeography. Traditional Elwha lands bordered those of the Quileute in the north-central uplands of Washington's Olympic Penin-sula. This story takes place in the liminal region of peaks and rain-forested riverine headwaters where Elwha and Quileute country come together.

Like most stories, this narrative has its own story. In May and June of 1978, Jay had the good luck to work at LaPush, Washington, with the eighty-four-year-old Hal George, who was the same man to whom Manuel Andrade re-ferred in the preface to *Quileute Texts* (1931): "The last 44 texts of this col-lection were obtained by Dr. Leo J. Frachtenberg in the summer of 1915 and the fall of 1916. [. . . .] Dr. Frachtenberg's chief informant was Hallie George, a half-blood Quileute." Thus, Jay was working with the same knowledge-able Quileute that Leo Frachtenberg had learned from sixty-three years earlier. Hal was born August 15, 1894. He had been twenty-one at the time he first told Quileute narratives to Frachtenberg, and at eighty-four he was still good-humored and acute. Hal had been a boy at the turn of the century, during that critical decade when traditional Quileute life was changing. The upriver villages and fish traps were falling into disuse and being torn down; staples of the traditional foraged diet were being replaced with spuds and rice, sugar and flour; and traditional medicine and belief systems were being impacted by whiteman's religions and worldview. At one point, Hal narrated again for us in Quileute several of the stories he had told Frachtenberg, and for many of these he told the stories almost word for word, line after line verbatim as Frachtenberg had recorded them from his telling six decades earlier.

One afternoon we asked Hal to tell me a story in Quileute that he had not told Frachtenberg. He thought for a moment and then started right in. "*T'so sa?, hiqawóxáli . . . ,*" the customary starting formula for a Quileute story ("Well, now, I'm going to tell the story about . . ."). We later transcribed and translated the story. It was a traditional telling of the story that follows but, because he told it in Quileute, it was not the telling that appears below. That form of the story, also told by Hal George, occurred several days later, when Hal agreed to tell a Quileute story to a non-Quileute-speaking family that was visiting on the reservation and had asked permission to "sit in on our fieldwork session." In fact, we almost didn't tape-record this telling of the story in English, because we knew that we already had a recording of him telling it in Quileute. As Jay recalls, "I am glad that I did record the English version, because it differed from the Quileute telling in ways that, upon reflection, we now find interesting and revealing."

The version of the story that Hal George produced in English for non-Quileutes differed from his Quileute version in some generalizable respects. First, the English version showed discursive contexting for outsiders. In almost every regard the English version is longer than the Quileute version because information has been inserted parenthetically to provide background and explain what a non-Quileute could not be expected to know: (a) place names are explained, (b) tribal histories are clarified, and (c) aspects of the spiritual world are expanded. Second, the English version has been shortened only where actions happened in fours (the traditional pattern in Quileute).

This story was transcribed from a tape now in the collection of the archives of Quileute Tribal School in LaPush, Washington. It is a narrow transcription in that it attempts to characterize Mr. George's actual usage, including Quileute interference on his pronunciation of English words with initial *cl*-clusters (e.g., "clouds" is pronounced with an initial *kɬ* cluster and written *kɬouds*), and syllable final English *-ng* sounds are pronounced [n] rather than [ŋ]. Statements that do not occur in the Quileute version are given in italics. A few editorial additions have been added and are in parenthesis.

The Border Monsters

T'so sa?. I'm goin' to tell you the story of the border monsters that used to fight up at Boulder Peak at the place where Quileute country and country of the *ʔ4xʷat'* come together. You know Boulder Peak, bitsíkʷalas. *We call it bitsíkʷalas 'cause it's the boundary, the border, and our Quileute land goes that far*. And Elwha land starts there; everythin' beyond Boulder Peak is Elwha land. Q̇ʷáti made that Boulder Peak to show where Elwha land stops and Quileute land starts. He piled stones up there and marked the boundary the way a wolf does. *We call that dóxʷalas (to mark territory by urinating)*. Q̇ʷáti piled up stones and that's the reason that Boulder Peak has all those big boulders big as houses. Q̇ʷáti did that, made that border so the Quileutes and Elwhas would know where the border was, cause the Quileutes and the Elwhas used to fight sometimes about the border. *They used to fight in the valley where Lake Crescent is now, used to be a big meadow there and the Quileutes and Elwhas used to fight over there until Stormking Mountain had enough of it and tore off a big stone from his head. He threw it down into the valley and it killed the warriors, killed the warriors and made a jam, a dam in the river at the end of the valley and so (that's the reason) Lake Crescent is there.*

Well, Q̇ʷáti made Boulder Peak. He marked the boundary of Quileute country with Boulder Peak. *It was Q̇ʷáti (who) made the Quileutes from wolves. And he also went over there in Elwha country and found the Elwhas were little people, real little and they only had little salmon in their waters. So Q̇ʷáti made a big king salmon out of lots of little ones and gave it a name and set it loose in the Elwha River. And then he stretched the people there so they would be big enough to handle them big kings in their river. And so the Old People would know where the border was, Q̇ʷáti made that big pile of rocks for a border between Quileute and Elwha country.*

Well, then . . . so Q̇ʷáti made Boulder Peak to mark the boundary between Quileute country and Elwha country. He piled up those stones and marked it like a wolf does. And there was a border monster who lived on the Quileute side up in the woods. He lived in a cave in the woods. He used to fight with another monster that lived over on the Elwha side. When they came out to fight, they always met at Boulder Peak and fought there.

Both monsters were fierce, like martens, and strong and wiry and real smart because they were old. They had big mouths full of teeth as big as a man and sharp toenails. And their breath was like a hot wind that could burn you if you stood close, and they cooked their meat by just blowing on it. They were real big; when they walk through the woods you can see their heads and backs above the trees. When they fight they whip their tails on this side and on this (other) side and roll around. Their tails break off trees. And when they roll they flatten the trees they roll over. And sometimes the hard breathin' sets the woods on fire around the battlefield. So that's why nothin' grows on Boulder Peak.

Well, then. Those two monsters are just covered with scars. They have scars all over their bodies from fightin' because they have been meetin' to fight for a lon' time. They have big scars where their skin was ripped and tore. Every time they fight, they fight until they are bloody and tired, all bit, bones broke, skin ripped and burned. They have scars on top of scars.

But, they are even matched so one of them can never kill the other one. Neither one can kill the other one. *We say they have* łibiti taxílit, *real stron' spirit power. If you are a good warrior, you need that power*. Neither one can kill the other. But they cause real bad injuries to each other every time they fight. Often them fights went on all day until night and it got dark. Then, they stop and roar. Both of them roar and roar and sin(g) a victory son(g). The Quileute monster san(g) his son(g): "łipílli ʔabiʔ łibíti ti'l. łipítilawli. ʔAhi-i-i. ʔAʔaʔaʔa-a-a." (four times) *He's talkin' about havin' a strong power and that's why he is always winnin'*. The Elwha monster sin(g)s, too. And then they roar some more and go home. They go to their cave.

Each monster has a cave in the woods. The Quileute monster lives on the upper Sol Duc and the Elwha monster lives over on the Elwha.

Well, then. They go in their caves and move a rock over the hole. And then they lick themselves. And they cry. They cry and cry because they are hurt bad. And their tears are hot, too, and make a creek of hot water. That hot water runs out of the caves. It runs and runs. And the Quileute monster cryin' causes the Sol Duc Hot Springs. And the Elwha monster cryin' causes the Olympic Hot Springs. We call that monster ʔaʔlatkił. "That means the monster who cries in the woods." Bitsas saʔ. *That's what we say at the end of a story. Bitsas saʔ. That's all there is to that. That's the story of the border monsters*.

Historical Events

Battle at Sea

A Northern Lushootseed Historical Narrative

Told by Wilson George

Edited by Vi Taqʷšəblu Hilbert and Thomas M. Hess

The story that follows is the translation of a transcription of Wilson George's tape recording telling a bit of the history of his people. The recording was made by Leon Metcalf in 1950 and later donated to the Burke Museum at the University of Washington. Metcalf himself made no attempt to either transcribe or translate the text. Hilbert did the transcription some thirty-five years later, and from this Hess made the translation that follows. We chose to present this particular text from the many elicited by Metcalf, Hilbert, Hess, and others, because it is one of the very few that presents Native history without the influence of European contact and because the quoted speeches illustrate a formal style rarely preserved in Lushootseed Salish.[1]

Wilson George was living on the Tulalip Reservation when the recording was made. He was, however, originally from the Suquamish people (located on the Kitsap Peninsula). Their most illustrious member was the man Kitsap, whose story is presented here.

Battle at Sea

These were my forebears, these people whom I'm going to tell you about. They were my ancestors. One time they were visited by a large party from Ɂəhiw̓ and elsewhere about the southern reaches of Puget Sound. They addressed my famous forefather.

"We ought to raid those people from up the coast! We should all combine our forces. Let us be the ones to avenge their attacks. If you, esteemed sir, are of like mind, your warriors and ours could go; we could retaliate."

Then the great Kitsap replied, "Yes! I understand. I hear what you worthy leaders are saying. I hear your counsel about raiding those notorious people to the north. They believe they can lord it over all of us with impunity. Not so! We have our own view of things—our own! Whoever thinks to fight us should know that we too can fight.

"If your minds concur in this, then I too will go. I and my warriors will accompany your leaders. If they go, we go. We will go and we will fight."

So they went. They set out. First they went to the Klallam who were invited to join this force. They crossed the Straits of Juan de Fuca. They came to Sooke. The warriors there were also invited to join forces. They were told, "You ought to accompany us. We are going after those arrogant ones who have been raiding us."

Their destination was there—what is called Vancouver today. The Native People's name was different, but I can't call it by its real name because my memory has grown short. It is short. I don't remember things well. And I don't remember the name of that place belonging to those people. But they were the ones to be raided. They were the ones my forefathers were seeking for revenge.

Now it was discovered! It was their own land that was to be raided—not someone else's. But, they too were on their way to perpetrate yet another attack on the Klallam.

The two war parties met each other. The two large groups intent on harming each other met out on the Straits. Those from Vancouver spoke. "Oh, let us not fight. We are too far from our land and you people also are too far from your land. It is better not to do battle here. If you give us a young man, it would be good. Or if it be a woman, we could be the ones to provide a young man for a marriage."

Some of our party replied, "We do not want it that way. We have come for revenge. We will fight you people. If you are good enough to give battle, that is what we should do. We will fight right here on the water—out from shore, here. In our canoes we will fight."

Then the wise Kitsap addressed his people. "Beware! These, our adversaries, are from this region and they are strong at sea. We cannot prevail in a battle with them on the water. And yet, we are the mighty ones with reputations to uphold. We have come to fight. We cannot simply go home without so much as a shot. That would not be good for our name. Therefore, I think that we must engage them in battle for that is what we have come to do."

Those from Vancouver answered. They spoke, "So be it. The heart of the worthy Kitsap is good. We too are willing to join battle. If they fight us, we fight!" Then they fought. The battle began on the water. There they fought. And always the people of ʔəhiw' were overwhelmed. Always they were outmaneuvered. Also their spears were too short. (Sqʷiƛ̕əb is what we call them; "spear" is the whiteman's word for them.) And ours were too short. But those belonging to the warriors from Vancouver were longer. Our spears were inadequate but they used theirs to overturn our canoes. And our warriors drowned.

As for Kitsap, he fought with bow and arrow. Once his arrows were spent, he would go to where the currents eddied in the riptide, and he gathered up the arrows that were floating there. He would grab a lot of arrows drifting there to reuse. He could refill his quiver. Doing this, Kitsap got the better of his foe. The ones from the north could not prevail over him.

He would feign a retreat, and they would come after him. He would pretend to flee and they would give chase. That way he would draw one enemy canoe after another away from the protection of their fellows, and he would pick off the man in the stern of each canoe. And these steersmen, shot by Kitsap's arrows, would roll out of their canoes. Without a man to steer, the canoes would swing broadside. Then Kitsap would pick them off one by one as they sat in their canoes. They would die. Kitsap was slaughtering them. His own people did not die. Those with him survived—all but one.

Only one was shot. He was shot right in the eye, the one in the stern of one of Kitsap's canoes. He grabbed that arrow and pulled it out. With it came his eye. It came out. His name was Təlibut. Təlibut was the name of the man whose eye came out. He was Kitsap's brother. He paddled a couple more strokes, then toppled into the water. But a man sitting near him caught him and pulled him back into the canoe. He didn't have an eye. He was dead. The seating shifted. A new man took the stern. Someone else took the place of Təlibut.

Meanwhile, Kitsap fought on. He was pursued. He would retreat; and they thought he was trying to leave, to retreat. As they would draw near, he would shoot the man in the stern, who would slump down dead and be pushed over the side.

As his arrows were used up, Kitsap would go to the spot where many floated in the tide. He gathered them up and used those enemy arrows to kill them.

Finally, someone among the enemy realized what was happening. He called out. "Kitsap is not really retreating! On the contrary, he wants to be chased. And as for me, I've had it. I'm finished. You should stop too. No one can kill Kitsap. His spirit power is too great. It is ferocious. It is not like that of ordinary men.

"You guys see how he is shot at? He just flips our arrows away. They do not enter his body. Or else it is his hair. It's only his hair. All our arrows just lodge in his hair. He pulls them out and reuses them on us. We're just giving him arrows to kill us with!

"Quit now, you guys. Kitsap has beaten us. Stop now, my people. This battle should end now!"

Then Kitsap stopped too and went home.

I'm finished. This ends my telling.

Notes

1. When making speeches in English, some few people from other Salish tribes still maintain this style of formal speech.—Eds.

Qeyqeyší's Marriage

A Humorous Pend d'Oreille Story

Told by Pete Beaverhead

Edited by Sarah G. Thomason

The story of how Qeyqeyší managed to get married is a comic account of a young man's brashness. Its humorous effect is evident not only in the content and storyteller's style but also in his audience's reaction: their laughter at the high points in the tale sometimes drowns his words. The translation below is inevitably a feeble reflection of the oral version; much of the texture of the story is lost in the switch from Salish to English and from oral performance (as recorded on tape) to the written page. The ideal audience for this story would be able to understand and appreciate the storyteller's words on tape. Providing such an audience is a major goal of the community's ongoing efforts to ensure that current and future generations can learn their ancestors' language. But for those who do not know the language, this translation at least will give a glimpse of the community's traditional oral literature. The story may be true, or it may be fiction, or (probably most likely) it may be a combination of the two. But regardless of its origin, it is a fine example of the storyteller's art, and a fine illustration of a people's good-natured humor.

The story must have been passed down through six or seven generations of storytellers of the Pend d'Oreille people of Montana.

The name Salish[1] is used by some modern tribal members to refer to all three Salishan tribes of Montana: the Bitterroot Salish, the Pend d'Oreilles, and the Kalispels. It is now more common, however, to refer to the (Bitterroot) Salish and the Pend d'Oreilles by their separate names, as reflected in the current name of the tribes' Culture Committee: Salish–Pend d'Oreille Culture Committee.

The Story's Background, Setting, and Characters

St. Ignatius, the site of a handsome mission built in the nineteenth century, lies in the Mission Valley of northwestern Montana, in the heart of the Flathead Reservation. In the main hall of the St. Ignatius Community Center, with painted portraits of Bitterroot Salish and Pend d'Oreille notables on all the walls, tribal elders began gathering in early 1975 to tape-record tribal history, historical tales, and myths. Except for the presence of the tape recorder and the absence of children, the storytelling scene must have been similar to traditional storytelling sessions—a major source of winter entertainment for tribal members from the earliest times.

Pete Beaverhead, who was born in 1899 and died in August 1975, told the story on February 24, 1975. It is on a tape recording among other historical tales, including some from the early reservation period; but this story and the one that follows it on the tape, about the escapades of a wild young man named Qeyqeyší and his equally wild friend One-Night, are set in prereservation days. This is clear from Pete Beaverhead's identification of the Qeyqeyší in the stories as "the father of the one in the picture." Probably he gestured toward the portrait on the wall as he said this. It still hangs in the Community Center's main hall, showing an imposing elderly man with long white hair flowing free around his shoulders.

The Qeyqeyší of the portrait was born about 1837, and he died in 1922; some present-day elders remember him in his last years. He is called Baptiste Ka-ka-she, son of Baptiste (or Tenas) Ka-ka-she, in the allotment records, which list all tribal members to whom eighty acres of reservation land were assigned in about 1905, several years before the rest of the reservation was opened by government decree to white settlement. The elder Qeyqeyší was therefore probably born between 1800 and 1817, though he could have been born well before 1800. Because he was a man of marriageable age at the time the story takes place, and because men usually did not marry until they were at least twenty years old, the story is set sometime before 1837, and quite possibly twenty or more years earlier. (As the story makes clear, the usual economic reasons for waiting till age twenty or so to get married did not apply to Qeyqeyší, so he could have been a bit younger; but this factor would not skew the very rough time estimate seriously.)

The elder Qeyqeyší, then—the Qeyqeyší of the story—was a young man not only before the reservation was established by the Hell Gate Treaty of 1855, but before the Salishan tribes of Montana had had any sustained contact with whites. Indeed, he may have been born before the people (*sqélix^w* "person, Indian") even saw many white men (*suyápi*): the first recorded contact between them and whites was when they provided members of the Lewis and Clark expedition with horses in 1805, although they must have met individual trappers before then. Whites set up trading posts in the region a few years later, but contact between the people and whites was limited until Jesuit missionaries arrived in the region, founding St. Mary's in the Bitterroot Valley in 1841 and the St. Ignatius mission in 1854.

Both the storyteller and the story's main character were Pend d'Oreilles, so Pete Beaverhead presumably heard tales of Qeyqeyší's youthful adventures from Pend d'Oreille elders during his own youth. There is, of course, no reason to suppose that the Qeyqeyší stories record actual events with precise accuracy, but it is at least likely that the young Qeyqeyší of the stories was less dignified than his mature son, the Qeyqeyší of the portrait, who was widely respected as a leader of his people. As a young man, in any case, the elder Qeyqeyší was apparently viewed by his people as irresponsible and unworthy of respect. And even if the stories are wholly fictional, they must at least reflect culturally plausible behavior and events.

The story is set in a camp, most likely a hunting camp on the plains east of the Rocky Mountains. Details of Pend d'Oreille customs are hard to find in early accounts of tribal life; the better-known Bitterroot Salish tribe was most often the subject of descriptions by both travelers and scholars.[2] It is certain, however, that Pend d'Oreilles' daily lives in the first decades of the nineteenth century closely resembled the lives of the Bitterroot Salish people. In spring and early summer the women dug roots and gathered berries while the men fished; family groups camped in separate locations for these activities. Later in the year the entire tribe would move eastward in a body, crossing the Rockies to the plains for the annual buffalo hunt. Because the setting for the Qeyqeyší story is clearly a large tribal encampment, and the tribe is breaking camp and moving on (which they would not be as likely to do if they were at home in what is now known as the Mission Valley), they are probably in the eastern hunting grounds.

The buffalo-hunting expeditions were also military expeditions, because the warlike Blackfeet and other Plains tribes made traveling east of the mountains extremely dangerous. The Salishan peoples had acquired horses earlier than the Blackfeet, certainly before the mid-eighteenth century; but by the late eighteenth century the Blackfeet had horses too, and unlike the Salish they also had firearms before the end of that century. They were therefore militarily dominant until the Salishan tribes received firearms shortly after Lewis and Clark's visit.

The widow who attracts Qeyqeyší's attention in the story belongs to a group that would have been fairly numerous in any Bitterroot Salish or Pend d'Oreille camp of the era: young men, married and otherwise, were frequent casualties in the battles over buffalo-hunting grounds. The emphasis on her horses would also have been a common cultural theme, because horses were wealth—they offered mobility, they enabled men to kill the buffalo that provided hides for tipi covers as well as meat, and in short they gave access to all the necessities and luxuries of life. The people made a distinction between ordinary horses (such as pack horses) and buffalo-hunting horses: the horses ridden to the hunt were by far the most valuable animals.

It is not hard to understand why Qeyqeyší would want to marry the widow; she is very rich, because her husband left her many horses. It is not so easy to understand why she would want to marry someone who is not respected by his tribesmen and who has neither horses nor anything else of value. That, no doubt, is why One-Night laughs so uproariously at the idea of Qeyqeyší's presuming to address this woman, and why Qeyqeyší's own mother assumes that he is lying when he says the woman has agreed to marry him. It is of course possible that Qeyqeyší appealed to her because he was an attractive man, though her own words in the story suggest that that was not a factor in her decision. Another possible motive might come from the fact that a widow's position in the tribe was unenviable. With no man to bring buffalo to her, a widow was forced to follow the men to the hunt; if she were lucky a relative or a friend would kill a buffalo for her, but even then she would have to butcher it and haul it back to camp herself. A rich widow was probably able to get more help, and because this woman was living with her parents she could presumably expect help from them too. Still, having an able-bodied husband meant a much easier life for a woman. She herself declares in the story that, after her husband's death, she decided to marry the first man to come along; and Qeyqeyší is the first man to come along with a marriage proposal.

Qeyqeyší's marriage rites are typical (though there were also other traditional ways of getting married). Early in the morning the crier rides around the camp urging people to get ready to move, and the people take down their tipi poles, catch their horses, load their belongings on their packhorses, and line up to move on to their next camp. The new husband leads a good horse to his bride's tipi for her to ride on, and they set out together, thus announcing their marriage to their fellow tribesmen.

A final small point: when Qeyqeyší finds the widow's tipi all lit up, the light would come from the fire in the center of the floor, below the smoke hole in the top of the structure.

Other details of the story require no background information, because they are universals of the human condition, not features specific to Pend d'Oreille culture.

The Story's Form

Most of the story is told in dialogue, though there are also some narrative passages. The storyteller makes use of variations in loudness, in length, and especially in pitch to highlight parts of his tale; in particular, he uses high pitch for emphasis, and he shifts into falsetto for some of the funniest parts. Most of these variations cannot be represented in the translation without distracting from the story's smooth flow, but lengthened words are sometimes indicated here by multiplying an English letter.

Pete Beaverhead also uses different voices for the various characters: Qeyqeyší speaks in the storyteller's normal voice, neither especially high nor especially low; his friend One-Night has a high and reedy voice, a frivolous voice, in keeping with his character; Qeyqeyší's mother speaks gruffly, sometimes almost in a whisper but always sounding firm and adult; the widow's voice is rather high and loud. Only the widow's parents have indeterminate voices, though they do sound different from the other characters. Unfortunately, the distinctive voice qualities cannot be conveyed directly on paper, so I have been forced to add "he said" and "she said" in some places to identify the speakers. (Some of these indications are already in the Salish text; only a few additions were needed.)

Otherwise, the translation is as close to the original as possible—which does not mean a literal translation, but rather a free English version that is meant to preserve the lighthearted spirit of the original Salish. The translation has two sources. First, I have used the translation that was prepared for the Culture Committee by tribal elder Dolly Linsebigler some years ago, adopting her phrasing in many instances. In addition, I transcribed and translated the tape with the help of Culture Committee members in the early 1980s, and those word-by-word translations have filled in a few gaps and provided a more precise rendering of some parts of the story.

Because Clarence Woodcock, late director of the Culture Committee, graciously gave me a copy of the original tape years ago, I have been able to follow Pete Beaverhead's lead in organizing the text of the story. To some extent the switches from speaker to speaker, and from narration to speech and back, impose their own patterning on the text. Further patterns also emerge, however, and I have therefore divided the story into lines for this translation. The organization below is based primarily on pause phrasing (as discussed, for instance, in Tedlock 1972, 1983) and secondarily on prosodic phrasing. Pauses are the main cue for a transition between lines. I have started a new line after each of the storyteller's pauses, except in a few instances where he was clearly searching for a word or where he was correcting a mistake, such as starting to say one name and then switching to another. At some important transitions he gives a cough, apparently not a throat-clearing cough but rather a cough meant to emphasize a break in the story. At the risk of distracting the reader from the progression of the story, I have indicated these emphatic coughs by an italicized *hm*.

Prosodic phrasing is important for dividing lines in cases where the story-teller does not pause at an obvious transition point—obvious because of the sentence structure and a dramatic change in pitch, from low to very high or from high to very low. In some cases these are transitions between speakers or between narration and a speaker, as when the narrative sentence "He said to his friend One-Night" is followed immediately by "I'm going to tell you something, so listen!" spoken in a high emphatic voice.

Syntactic constituency and speakers' turn-taking generally coincide with prosodic phrasing in the story, making line boundaries easier to find. There are some exceptions, among them very short acknowledgments by one speaker of something just said by another; for example, Qeyqeyší's announcement "I'm going to tell you something, so listen!" followed by One-Night's laconic response "Ah." I've put such responses in the same line as the statements that motivated them. In a very few instances it was necessary to place a line break because of English sentence structure, a break that would not appear in the Salish text.

The story has some instances of syntactic parallelism, but not many, and I have found no clear groups of lines that might reflect underlying rhetorical form of the type described by Hymes (e.g., 1981) for texts in some other Native American languages. This does not, of course, mean that such patterns do not exist in the Qeyqeyší story; but if they do exist, they do not leap out at the observer, or at least not at this observer. The "paragraphs" I've set up are therefore groups of lines separated by major breaks. Some of these are prosodic breaks marked by extra-long pauses and some are discourse breaks marked by a change in topic, a change between narration and speaker, or a change from speaker to speaker.

Qeyqeyší's Marriage

One day, towards evening,
two young men were lying around.
One was Qeyqeyší—the father of the man in the picture there—
and the other was his friend One-Night.

Qeyqeyší said to his friend One-Night,
"I'm going to tell you something, so listen!" "Ah."

These young men were always laughed at, they did crazy things,
and their fellow tribesmen didn't like them at all.
Qeyqeyší said,
"In the morning I'm going to get a wife."
"Ah! Ah! So you're going to get a wife, my friend?" "Yes."

There was a woman, she still had her father and mother,
her husband had been killed in a battle the year before.
He had owned lots of horses,
he had a tipi, and he had everything,
packhorses, who knows how many horses.
When the people would move camp, she'd go along herding her horses.

Qeyqeyší named this woman and said, "That's the one,
the woman whose husband got killed,
that's the one I'm going to marry."

One-Night laid back—
"Ah, ha! Ha! HA! HA HA HA HA HA HA!
HA HA HA HA HA!
So you think this woman is saying,
'Oh boy, I'm going to be Qeyqeyší's wife!'?
You sure have a lot of nerve to think that.
HA, HA, HA!
Say, do you think she'd have anything to do with ME?
Haaaaaaa!"

Qeyqeyší's mother was sitting there looking at them.
"What are you two up to?"
One-Night said,
"You're going to get a daughter-in-law, your Qeyqeyší is going to get a
wife. Haaaa!"

"Mmmmm my little son, you must be lying."

He didn't say a word, he just sat there.
One-Night laughed and laughed and wouldn't quit.
Hm!

Qeyqeyší got up and went out and walked around the camp.
"When my friend stops laughing, I'll go home and go back in."
Hm.

Aaaah. So he walked around the camp,
and here he was before those people's tipi, and it was all lit up.

When he said he was going to get married
he was lying to his friend, it wasn't true.
Now he got there and stood a while, watching.
"Okay, I'm going to go in and propose."

He went into their tipi and they were all sitting there,
the woman was there,
and her father was there, and her mother too.

Her father said,
"Well, come in, sit down over there."
So he sat down.
"All right, come on now, what are you doing here?
You never came into my tipi before, but tonight you've come in.
You must have something on your mind."

"Yes. You'll find out, don't be in such a hurry.

It's your daughter I've come for.
You're going to give her to me for my wife.

You know me very well."

The three of them sat there real quiet for a long time.

Finally the mother said to her husband,

"Ehhhh,
Say something, be sociable, don't just sit there!"

He said,
"Hm.
It's not ME he's proposing to, it's our daughter, he's come for her,
not me.
YOU think of something to say to him, you should be able to think of
something."

The woman sat there a while and then said,
"Why talk to us when you should be asking her?
Ask her—after all, you came to propose."
Hm.

He said, "Yes,
you, woman, you already understand.
You saw me come in just now.
I don't have anything at my mother's.
I had everything I own with me when I came in—
all I have is my moccasins and my leggings and my shirt.

Don't go thinking
that I have anything of value,
that I have horses for you to ride on,
even though a man is supposed to bring one for his bride
when he gets married."

She sat there for awhile and then told him, "Well.
Here's what I said after my husband died.
I said, if I'm sitting here
and a man comes into our tipi to propose,
even if he's poor,
even if he's a good-for-nothing,
even if he's a laughingstock,
I'll take him.
So okay.

Remember, when we break camp in the morning, that's when the people
get married.
So tomorrow morning
we'll get married, and a-a-a-all
the people will see us."

Qeyqeyší said, "Okay, thanks."
He got up and walked out.

He went home and walked in with a bi-i-i-ig smile on his face.

One-Night asked him,
"Have you been visiting your wife-to-be?!"

Qeyqeyší didn't tell him he had just got through asking her.

"Have you been visiting your wife-to-be?"
"Yes." "Ah!
So why did you come back here?
You should have stayed there."

"No. You know our people's ways.
When we move, that's when we'll get married."

His mother said to him, "Ehhhhh!
You have a nerve—-
you mean to say that you went proposing!
Nooooo!
Pitiful!"
Hm.

"NO, she accepted me already,
and I'm not going to back out now."

She said,
"Well, okay."
His mother had a real nice horse,
a good buffalo-hunting horse.

She told him, "In the morning
you can lead him for your bride to ride on,
if you're telling the truth and not lying."
Hm.

So in the morning the crier got on his horse and trotted around the camp
telling everyone, "Come on! Get ready, we're going to move!"
Hm.

Qeyqeyši led the fine bay horse.
He walked around the camp,
And as he walked around the camp,
everyone was watching.

"Hey look, Qeyqeyší's going to get a wife, wonder who it is!
Watch him so we'll know."

So-o-o-o they had already taken down their tipi poles,
they were packed and ready to move.
The woman told Qeyqeyší,
"Here's my saddle,"
and Qeyqeyší put it on the horse.

The people were already lined up and moving out of camp.
Hm.

She said to Qeyqeyší,
"Pick out a horse to ride on from these here,
they're all the same,
they're walking along and not in use, they're all tame."
Ah. So they both got on their horses.

The people who were moving lined up and then walked alongside of
them.
Qeyqeyší glanced back at his friend.

"Hey, my friend really did get a wife!"
He went up to Qeyqeyší and said, "Here, give me your hand.

Friend, how did you do it, how did you manage to get a wife?!
I ne-e-e-e-ver thought that woman would tell you,
'Okay, let's get married!'"

And that's the end of the story about Qeyqeyší and One-Night.

Notes

I am very grateful to the Flathead Culture Committee for giving me permission, in June 1995, to edit this story for publication in this volume. I also owe a great debt of gratitude to the late Clarence Woodcock, the former director of the Culture Committee, to Tony Incashola, the present director, and to Bitterroot Salish and Pend d'Oreille elders and members of the Culture Committee for offering me the opportunity to work with them on Salish language materials over the past twenty years. It was Clarence Woodcock who first gave me a copy of the tape that contains Pete Beaverhead's Qeyqeyší stories, and he and Lucy Vanderburg helped me transcribe the Salish text.

1. The Salish group in Montana was probably the first group in the Salishan family to be encountered by early white explorers coming from the east; thus the name was used in English to refer to many of the groups west of there.—Eds.

2. The information in the following paragraphs is drawn—with due caution, relying mainly on converging independent accounts—from a variety of sources, but especially Teit (1927–28), Flathead Culture Committee (1979), Turney-High (1937), Malan (1948), and Ronan (1890).

Sametl

A Chinook Jargon Rendering of a Saanich Story

Told by Thomas Paul

Edited by Dell Hymes

In the nineteenth century the Chinook Jargon spread widely in western North America, from northern California to Alaska, as a lingua franca among Indians and whites, and among Indians of different languages as well. A good many stories evidently were transmitted by means of it. The story that follows was recorded near Victoria, British Columbia, in May 1930 by Melville Jacobs (1936:21–23). The narrator was Thomas Paul, a Saanich Coast Salish past middle age. The territory of the Saanich is north of Victoria, as is Mill Bay, the place where the wolf cubs in the story were captured.

The pattern number of the Saanich is four, and texts from older speakers today show two- and four-part patterns (Montler 1986, personal communication; cf. Hymes 1990:73, 75). So does Mr. Paul's account of Sametl. Both the substance and the form of the story thus have traditional roots.

A detailed account of the text and its translation is given in Hymes (1990). Note the frequent occurrence of the Jargon equivalent of "Well" at the beginning of groups of lines, and of "and" at the beginning of verses within groups. The four- and two-part relations commonly convey an implicit sense of "this, then that," of initiation and outcome. (Lines with "enough," Jargon *kabit*, stand outside the four-part relations).

Most of the story is taken up with preparation and patterns of movement (departure, travel, arrival, what is seen). Such preparation, ritual-like, fits securing a relation with a source of good. Taking the two cubs brings that source near. Decorating the cubs with cedar bark (a part of regalia in dances of the sacred winter season) honors them and their parent. So doing, Sametl uses his rapidity to initiate reciprocity with Wolf, who will provide him with deer.

Sametl

I. SAMETL PREPARES |

He was a powerful man long ago.   i. |
    NO WAY at all they could beat him.

REALLY knew how to go fast.
He would come to this side,
come to some one village,
want to fight,
mean.
And people come together:
"Good we hurry to that man's house.
And then we fight his people."

And the people hurry,
two canoes go back,
full of people.
And they hurry,
go to the other side,
not far from shore:
Sametl is waiting.

Like that enough.

Sametl saw a small wolf
and he thought,
he would get that small wolf.
And Sametl ran on home,
he went to his house.
And he fixed his house well,
he made his house strong.
Well, enough like that.

He took a small canoe,
ran to his canoe,
and waiting in the canoe was his paddle.
He hurried to Mill Bay,
and he reached Mill Bay.
And he saw the water,
it would run (out).
And he stayed waiting for that tide,
it would go (out), that tide.

ii. |

Well, that water went (out) now.   iii. |
And he hauled out his canoe.
And Sametl jumped.
And he went too far across.

Well, in a little while, he hauled it out a little.   iv. |
    He jumped again.
He again hauled it out
He again hauled it out,
    he jumped again;
And he got straight to his canoe.

And he took his stick (pike pole),
    he stood his stick (in the water),
        he made the stick stay.
And Sametl took rope,
    he tied it to the stick like that.

And he ran,
    went ashore.
And he waited,
    the tide would come.

He STAYED,
    I don't know how long.
The water came,
    full now.

II. SAMETL SUCCEEDS |

Well, Sametl ran,
    went toward the wolf,
        to where that wolf stayed.
And he arrived,
And he stood,
And he saw two small wolves.

And he went,

he walked slowly.
And he took the two small wolves.
And he took (them),
And one in the right (arm),
    and one in the left (arm).

Well, he ran now,
    he ran hard.
(Once) he could get to the beach,
     now he jumped.
He got to his canoe,
    he took that rope,
And he paddled,
    he paddled hard.

Ran to his home;
    (once) he could get to his house—
        he brought back those two small wolves—
           he ran into his house.
He just got inside,
    he made shut the door.

Now the big wolf came to his house.
And the wolf was mean,
    he ate up (everything) around the house.

Well, Sametl thought   vii. |
    he should get cedar bark;
        RIGHT AWAY he fixed that cedar bark just right.
And Sametl tied it on the arms, that small wolf,
    here on the arms and here,
        left and right,
            he tied again.
And on its legs,
    two legs he tied to the cedar bark.
And he tied it on his chest crossways.

And again he did it crossways.
He finished one.
	He took (the other) one.
He again did it that way.
	He could finish doing it that way.
And took back outside those two small wolves,
	he went back outside.
Enough.

The wolf took [accepted] his small ones completely.	viii. |
The wolf took his small ones back home.

The wolf (was) a true friend to Sametl.
The wolf sometimes gave deer to Sametl,
	good friends now.

That's enough.

Chairman Roy Wilson's Cowlitz Desanctification Ceremony

Edited by Judith Irwin

Heading east into the Cascade Mountains on June 21, 1981, three men and three women, including me, left our cars near southwest Washington's Highway 12. It was Sunday and drizzling a little as we trekked down the muddy logging road. The ceremonial site lay near a narrow neck of fast water on the Cowlitz, a river that drained much of the south side of Mount Rainier (called "Tacoma" by most Indians). Snowmelt, pummeling boulders in that rushing two-mile stretch of falls, had hammered out footholds where generations of Cowlitz fished. That narrow passage had been selected by a hydroelectric company as the ideal place for the construction of its next dam.

Earlier, still federally unacknowledged, the Cowlitz Tribe had been unable legally to stop this new affront to its fishing and sacred burial grounds near their ancient village Koapk.[1] Here salmon and steelhead (an ocean-going rainbow trout) paused in the quieter pools before leaping over the huge boulders and ledges that separated them from their upstream spawning grounds. Eels, another valued food resource, clung to the boulders. At the Cowlitz Falls, the Cowlitz people and their relatives from both sides of the Cascade Mountains gathered annually to fish for winter provisions. In the 1920s, without authorization, some non-Indians had desecrated the area by blasting out sections of the Falls.

Difficult to access, these Falls were special. To avoid another desecration of sacred tribal ground, the Cowlitz tribal chairman, Roy Wilson—a descendant of the historical Cowlitz Chief Kishkok—led our party of six toward the area to be desanctified.

Having previously been on eight vision quests, Roy Wilson explained that to receive the spirit guidance he needed for this ceremony, he had gone again into the high mountains to fast and pray for four days and nights. "Chief Kishkok, my ancestor, came and taught me the ceremony with its prayers and song," he said.

To prepare the ground for this day's desanctification ceremony, he had come into the forest one week earlier to mark the boundary for "this very important ceremony for our people and our ancestors." Then he had fasted for the rest of the week. The fasting was to cleanse his body and sanctify it. Meditation cleansed the spirit. The purpose of the desanctification ceremony was to desanctify or purify the sacred ground before the earth-gouging machines tore up the site of a tribal village and sacred burial grounds. It is an aboriginal belief, he said, that "spirits are still in the area, thus, we cleanse the area before they [the dam builders] arrive." He added that later, with a different ceremony, the spirits would be invited to return

One of the men carried Roy Wilson's big drum. The rain had stopped. The air was moist and fresh. Beside the road, alder competed with spruce and big-leafed maple. Underneath, among luxuriant ferns, bleeding hearts and slender therofon bloomed.

The heavy rains had drilled and filled a stream that tumbled across our rocky road. Clambering over logs, all of us crossed the stream except Leslie, Roy's wife, who wore a white ceremonial buckskin dress and shawl. Roy took her up piggy-back and, taking care with his footing on the stream's tumbling rocks, carried her safely over.

At a smoother and less wooded area, Roy spotted one of the cedar boughs with which he had earlier marked the ceremonial ground. He explained that he had gently cut off the short cedar bough, praying to the tree's spirit for forgiveness for taking a portion of its life. He said, "I told it that I needed its help in this very important sacred ceremony for our people and our ancestors."

Pointing out the other three cedar markers, he indicated the limits of the ceremonial circle. He explained the symbolism of each marker. "As we look to the north," he said, "I'm addressing the Spirit of the North, the Spirit of Wisdom, and the Spirit of the Earth, Mother Earth, from which comes all life. The red arrow points to the north.[2]

"As we look to the east we see the Spirit of the East, the Spirit of Innocence, for that is where the sun arises. This is represented by the yellow arrow.

"As we look to the south, we see the sun at its apex. The hunter seeks the Spirit of the South, for then he can see for great distances, and the prophet, who sees ahead, also seeks the Spirit of the South. Here points the white arrow.

"As we look to the west, we look within, to the Spirit of Meditation. It is the end of the day, and the arrow is black.

"By addressing the four spirits, we ask the guardian spirits watching over the area to leave the area. At the close of the day, they leave the ground free so there will be no molestation. Others have dug into village sites without ceremony and it brings bad *tomanawas* (spirit power).[3]

"The cedar," he explained, "is at the heart of our culture. Mother Earth gave us cedar to split into great planks so that we would not have to live in tipis but could live in houses, and so that we could hollow out cedar logs for canoes to travel in, and also so we could have water-resistant clothes. By pounding the inner bark we made clothing. From the boughs we made rope and nets. From the bark and roots we made baskets so watertight that we could bring water and cook in them. Cedar is sacred to our people. I use the fresh cedar bough to cleanse the area of spirits in the desanctification ceremony.

"At the very end of the ceremony," he added, "because we Cowlitz are aware of our cross-culturalization with the white people and for the sake of our Christian Cowlitz people, I will end with the Lord's Prayer in Indian sign language."

Roy then took a position in the center of the ceremonial circle. We observers each moved carefully to place ourselves outside the sacred circle so as not to profane the ceremony. Lifting his eyes to the tops of the trees and to the sky he began a soft drumming. After two loud pounds, he sang to the Spirit of the North.

Thus announced, he began the desanctification rite during which he swept the ground in front of him with the cedar bough as he moved. In front of the tree on the north, he held the bough before him in both hands as if to consecrate the tree. Raising his right hand toward the tree, he addressed the spirits of ancestors in the north. Then he slowly stepped backward from the tree to the center of the circle again.

Repeating this ceremony in each direction, he finally laid the cedar bough upon the ground in the center of the circle, where it remained.

Again, he beat the drum and sang. He concluded with the Lord's Prayer in Indian sign language. Raising his arms toward heaven, pounding one fist into the open palm of his other hand, circling and bending with his body, arms, and hands, he enacted the meaning of the words.

Klatawa sahale, he said at last. The ceremony was completed, and Roy Wilson stepped to where his wife was standing.

He explained, "When I said 'klatawa sahale,' I was telling the spirits to go." He told how, when he was a youngster and liked to be near his father, to watch what he was doing, his father would tell him, "klatawa!" That meant Roy should move back to arm's length. By drawing out the syllables, his father meant Roy should move farther away but still be where he could see. However, if his father also emphasized the syllables, it meant that Roy should now go somewhere else. "So," said Roy, "I told the good spirits to go somewhere a way off, but not too far away."

The ceremony completed, the six of us moved to go "somewhere else"— back to our cars. As we left the site, the rain came down like pellets. Roy said he had made a prayer on the way to the site that the rain might stop during the ceremony. Up the hill, we moved through rain-soaked underbrush.

At hilltop and under the protection of our parked cars, we broke our fasts with fresh strawberries and cantaloupe, cheese and crackers.

Many months later, Roy Wilson sent out an invitation to the Cowlitz people to join him on another trek—this time to reconsecrate the ceremonial site and invite the good spirits' return.

Notes

Judith Irwin is an honorary member of the Cowlitz Tribe.

1. On Valentine's Day in the year 2000, the Cowlitz Indian Tribe was finally granted federal acknowledgment.

2. Other Indian tribes may give different symbols import to the directions and to the colors representing them.

3. The Indian words in this story are Chinook Jargon, which many people still understand into the twenty-first century.—Eds.

Three Lillooet Stories

Told by Sam Mitchell, Martina LaRochelle, Rosie Joseph

Edited by Jan P. van Eijk

The Lillooet[1] inhabit an area 160 to 300 kilometers (100 to 185 miles) northeast of Vancouver, an area they have called their homeland for an untold number of centuries. It is a strikingly beautiful piece of earth—with soaring mountains, wide lakes, dense forests, and fast-flowing rivers—that has provided the Lillooet with ample sustenance during their wise and respectful occupation of this land and has also provided the setting for their magnificent oral literature.

The first story, "The Swimmer," told by the unforgettable Sam Mitchell, shows the importance of tobacco in the traditional Lillooet culture. Of course, this was original tobacco, possibly enriched with kinnikinnick, and not the nontraditional, store-bought variety. Anyone who has ever seen the churning hell that the Fraser River turns into each spring cannot help but marvel at the main character's desire for tobacco that compels him to swim the Fraser at its most dangerous time.

The second story, "The Smallpox," told by Martina LaRochelle, deals with the cataclysmic epidemic that ravaged the Lillooet community, together with many other Indian communities. No rendition on paper, either in the Lillooet original or in English translation, can do justice to the sweep and drama with which Martina tells this harrowing tale, her voice a sequence of beautifully controlled cadenzas, rising and falling with each stage in the story.

Finally, Rosie Joseph weighs in with her delightful anecdote about how she and her cousin Tom were chastised for misbehaving at the dinner table. Typically, this story combines amusement with a moral lesson: good manners and proper behavior are of the highest importance to traditional Native elders, and anyone who violates the code is corrected in a gentle but firm manner. (Note that in this story even Rosie's uncle is not above the law, so he manages to stifle his laughter in order not to be punished by Rosie's grandfather.)

These stories were originally tape-recorded in Lillooet and then transcribed and translated into English by me, and the transcriptions and translations checked with the storytellers. Of "The Swimmer" there is also an English version by Sam Mitchell, far better than the one I give here. However, I have opted for my version because it is a literal translation of the Lillooet original and as such would allow students of the language easier access to the Lillooet text. The transcription used in the above examples is the practical one, in use since 1974 by the Mount Currie Community School and now also by the Upper St'át'imc Language, Culture, and Education Society. The Lillooet originals of these stories and their English translations, together with a number of other Lillooet texts, are available in Van Eijk and Williams (1981).

Well then, the white man has spoken far too long (as is his wont), and it is time to yield the floor to my Lillooet teachers who will instruct, enlighten, and amuse the reader in their customary way.

The Swimmer

He was over there, and he caught sight of some people fishing on the other side, they were having a smoke. So he hollered over (this Fraser River is pretty wide in summer, when there is lots of water), he hollered over to his friends, and he said: "Put out that pipe, you guys, I am going to get a few puffs."[2]

So he took off upstream along the Fraser. He got to a certain spot upstream and he took off his pants and everything else that he was wearing. He wasn't wearing too many clothes at that time, I guess. Next, he tied his clothes to his head.

Then he swam off, he got ashore, and he put his pants back on. He got to the place where they were fishing, and he had a few puffs there. He had just a few puffs of the tobacco, and then he went back again. He swam off, and he went back to his house.

That was Ntsaqwemlha7, that's his Indian name.

The Smallpox

The underground house over there, there was this one group of people living over there. This one group of people was living over there. That is where they were, there were many of them it seems.

So they were living there, and then one man set out from there, from the underground house. He set out from there, he went down, and he carried on until he almost got to the brow of the hill, there at Lillooet, what is Lillooet now. So he got to the brow of the hill. There was a pair of long johns lying there, a pair of underpants. He saw them, and he picked them up, they were good!

So he thought: *I'll take these home to the underground house*. So he took those long johns to bring them to the underground house, to his children and his relatives. So he took off again and he went down.

While he was going along he met somebody, whoever it was that he met, and he said: "Hey, I found a pair of long johns here. So I took them, and I am taking them home." So they were talking there, but they didn't know who had thrown them away, whether it was a white man or whoever. Well, a couple of days went by, and then one of them fell ill. The one who had thrown away the long johns must have been sick. That is what the white people call "smallpox." So we Indians call it the same, we say "smallpox."

Anyhow, that one person got sick in a few days. They didn't know any medicine for it. They didn't know what was the matter with him, he was just sick. And then he died.

A few days went by, and then another one got sick. The same thing happened, he died. And so they went, one after the other.

The people from T'it'q̓et heard about it. There were a number of them living in another underground house, and they heard about it. "They say that those people down there are all dying."

So one of them came over to the underground house to have a peek: the sick were just lying around, they did not have any strength left. Then he got scared, the one who had come to the underground house to have a peek. He did not want to go inside, because some of the people in that house were dead already.

So he went back home again, to T'it'q̓et, and he told his relatives there at T'it'q̓et: "Say, those people down below are having a hard time. They are sick, whatever their sickness is." My, then they talked about those sick people there.

A few more days went by. The one who had come before to take a peek came again. Everybody in that house already was dead. There only was a child of about two years left. It was just tottering about. Its mother already was dead. It must have been hungry, that little boy or girl. It must have been hungry, because it went and grabbed its mother's breasts and sucked at them, but its mother already was dead.

The one who had taken a peek before came again, but the child wasn't around anymore. It must have died already.

So they caved in that underground house. They did not dig out the people. So that is when the underground house got caved in. The bones and everything else that used to be there in the underground house must be still there. The underground house is still there.

This story was told by Harry Carey's wife. It is a story she told to the people. It seems it was a white person who told it. That was the first half-breed woman here in Lillooet, Harry Carey's wife. However, I have forgotten her name.

That is what my mother told me when I was a child.

That is the end of my story.[3]

Cousin Tom and Rosie

One time my cousin Tom came and visited us. We were children of the same age and size. He came to play with me, so we played.

An it not evening we told him: "You'd better stay, we are going to eat soon." So he stayed and we sat down at the table. When we were about to eat, the pup of our next-door neighbors barked. His name was Wepel'qen.

So he barked, and he said: "Woop."[4] Thomas looked me in the face and he started to giggle, so I giggled too. There he was, he didn't want to laugh, yet he kept on eating.

He was doing that, and then he suddenly squirted out his food.

He couldn't stop laughing, and it didn't take long before I squirted out my food too, and we both got carried away laughing.

One way or another my grandfather got mad, so he made us go outside, and he told us: "Go outside and laugh there!" So we went outside. Well, there we stood. We couldn't laugh, so we went inside again.

We were just about to eat again, when Thomas burst out laughing like before. I burst out laughing too, so right away we were told to go outside again.

The same thing happened to us as before, we just couldn't laugh while we were outside.

After a while we went inside again, and we started to eat once more. I did not want to look my cousin in the face, because I didn't want to be thrown out again. I looked at my grandmother and my grandfather, but they just kept on eating. My uncle was there too, and I looked him in the face. I knew that he was about to laugh too, but he kept on eating, he wouldn't laugh.

That is a funny thing that happened to me and Tom, my cousin.

That's all.

Notes

1. In recent literature, the label *Lillooet* is consistently replaced with *St'át'imc* (for the people) and *St'át'imcets* (for their language). Although *St'át'imc* originally only refers to the northern bands, it now seems to have been adopted as an overall designation for all Lillooet-speaking bands.

2. That this event happened many years ago is illustrated by the fact that the fishermen are not smoking cigarettes or cigars, but are sharing a single old-style pipe.

3. The above translation omits a brief segment where Martina tries to guess the date of the event by referring to the year rings on the stump of a tree that grew on the spot of the underground house and was later chopped down. From the way the story is told it seems more an aside than an integral part of the story.

4. The name of the pup translates as "hairy head." What causes the children to have so much fun is the fact that his bark, "Woop," sounds like the first part of his name.

Reminiscences from the Shuswap

Told by Lilly Harry

Edited by Aert H. Kuipers

The texts that follow were recorded with Mrs. Lilly Harry of Dog Creek, British Columbia, after the publication of *A Report on Shuswap* (Kuipers 1989), which contains four texts also told by her. Lilly Harry was one of the most knowledgeable speakers of Shuswap I have met, which is why I paid another visit to Dog Creek in the early 1990s. Mrs. Mary Palmantier, also of Dog Creek, as usual assisted in transcribing the material. Both Lilly and Mary have passed away since then.

Tanning Hides

How did the people of old times treat hides? The old people shore off the hair, and when they had finished shearing off the hide they took it and put it in water; they put it in water for a long time, took it out, put it on a scraping rack and scraped it. The shinbone of a deer, that was the scraping tool; there was no iron. They scraped it. After scraping it they washed the hide, removed the blood from it. Washed it thoroughly. They took (animal) brains and boiled them. They twisted the hide, and when they had finished twisting it, they pulled and pulled it (to stretch it) and then took it and put it in that brain extract.

Then they put it down. It was probably a *mim'x*-basket they put things to soak in. Then they went and took it out of the brain extract, took it and twisted it, scraped it on a rack. After scraping it, they softened it by poking it with a tanning stick for a long time, and when the stretched hide was dry they took it off (the rack).

They gathered a lot of pinecones and smoked the skin until it was ready. If you want the skin to be yellow, it will be yellow; if you want it to be red, you take an alder tree, cut off a branch. You boil it together with the brains into which you put the skin, then the skin will be red, not yellow. It is the alder that produces the red color.

Getting Rid of Gall

If you want to vomit, if you are in training and you haven't eaten for a long time, then the gall, if you have gall and you want to get rid of it, then to throw it up you must carefully prepare two branches of the red willow. They shouldn't go just here (showing) but here, halfway down your throat, and the gall will start to emerge and come out. You'll throw it up until there is none left, then you'll drink some lukewarm water, do it once more; twice you do it, and that'll be enough. Then it's enough, wherever that stuff (gall) is produced. It arises here somewhere (pointing), this particular type of sickness.

Just look at some of those people, their flesh all yellow; it'll be yellow, the doctor cannot find (the cause of) a person's disease. He is giving them medicines, but without effect. And if you don't want that red willow for making you vomit, then you get some pitch of the white poplar, that you can chew at any time.

Look at Tswinek at Alkali Lake, she no longer spits gall. We were walking along the road—retch, retch, retch. I said to her: "What are you spitting out?"—"Oh," she said, "gall." I told (grandson) Larry: "Collect some for her so I can cure her." He gathered her just a handful, I gave it to her and told her: "In your daily round always have this with you like chewing tobacco, and swallow (the juice). When it loses its taste, then spit it out and put some more in your mouth. The source (of the gall) will then dry up."

I say to her when I see her now: "Are you spitting gall?" "No, that's finished," she said, "I've used it all up," she said, "I'll get some more," she said, "it's all gone," she said, "there is none left." See how fat she is!

Steam-Cooking

Fresh swamp hay is what they put the lichen on, but the balsam root is different, they (both) were steam cooked. The swamp hay was cut from the water, the green swamp hay there, it was put down for the lichen to be put on top, swamp hay is what you work with (use) for lichen.

The lichen is (used) just by itself, it doesn't have a companion (another ingredient); if you put anything in, it'll never turn out. It'll be messed up (lit. unraveled) like a person's hair, why I don't know. (If) it doesn't get cooked (done), it becomes kind of tough. You see, if you put it in a pot, if there it doesn't get cooked you fix it and give it some more water and let it boil. Before long, if you look at (check) it, it'll have the appearance of chewing tobacco. But if you prepare it in a cooking pit then it won't pack (lit. it will fly apart) if you mix in cactus or anything. Cactus goes with balsam root.

And the wild onion is likewise (used) by itself, nothing is mixed in. You might steam cook it sometime when you are hungry.

When you are digging for balsam root when you are root digging, if there are children around they collect them for you and make you a big pile of them where you are digging. You'll go there in the evening, you beat (the dirt) off them, you take off the hard-cover-like stuff (*speaker searches for the word "[outer?] bark of root," see end of sentence*), you take a long time taking off the what-do-you-call-it, you do all of it and you collect the balsam root bark. And the balsam root itself you put down where you have made your preparations and arranged the stones on which you are going to steam cook them, all is in readiness.

You light a fire at the bottom (of the cooking pit), it will flame up like a sweatbath until it's all gone and the stones collapse. You get some earth, you put it on and cover those stones well. You get some pitchwood and chop it up, you put a piece here and a piece there, that's what you do with it. When all that is done you spread on the balsam root bark and you sprinkle it. You take the top of a jackpine, one piece, and you put it on there. You get those flowers that grow there, you pick a lot of them and you pile them up on top. You leave those as your covering, and that's how you finish it.

You take old pine boughs, you cut down an old tree and break off the branches, you arrange those nicely in there, and finally you take the balsam root and pile it on. It doesn't matter how many sacks of balsam root you prepare, the balsam root doesn't care when it is in a good mood. You take cactus, a few containers full of cactus you have collected, you put those in, you'll have prepared a place for them. You then take the pine boughs and spread them on there, arranging them well so that no earth will get in. Finally you take the jackpine and put that on, too, you take the pitchwood and do likewise with it. A lot of stuff goes in there before it is covered with earth.

Incident with a Lynx

Our grandmother, she was coming from the snow mountains hauling a deer. She came down and saw an elk. They were there with three sisters. They were hauling a deer from a long way up there, for their food in the snow season. There was an elk lying there. My grandmother said: "It must have been a lynx that killed that one lying there. Let's take it, it's good, it's not damaged, it has just taken it by the throat and bitten it, it's still warm." So they skinned it, and as they were skinning it some acorns fell and hit the ground. They became aware that something was the matter; the lynx was getting ready to jump at (the women) skinning there. Then my grandmother said: "Get out of the way! It's getting ready to spring!" And then they saw it, too. They ran away there. They had wanted to steal food, they had wanted to rob the hunter of his kill, but it was they that ran off from there.

When the Animals Were People

Lady Louse

A Traditional Northern Lushootseed Story

Told by Vi Taqʷšəblu Hilbert, based on Elizabeth Krise's version of the story

Edited by Vi Taqʷšəblu Hilbert

When Thom Hess did fieldwork on the Lushootseed language at the Tulalip Reservation, Elizabeth Krise told him a ten-line story called "Lady Louse." This little story was told by many different storytellers in many languages spoken in this area.

When I began teaching Lushootseed at the University of Washington, people expected me to be a storyteller. I began to tell this little ten-line story to introduce our language to the general public[1] and to give them an example of important lessons left for us by our ancestors.

Lady Louse

Lady Louse lived there
She lived in a great big house
All alone—*all by herself*
She had no friends or relatives
So, she took it
And, she swept it
This great big house
When she got to the very middle of it
She got lost
And that was the end of Lady Louse.

And how could this simple little story teach us anything? Our culture demands cleanliness in all areas—physical, mental. Our culture values family. No one is ever left alone.

So she took it and she swept it—*Swept what?*

The First People taught through metaphor and symbolism. Here they present a beautiful lesson in a philosophical package called Lady Louse. Because I was taught never to insult the intelligence of the listener, it has never been my practice to tell an audience what this story means. They tell me! Hundreds have told me what the story means to them. They have then been given the assignment of creating an original story portraying a Lady Louse that presents herself from their philosophy.

Notes

1. Vi Taqʷšəblu Hilbert became internationally famous as a storyteller, telling stories in Lushootseed (Skagit) and English, using a very effective technique. She said a sentence first in Lushootseed, with a seamless transition to the same sentence in English, then back to Lushootseed, somehow giving her English-speaking audience the illusion they were really understanding Lushootseed. She always said her language was so beautiful she wanted others to share it.—Eds.

Black Bear and Grizzly Bear

A Traditional Upriver Halkomelem Story

Told by Dan Milo

Edited by Ralph Maud

The following "Adam and Eve" story was obtained in July 1964, from Dan Milo of Scowkale, Chilliwack, British Columbia, by Oliver Wells, a third-generation pioneer farmer of nearby Edenbank Farm, who had decided to tape-record some of the elders he had known all his life. He was a sincere man, trusted for an understanding arising from a shared knowledge of trails and animals, the annual cycle of plowing, and salmon runs. The nonprofessional but authentic ethnology that resulted from Oliver Wells's efforts can be seen in his book (Wells 1987:89–90), published posthumously. Born on October 10, 1867, Dan Milo was the oldest person interviewed; he was also, as the tapes testify, a born storyteller.

The story chosen from his repertoire is a classic of the area. Franz Boas got the essential element of it when he stopped briefly in Lytton, British Columbia, in 1888. The Transformer once met "a man who lived all by himself," his anonymous informant told him. "So he changed a cottonwood tree and a birch tree into women and gave them to him" (Boas 1895b). If Boas had had time to look around for the local Homer, as Charles Hill-Tout did about seven years later, he could have obtained from Chief Mischelle the very full version found in Maud 1978, 1:21–39, which includes all the myth elements that Dan Milo remembers and a few that have faded with time.

Hill-Tout called it the Oannes legend of the Salish people, referring to the god who came out of the sea to give the Sumerians their skills and mores—a sort of Prometheus. The Salish epic Transformers roam the myth world and make it over into the present known landscape and inhabitants. By Dan Milo's time the etiological emphasis is concentrated at the end, and is associated in his mind with the Christian Genesis story. The Lillooet used the myth to explain something about the neighboring Shuswap, said to have originated from a man who had two knot-hole wives, a cottonwood and an aspen-poplar, so his children had both dark and light skin (Teit 1912b:357). Dan Milo has his own variation on that theme. When he told Oliver Wells this story he was ninety-seven years old, and blind. But he knew that the Chilliwack bands were healthier and happier than at any time in his lifetime, and that spirit dancing had come again to the Sto:lo (Halkomelem). Listening to the tape, one hears a confidence, especially in the statement "I want it *my* color." The first man of his people, Dan Milo seems to be saying, had a choice, and made it emphatically. The world as it is has a rightness to it.

Oliver Wells first asked Dan Milo for the story in his own language. Brent Galloway made a phonetic transcription of this Halkomelem version with the assistance of Edna Bobb and Amelia Douglas at the Coqualeetza Educational Center, Sardis, British Columbia. Their word-for-word and fluent interlinear translation is available in typescript. Immediately following this version on the tape is Dan Milo's rendering of the story in English, transcribed by Ralph Maud, Brent Galloway, and Marie Weeden, published in Wells 1987:89–90. For the present volume, Ralph Maud, with the help of Marie Weeden, has fused together these two complementary tellings.

Black Bear and Grizzly Bear

My dear friends, whoever will be listening to this story, the story of what must have been people, the Black Bear and the Grizzly Bear. That's the older sister, the Grizzly, to the Black Bear. One child of the Black Bear is an older girl. There is also an older boy and a little child. The Grizzly's children are all girls.

Well, every day these two women go out to do some hunting for what they eat. Well, one night the Grizzly came home, and all of the children were sleeping, but the older girl of the Black Bear saw her aunt cooking. She saw the breast of her mother in what the Grizzly was cooking. She took a long time to sit down. And the big girl, she spoke to her aunt: "Where is my mother?"

"Oh, she is going to stay there for the night. She'll be coming home later."

So she let it go at that. She knew her mother had been killed.

The next day the Grizzly went hunting again. Then the Black Bear's children coaxed the Grizzly's children to play in the river. Well, I tell you that the grizzly bear doesn't swim at all, can't swim. So the Grizzly's children were all drowned. The others went to work and picked up some rotten logs, and that's what they laid in the bed of each of these Grizzly's children. Then the girl's brother said, "We'd better leave or she will kill us." Thus he got them going and they went along. It was the girl who took care of the younger brother, the little child.

Well, when the Grizzly came home, all her children were in bed, and she tried to wake them up. No, they wouldn't move at all. She went there and picked them up, but they were not children at all. It was rotten wood.[1] And the Black Bear's children, they're gone.

So first thing in the morning the Grizzly she followed them. The Black Bear's children, they thought they'd climb a tree. They gathered the stuff that's prickly that is sometimes in the bark of fir trees, and wrapped it in a blanket. Then they climbed high up. Well, the Grizzly Bear came along following their trail.

"You there, what did you do with my children? What did you do with my children?

"Oh, we have them here," the girl said. "You lie down, down there, and I'll lower down your children. You open your eyes wide. I'll lower down your children."

She did, and they poured down the stuff from the trees, dust, and she got it all over in her eyes. She got blinded. She couldn't see.

They came down. They hollered across the river to someone working on a canoe. He came across and took them over.

"There's the Grizzly is chasing after us. If she calls you to bring her over, you can drown her for us. She doesn't swim. If she gets in the water she'll die."

Then they got out of the canoe and traveled on from the river. So this man he went to work and made a high seat for the Grizzly to sit on. On their way across, about half ways over the river, he shook that tree [seat], and the Grizzly tumbled over, you know, and she got drowned.

And they just kept on going, the Black Bear's children. They came to a place, you know, and they make a fire for the night. The little boy's got a cap on, and it's all on the older brother's way, you know. He got hold of his little brother's cap and threw it in the fire.

"It's always in my way," that's what he said.

So he threw it in the fire. The child woke up, but his cap was already burned up. Then he cried and cried. They say it wasn't long before the water began to rise from the river, and the older boy and girl ran away. By gosh, they had to run to get away from the water. They looked down there, and the boy was still sitting down there, and the fire's still on under the water. But they kept on a-going to be saved.

Well, that boy, he was there by himself. He saw a man come down the river with a pole with a hook on it. The kid, he sees that the man is doing some fishing. *I'll go and fix him*, this boy said, and jumped in the river and turned to be a nice pretty-looking fish, this boy did. The man aimed down at the nice pretty-looking fish to hook it. Well, that kid he grabbed the hook before it hooked him, and was pulled out. Immediately he was out the kid looked for the club that he kills fish with, and the kid, he kicked that stick, you know, that club. It went quite a long ways. Well, that kid he went to work and he cut that hook, and he jumped in the river again.

When that man came along, his hook was gone. He didn't have any more. It was his only one. So he went home. But that child began to think: *I'll go look for that guy that's doing the fishing*. He got there, and the man was lying down, which meant his feelings were hurt.

"Hello, grandpa," he says. "You look to be sad."

"Oh, I lost my hook, sonny. I lost my hook. A fish took it away."

"Oh . . . here's your hook, grandpa. I found it."

By gosh, that man is sure glad.

"Where do you stay, boy?"

"I've got no home, grandpa. I got no home. I just wandered around."

"Oh, you stay with me."

And one morning while the man was outside doing some work the child went to fix up the man's bed, fix up his blanket. And they say there was a knot-hole lying under his blanket. The kid took it and threw it in the fire. Pretty soon that man came in.

"Oh, my gosh, my wife must've gone and got burned."

"Is that your wife?" this kid says.

"Yeah, that's my wife. I was the first man created here," that's what the man said to him. "I was the first man created, and the Great Man forgot to leave me a wife."

"Give me an ax; I'll get you a wife."

So this man gave him an ax, and he went out. And there's a nice tree, a birch. The next one is the alder. He cut them up, about the height of a person, and he split them and laid them down outside of the man's house. Well, he hollered at him to tell him to come out: "I've brought you a wife. I am going to make a wife for you, whichever one of these sticks you want for your wife."

"I want it my color." That's what the man said. "That's the alder."

"Oh, all right. You go inside and I'll bring in your wife."

Well, this boy he went to work and made a nice pretty-looking girl, hair hanging down to her knees. Took her in the house. So he got a wife. Then he told that he was the first man created, but the Man forgot to get him a wife like he had done with Adam and Eve.

That's the end of the story, my friend.

Notes

1. Rotten wood being substituted for a child is a frequent theme in these stories.—Eds.

Beaver and Mouse

A Traditional Nooksack Story

Told by George Swanaset

Edited by Pamela Amoss

The Nooksack tribal leader, George Swanaset, told me this story in 1954, when I had just begun my fieldwork with him on the Nooksack language. Later I tape-recorded him telling it in Nooksack and English. I chose it for this collection because it was the first text I transcribed, and because it has a clear moral, both universally and culturally relevant. It was also one of George Swanaset's favorite stories, and he always chuckled wickedly when recounting Beaver's discourteous retort to the repentant Mouse.

George Swanaset was dedicated to preserving the Nooksack language and to working for the welfare of the Nooksack people. He had struggled to preserve the language since the early 1930s, when he had served as an informant for Thelma Adamson, who eventually abandoned the project when her health deteriorated. Unfortunately, Adamson's notes have been lost. Later, in the early 1950s, George began working with Paul Fetzer, a graduate student at the University of Washington, who recorded much material but who tragically succumbed to cancer before he was able to complete his analysis. When I appeared, George was delighted to take up his task again and worked very seriously to help me with his complex and difficult language. At the time, I believed he was the last person to have any real knowledge of Nooksack. Although it turned out that there were a few other people with significant knowledge, and other scholars and I were able to collect additional information, by 1990 all of the people who knew the language had died. The Nooksack tribe has made an effort to revive the use of Halkomelem, since a number of the older members spoke it when they were young, and more recently some tribal members are using recorded material to study Nooksack as well.

Although I have taken some liberties in the translation, I have tried to keep it close to the original. I returned to the oral recording to hear where the speaker had paused so I could use the pauses to define line breaks. Paragraph breaks are based both on pauses and on what I judged to be the organization of the narrative content. George Swanaset had a special cadence to his recitation of myths that I have tried to suggest by arranging the lines in verse form. I have also tried to make the stress patterns of the English mimic the rhythm of the song, in the process taking serious license with the syntax and grammar but staying close to what I understand of the spirit.

According to George Swanaset this is one of several Nooksack stories whose telling would have been limited to particular times of the year. As he explained, telling this story about Beaver would bring on a heavy rainstorm, so people were very careful with it. Unfortunately, although I dutifully noted the information George volunteered, I did not ask him to expand on it. It is possible that on one of those days in the winter when the cold wind from Canada blows down the Nooksack Valley and the temperature drops well be-low freezing, this story would have been told to promote the return of wetter and warmer winter weather. The Nooksack had another story that explains the northeast wind that generates those arctic interludes, and they told that story only when the northeast winds blew.

Unique among the Nooksack stories I collected, Beaver has a song as an in-tegral element. When he told the story, George sang Beaver's *syowen*, or spirit power song. In its cryptic lyrics—one line repeated—Beaver's song is like the few spirit power songs in the native Nooksack language that I have transcribed as dictated by their owners. Again, I did not think to ask George Swanaset if he had heard of anyone using Beaver's song as his spirit power.

Clearly, the story addresses a universal human problem: how to deal with rejection by a potential lover. Anyone unkindly rebuffed can easily empathize with Beaver's chagrin and rejoice in the punishment visited upon the uppity Mouse. But the story also speaks to the particular problems of aboriginal Coast Salish, the anxieties and dilemmas people experienced when they sought suit-able marriage partners. Since marriage was a contract between families, the usual young woman, unlike Mouse, would have had little chance to refuse a suitor her family found acceptable. Nevertheless, from the man's perspective, the process of negotiating a marriage always involved the risk of rejection, if not by the girl herself, then by her family.

A young suitor was expected to sit outside his intended's house until he was accepted and invited inside. Even if the girl's family liked him, it was custom-ary to keep him waiting several days and nights as a way of underscoring the high social status of the woman's kinfolk. But if a more desirable suitor were in the running, a young man might find himself waiting in vain and forced to eventually return home, like Beaver, with his amour propre seriously chal-lenged. In their turn, the family of the girl faced the danger of arousing the enmity of the rejected suitor and his family, represented in the myth by the deluge the offended Beaver called up to punish Mouse.

The anxiety generated by these risky negotiations, as well as other delicate social maneuverings, was symbolized in the fear of retaliation from the guardian spirits of those intentionally or unintentionally wronged. Every adult person was assumed to have some sort of spiritual help, and even the least prepossessing person might have lethal spirit powers that could be called upon to avenge him.

Although arranged marriages had been largely given up by the time people of George Swanaset's cohort came along, belief in individual spirit powers persisted, and so the story continued to resonate for people of his generation. In fact, since Coast Salish people continue to believe in the possibility of special spiritual experiences, the story should still speak to Native people in the twenty-first century. Although the story is about rejected lovers, the moral applies more generally. The message, relevant now as it was when the Nooksack first told it, is that everyone should be treated with respect, and one who fails to show respect does so at his or her peril.

Beaver and Mouse

There is this fine woman, a single girl.
And Beaver goes to get her to be his wife, that single girl, Mouse.
He goes over there to get her to be his wife.

And then Mouse gives her answer.
(No, No, it won't be what Beaver has in mind, that he'll get together with Mouse.)
And Mouse is mad! She reviles Beaver because he is ugly.
And then she says,
"You are so pot-gutted, so wide-butted; your tail is ugly."
And so Beaver gets turned down.

And so that's the way it is, the way Mouse says it.
And then Beaver turns back.
And then he heads home.
And then he calls for rain.[1]

And then he dances his syowen.
And then it rains many days, many nights.

And then he dances.
And then he sings his syowen,
"Pelting down rain drops,
Let rain come!
Pelting down rain drops,
Let rain come!
Pelting down rain drops,
Let rain come!"
That Beaver, that's what he sings.
And then the high water comes and it gets deep everywhere.

And then, Mouse, she climbs, she climbs up a tree.
And then the water gets still deeper, the water is deep.
Then Mouse, she yells,
"Oh, Beaver!
Come, come and get me.
I'll accept you. You'll be my husband.
Come and get me!"
That Mouse, that's what she's yelling.

Then, Beaver, he hears what she's yelling.
And then Beaver answers back,
"What are you scheming for, you scald-ass?"
That's what Beaver answers.
And so, Beaver, he doesn't go and get her.

And that's it.

Notes

1. A Thompson story with the same motif has Beaver's power song in what is considered foreign speech, the way Beaver talks, which is obviously based on a Coast Salish language (see Egesdal 1992:53–54). The motif is also in the Pentlatch story "Beaver and Frogs" (Kinkade, this volume). —Eds.

Crow, Her Son, Her Daughter

A Traditional Southern Lushootseed Story

Told by Marion Davis

Edited by Dell Hymes

This myth begins with the popular theme of a younger sibling or child who misunderstands instructions. Sometimes the consequence is merely embarrassment, sometimes, as here, a death. Usually, as here, the consequence is remedied.

This version of the theme was told by Mr. Marion Davis to Thelma Adamson in 1927 (see Adamson 1934:361–64). Mr. Davis learned his stories from his mother, who was from the White River region of Puget Sound, and was brought to Upper Chehalis territory when he was about five years old. His version is especially interesting because it changes formal pattern with a change in the role of gender. The first scene tells of the son's mistake and his denial of it. It has five stanzas, and they in turn have five or three verses. The second scene tells of the mother persisting in getting the truth, and, as a doctor (shaman), singing until the girl is restored. It has four stanzas, and they have each four verses. (Notice that the story mentions interrogating the son five times, but shows only four. Showing a fifth time would have required a fifth stanza.)

The association of female-centered, or controlled, activity with four, male-centered activity with five, has a parallel in an analogue of this part of the White River (Southern Lushootseed) myth among the Tillamook on the Oregon coast (Hymes 1993). Perhaps the association was part of a widespread Salish tradition.

Mr. Davis's story has a second part in which Crow's son makes a second mistake, and now is himself killed. Like the daughter, he is healed, but in response to his own petition. And he goes on to success in fishing and revenge.

In effect, Mr. Davis has interwoven two cycles of death, restoration, and punishment. Both punishments come in the second part—that of the son, as a culprit, in the second scene of the second part, that of Raven, as responsible for the son's death, in the last. And the second part is a rich use of five-part relations associated with males. Its third scene is its pivot. It completes a sequence of three with the son's mistake, death, and recovery, and begins a sequence of three, as he starts toward home, thinking of reprisal. And as the son succeeds in getting fish, his fifth try, that point in the sequence is amplified into three stanzas of its own.

Raven, of course, is the well-known Transformer and Trickster of the Northwest Coast. According to Adamson (1934:361n6), the daughter in the story has no name. No English name is given for the son. I suspect it is a bird, because of the reduplication, and because in an analogue among the Clackamas Chinook, the son is Cock Robin.

Crow, Her Son, Her Daughter

Crow had one son, Ts'ítsixwun, and a daughter.   PROLOGUE |
They lived in a village close to the bay.

                                            I. i. CROW'S SON ROASTS HIS SISTER |
One morning Crow said to her son,
      "I'll have to go to the bay
            and try to get some more clams."
She had a few small clams in the house.
      "If your little sister wakes up and cries,
            get some of the clams and cook them.
      You must roast them
            and give them to her."
"All right, I'll do it," Ts'ítsixwun said.

His mother went to the bay to dig clams.
When she got to the house,
      both her little daughter and Ts'ítsixwun were gone.
In a short while the boy returned.
"Where's your sister?" she asked.
"She's outside," Ts'ítsixwun answered.

"Go get her," she said.
The boy went out.
"She's not there," he said.
"Well, where is she?" she asked.
"Perhaps she's over there where the children are playing dolls," he said.

The girl was not there,
     for Ts'ítsixwun had roasted her.
His mother had said to him,
     "t'et'sápcid tcax^u ts'a'a tsútsuq'wa aq'sáxo' "
     (Roast some clams for your little sister).
He had understood her to say,
     "t'it sápud tcax^u tsaat tsútsuq'wa"
     (Roast your little sister's backside).

And so when his little sister had awakened,
     he had roasted her before the fire
          until she died.
He had lied to his mother about his sister,
     he was afraid to tell her the truth.
He had thrown her in the gooseberry bushes,
     where Crow could not find her.

ii. Crow's Song Restores Her Daughter |

When Ts'ítsixwun came back for the second time,
     he said, "She isn't there,
          I can't find her."
"Well, where is she then?
     You should know where she is!" his mother said.
"Maybe she's over there
     where the children are swinging," he said.
"Well then, go after her and bring her home," Crow said.

In a little while he came back and said,
     "No, she's not there.
     Maybe she's over there
          where the children are playing the laughing game."
"Well, go get her," she said.
He ran to the place,
     he was afraid to tell his mother the truth.

The fifth time, he told her what he had done:
     "Why, mother," he said,
          "you said, 't'it sápud tcax^u tsaat tsútsuq'wa.'"
"No I didn't," Crow cried,
     "I said, 't'et'sápcid tcax^u ts'a'a tsútsuq'wa aq'sáxo.'

What did you do with her?" she demanded.
"Well, when she woke up
    I roasted her before the fire
        and she died," he explained,
            "then I threw her in the gooseberry bushes."
"Well, go get her," she said.

The boy brought his little dead sister home.
Crow tied her packstrap around her middle,
    wrapped her hair around her head
        and tied it on her forehead.
            [getting ready to doctor]
Then she began to sing,
    holding her right forearm against her forehead,
        "ɬaɬaᵃ babálxweis
        ɬaɬaᵃ babálxweis."[1]
She sang the song over and over
    until the little girl came to life.

II. i. CROW BRINGS HOME A SEAL TO ROAST |

Crow went to the bay five times to dig clams.
The fifth time, while digging,
    she noticed that the tide was coming in.
There was a seal in the water right in front of her.
Oh, what can I do to catch him?
    I wish he would come close,
        then I could club him.

She wished and wished that he would come ashore.
Finally, she began to sing.
    "*tc'étc'i tásxᵘ*,
            dédi sxwádatč̓"
    [Come near, seal,
        go down, bay.]
The seal came nearer.
The water began to withdraw
    and left the seal marooned in the sand.
Crow got a club
    and ran after him.

She struck him with the club
    and killed him.

Then she carried the body back from the shore
    and resumed her clam digging.
When she had finished,
    she packed the seal home.
First she rolled it in the fire
    to singe the hair off.
Then she rolled it out
    and scraped the burned hairs off.
Then she butchered it
    and roasted the meat in a pit over the rocks.

ii. RAVEN IS OFFENDED AND TAKES REVENGE |

When the meat was done,
    she invited all the people to come to her house
            and eat it.
Everyone came
    and had a good time
            eating seal fat.
Raven (qwáqᵁ) heard
    that his sister had invited everyone to her house to feast
            except himself,
                and this made him angry.
But she had not forgotten him;
    right away she had sent Ts'itsixwun
            with a large piece of fat for his uncle.
But the boy had turned off the trail
    and eaten the fat himself.

Raven went to see Crow.
She saw by his eyes
    that he was angry
            and asked if he got the piece of fat she sent.
"No!" he said.

Ts'itsixwun's stomach looked rather distended.

You've got it all in your stomach!
  Raven said to himself.
I'll call him to look for my louse, he thought.

They say that Raven's knife was pretty sharp.
"Come here, my nephew, and look for my louse," he called,
  "It's right in the front of my head."
Crow did not see what was going on.

Ts'itsixwun went close
  and Raven pointed his knife at the boy's stomach
    where it was bulging out.
Then he ripped his stomach open
  and the piece of fat came out.
Ts'itsixwun died right there.
Raven ate the piece of fat
  that had been in the boy's stomach.
Then he thought,
  What shall I do with him?
  I guess I'll throw him in the river
  and let him float down.
So he took hold of Ts'itsixwun
  and threw him in the river.
The boy floated down.

iii. CROW'S SON IS HEALED |
(I think it was still the fall of the year,
  for the leaves that were falling from the trees overhanging the river
    were floating down.)
Ts'itsixwun was still alive in his heart.
Oh, he thought,
  I wish the leaves would come right into my stomach
    and heal me.
He floated down and down,
  thinking this all the while.
Finally a leaf fell right into his wound
  and suddenly it knit together.

He swam out to the riverbank
  and stayed there quite a while.
Perhaps I can walk now,
  he thought.
No, he could not do it.

He tried five times;
  then he stood up and walked.
Then he thought,
  Oh how shall I get even with the fellow who killed me?
  I'll surely get even some way.
And so he turned toward home.

iv. HE BRINGS HOME MANY FISH |

He walked a long way
  and finally came to a lake.
Perhaps there is a fish here,
  he thought.
No, there was no fish,
  so he kept on going toward home.

He came to another lake.
Perhaps there is a fish here.
No, there was no fish there,
  so he went on.

He came to another lake, the third one.
Perhaps there is a fish here.
No, there was no fish,
  so he kept on going.

He came to another.
Perhaps there is a fish here.
Yes, there was a little fish in the lake.

He went on.
When he got nearer home,
  he found a larger lake.
There was a big fish there.

Oh, what could I use for a hook to catch it with? he thought.
He went to a gooseberry bush
 and pulled out a sharp thorn.
Then he got something to use for a string
 and tied it to the thorn.

He caught one fish
 but threw it back in again.
Then he caught a second fish
 and threw it back in also.
The third time,
 a whole school of fish came.
He soon had a large pile.
He broke off a forked stick
 and slipped the fish on by their heads
  until both prongs of the stick were full.
The stick was so weighted down with fish
 he could hardly carry it.

v. He Overcomes Raven |

He kept on going toward home
 and finally arrived in front of the house,
  where Crow saw him.
They now had a lot of fish
 and started to roast them.
While the fish were roasting,
 Raven came along.
He noticed the fish
 and became very happy.
  "That's the kind of boy I wanted you to be!
  That's why I killed you," he said to Ts'itsixwun.
  "I sent you floating down the river
   so that you would get such a *tamanowas* [power]."
Raven was happy
 because he thought
  he would have some fish to eat before long.

When the fish were done,

they put almost all of them on a mat
and gave them to Raven.
He ate and ate and ate.
When the fish were about gone,
he began to say,
"æ', æ', æ'."

The bones were sticking in his throat.
He kept on gagging
and finally died right there.
Ts'itsixwun got even with Raven.

(Ts'itsixwun was a great eater like his uncle Raven.)

Notes

1. Adamson (1934) notes "The narrator did not know the meaning of this song."

The Whiteman as "Other"

The Sailor Who Jumped Ship and Was Befriended by Skagits

A Lushootseed Historical Story

Told by Susie Sampson Peter

Edited by Jay Miller and Vi Taqʷšəblu Hilbert

This historical narrative, told by Susie Sampson Peter, is a good example of the Native view of the whiteman as "other." It is a reminiscence of something that happened during her childhood, a very sympathetic story of reciprocal help in time of need.[1]

A survey of the booster biographies of Skagit County pioneers (Anon. 1906:493–824) suggests only one possible match with the cook in Aunt Susie's story. Still alive in 1906, Michael J. Sullivan was born in Massachusetts of Irish parents, but was left an orphan who, at twelve, became a cabin boy on a ship that took 112 days to round Cape Horn from Boston to San Francisco. In 1866, he came to Puget Sound and found work at the Utsaladdy Mill on Camano Island. In 1868, he took squatter's rights on Swinomish Flats, at the site of the future town of La Conner. He cleared, diked, and drained prime farmland, attracting others to settle nearby. By 1880, all the flats were claimed. He filed a preemption claim and proved up on 315 acres of land, building a fine house but preserving his first cabin. In 1903 in Seattle, he married Josephine Smith, the Irish niece of Patrick O'Hare, another La Conner pioneer, in a Catholic ceremony. "The homeless cabin boy on the quays of 'Frisco has become a leading and wealthy citizen of one of the best counties in Northwestern Washington, successful in business and respected by all" (Anon. 1906:668).

While not identified as a cook, Sullivan best fits the profile of a young man fleeing a life of hardship at sea. As a fellow Catholic, he would have had a link with Natives that other settlers lacked. His late marriage also fits this account. All the others came to the Skagit with practical skills as farmers, miners, traders, railroad workers, or handymen. At a later time, others settled after careers in the Navy or at sea, but none of these men came alone or at the right time.

Natives are rarely mentioned in these 1906 biographies, except as impediments to progress, owners of hordes of dogs, or suspected murderers. A separate chapter summarizes their traditions, but Aunt Susie does much to set the record straight with her own account.

In 1856, the Camano Island partnership of Lawrence Grennan and Thomas Cranney began supplying pilings for San Francisco wharf construction. Then they shifted to selling ship spars and masts for export around the world. Their Utsaladdy Mill was operating by 1860, providing special orders for, among others, a British Cunard Line steamship and the 200-foot flagpole for the 1866 Paris Exhibition (White 1980:81–84).

The Sailor Who Jumped Ship and Was Befriended by Skagits

My family was then living at Utsaladdy on Camano Island. A lot of people were working there. They worked at the lumber mill. And my father worked there. Ships would come from what they called California to get lumber from the mill. One after another they came.

Once, two ships came toward Utsaladdy. One of them had all of its sails straightened, filled by a gust of wind and moving very fast, when a sailor fell overboard. This ship was unable to stop. Someone rushed to the side and a life preserver was thrown overboard. It was thrown. The one who had gone underwater grabbed it right away and hung on. At the same instant, a signal was hung up from the stern so that the other ship coming behind would know that someone had gone overboard from the preceding ship.

Those on the second ship waved. They waved. They waved, to show that they understood the signal. They watched the water to determine if the one who had fallen in had been retrieved. They too threw a life preserver into the water.

The man in the water now had two floats and he was able to stay on top of the water. He was rescued, but the two crews began to talk about all of their other comrades who had not been as fortunate. Many had been lost in death by drowning.

In particular, a teenager who worked on the ship as a firewood cutter began to cry. Perhaps he was thirteen years old. He was very strong from his work. Yet inside, he was a tiny boy who still mourned his brother who had worked from the mast of the ship in the rigging. His older brother unfastened the sails. He had the job of dropping the sails to catch the wind. It was a necessary but dangerous job. One day, he fell or jumped overboard and drowned. For these young boys, life was hard. Sometimes they gave up and managed to kill themselves because they felt trapped by a life on the sea. So, the younger surviving brother, recalling again the loss of his brother, cried and cried.

Meanwhile, at our own camp, we used to fish with a line and we traded fish for hardtack crackers at the store. For a whole fish we got half of a bucket of hardtack. We fished every day and traded two fish for a full bucket of hardtack.

At this time I was really a child. Other people now very old were then children too. We fished and watched the activity at the mill. These white people lived there permanently. They did not run away or move around. These particular white people became known to us. We grew to know each other well.

Only the ships came and went. A ship would dock and wait until it was full of boards and posts. Then they sailed back the next day. These ships waited for a full load before heading back to California. They stayed as long as it took for a full load.

While the ship was docked, the sailors would go over to the point of land where there was a tavern. These idle sailors went to the local bar, getting drunk, causing trouble, and killing time until their ship was loaded. They spent all their time at the bar. As long as the bar was open, they stayed. Maybe it would be three A.M. by the clock, according to today's time. This was more than enough time for them to become very drunk.

Now the man that I want to talk about, their cook, also went along, but he did not like all the rowdiness and fighting. He decided to jump ship and start a new life. My father, Doctor Bill, worked at the mill and was a famous native doctor (shaman). Everyone knew and liked him.

The cook said to my father, "Oh, I am going to run away. Can you take me to shore, away from this island?" My father did not like the way the sailors behaved at the tavern, so he agreed to help, saying, "After a while, I will be going over that way and I will come for you. I will pick you up as I go upriver."

The cook was pleased and encouraged Doctor Bill by saying, "My things are already prepared. My things are packed to put into your canoe as soon as you get to the ship."

I knew that my father was going to help the cook because he pledged us to secrecy. He knew that children might give the plan away, so he came to us and said, "You are not to say anything. You are not to say anything about this Boston [American].[2] I am going to take that Boston to our older cousin, because he says he is going to run away." Then we knew the plan and kept silent.

My father and the cook went back in his canoe to the ship. The cook quietly went on board and loaded his things into the canoe. He really had a lot of things. He loaded and loaded and loaded. He just kept on loading. They had agreed that a bucket worth of hardtack would be my father's pay. That was one full gunnysack. After he had unloaded all this stuff from the ship and piled it in the canoe, they went away in secret.

They broke away from the ship. They cast off. They went toward the mainland. In time, this overloaded canoe arrived at the place called Lebadi?. It was late at night. The heavy canoe was beached. It was pivoted at the ends to move it onto dry land. The cook's things were unloaded quickly. Then my father said to him, "Just tell my niece that I brought you, just tell my niece that I sent you here for safety. Just go to the husband of my niece, Jack Moore, and ask him where it would be best for you to settle." They were safe there. Father and the cook slept when and where they were. During the night, my father got up and paddled home.

No Bostons had yet visited or settled in the region. No one from the mill or the ship would know he was there.

Meanwhile, the next morning at the ship, longboats were sent ashore. They beached and brought the other sailors back in relays. My, but they were very drunk. These longboats came from the ship to ferry the drunk sailors back on board. They arrived and went to their hammocks and bunks to sleep. They slept. They slept. The night before at the bar, they had told the cook what to prepare for their breakfast. He was supposed to get up in the morning and cook for them. They wanted a big meal because that was the day they were hoisting sail and going back to California. They were set to sail into the sea, to go seaward. They had gone to bed and they slept on, expecting a big breakfast.

They awoke but there was no fire. There was no food ready. All was quiet. They wondered, Oh, no! Where was their cook? Then they realized, he was far away! He was there at the place called Abadach.[3]

Indeed, that is where he was. The next morning, the sleepers in the longhouse began to stir. People woke up. Right away, the cook asked to speak to Doctor Bill's niece. He met her husband and asked if there was any place where he could bring his things from the beach and store them indoors.

Jack Moore asked, "Who brought you here?" The cook replied, "Oh, it was Doctor Bill who brought me here. He directed me to his niece here and said that her husband was very good and helpful. Jack Moore, it is said, is his name. He will tell me where I can put my stuff." Jack pointed to a small cedar-plank shed, saying, "Over there is the place where my mother keeps busy. It is her shed for drying and smoking fish. She is not using it just now. You can go in and out of it freely. Your things will be safe there."

So, this white man put his things inside. He worked all day long and finally went to sleep very tired. People were amazed at all that he possessed. He had a hammer. He had nails, a saw, another saw, two different kinds of saws. He had a hand saw and blanket, too. He used these when he traveled.

His possessions were safe in the shed. He rested for a few days. Then he was anxious to find a homestead. He went to Jack Moore and asked, "Where can I settle? When can I go from here and have a place of my own? I want to be out of the way. I want a place of my own. Where do you think it would be best for me to move? Doctor Bill said that you would know where I could be safe and not bother you."

Jack thought for some time and decided, "There is a good place for you, an upland marked by a big fir tree. No one has laid claim to the land on the other side of that tree. It could be yours."

The cook was delighted, "Yes, that is where I shall go. I will look at it and decide." So, he went and indeed found this to be a nice place. He had found where he could live. It was marked by a fir tree, fallen over. It must have broken and blown down in a storm. It was a good tree to use for building. He decided to stay. He gathered up the dried stuff (needles) from under the trees and he piled it up enough to make a bed where he could lay down when night came.

The next morning he began to clear the land. He fixed it up where he was. He began preparing his homestead. He fixed it. He fixed it up, leveling a spot for a house foundation. He dug a root cellar where he could put his food and store his possessions.

Then he went back to Jack Moore's town and he began to pack away his things. He really and truly had lots of things, he was not poor, destitute, or unfortunate. People saw that he had a frying pan, teakettle, and pots. He was set to move to a new location by himself.

Now he was settled, still working all the time. He needed more things to work on his place. He did not know where to buy them. So he went back to Jack Moore and he asked, "Is there a store around anyplace?" Jack replied, "There is a store, but it is a long walk. At the fish trap, go beyond a little creek where there is a log bridge that will take you across to the path to the store." The white man understood. He walked there.

At the store, the cook said, "Oh, I want a saw, but not a very long one. And nails, just enough for me to carry. Give me some food, too." Then he took his tools and food and he walked home. It was night when he arrived and he went to sleep. The next morning, early, he cleared more land. Much land.

He worked for himself. He did not work for money. He just made a house for himself. He split the boards. He worked, worked, worked. Another day came, he worked. Another day came, still he worked.

Everyone admired his determination and dedication. Other settlers heard about his land and a few homesteaded at a distance. As a wonderful gift, he was given a cat. He was given a cat by one of these neighbors. Then another whiteman asked, "Would you like to have a dog? I have two little dogs." The cook agreed, "Oh, I would like that. I will keep it tied up so it will not run away." Now the cook was not alone.

A year went by. By then, he had cleared land and planted large fields. He even had chickens. He was such a hard worker that people liked to give him things because he so appreciated them. He was given two chickens, three. One was a male and two were female. He had a rooster and two hens. He had them fenced and protected. He was on guard.

One night a raccoon went after his chickens. The dog barked a warning and he shot the thieving raccoon. (I guess that means that the cook had a gun now. My father said that the cook owned a whiteman's gun, a pistol, a hand gun. He did not have what we call a real (two-hand) gun, a rifle to kill big game.) The raccoon was killed. The man butchered it, butchered it for his little dog and his little cat and his dear chickens, all three. They had warned him of the threat and earned a treat of fresh meat. The man truly owned these pets because he cared for them so well.

It was very good the way he was finally fixed up, settled, established, and set. He had a (wooden) floor in his house. He had a fireplace chimney. He made the chimney himself.

Another year passed. It became summery warm. He planted now. The field had been prepared thoroughly. He planted everything. He had plenty. The other white people liked to talk to him when he went there, where the store is. There, upriver, way upstream.

One day, he considered another, easier way to get to the store. *Oh, I could go by water when the water rises. I could go upstream and get to the store quicker.* So he went down to the water because he now had bought a boat. He earned money by working at a logging camp. He was working now. He worked for money during the week. Every Sunday, he worked in his garden, which is why it grew so well.

He was very well off, yet he did not forget his friends. He began to think about my father and how he was rescued from the harsh life aboard the ship. He asked aloud, *Oh, I need to find out about that Indian who brought me away safely, to learn how he is. Did he die, is that the reason that he doesn't canoe over to visit? He never visits his nephew Jack Moore.* He decided to ask about Doctor Bill the next time he went to the store.

Meanwhile he was very busy. He was so busy he did not go anywhere. He was building a fence. He split his own fencing posts from cottonwood. Mmmm, lots and lots. He hired out to fence the lands of other white settlers.

My family was still at Utsaladdy. The Gage brothers, Bill and John, hired my father and took care of my relatives by giving them wages, bulk foods, and trade goods. My family also continued to gather Native foods. In the spring, my mother dug up roots to eat. Everyone dug them at that time, enjoying themselves. Women worked hard and had fun.

Men were paid to work in the mill. Every man earned three quarters (three 25-cent pieces) a day, plus lunch. But we children were too small to earn wages or work hard. We were no good for anything. The only thing we could do was help our father when he was putting up fencing. Our job was to pull the fencing rails around. A bunch of us would pull one at a time. Each one was heavy because it was green cottonwood. We all were doing this at Utsaladdy one nice day when the former cook came there in his boat.

It was hot when my father, Doctor Bill, asked us, "Oh, my children, would you dip me some water. I am very thirsty. Go quickly and the water will still be cold when you carry it up to me. Do it now. Don't fool around. Don't play along the way."

We liked to help our father so we took the water jug and ran downhill. We intended to go all the way down to a shaded section of the stream where the water was sure to be cool. At the store we stopped because, right away, we recognized this whiteman. We said, "Oh, he is the one that we helped out, this whiteman here. He must be coming here to check up."

The cook also saw us. He turned to John Gage at the store and asked, "Where are those children from? Is their father here?" Mr. Gage became suspicious, but replied, "He is here, he is working upland." Mr. Gage was not used to having whitemen ask about Natives unless something was wrong.

The cook kept on, "Oh, do you think that Doctor Bill might be coming back here soon? Who is his boss? Who is he working for? How far away is he working? I would really like to see him."

By now Mr. Gage was thinking hard. Could Doctor Bill have done something bad? He is such a good man, it seems unlikely. What in the world could he have been up to?

Mr. Gage turned to me and said, "Susie, this man wants your father to come. He wants to see him." I was startled, but I knew Mr. Gage and I said, "Oh, all right." We children turned right around and ran uphill with the water that we had fetched.

My father took it and drank. We waited a minute and then I said, "Daddy, there is a white man here that we helped." My father looked up and asked, "Where, my children?" I answered, "He is at the store. He calls specifically for you." Father put down the cup, saying "Let us go. I will see him. You children run on ahead, take us forward."

We ran down the hill. My father also went quickly, quickly. Right away the former cook saw him. He ran up to hug and embrace my father. The whiteman was crying, "Oh, brother, why did you forget me? I am very lonely now."

Seeing my father reminded him of his life aboard ship and the crewmates who had drowned along the way. Vividly, he recalled a time when a life preserver was thrown to a friend overboard but it did no good. His friend drowned in front of his eyes. Such sadness reconfirmed the wisdom of his jumping ship on the night before it sailed away to California. Like others before him, sailors came to dread the day that their ship left port, and they were at the mercy of the sea and crew. The hours before departure were when sailors, who would rather die than sail, risked their lives to jump ship.

These good men were the first whitemen that our people saw. They were running away to freedom. We helped them all that we could. They did not deserve such a life of hardship and brutality. These deserters increased. After the cook, there were others. One became two, then three, then more. They decided to run away from their ships.

But the cook was the first one, and we admired how he had remade a life of his own. He worked hard, owned much, and was still a friend. He turned to Mr. Gage and noted that he had again found his good friend, his younger brother. He told the trader, "You give my brother all that he needs. Give him one sack of flour, a bucket of hardtack, two dollars worth of sugar, some beans, some bacon, some lard, tea, coffee, rice. I do not care what it costs. Charge it to me. Oh, and give him a cask of molasses." All these things were put in a box for my father while we watched. The man counted out his money and paid the bill there and then. We knew then that it was all ours.

Then the former cook went further. He said, "I have chickens. I have a hen, but it hid its chicks. There are lots of them. Raccoons sometimes get one or two, but they hide pretty well. I have a dog and a cat at my house. I am working now at the logging camp. I have done well since you first helped me.

"I have fields of plenty. Have your children come and pick everything that they want. There is lots of corn, carrots, and potatoes. It would be best if they came on Sunday. They could bring back cabbage. I have lots of things planted."

We children were surprised by such generosity. We went on Sunday, in the evening when it was cool, and we filled a canoe with food. We took it home. Mother was very pleased, "Now we have lots of fresh food. You folks have taken lots of food." Indeed, we had helped ourselves. But there was much more left there for the man.

My mother, her voice rich in sarcasm, could not help reminding my father that, even though he was not really a relative, the former cook was more generous to our family than our own blood kin. He paid for five dollars' worth of staple foods for us from the store and also provided us with fresh food from his garden. He was truly a great man.

The next time my father went to the store, John Gage took him aside and said, "I got very frightened for you when that man came asking for you. All I could think was 'What did Doctor Billy do wrong that a whiteman wanted to see him? What could Doctor Bill have done to attract the attention of a Boston?' Now I know that the man had run away from a ship as a boy and you gave him help and direction. He has done much for all of us."

Now in my old age, I still think of that cook who jumped ship and was befriended by my family. That whiteman was very nice. He had lots of food, and he fed us well. He even gave us a meal when we arrived there on Sunday to pick from his fields. It was late at night before we got all of it home.

So, you see, that is the way it was with the very first white people. They came in ships but were unhappy. They ran away, and sometimes they died in the attempt. Those are the ones we still mourn. Many were too young to know better or find a better way to survive. Sometimes they drowned in front of us in the bay at Utsaladdy.

These first whitemen were desperate. They had nothing when they escaped. They were extremely poor. They were despairing, destitute, and desperate. We took pity on them because they were much poorer than we were. They just ran away and left everything behind. They did not choose to come here. The ships brought them. They were like prisoners. There were lots of white people running away, lots of them. In particular, the first of them was a pal of my father, a Boston who had been a ship's cook brought from California. My father called this man his *bleda*, his brother.

Now I am finished about him. Yes, done now, finished.

Notes

1. Recorded on tape by Leon Metcalf, this story was translated from Skagit (Lushootseed) by Jay Miller and Vi Taqʷšəblu Hilbert.—Eds.

2. Lushootseed and some other Native peoples of the Northwest used "Boston" as the designation for all Americans since so many of the sailors who visited them came from that port. In spoken Lushootseed, however, the term is pronounced *pastəd*. (Lushootseed lacks nasal sounds, so the *n* in *Boston* is realized as a *d.*) The term makes sense because Natives identified people by their home town.

3. In her version of the Star Child epic, Susie Sampson Peter indicated that Abadach was near the town of Sterling, between Burlington and Sedro Woolley on the lower Skagit River.

Circling Raven and the Jesuits
A Traditional Coeur d'Alene Story

Told by Margaret Stensgar

Edited by Ivy G. Doak and Margaret Stensgar

"Circling Raven" is a historical tale of special importance to the Coeur d'Alene.[1] Circling Raven, a revered elder and Margaret Stensgar's great-great-grandfather, foresaw the coming of the Jesuit priests to the northern Idaho region, and persuaded his people to welcome them. When the Jesuits arrived in the northern Idaho Territory in late 1842, they were accepted, and by 1845 the Mission of the Sacred Heart was established on the St. Joseph River (Point 1967). In 1846 the mission was moved to higher ground at a site on the Coeur d'Alene River that is now called the Old Mission at Cataldo (De Smet 1905). The story of Circling Raven is performed as a pageant every year in mid-August at the Old Mission.

Mrs. Stensgar told me this story in the Coeur d'Alene language on several occasions during our years of working together, this version in August 1986. In 1991 we worked through the recorded text line by line; the resulting translation is presented here.[2]

Circling Raven and the Jesuits

It was a long time ago. I wasn't even born yet. My great-great-grandfather, Circling Raven, that's his name, he told them he went to sleep and dreamed. He saw this Blackrobe. This Blackrobe told him, "You tell all your people . . . I'm going to tell you about the Great Spirit: That is the one to believe in.

"All of you my people, after a while I'll be gone. I don't feel good. I am going to teach you, I'm going to tell you what I've seen when I slept, in my dream. Then I'm going to tell you, all of you menfolks, all of you my people, that is the one to look for. That man will be a Blackrobe; he will have a black hat. He will have a necklace with a crucifix. He will have a white body and face. That is the one to look for, the one to believe in. He will be riding on a horse. Go, look for that man. Now I am short of breath. Soon I will die."

Then he died, this man. Circling Raven died. Our people felt awfully bad, they cried. Our chief died.

They said, "We will go look for him, that man."

After they buried the chief, then they went to look for him, the Blackrobe. Then they went (a long way), and all of a sudden they saw the Blackrobes. The Blackrobe, he's got a black hat, he's got a white face. And he's got a crucifix. That is the man to believe in, the Blackrobe.

"I will tell you (folks) about the Great Spirit."

Then he came and he told his people, "Hey! I've seen him. I've seen this man. He's got a white body, got a black robe, and a hat."

And then, "He is coming."

They all gathered, our people. The Father came in. The Blackrobe got here, and he was told, "Ah, Blackrobe, you got here. Come in!"

That Blackrobe, he was thankful. He shook hands with his people. The people were really glad. Happy, our people were happy.

Then this Blackrobe said, "You build it, you build a church. Later on, I will be back. Then I will teach you, I will teach you about the Great Spirit; he is the one to believe in.

"You are to put all your heart in it, and you pray. All of you that are sitting here. Soon all of you children who sit here, you are to learn about the Great Spirit. His name is Jesus Christ. He is the one to believe in."

The people agreed.

"Now I will leave." Then he got back on his horse and he left, the Blackrobe did.

Now the chief spoke. He told them, "Go to Cataldo. Go. We'll build a church."

Well, the old people, the men, the children, they all worked. They went to work. They went down to the creek with the horses. They had horses and they took . . . wood and they tied it to the horse and they took hides and tied it to the wood [I don't know what it's called] and they went down to the creek.

They put stones and rocks there (on the hide). . . . Then mud, clay (white mud), they put it on and took it there. When they finished there, they went back up on the hill there and built with it. And they went back (down again) and they got some more rocks and things, you know, and broken sticks and stuff, and hides. Then they went back there and built the church with that.

They built the church, and they finished. They didn't have anything, and to this day the church is still up. It's been a long time since they built it, and it's still there. They did it in two . . . maybe in five days . . . here they built the church.

When you go to Cataldo, look at what the Indians made, what the Coeur d'Alene built. It's really something because we are lucky to have that from Jesus Christ; and then he helped us and we built that.

Now the priest [Blackrobe] came back. Then when he came, he saw the building. He knelt down and he was glad, he was thankful, he was happy. He told the people, "It's good that this church is built. It's good, really beautiful." Then he started teaching the Coeur d'Alene about Jesus Christ.

And now we learned to pray to adore Jesus Christ.

I don't say anything more

Now we are all happy, us Coeur d'Alenes.

Thank you.

Notes

1. The neighboring Flatheads have a similar prophecy about the coming of the Jesuits by a man named "Shining Shirt" (Woodcock 1996).—Eds.

2. Margaret Stensgar passed away in April 1996, and did not see a final version of this paper.

Oratory

The Two-Headed Person
A Colville-Okanagan Oratory

Speech by William M. Charley, translated by William M. Charley,
Clara Jack, and Anthony Mattina

Edited by Anthony Mattina

my old heart to keep the native language for our youth

Around nine o'clock the morning of Friday, June 24, 1988, a group of about
one hundred individuals gathered on the east bank of the Columbia River near
Bridgeport, Washington, to break the ground at the site of the future Colville
fish hatchery—a project in partial reparation of the fishing losses suffered by
the Colvilles after the installation of the various dams on the river. I was invited to attend by my friend and then tribal councilman Mike Somday. Because elders would be speaking in the various languages and dialects of the
Reservation, he encouraged me to record the proceedings. When I arrived at
the scene a few minutes before 9 A.M., Mike introduced me to the elders I had
not yet met, and we received permission to record their speeches.

I had intended to record only the elders' speeches, but in fact the tape recorder ran throughout the ceremony, interrupted temporarily once by the end
of the tape, and once by a recess. Each speaker, with his/her back to the river
and facing the crowd, held the microphone in his or her hand, and passed it
back to the master of ceremonies when finished. The recorder remained on the
ground the whole time. The master of ceremonies was a Colville official representing the Tribal Department of Fish and Game who introduced the various
speakers and made other appropriate comments. Besides the MC, a total of
twelve individuals made remarks, and two of them spoke twice, for a total of
fourteen speeches, each preceded by the MC's introduction, in a ceremony that
lasted three and one half hours.

The opening prayer was delivered in Colville, the only speech not to be
followed or preceded by an interpretation in English. Six speeches, three by
tribal members and three by non-Indians, were delivered in English only. One
speech was delivered in three languages, Colville, Moses-Columbian, and
English; and another was delivered in Moses-Columbian and English. The
remaining five speeches were delivered in Colville and English, and one was

preponderantly in English. William Charley's Colville portion of the speech was just over seven minutes long; the English that followed was one minute and twenty seconds less; the transcription of the Colville speech came to 750 words. The speed of delivery of the Colville speeches, calculated in words per second (WPS), ranged from a low of 1.0 WPS, to a high of 1.74 WPS. Because the second highest speed of delivery was 1.32 WPS, I conclude that the fastest delivery, which happened to be William Charley's, was considerably faster paced than those of the other speakers, and probably at the upper limit of what would be considered normal range.

Before the Colville hatchery groundbreaking ceremony, I had occasion to listen to public speeches in sylxcin (Colville-Okanagan) in July 1981. The Okanagan Indian Curriculum project, inspired by tribal elders and funded by the Okanagan Tribal Council, held a three-day Historical Symposium on the Okanagan Reserve in Penticton, British Columbia, "for the benefit of people interested in the accurate history of the Indian Nations . . ." The speeches, by Okanagan elders and other invited speakers, were to generate discussion about "the true representation of Indian history from before the time of European settlement."

At the Historical Symposium the elders spoke to a mixed audience of over two hundred from a covered platform through loudspeakers. Each spoke in his/her native dialect, stopping after each sentence to allow the interpreter's rendition in English. The entire proceedings were tape-recorded and partially videotaped, and the English transcript of the symposium was copyrighted in 1982 by the Okanagan Tribal Council. Common to all the elders' speeches are the lamented loss of aboriginal lands at the hands of Europeans, and the consequent loss of lifestyle. These themes pervaded these speeches, which often made reference not only to a historical past but also to a mythological past.

What we know about traditional Colville-Okanagan oratory that predates modern events like those I have witnessed, we know from secondhand reports of ethnographers, missionaries, and travelers. In Raufer (1966) we read of the Moses-Columbian tribal member Dr. Paschal Sherman's report that in the early 1900s, at St. Mary's Mission in Omak, Washington, on occasions such as the feast of Corpus Christi, the tribal chiefs gathered to "deliver addresses." Dr. Sherman writes that he was "thrilled by . . . addresses, delivered in different Indian dialects, eloquent, some fierce and forceful in manner, always inspiring and moving in the sentiments and counsel so warmly proceeding from the heart" (Raufer 1966:373). We have George Bryce's quotation (1907) of the translation of a speech made in 1841 by Okanagan chief Nicola, and earlier we have Alexander Ross's report (1811–12) that councils were held to discuss matters of great weight, and that at such councils the Okanagan chief "opens the business of the meeting with a speech, closing every sentence with great emphasis, the other councilors vociferating approbation. As soon as the chief is done speechifying," continues Ross, "others harangue also; but only one at a time" (p. 293 of original, p. 279 of Thwaites's reprint). But while we have these reports from which to imagine the actual delivery, content, and context of these speeches, we have, to my knowledge, no record of a single original Colville-Okanagan speech delivered by anyone, chief or other, until the Historical Symposium, and now, William Charley's speech.

William Charley wanted his speech to be widely known. After Clara Jack and I had transcribed the speech, I sent him a copy of the transcription along with the taped speech, asking him if he would care to make his work known. After we collaborated on the presentational format of the speech, he wrote to me:

> My dear Sir:
> Thanks for been so nice toward me and I enjoy the "cassette" the speech at the big doins June 24. 1988. To play this for my fellow-Elders who were very impressed with this "cassette" and mention the change of time to be well=word and get over the "message" I will get in touch with the adult education project and find the way to attend the [XXIII International] conference [on Salish Languages] Eugene Oregon Aug. 11–13 my old heart to keep the native language for our "youth."

Here is the English translation of the speech.

The Two-Headed Person

Thank you my relatives, you are gathered here.
    This is a big day.
    A long time ago before the white people got here to us, the Indians were truly happy on this earth.
    They survived, the Indians ate from this land, from bitterroot, camas, all food from the earth, from the water, fish, spring salmon, everything good from the water.
    Time went by, and the white people got here to us.
    They fenced in the Indians on undesirable land.
    They told them, "You will stay there, and you will die there."
    They told the Indians.
    From the fenced-in land the Indians went on to school.

They went to school, and they wrote, they learned the language of the whites.

It was then that two heads were born, the Indian's heads, one white, the other Indian.

Both heads were good.

The white head, that had white language and white knowledge, and the Indian head was equally good.

These are our Indians' values, our Indian culture, our Indian philosophy of life.

Everything Indian was good before the white people arrived here.

We had medicine men, they took care of our relatives.

Now I am glad that there are two heads.

Time went by, and the two heads had a quarrel.

The white head told the Indian head: "You are Indian, you are ignorant, you don't know anything.

I teach you things.

And now you speak English.

I teach you that."

And the Indian head told the white head: "Wherever you came from," it said to it, "it's best you go back there.

I am Indian, this is my country, I was happy here, I was happy in my country.

You got here and you turned everything bad.

It's best you go back."

Look, our heads are two, Indian and white, and the heads fight.

It's bad that it's like that.

If we are wise we'll make both heads work towards good.

And we will do good.

Now I am glad that our smart children are our councilmen, our children do everything.

They know the white people's language, they have the white people's knowledge.

We will turn this white knowledge to do good for our elders, we elders are glad that our children are educated, that they have schooling.

I have always said, the whites took away our land, the whites took away from us, they took everything from us, and last of all the whites took my language.

My language is gone.

Nobody is left that speaks Indian.

Our teachings from our elders are that whatever we see on earth understands and talks Indian.

Not only our Native language has died, this whole world is lonesome.

It never hears the Indian language spoken.

The world is lonesome.

When a person speaks Indian this whole world stops, and listens to the speaker.

That speaker is the world, that speaker is alive, that speaker is knowledge, that speaker is part of us, the world.

And now I am teaching the Indian language, I work at St. Mary's Mission.

A long time ago St. Mary's Mission . . .

There was a very educated Moses man, Paschal Sherman.

And now they call this school Paschal Sherman.

There I teach the Indian language to the children

I teach the children.

"You," I say, "in a while you will be grown, you will be a leader, you will be speaking not for yourself, but for your own people.

"Your heart is for your people, and that is good."

Now when the children have grown, they will know the Indian language.

A long time ago my desire . . .

In a while . . .

People were at church at St. Mary's, they were walking, and they stopped.

And if I talked, and I said, "My heart is sick.

"Long ago our leaders were like that, the man talked, he'd talk a while, he talked Indian.

"When a speaker is done talking, they would reply 'Ah . . .'

"The Indians liked what he said, because it was good."

I see it, it's coming near, it's coming near, it won't be long from now, we will see a young one stand up and talk Indian.

[One head] will stop talking Indian, and translate what he said in English.

That is Indian knowledge, his two heads, the English language, and the Indian language.

They should be glad.

Now I am glad when the students stand up.

They shine, because they's Indians, this is their land.

I teach the children at Paschal Sherman school.

Many white people have said to me that our children are different, the little ones are different.

They are not careful, whoever they see they'll talk to.

I say they find out who it is, they find out he's Indian, it's our way to do so.

This is our Indian belief.

When we pass our Indian beliefs to our children, the Indian language will continue.

This land is sad that it never hears Indian spoken.

When Indian is spoken the land is glad, the Indian is glad, and now my fellow elders and I talk about fixing the Reservation.

We fix it so it will grow spawning salmon, and squaw fish, spring salmon, and everything.

My fellow elders say to me, "What are you making?

"Are they making a spawning facility?"

"I guess so."

And so they're changing the earth.

The white people thought of it.

The knowledgeable children went along.

They all agreed.

Now I quit talking.

In a little while I'll translate into English.

I'll translate what I said, I am sorry when I speak English I get lost for words, because English is not my language, no, Indian is my language.

It's recently that I've learned the English language.

That's how it was made, one of my heads English, and one of my heads Indian.

Following the Colville recitation, William Charley rendered his Colville speech into English, remaining remarkably close to the original, and then he concluded his talk as follows:

> Before I end my talk I'd like to add a little Indian legend. A lo::ng time ago a chief was dying from old age. He was in his bed, and he had five sons, and the five men came to see their dad, and the chief tell the five sons to "get some willow sticks about that long, about the size of your little finger and bring them back to me for some advice." The five

men went out and got them willow sticks and came back to the chief, and the chief put these five willow sticks together and bent them like a horseshoe. When he let one end go it snapped right back in shape again, and he [inaudible] advice to his five sons. "In life don't ever do something by yourself. Whatever you see that is good, get others into it, talk on it, plan on it, and work together and it can be done. You know that these five willow sticks supporting one another you can bend them like a horseshoe. Now if you did that with one stick, it may not have worked."

William Charley died without seeing his speech in print. In a letter to me he had said:

I think that we are doing so well . . . and I feel that what we are doing is for our youth.

. . .

I am happy and I am honored and I pray that I get a little credit for this because my heart is for my people.

So this is William Charley's story.

Funeral Address of Chief Tiʔɬníc'eʔ to the Mourners of a Dead Child

A Thompson River Salish [Nɬeʔképmx] Oration

Spoken by Chief Ti ʔɬníc'eʔ

Edited by Laurence C. Thompson and M. Terry Thompson

In 1913, James Teit, of Spences Bridge, British Columbia, accompanied a delegation of Chiefs from British Columbia to Ottawa, the capital city of Canada. At some time during that visit, they called on Marius Barbeau at the (then) National Museum of Man. Barbeau made some wax cylinder recordings of a number of songs in Nɬeʔképmx (Thompson River Salish) and other languages, and two Nɬeʔképmx orations. There are only these two known sound-recorded examples of the old-fashioned style of Nɬeʔképmx formal oration available,[1] both given by Chief Tiʔɬníčeʔ from the Spences Bridge area.

In 1972, Laurence C. and M. Terry Thompson visited the National Museum of Man[2] and were given tape-recorded copies of most of the Nɬeʔképmx wax cylinders. In 1979, Laurence C. Thompson worked through the recording of the "Funeral Address," writing it in phonetic transcription and translating it with the help of Annie Z. York, of Spuzzum, British Columbia.[3] In 1995, M. Terry Thompson listened to the tape recording, referring to the written transcription and translation, and with the help of Steven M. Egesdal, made this analysis of the oration in English.

This is a formal speech, spoken in firm and ringing tones by a man who was obviously accustomed to speaking with authority and in public. The rhythm and cadence of the language is very accomplished and polished, and the entire oration was spoken without hesitation. The spacing gives some indication of the cadence of the oration.

Funeral Address to the Mourners of a Dead Child

My children, you just hold on!
While we're pitiful, we're not the only ones that are pitiful like that.
> Every place on earth it's like that,
> There are pitiful ones like that.
You look at it, what happened to us.

We're surely pitiful.

But it's not only here that it happens like that.

In every place death exists.

That is the way it has been since the world was created.

A person eventually dies.

A child is born of its mother and grows up.

It isn't long and then he dies.

We couldn't stop it.

We are powerless to do anything, my children,

I guess that's what He thinks.

That's what He thinks who created us here.

Keep your hearts slow when you hang your heads in sadness.

You should look after each other.

Although we're pitiful, don't get angry at your friend!

It would be good if you take care of your friend.

We're all taking care of this earth.

Many people suffer the same way.

We're not alone in this world.

You see what happened to us, my children,

See what happens and look at it,

And take care of it—you watch.

It would be good for you to know what happens.

You're not the only one that's pitiful, that suffers like that,

You're not the only one here that's pitiful, that's suffering like that.

People are never without trouble,

People are never without trouble, that's your sorrow.

That's what I'm telling you, my children.

I'm through speaking to you,

Giving you my kind sympathy.

REPLY: That's what you've been speaking.[4]

Notes

1. The other oration, of advice to an adolescent about to begin a search for spirit power, is cut off before the end due to the shortness of recording time possible on the wax cylinder.

2. This travel was performed as part of a research grant from the Guggenheim Foundation.

3. Research during this period was accomplished with funding from the National Science Foundation and the National Endowment for the Humanities.

4. This formal reply was given by Chief Pətcinéyt, another member of the delegation.

Humor

The Two Coyotes

A Humorous Lillooet Story

Told by Bill Edwards

Edited by Jan P. van Eijk

The Lillooet inhabit an area 160 to 300 kilometers (100 to 185 miles) northeast of Vancouver, an area they have called their homeland for an untold number of centuries. It is a strikingly beautiful piece of earth—with soaring mountains, wide lakes, dense forests, and fast-flowing rivers—that has provided the Lillooet with ample sustenance during their wise and respectful occupation of this land and has also provided the setting for their magnificent oral literature.

This story, "The Two Coyotes," is a classic Lillooet myth that deals with one of the main characters in Lillooet cosmology. As a Trickster, Coyote displays the entire range of human qualities, from lust and greed to courage and resourcefulness. In this story he dupes his namesake by playing on the word *pépla7*, which translates as "one animal" or "another one" (i.e., another animal). Not only is this short story an amusing one, especially in Bill Edwards's masterful rendering, but it also shows how Lillooet, no less than English, can use word-play in a very sophisticated manner.[1]

The Two Coyotes

Two coyotes were going along. Then one of them said: "I am a Coyote, everybody knows that I am a Coyote. But you are not a Coyote, you are 'Another One.'"

"No way, I am also a Coyote," the other one said.

"Not at all, you are 'Another One.' Okay, you will find out right now. I am going to cross this garden, you listen to the people."

Well, he went across, and while he was going across he was seen by the people. "Hey, there is a Coyote going there, it is a Coyote that is going there." He carried on, and he went out of sight.

Then the other one took off, he suddenly appeared, and they noticed him. "There goes another one, it's another one that is going there."

He carried on and he got to the other spot, where he met his friend.

"See?" he was told, "See? did you hear them? I am a Coyote, but you are 'Another One.'"

Notes

1. This same story and similar word-play occurs in at least Thompson River Salish and in Spokane, and we have been told it is widespread.—Eds.

The Story of Mink and Miss Pitch

A Traditional Upriver Halkomelem Story

Told by Susan Malloway Jimmy

Edited by Brent Galloway

This story is a translation of a traditional Upriver Halkomelem story. Halkomelem has three dialect groups: Upriver Halkomelem, Downriver Halkomelem, and Island Halkomelem. In Whatcom County, Washington, some members of the Nooksack Tribe also speak Upriver Halkomelem. There were fewer than 150 native speakers of Halkomelem in 1996. Thanks to language revival efforts, there are now at least several new young or middle-aged moderately fluent speakers in each dialect group.

There are several types of Upriver Halkomelem stories: news of recent events, stories of historical events, and $sx̌^woxǐ^wiy\acute{\varepsilon}m$ ("myth, legend, fable"). Most $sx̌^wox̌^wiy\acute{\varepsilon}m$ are set in a distant past before or during the time when the Transformers walked the earth. This was a time when most living creatures were people, but many of them had the odd habits of nonhumans. The Transformers in Halkomelem stories were originally two daughters of black bears, whose mother was killed by Grizzly Bear,[1] and who wandered to the land beyond the edge of the world and gained great powers. When they returned, they traveled the Pacific Northwest, sometimes together, but usually singly, noticing the habits of people and turning them into the animals we know today. Sometimes they turned people and already-changed animals into stone, usually because of some mischief they got into in confrontations with the Transformers in these legends; the stones were then named for the people or animals they were originally.

This story is set in such a time, when Mink and Pitch were a man and a woman, respectively, but had some of the habits and characteristics of the real animal and of real pitch. The story was tape-recorded on May 3, 1978, in Upriver Halkomelem, by Mrs. Susan (Malloway) Jimmy, originally of Sardis, British Columbia. Her daughter, Mrs. Maria (Jimmy) Villanueva, had heard the story from her mother and offered to tape-record it for me. On the tape, Maria occasionally chuckles in anticipation of certain parts of the story, and this reflects the authentic nature of the performance and the audience. Usually these stories were told many times to children as bedtime stories, and the children would also know and anticipate humorous parts.

The story is about Mink and Miss Pitch (Susan Jimmy's English name for the story; she did not give it a title in Halkomelem). In fact, the story is told completely without using the Halkomelem word for pitch or any proper name for Miss Pitch. Thus, a listener who did not know the story would be guessing about the identity of the beautiful heroine in the story. In Halkomelem legends, as well as legends of a number of other Coast Salish languages, Mink is a notorious and inept womanizer. Mink usually gets caught in stupid and embarrassing situations, often of a sexual nature.

This story was wonderfully told, with excellent humor, characterizations, and plot details. It has more vivid descriptions than many Halkomelem stories. I doubt this indicates that it was anglicized, because some other traditional stories also have this degree of description. I transcribed it with Mrs. Edna Bobb of Seabird Island Reserve, and Mrs. Amelia Douglas of Cheam Reserve, in 1978–79. Later, when I analyzed it, I saw that it was also an excellent example of a sophisticated use of discourse conjunctions, timing, and repetition for humorous effect, all within a traditional style of storytelling.

This presentation of the story follows the ethnopoetic approach of Hymes (1981). While I use that approach, I would not characterize the story as poetry. There are no rhymes or tight meters, for instance, and no feeling of poetry. Close study reveals artistry and tradition, however, and an ethnopoetic presentation helps to bring the story more authentically alive in translation than by adding storytelling techniques from English not present in the Halkomelem. Three raised dots within a word or after the *o* in "so" is used to represent Halkomelem emphasis, rhetorical vowel lengthening, and can be read in English by pronouncing the vowel preceding it three times as long. It has a similar force in both English and Halkomelem.

Two additional comments about content are noteworthy. This is a humorous story told by a mother to her daughter; both participants enjoyed the story immensely, as can be heard on the tape. Mink, in his lust, makes a real fool of himself, as usual. Toward the end, Mink punches and kicks his "wife," but he is kept stuck all night long and throughout the first half of the next day, with Miss Pitch telling him off. So a subtheme of the plot is that wife battering does not pay. I have not attempted to discuss this further, nor to deal with how it violates Halkomelem cultural practice. However, as Mink usually violates at least one cultural practice in each story about him, this may be a case of that violation, as well as of his usual stupidity, obsession, and other character flaws.

The Story of Mink and Miss Pitch

Little Mink is traveling, going along, they say.
    He is a handsome man.
        He is traveling on foot/walking along.
            He is traveling along the edge of the river.

And an adolescent virgin girl is sitting.
    It is on a hill that the beautiful woman is sitting.

So that young man, Little Mink, walked.
    So··· he just walks there.
        It is for three days that he walks.
            He has his hands behind his back as he walks
                along.

So it just got to the fourth day.
    And so he thinks to himself, *Oh, it might be good if I go see the
        girl.*
        He's going to talk to her, they say, that Little Mink
            says.

So··· he just goes to climb the hill.
    So he managed to reach the girl there.
        He went up to the place where the girl was.

So he says to her, "Oh, you are really very beautiful.
    Your clothes are nice.
        So why don't you ever walk a little?
            You always just sit there every day."

So the girl said, "Oh that's the way I am.
    That's the way I am, sitting every day.
        So it is that I'm just sitting here."

So it is that he said, "Oh, you're very beautiful.
    Oh just stay sitting."
        "Yes, that's the way I am every day."

"I'd better get home.
     It's already getting dark."

So he just goes down the hill.
     So he just goes down on the flat.
          He got to the edge of the river so he walks.
               He walks there.

It gets daylight and he was already walking again.
     Again he's traveling by the edge of the river as he walks.
          He's a handsome man, that Mink.

So·· · he just thinks to himself again,
     It would be good if I went to see the girl, see whatever
          she is doing.

So again he just climbs the hill.
     He reached the girl there.

So he said to her, "Oh, your clothes are really nice.
     You are beautiful.
          Why don't you ever walk to the edge of the river?"

"Oh, that's the way I am. I'm like that.
     Just always sitting.
          I've got lots of work, so I'm sitting here."

So·· · then it is that he just coaxes her.
     "It's good that we go walk."

"No.

So it is that the sun will just start to appear, when I sweat already.
     So it is that my sweat drips.
          So my sweat drips until they say it reaches the ground.
               So that is just my daughters,
                    my sweat starting to grow on the ground."

So he says, "So why do you just have children and no husband?
    Why don't you pity me?
        I'll take care of you.
            I'll give you everything that you're eating.
                Whatever you might wish for to eat I'll give
                    you."

"No," says that woman, says that girl.
    "It would be impossible.
        So it is already that it just starts to get hot when I
            sweat already.

Nobody gets near it.
    So it got late at night,
        and so my body gets hard.
            I guess it's impossible for anybody to get near me
                when my body is hard."

"Oh, it's no matter.
    You better accept me."
        "No," she said.

So· · · he just walks home.

Morning comes.
    Again it gets daylight.
        Again he's walking.

So again he just came to arrive.
    Again he comes to see the girl.

He was just told repeatedly it would be impossible.
    So· · · she's just there.

It is on the fourth day
    and so that Mink thinks to himself, *It would be good if I camp.
        Then it is that I'm going to hug that girl.*

So· · · he just climbed up the hill.

He lays down beside the girl.
    It was just getting dark a little when he takes her arm
        and so he hugged her.
            So· · · he just stays like that until it comes to be
            day.

It starts to be day and he's stuck.
    He's stuck on the girl.
        He isn't stuck too hard because he manages to get himself
        loose.

So· · · he just goes home again.
    He goes home.
        He goes to wherever his house is.

Later in the morning he's walking again.
    That man is handsome, that Mink.

So· · · he just climbed the hill.
    So he reached the girl.

So he proposed to her.
    So "No," that girl said.
        "It can't be.
            And nobody gets near to me when it starts to get hot
            because I sweat."

So· · · he just thinks to himself,
    Oh, it would be good if I hug her.

So· · · he just hugs the girl.
    So he stayed like that a long time.
        It was already getting night.

Again that girl got hard.
     Again she got frozen.
          So he got stuck.
               He can't get himself loose.

So· · · he just thought, *Oh I've gotten married.*
     The girl accepted me.
          So he stays like that a long time.

It starts to get light again and again it gets hot.
     It already started to get hot.

So he just came loose.

So· · · he just says, "So it will be that I'll stay together with you.
     I'll stay here."
          So he laid on his back right beside that girl.

He's on his back a lo· · ·ng time there in the hot sun.
     So· · · he's just there I don't know how many days on his back.

So· · · he just gets mad.
     She'll learn how it feels!
          I'll beat her up.
               She can't do that, not pay any attention to me!

So· · · he just punched his wife in the face.
     He had already gotten a wife he felt.
          So he punched her in the face.

And so his hand stuck in the face of that girl.
     So· · · he just stays like that.

He's wondering, *I wonder what shall I do?*
     Oh she'll learn how it feels.
          It'll be now.
               Now she be hurt this time.

So he punched her in the face left-handed.

So· · · he just sticks.
    So he gets really stuck.
        So he's like that a lo· · ·ng time.
            The woman was already getting a little frozen.

So· · · he just thinks to himself, *She'll see how it feels.*

I'll kick her.
    It'll be in her stomach that I kick her.
So he kicked her.

So· · · he just gets stuck.
    His foot is stuck in the stomach of his wife.
        So· · · he's just sitting there.
            He's stuck.
                He can't manage to get himself loose.

So he just thinks to himself, *Oh now she'll get hurt.*
    Now she'll get hurt this time.
        I'll beat her to a pulp.
            I'll beat her body to a pulp.

So he used his left foot.
    He kicks her.
        It's really hard that he kicks her until it goes deep.

His foot stuck.
    So· · · he just stays there.
        So he gets all doubled up.
            He's all doubled up.
                He can't manage to get loose.
                    So· · · he just stays like that.

He's thinking, *What will I do so I can move?*
    Now I'll hurt her.
        Oh it'll be good if I butt her with my face.

So his wife got butted on her forehead.

So his forehead stuck on his wife.
 And so he's there, all doubled over.
  All that night he's all doubled over.
   He can't get himself loose.

It started to get daylight.
 Then it got day
  Then the sun appeared.
   He's sitting.
    His arms got loosened up a little.

I'll manage to get myself loose!

So· · · he just tries hard.
 So his arm on one side came loose.
  It isn't long until his other arm came loose.

It already started to get hot.

So· · · his feet just came loose.

And so suddenly he drops to the ground.

So he's there on his back o· · ·n the ground for a long time.
 His arms are stuck.
  His legs get stuck.
   So he's all doubled over there.

So the woman just says, "You went until you found out how it feels.
 I told you that I am bad.
  I can't walk.
   It's just the way I am like, sitting here.
    It's all day, all night that I'm sitting
    here.

And so when it starts to get hot

then I start to sweat.
              So when it gets dark and then it gets frozen."

So there was nothing that Mink could do.

Notes

1. One of the Thompson River Salish Transformers was the youngest of four Black Bear cubs, whose parents were killed by Grizzly Woman. (See Egesdal and M. T. Thompson 1994.)—Eds.

Broke-Her-Nose Woman (or The Stupid Daughter-in-Law)

A Humorous Nɬeʔkepmxcín (Thompson River Salish) Story

Told by Mabel Joe

Edited by Mabel Joe and M. Terry Thompson

Word play is often used in Nle'kepmxcin (Nɬeʔkepmxcín), sometimes for poetic effect, and often for humor. This short humorous tale uses word-play based on a lexical suffix[1] with the basic meaning "nose." The meaning has been extended over the years and has come to mean a number of things: nose, beak, front end, prow or bow [of boat], torch, wick, point, sharp end, hook, flower, bud, joint, knuckle, and such; in this case it should have been understood as "the end of a branch."

This traditional story was told in the Thompson language by Mabel Joe at the Elders' Day gathering, August 20, 1978, at Quilcene, near Merritt, British Columbia, and won a prize as the most humorous story.[2] The spacing roughly approximates the cadence of speech.

Broke-Her-Nose Woman (or *The Stupid Daughter-in-Law*)

I'm going to tell you a story
about the people a long time ago,
what work the women did.
One time they said, "We're going to go for moss."[3]
So they went to get moss.
They said, "We're all going to get moss."

One old lady said to her daughter-in-law,
"Go along with the other daughters-in-law.
You break the end of the branches."[4]
She said, "Go with them, the sisters-in-law."
They were around there,
they were working.
She was supposed to be breaking off branches,
but instead she twisted her nose.
Breaking branches—she didn't help.

Instead she was there breaking her nose.
When she came back her nose was all swelled up there.

"Why is your nose swelled up?
Daughter-in-law, WHY is your nose all swelled up?"

"You told me, 'You're going to go,
you're going to go around there
and break your nose.'
So· · ·, I broke my nose,
I broke my own nose."

She was supposed to be HELPING,
but she was breaking her nose.
Her nose was swelled up there for a few days.

That's my story.
It's like that now.
If we tell them something,
"You're going to help out,"
she doesn't know how to do things, she's
stupid.

There is the stupid daughter-in-law.

AUDIENCE: [Laughter and applause]

Notes

1. Lexical suffixes are found throughout the Salishan languages. These suffixes have no grammatical content, and are not complete words, so that the words incorporating them cannot be called compounds. The terminology "lexical suffix" is used consistently in modern linguistic descriptions of the languages. They add precision of reference and a variety of nuances, sometimes very subtle and highly specialized ones (Thompson and Thompson 1992:112–14; Thompson and Thompson 1996:535–43).

2. It was recorded on tape by Sharon Mayes and Yvonne Hebert (Mayes and Hebert 1978). Working together, Mabel Joe and M. Terry Thompson (M. T. Thompson and Joe 1989) transcribed it phonetically from the tape recording and translated it on July 22, 1989.

3. Black tree lichen, or Spanish moss, *Bryoria fremontii,* an important food for all the Interior

Salishan people. It grows on the branches of coniferous trees such as larch, pines, and Douglas fir (Turner et al. 1990:71–75).

4. q'w'áqsm "break the end of branches," or "break your nose." (=aqs is a lexical suffix with several meanings, including "branch" (protruding from the tree) and "nose" (protruding from the face).

Songs

Three Thompson River Salish Songs from Spuzzum

Sung by Annie Z. York

Edited by Andrea Laforet

In the early 1980s Annie York, who lived in Spuzzum, the southernmost Nle'kepmx (Nɬeʔképmx, Thompson River Salish) village, shared three songs: "A Song of the Seasons," "Simon Fraser's Song," and "The Song for Mount Baker." For each song, she provided the Nle'kepmx text and an English translation designed to give the poetic sense as well as the literal meaning of the words.

A small community situated beside Spuzzum Creek on the western bank of the Fraser River, Spuzzum has long been a gateway to the rich and diverse country of the Nle'kepmx. The river here is narrow, deep, and turbulent; the Coast Mountains rise behind the village, and the Cascades are just across the river. The Fraser Canyon is a dramatically beautiful place to live.

During the nineteenth century Spuzzum found itself in the path of virtually every major colonial initiative undertaken to form what is now British Columbia. Fur traders, gold miners, railroad builders, merchants, administrators, missionaries, and settlers all came to, and through, Spuzzum, all of them intending to reshape at least some part of the landscape or some part of Nle'kepmx life. The songs presented here reflect some of those events and testify to the enduring creativity of the Nle'kepmx who witnessed them.

Annie York was born in Spuzzum in 1904 and visited the community for various periods during a childhood spent with her parents and great-aunt in the Fraser and Nicola valleys. She returned to Spuzzum in 1932 and lived there until her death in 1991. The first two songs came to Miss York from another Spuzzum resident, Annie Lee, Kwəsəmitétkʷu, who was born in the 1860s and died in the 1930s. Annie York learned "The Song for Mount Baker" from Bob Peters, a relative whose ancestors were from Spuzzum, although his family was living at Yale, twelve miles downriver. Bob Peters originally played this song for Miss York on his flute.

All of the songs are attributed to Kəsnén, also known as Kətyén, a woman who lived in Spuzzum in the late eighteenth and early nineteenth centuries.

She was a cousin of Miss York's grandmother, Amelia York. The "Song for Mount Baker" refers to events that took place in the mid-nineteenth century, and although Kəsnén could easily have had a lifespan that stretched from the 1780s to the 1860s, it is possible that more than one original composer was involved, and also possible that the songs acquired shape and intonation from each person who passed them on. The songs were originally composed and sung in the Nle'kepmx language. They did not have formal titles; the titles used here reflect the way in which Annie York referred to them. At least one was written down by Annie York in English to preserve it at a time when the use of Nle'kepmxcin in Spuzzum was in decline.

These are not the only Nle'kepmx songs to have been recorded. In the early twentieth century several Nle'kepmx people from the Thompson and Nicola valleys recorded songs for James Teit, a long-time resident of the region who did ethnographic work under the direction of Franz Boas. Teit compiled these in an unpublished manuscript, "Notes on Songs of the Indians of British Columbia." Recently, Wendy Wickwire has recorded and studied songs preserved and sung by contemporary Nle'kepmx people.

For the Nle'kepmx, song has traditionally been the medium of communication between human beings and the other beings inhabiting the world. For people educated in the old ways, the concept of people (*séytknmx*) includes beings who appear in the waking world as grizzly bears, salmon, or water, but appear to human beings in dreams as people with knowledge greater than a normal human being could possess. Anyone meeting a nonhuman being, for example, the Grizzly Bear, or Crane, in a dream might have a song given to him as a sign of the encounter and as a part of the gifts that came from it. In every generation certain people also have been recognized as especially good singers or composers of songs.

In addition to the songs received in dreams, Xʷəlínek, Yupétkʷu, Tiʔɬníče? and others who worked with Teit recorded love songs, cradle songs, and songs for singing while playing lahal (stick-game), a gambling game known throughout the Salish-speaking world and the entire Northwest Coast. The words of the songs express the loneliness of separation, a prayer for protection, or a lullaby for twins. Sometimes they are entirely without explicit meaning.

Like many of the songs recorded by Teit, the three songs preserved by Annie York incorporate themes of life after the arrival of Europeans, but they also center on images significant in Nle'kepmx thought. Although the songs differ in length, purpose, and content, there are similarities in imagery and concept from one song to another.

All of the songs voice concerns important in the traditional world. "A Song of the Seasons" is a contemplative lyric on the themes of the changing seasons, life and death. The other two songs were composed in response to events directly connected with European contact, specifically the visit of Simon Fraser to Spuzzum in 1808 and the establishment in 1859 of the international boundary, which placed Mount Baker in the United States.

A Song of the Seasons

When spring comes to the earth
The mountains have a snowy top
When spring comes to the earth
When the plants bud out
Then the birds sing
When spring comes to the earth
When the lonely forest turns green on the side-hills
The running-place of the black bear and the grizzly
In the high places.
Then the trees are blown by the wind
The fir and the cedar
Then the creek flows
On the green side-hill.
Then the flowers bloom
On the green side-hill.
There are flowers like the stars in the sky.
Then the sun shines when it comes out.
It is God's work, toward (his) real thought.
Of all the plants
Here on the earth.
Then it is autumn.
Then the leaves turn red.
Then the leaves turn yellow
Then autumn comes
Then in that last day
Then the leaves are finished falling in that lonely forest
In the last day of my life
When my life is over, it's going to float
Like an old Indian canoe
Until my tears here are finished

It's going to be a memory—my thinking
It will float toward the ocean
When my life comes to an end and the sun turns red
The sun, as it goes down.
In the west as this life ends
The real work of God
Then he thinks about everything
Here on earth.
Then this life is going to be finished
Then my friends will remember me.
My tears are really finished, they'll stay here on earth
I will not return to this life here
When God will judge me
On this life.

The Nle'kepmx text begins with *nxʷúy̓t us e tmíxʷ*, the insistent push of the coming of spring captured in the bouncy rhythm of the phrase. The English, "When spring comes to the earth," brings a more measured quality to the translation, but the English rendition preserves the structure and imagery of the original text. The song is in two parts, the first dealing with the coming of spring and the renewal of life, and the second dealing with autumn and the approach of death.

The nine introductory lines contain images of states of being and becoming associated with spring,

When spring comes to the earth
The mountains have a snowy top
When spring comes to the earth
When the plants bud out
Then the birds sing
When spring comes to the earth
When the lonely forest turns green on the side-hills
The running-place of the black bear and the grizzly
In the high places.

followed by action imagery:

Then the trees are blown by the wind...
Then the creek flows . . .
Then the flowers bloom . . .

The first section of the song is summed up with the rhythmic phrase, "Here on this earth" (*n ʔéye tək tmíxᵂ*), a phrase heard as well in certain songs Teit recorded upcountry[1] (Teit n.d.: Song 49), where it sums up and provides a conclusion to what has gone before.

The second part begins with the idea of encroaching autumn, conveyed in three lines of identical structure:

> Then it is autumn;
> Then the leaves turn red,
> Then the leaves turn yellow.

Meaning is given additional force through repetition. The repetition of "When spring comes to the earth" gives incremental force to the lines that follow it, and the refrain, "Here on this earth," repeated in the second half, conveys the inevitability or immutability of the process being evoked.

The connection between the seasons and human life is presented in two principal images, which link a person's life with a canoe and the end of life with the sunset. For some Nle'kepmx people, canoes have also been linked with life, or the end of life, in dreams foretelling the death of a family member. Annie York said, "If someone in a family was going to die, you saw canoes in a lake. You dream about it too. That's not a good dream." The use of sunset as a metaphor for the end of life was perhaps even more common. The souls of sick people were drawn to the west, away from life, by the sun (Teit n.d.: Song 106), and the progression of sunrise to sunset, beginning of life to end of life, was reflected in the movements of the dancers in the circle dance (Teit n.d.: Song 40), performed by Nle'kepmx people at the summer solstice and other times of the year.

"A Song of the Seasons" expresses the thoughts of a single person, and this, too, is in keeping with Nle'kepmx traditional practice. Except during the circle dance—considered a kind of prayer—Nle'kepmx people expressed their relationship with the supernatural as individuals. The Christian churches established in the 1860s required a more collective practice, followed by the many people who became converts, but Christianity had a varied impact on individual belief.

Nle'kepmx thought affirmed that connections with the supernatural were a natural and normal part of the life of every person. Nle'kepmx society supported an interest in the fundamental nature of the world; an interest in Christianity was an extension of this, and many devoutly Christian Nle'kepmx people, including Annie York, have combined Christian belief and an Nle'kepmx understanding of the nature of things. The lines near the end of the song, concerned with God and judgment, clearly show Christian influence. However, the references to high, lonely, places, to movement from east to west, and to images of canoes and sunset, all reflect traditional religious beliefs.

Simon Fraser's Song

Simon Fraser passed through Spuzzum in June 1808. He recorded the visit in his journal (Lamb 1960), and probably was unaware that his trip downriver through Nle'kepmx territory also was recorded in Nle'kepmx oral narratives (Teit 1912a:414–16). This song composed in Spuzzum, however, was not a record of his visit, but a song sung for his protection as he left to go downriver into Halkomelem territory.

> We'll meet you again
> When the leaves are turning red and yellow
> And when our chief asks us to pray
> We'll pray for you when the sun rises
> And when the sun rises we'll bow our heads
> And face to the sun
> And we'll pray for you.
> And when our chief takes his pipe
> And smokes his pipe
> His smoke will drift down the river to follow you
>   and will accompany you.
> And when all the trees sway along the beach
> The green leaves and the green boughs
> And with all the emerald wings will sway around you
> And the silvery circle, the eddy, the pool
> And you will be safe when you go through this channel
> And when you are in the woods, in the forest we'll always
>   pray for you
> And our prayers will always remain with you
> And all our tribes from Spuzzum will always pray for you to
>   return
> And one day your flag will fly over us.

Annie York provided this English translation in a discussion of a somewhat shorter Nle'kepmx text recorded by an earlier interviewer (Orchard n.d.). She affirmed that in the song Simon Fraser is being addressed as the son of the Sun. The narratives about Fraser's journey that Teit recorded indicate that the Nle'kepmx people who encountered Fraser saw him and his crew as Transformers returned to earth. Fraser was variously seen as the son of the Sun and as Coyote. Coyote was not only a Transformer and Trickster in myth-time but also the figure who was to return at the end of the world, traveling with the Old One and the souls of the dead, surrounded either by tobacco smoke or a red cloud. It is clear, too, that Nle'kepmx people saw Fraser as sharing Coyote's gullibility and vulnerability, and his journal indicates that they had ample reason to do so. Fraser appeared suddenly in Nle'kepmx territory, on a journey that took him from one end of the country to the other, and back again. Although the Transformers were known as Coyote, the Black Bear Brothers, and Hog-Fennel Root, they, too, moved through the earth in human form, constantly traveling.

The original Nle'kepmx text is reminiscent of prayer songs recorded by Teit (n.d.: Song 69). Although the English version contains more images, prayer is still a strong theme. For Annie York the imagery was pivotal to the meaning of the song as a promise of supernatural protection for Fraser. To the image of people bowing their heads before the sun in prayer is added the image of the chief smoking his pipe, the tobacco smoke drifting down the river. Smoking was a means of communication with supernatural beings analogous to prayer; tobacco, and, by extension, drifting smoke, were xaʔxáʔ; that is, suffused with immanent supernatural power. Water, "the silvery circle, the eddy, the pool," also was a medium for prayer, as were fir boughs, "green boughs." Fir boughs were also used by specialists in arranging for the ritual protection of patients.

The last lines of this translation contain a reference to the establishment of European sovereignty that is not in the Nle'kepmx text, and it may be a reference to the kind of prophecy made by some Nle'kepmx people who experienced early visions of postcontact life (Teit n.d.: VI M 51), or simply an added commentary.

Song for Mount Baker

Whether the reference to the flag in the Simon Fraser song arises out of conviction or courtesy, the "Song for Mount Baker" carries a different message. Like "A Song for the Seasons," it is contemplative and reflective, but, more than that, it is a song of mourning. Annie York classified it as *yémit* (prayer).

> This is the song.
> This is the song.
> I'm going to sing.
> We won't face again to that mountain to pray.
> When it's sunny, then it begins to shine, that mountaintop
> that glitters.
> We won't bow to pray toward that mountain.

Our chief won't smoke his pipe again.
The eagle flies at its top.
In spring the mountain goats run on its slopes.
Then the baby goats are born.
But the chief is finished smoking his pipe there.
Finished is the smoke rising from his pipe, the wind blowing
     the smoke.
The flag across the line flutters
The red, the white, the blue and the stars.

Although it shares with "Simon Fraser's Song" the images of prayer, of smoking and blowing smoke, and of the wind blowing, the "Song for Mount Baker" is closer in structure to "A Song for the Seasons," and although the word *tmíxʷ* (land), is not used, that is its theme. Like songs recorded by Teit, the "Song for Mount Baker" has an initial set of lines announcing the singer's intention, the intention emphasized by the parallel structure of the first two lines,

> This is the song
> This is the song
> I am going to sing

and by the use of the two words for song: *snéʔm*, which carries the connotation of supernatural helper as well as the song that is its gift, and *sʔíƛ̓m*, which evokes the process of singing. The first three lines are a component unto themselves. The completely different structure of the fourth line announces the beginning of the song itself.

The entire text carries the message that Mount Baker has been removed from the Nle'kepmx world as it has been known, with images of renewal,

> In the spring the mountain goats run on its slopes
> Then the baby goats are born

contrasted against images of ending, of termination. The similar rhythm and identical meaning of the fourth and sixth lines reinforce the overall message:

> We won't face again to that mountain to pray.
> We won't bow to pray toward that mountain.

The newly born goats signify the renewal that is a quality of the land, but the mountain itself has been removed from the Nle'kepmx people as a place where communication with the supernatural, a communication that is essential to life, may be held. "Finished is the smoke rising from his pipe." The flag in this song is part of the essential message; it symbolizes the change that has come to the land.

These are songs held a long time in memory, without being performed. The Nle'kepmx texts for all three convey a strong poetic sense on the part of the composer, and probably, as well, on the part of those who kept the songs.

Ironically, although "A Song for the Seasons" contains no imagery from European contact, it is the most unusual in terms of Nle'kepmx song. Although diverse in form and purpose, the songs Teit recorded focus on relationships among people, or between human and supernatural beings, with virtually no imagery descriptive of the country. This may simply be an accident of the history of collecting, or "A Song for the Seasons" may be a novel and highly personal poetic expression.

The very fact that they arise from experiences of postcontact life connects the "Song for Mount Baker" and "Simon Fraser's Song" with other forms of nineteenth century Nle'kepmx experience and expression. Ti?ɬniče, a chief and colleague of Teit who lived at Spences Bridge, acquired a song during a dream that took place in a mine shaft (Teit n.d.: VI M 49, VI M 50). Another man had as his supernatural helper the report of a gun (Teit n.d.: VI M 44). Praying songs of upcountry chiefs incorporated visions of European houses, and European goods, such as stoves, that were to become part of Nle?kepmx life.

The time from which these three songs have come was a dynamic period in Nle'kepmx history. In keeping them and passing them on, Annie York has enabled a new generation to appreciate not only aspects of Nle'kepmx song but also something of the experience of the people who lived through that time.

Notes

1. North, "up" the Fraser and Thompson rivers.—Eds.

Modern Poems and a Story-Poem

The modern poems and the story-poem included in this volume originated and were written in English by Duane Niatum, Klallam, who does not speak the Klallam language but understands the culture; and by the late Jack Iyall, Cowlitz, who lived in his culture but wrote his poetry in English.

Both writers share some of the wistfulness about the decay of their ancestral cultures, along with their optimism, and their delight in those same cultures.—Eds.

Growing Old

Jack Iyall [Cowlitz]

Today, I'm a dirty old man.
Yesterday, growing old was beautiful.
Today, I'm in the welfare line.
Yesterday, there was a place for me.
Today, I'm getting old and things are getting worse.
At sixty-five, I witness the mysteries of the universe.
At seventy, I could talk to spirits.
At eighty-five, I'm preparing for my trip to the spirit land.
The preacher said I can't go 'til judgment day . . .
The new and the old within.
Wrap yourself in memories
As a warm bright colored blanket
Against the chill wind of progress.

The Salmon

Duane Niatum [Klallam]

Mother of salt and slate,
foam and storm, eye of columbine;
sea flower carried by our shadow people
in a canoe on a horizon of mud and slime,
under the forest floor;

mixer of scale, bone, and blood,
nose of Thunderbird who answered her wave
as it passed our rainbow mountain;
mother of calm and deliverance,
the tongue's drum from the cliff.

High above the raven valleys
near the sea, dream fox
with the thread of the current in its mouth
touches the Elwha river twice
as she nestles her eggs in the gravel.
The roots of the wind's hair
builds the birth cradle out of moon and tide.

Salmon Woman, a streaky
thrust at fertility, edges like Dawnmaker
up the slope, the thinning trail of the river.
Fever rattle of joy and tenacity,
gills bellow fullness and emptiness:
the songs of grandmothers
around Hadlock village fires that wove
our daughter into blankets and water dreamers.

To Our Salish Women Who Weave the Seasons

For Mary Peters

Duane Niatum [Klallam]

I try to sleep
on a tule mat to see what the dream shows

of the last Klallam grandmother to weave
such bulrush grass. I drop a red cedar

     wreath into the Hoko River
to put the family ghosts to bed.

Grandmother weavers circle our struggle,
come to witness people falling out

     of their skins, nourish those
shaking with madness or chronic disease,

soften our yoke to the years-wheel.
The story carved on the elders' staff

     of my nomad pantomime lives
on when the spindle whorls dance.

     How to speak with these women
in bark capes and hats who spin in

and out of my life like a wedding on fire?
How reach the hands of these elders

     the Transformer promised a healing
path out of darkness and despair so the words

of our storyteller would be caught in the sunstone net,
at the long pauses of the short notes?

  These women clack humor-rattles
and teach us the power of laughter and tears

to switch the light back on, soothe our fears,
tie our family and the villages to the center

  of the basket. They taunt enemies
into self-destruction before our ancestral mountains

the ravagers have made as barren as the backs
of mangy dogs. O these sea and river weavers

hum and sing until our grief turns to frog song
on Crow's mirror. These dancers tell me in

their own snow-water voices to sing morning,
noon and night to Crow, first maker

before his baskets were offered as clamshell
gifts so by the next moon the sun will ripen

the heart's chokecherry. O these women in
Thunderbird and Wolf capes let me know

when I'm up to my neck in rapids and storm,
  I'm at home and a son

of their tribe as mutilated as the sea and earth
yet still half osprey and half salmon.

So every bone that wants to sing sings;
every nerve that wants to burn burns.

Sleeping Woman [Min-!sw-tun]

For Linda of Lower Elwha

Duane Niatum [Klallam]

The inspiration for writing an adaptation of this Klallam sacred narrative (myth) is to support all the Klallams at Lower Elwha, Jamestown, and Port Gamble who are encouraging the young people to learn the language, songs, and stories of their ancestors. I hope the modern context for the story helps draw the next generation into its world. Key figures in the story are youths, which should appeal to their interest. We can no longer ignore the fact that the Klallam language is endangered, and with it our oral traditions. For decades before I was born, the forces of Euramerican culture, particularly those of the missionaries, federal government, and educators, succeeded in convincing or shaming American Indian children and youth into ignoring or resisting all connections to their tribal heritage. Fortunately, out of more than thirty-one Klallam villages that existed on the Olympic Peninsula, the three that remain are making every effort to turn this trend around. Becher Bay, a village located on the southern tip of Vancouver Island, has been quite successful in keeping the language and traditions alive in the community. The old smokehouse religion is as strong today as it ever was in the past. Such Klallam tenacity gives one a thin ray of hope.

Sleeping Woman

Grandfather, who was handed the storyteller's staff, told us a story of our ancestors of the red cedar forest who lived long, long ago. His story starts from the claim that Sleeping Woman never slept. This was, at least, what five of the most cantankerous men of the medicine road tried to convince the people. Grandpa reminded us that these men failed to see that Sleeping Woman was just a woman who spent a good deal of her time fishing in dreams, where dreams brought her the herbs and plants to help us along the healing path. Grandpa said their gossip party was forever spreading rumors throughout the village and far beyond that Sleeping Woman was only a make-believe healer and her art was brewed in a basket of swamp sludge. Yet it didn't take long for the people to see that these men never carried a pouch of proof. Jealousy boiled in their blood for years, and Raven was ready to call in the wolves to quiet them down. Truth was something these shamans as slippery as candle-fish had lost sight of in their riptide obsession to possess Sleeping Woman. Their pride had reduced them to walking around with square heads and puff-ball feet in their not-so-clever game of one-upmanship. These medicine men that stepped on the heels of envy grew dimmer and dimmer in the eyes of the village elders. And before the mosquitoes finished their feast on this clan, not one person in any of the villages asked them for help in sickness or anything else. The strong people were convinced that these medicine men were headed for quicksand or the swirling pool at the beach that the sea had created for such men who chose the path to nowhere.

Grandpa said our ancestors saw that these men with eyes as dried up and vacant as crab shells in the wind had lost the ability to read the songlines of their blood. They had looked inward at the red river and its promise of story and cure and all they saw were stinkbug's juices, never the proper song or solution. The community and the elders saw how haggard and drained of spirit these carriers of the healing path had become. These men who had stumbled off the path began to look pitiful even to themselves, and this only added to their grief. Their schemes and lies had erased what animals from the inner depths had once whispered to them—the secret words to health. They were deaf to the dawn dancers and had only managed to fall into a sinkhole. Everything they touched broke into pieces before their eyes. The men shriveled into tiny grubs in search of a place to disappear in.

I remember one day as a small boy my great-uncle told a different story of Sleeping Woman, where it was the children who first rejected the gossip of these men. The children would hide in the bushes on each side of the village path and watch for her to appear from either direction. When they could see the sun light up the features of her spruce-root hat, the children would sing silently to themselves. Thunderbird played the major role in her hat design as well as her dress made of mountain-goat wool. The children could close their eyes and feel Sleeping Woman was close by because they could hear the deer-hoof rattles shake around her ankles. They loved most the amulet she wore around her neck with the face of Wolf carved in cherry bark and polished with salmon eggs. The children would leave an offering for her, baskets of blue-berries, blackcaps, or chokecherries, in return for a morning or evening song. The children would pick with wild abandon the song she offered from the air like a swallowtail butterfly and tuck it safely into their hearts.

The medicine men were driven to chewing away their wooden charms like beavers. With two right feet dragging in the ditch, they could never decide whether they wanted to be remembered in the stories passed on to each generation as spirit boards with river otter tails or in the mixed blessings of Trickster's fan of false-face mirrors. None of them would dare admit if they started to hate Sleeping Woman before the animals of the forest refused to talk with them, the birds to show them the waterfalls, or the stars begin exposing their shallow strut and eyeless looks.

Stump Wart was clearly the leader of this jealousy clan. He had wanted to marry Sleeping Woman in the worst way. When they were young and wild as the river and the blue and gray willows in the wind, he sang her a song of his love in the light of the strawberry moon. His heart twisted like a knee jerk as Sleeping Woman refused to hear a single note. Neither fasting nor bathing with hemlock brought her any closer to his longhouse. So the only warmth Stump Wart felt was the morning glow of water louse.

But what made him feel like a rock person without any ground to sleep on was the day he tried to stop her from going to the beach to dig clams for her family's dinner. He put his arms out for her to halt. She tossed him a smile and his skull slipped a notch from its axis. She then waved a flicker feather in a circle in front of his face; it blazed like a firestick into his body all the way to his toes. His eyes went white and his heart took away his breath. He stood paralyzed and could move neither arm nor leg. Sleeping Woman swirled into a coil of smoke as she sidestepped around him and vanished; his nerves squinched into little spasms and snapped like blackberry vines in the heat. Stump Wart began to wonder if he had only imagined her coming down the path. "This is not good form," he said, and began to gather plants for brewing some strong tea to bring him peace on his return to his lodge. He knew tonight's sleep would bring nightmares filled with little people on the warpath.

Gull's Foot had also loved her long ago, and he never hid his feelings from the community. As a self-proclaimed medium of the gods that could turn a swamp into a dried hazelnut and a bear into a smokehouse mat, he was positive that his powers would win her hand and add a ring to his potlatch hat. One afternoon Gull's Foot pounded his drum and sang his song from one longhouse to the next around the village. He hollered to each family he passed that Sleeping Woman was his dream girl and must be his wife. He promised the people that by the next moon she would rush into his open arms. But he never expected Moon would see him dancing away his passions and would laugh to herself at the one with snail milk for brains. Before Owl called for a round dance of mice, Sleeping Woman had sent a messenger to the season's foot mite with the words—"You must be joking."

The people learned in less time than it takes a crow to laugh that Gull's Foot had slithered away from the community like Snake into the land of stinging nettles. He stole out of the village one night to flee to a place where no one could tell his story back to him. During a feast a few days later, the entire village heard from the nearby trees a song that told them Sleeping Woman had enlisted the wasps to help him on his way.

Sleeping Woman was known to have a heart the size of a mountain lake, but her love had limits when it came to someone like Gull's Foot or Stump Wart. The people knew from the elders that she was the only creature the wolves would welcome into their trek as they traveled up the hills on their way to sing to the star family. The stories told of how Sleeping Woman loved and protected the village and would always be its shield, so long as the rivers run and the grass weaves the zigzag journey of salmon. The people of red cedar did wonder if a day would come when Sleeping Woman would refuse to turn the other cheek.

The other medicine men from neighboring villages who worked day and night to rid their homeland of Sleeping Woman were not as gifted. They tried as best they could to keep their hostility toward her wrapped in a concealed anger blanket. They walked on their tiptoes and kept their eyes on the food line of the ants. But the act that inspired the laughter drum throughout the village came while they tried to sabotage her healing ceremony for a very ill boy. These shamans without an entrance to even an outhouse had decided that as she was performing her medicine song over the boy, they would chant their song as close to the longhouse as they dare hide. They hoped this would drive her power up the smoke-hole. Unfortunately, the poison arrow from their bow simply came back to them and pinned their toes to the treachery pole. So these medicine men with elbows in their mouths ended up with surprise tattooed to their chests. And while their eyes rolled backward in disbelief, a rather large skunk proceeded to spray them upward, downward, and across their bodies until they vomited on one another. They wobbled away from the village like featherless ducks and quickly became thin wisps of slug blushes.

Yet not too many days later a few elders began to see these neighbors as family gone astray. They decided to ask the entire community to come together and sit in council from morning until sundown. The result was that they decided to have a feast during the next moon. The elders would ask the foolish men to sit in the center of the ceremonial longhouse while the villagers sat around them in a second circle. The men with their tails between their legs sent word to the elders that they would be honored to attend and would bring gifts for each child and elder in the village.

On that special occasion the elders walked around the men with red cedar branches brushing perfume into the air. The elders sang an old mountain healing song as they walked in the circle. As they returned from the opposite direction, the medicine men could not stop the tears from flowing down their faces. The guests sat very still until a grandmother motioned with her lips for one man to sing a song of the path back to his family and clan. The elders called the river a trusted ancestor who gave their family its song and the way to welcome such problem relatives back into the circle of their lives. A medicine man wearing a hemlock headband with eagle feathers called out and the people stood and raised their arms to the sky. The elders wanted their great family in the sky to know that they had not forgotten the stories and path of the heart. Sleeping Woman had told them that the warmth of the sun never brought as much pleasure as the warmth of forgiveness.

The shamans whose medicine canoe had become beached on a dry river-bed knew something strong and beautiful was in the air. They heard in the red-breasted woodpecker's drilling ceremony a small change to their downward spiral. The men felt the mystery inside their stomachs. They thought that Sleeping Woman was not through with their stories. She had been the moontide that brought them wandering the villages with beggar bowls. Yet one by one, each guest could see a patch of sunlight and the air clearing and growing as blue as a mussel shell. The men began to see themselves as part of this family of mountains, rivers, forests, and sea. They asked themselves if maybe someday they would be allowed to stand again as carriers of the medicine staff. They could feel in their stomachs that Sleeping Woman must have made this new turn in their journey possible. They watched their story unravel and saw that they would be spending the rest of their days as students of Sleeping Woman's path.

KoKoKa Ree, Gull's Foot's mother, told him how foolish he was to fall in love and chase after a woman who was obviously half spirit and half animal. She said Sleeping Woman was the daughter of the darker shades of the forest. Then again KoKoKa Ree thought she could be the daughter of two stars. The village people were aware of this possibility since her birth was covered with a shawl of the floating world that drifted like sea mist across the sky. No one was certain where or when she was born. The head chief wanted to claim her as his daughter but he seemed stuck in the place between yes and no. The people took his silence and shyness for a fear that he was a mere child in the long and supple stream of her sky blanket. Besides, she was a young girl before any person in the village noticed her. Several villagers said she walked near them without ever recognizing that they were there. She would appear and disappear as if in another dimension and pass the way Cougar does, but then they remembered the story of how she moved the way sea or mountain fog slips in and out of their lives.

Ish Boy's grandmother swore she saw Sleeping Woman return to their sacred river as an otter. His grandmother said her eyebrows and eyes glistened like water and were full of dream wishes. Grandmother said no otter she ever saw at the river ever promised that many ways to paddle through fog in the thick troughs of night. So Sleeping Woman lived among the people and practiced her art, and then again she did not. Yet the children were certain that she was bound to join them in at least one of their games during the day.

One day when a niece of Stump Wart's was sneaking home from her sweetheart's hideaway at the edge of the forest, she was amazed to see Sleeping Woman step from a crack in the moon. The niece came to a fork on a steep path near the top of a cliff above her grandparents' house and turned to see Sleeping Woman in a sky canoe among the stars. The yellow-iris moon was guiding her across the heavens. If Sleeping Woman was not the spirit of the moon, Stump Wart's niece surmised, then she was certainly daughter of the Moon and the Sun, her father. The niece thought there was no other way to remember the turning of the night. Yet she was convinced that Sleeping Woman's eyes held more sunlight than moonlight. The people began to believe that the magic in her journey was as potent as the dawn. Whenever the village was almost swept away in one of the icicles-on-the-eyebrows and silver-shaking nights, the children would chant for a story of Sleeping Woman. They took pride in knowing they never became lost in the haze of her coming and going and that she might be a reflection of the Northwest nectar that sometimes turns the day into night and night into day. Once more, their parents had taught them to speak with words that were formed from this whirling world of mist and fog. For this reason, Sleeping Woman became their favorite dreamwalker.

All the people agreed that from the very beginning they had known that Wolf, big brother of Coyote, was Sleeping Woman's protector of the path before light. As long as anyone could remember, Wolf had been known as the voice of the Klallam's night chants. Wolf told the people at their Thunderbird smokehouse the stories of Moon. Nevertheless, for every member in every village of the tribe, Wolf was best known from the deep-rooted stories as the healer of terrible times. Wolf's keen could reach the ears of the dead, and the swallow would stop in mid-flight to listen. The bats had all of Wolf's songs memorized by heart, and the people would sometimes hear them sing those gifts of night and longing as they swooped and glided up and down, in and out of the village sky, herding insects.

The stories about Sleeping Woman were as varied as the gray-blue and red clouds that floated above the mountains and their lives, but the people believed the best story about their special guardian was that she was more than a woman of sun-basket medicine full of roots and rose petals. The storytellers, now wandering along The White Trail in the Sky, had passed on to their river family how over the years they became enraptured with Sleeping Woman and her love for children, the elderly and outcast. Everyone in all the villages believed this was when the Sky Dancers gave her the gift of being the keeper of the animals and the dream song of First People. The story reveals that there was not a plant that grew on the green earth of their ancestors that failed to sing its power to Sleeping Woman on her long journey to the spirit lake of belief, trust, and good health. Grandparents would remind the children that she was known to bring nourishment even to the stones, beetles, worms, and skunk cabbage.

One night little Crow and other children from the village of White Pine were gathered around the storytelling fire on the beach. The entire village was one ear as they heard little Crow's grandfather tell another favorite story of this medicine woman. The children learned how Wolf, after a night of hearing Sleeping Woman sing several evening sunset songs, gave her the mask of a shy flower of the undercover forest to use in her dance ceremonies. The flower was one of the rarest, a tiny, white-faced and mysterious plant, beautiful and delicate, whose name still resists memory. Little Crow's grandpa said it was Beaver who first told the people the flower is present for such a brief bouquet of moments that only our souls can see, smell, or hold it. He reminded the other children that the mind was the first critter to write a jealousy song, and if it had half the chance, out of pure envy, it would plot for the flower's disappearance. Yet, the children discovered that the most remarkable thing about the story is that whoever sees the flower among the spots of light off a forest floor will watch it bloom again in their dreams. The flower has lit their destiny and way to the stars that stumble on and on as if heeding a path that will not forget them or end the journey any time soon. The children saw this to be true because Sleeping Woman heard their wishes to be birds and gave them wings as mighty as Eagle's for the flight to slip through the four windows of the Sky People and back to their evergreen births. All Sleeping Woman asked in return is that they promise to tell their parents and the rest of the village what they saw and what stories they heard.

Even though little Crow's grandpa had said goodnight and returned to his longhouse, the children could not stop thinking about the tiny flower. Before the sun was totally swimming in the horizon, and the moon above their homes, they walked to where the river joins the sea to ride in a canoe like madrona leaves in the wind. The children felt they had to see Sleeping Woman and they danced and sang a welcome song to her. After they completed their fourth circle, she appeared from an opening in the last wave to reach the beach. They continued the round-dance in joy and asked if she would give them a song of this forest flower that smelled of a mystery that was to remain a secret of the earth and the forest. They would not rest until they could imagine putting it under their pillows. They had hardly sat down on the ground when they heard her voice pass through the hollows of their bones and inspire their fingers to dance with the moon moths. In return, she wanted them to create a healing song and dance for each elder in their village. She said it would be best if they do this alone and away from the village. They would need to call upon the Song Sparrow clan who lived inside their hearts. Sleeping Woman assured them it would not be long when they could celebrate the elders' full basket of ancient bliss in the home village and along the entire trail of their ancestors in the sky. The children promised and placed red cedar boughs along her path back to the sea. Sleeping Woman stepped beyond them and began swaying in and out of the light and the dark, and as the children's eyes blinked with delight, she disappeared in the next rolling-back wave of the moon in a deep sea swirl of stars.

Note
Min-!sw-tun, pronounced Min-who-tun, is Klallam for Sleeping Woman.

Journeys to Other Worlds

The Kidnapping of Moon

An Upper Chehalis Myth

Told by Silas Heck

Edited by M. Dale Kinkade

This Upper Chehalis story was recorded on July 29, 1960, from Silas Heck, one of the last fluent speakers of the language and probably the last who could tell stories in the language. His repertoire of traditional tales was very limited, because when he was sent off to boarding school as a child his parents encouraged him to forget Indian ways and traditions. He remembered several and recorded them for me, however. He preferred to rehearse them to himself the night before he recorded them; thus, his renditions are generally quite artistic. Because he was extremely hard of hearing, it was not practical to play the recordings back to him for translation, but he would tell me a rough version of the story in English so that I would know its contents. Mr. Heck lived on the Chehalis Indian Reservation just outside Oakville, Washington. I worked intensively with Mr. Heck during the summers of 1960 and 1961, and supplemented this material with smaller amounts gathered subsequently from other speakers. Mr. Heck died in 1967, and as of the early 1990s there were no more than one or two speakers left, and the language is no longer used.

The translation offered here is thus my own, based on a careful transcription and analysis of the original Upper Chehalis version; I have tried to be as faithful as possible to the Upper Chehalis original, while at the same time trying to render it into reasonably straightforward English. Several features should be pointed out about this translation: (a) The usual narrative tense/aspect form used is imperfective ("he is going"), rather than perfective ("he went"), and I have kept this aspect in the translation. (b) Although it makes for awkward English, I have left in all conjunctions at the beginnings of lines; these are important discourse markers, and the text can be read ignoring them as appropriate. (c) The use of passive voice is common in texts, and I have retained that in most instances. (d) Mr. Heck did not distinguish between "woman" and "girl" in the first part of the text, but I have made the distinction for clarity. (e) A few odd sentences have been left in (e.g., "he is told by the people").

Most of the people who identify themselves as Upper Chehalis live today on or near the Chehalis Indian Reservation, although people from several nearby groups were also allotted there, and most current residents have mixed ancestry from the Upper Chehalis, Lower Chehalis, Satsop, Cowlitz, Twana, Nisqually, and so forth. The original territory of the Upper Chehalis was along the Chehalis River and its tributaries from just east of Elma to just north of Pe Ell. They fished in the rivers and creeks of the area, hunted in the woods and mountains, and gathered plants throughout the region. A particularly important feature of this area was and is the large number of prairies, large and small, that were kept burned off and free of forest. These prairies provided valuable grounds for berries and such important roots as camas and bracken fern (Hajda 1990:505–7). Prairies often feature prominently in the folktales of the Upper Chehalis, as in section II.B of this story.

This particular myth is one of the most important tales of the Upper Chehalis; it explains the origin of the current form of many of the animals and fish of the area, and the origin of the sun and the moon. It is their primary Transformer story. Other mythic stories were also very popular, particularly those involving Bluejay (who figures importantly in this story), x\ʷə́n (a kind of Trickster, who also appears here), and Wren. People today often know of the stories about x\ʷə́n as being "dirty" stories, but the Wren stories easily outdo them for outrageous ribaldry. Curiously, all versions (including Lower Chehalis and Quinault ones) begin with an episode about x\ʷə́n, who then disappears from the myth (although he reappears briefly in a few tellings), and the Transformer becomes the main character. Some semi-historic stories were also told, and stories about the Siatco (the local name for the sasquatch) were also very popular, although no one seems to have recorded or transcribed any.

A number of versions of this story are known, told by different people and at different times, although there are only two published sources of it. The earliest was published by Robert J. Jackson (1906) in *Washington Magazine*. Jackson was a Chehalis Indian, and the version he published is his own. It is lengthy and compares favorably with other versions in comprehensiveness (episodes of this myth were commonly omitted to save time or to accommodate a particular audience). Thelma Adamson (1934) published two Upper Chehalis versions, one very long one from Peter Heck and a shorter one from Jonas Secena; her book also includes a Humptulips (Lower Chehalis) version from Lucy Heck, and closely related stories in Cowlitz, Puyallup, and Twana (Skokomish). Both Jackson (1906) and Adamson (1934) are in English only. Other versions are unpublished, but are in Upper Chehalis. These are manuscript versions made in 1927 by Franz Boas from Jonas Secena (a very long version, which includes several introductory episodes about x̣ʷə́n) and Robert Choke; tape recordings made by Leon Metcalf from Silas Heck in 1951 and Murphy Secena in 1952 (both of which I have transcribed); and my recording from Silas Heck presented here. There are also unpublished Quinault variants of the myth among the "Xwoni Xwoni Tales" in Olson (1926) and Farrand (1897).

Of these narrators, I know nothing further about Robert Jackson. Peter Heck told many stories to both Adamson and Boas, and spoke an upriver dialect of Upper Chehalis. Silas Heck was his youngest brother (but spoke the down river dialect), and Adamson says that Lucy Heck was married to Silas Heck (1934:xi), although she would have been many years older than he. Jonas and Murphy Secena were also brothers.

Those familiar with the folklore of this area may also know the collection of x̣ʷə́n stories by Katherine Van Winkle Palmer (1925), which bears the subtitle *The Indian Interpretation of the Origin of the People and Animals*. At first glance this looks like yet another version of this Moon myth, but in fact has very few episodes that correspond to episodes in other versions. It is best considered a collection of x̣ʷə́n stories; this Trickster was capable of transformations, so some stories might easily be assigned to either x̣ʷə́n or Moon. Palmer's stories also appear to show heavy influence from Puyallup, and her source, George Sa[u]nders was indeed Puyallup. Many other stories about x̣ʷə́n are known, including many published in Adamson (1934) and Upper Chehalis versions transcribed by Boas in 1927 and recorded by me in 1960–61. Livingston Farrand collected some in Quinault in 1898 from Bob Pope; Ronald L. Olson also collected some between 1925 and 1927 from the same speaker.

This Upper Chehalis myth is also related in significant ways to the well-known Star Child myth of the Lushootseed and the Twana (and the Cowlitz versions seem to resemble the Lushootseed versions more than the Upper Chehalis ones). Many of the episodes involving the Transformer are the same, and the conclusion with the Transformer and his younger brother becoming the Moon and Sun are equivalent. What is different is the way the two traditions begin. The Star Child myths begin with two young women admiring two stars, who find themselves in the sky as the wives of these two stars and get back to earth with a baby fathered by one of the stars. The Upper Chehalis versions begin with x̣ʷə́n wanting a woman, creating them from salmon milt, their maturing and running away from him, and kidnapping a baby. This baby happens to be the baby that the women in the Lushootseed myth brought back from the sky country, and it is at this point that the two traditions merge. One version explains the presence of the baby and its mother and grandmother (who may be made from a rotten log) in the story, the other explains the origin of the kidnappers.

I have taken the title from the last line of the story. Mr. Heck never provided titles, but an Upper Chehalis story often begins with a sentence indicating what it is about. In this case the last sentence provides that information. For the long version told by Jonas Secena, Boas gives the title "The Adventures of x̣ʷənéx̣ʷəne"; this implies that x̣ʷənéx̣ʷəne is the most important character in the story, and in this respect is misleading and inappropriate.

The story takes place largely in Chehalis territory. Although no specific locations are mentioned in this version, in the one told by Jonas Secena to Boas, the baby's mother and grandmother are encountered on a prairie at Claquato (a small prairie where the present-day community by that name is found just west of the city of Chehalis); Claquato was a summer gathering place of the Chehalis. Other versions specify that the pursuit of the kidnappers ends further up the Chehalis River. Two other sites are specified in the story, both mythic. One is the land of the salmon, where the kidnappers take the baby; this is considered their home, since they were made from milt. The other site is the border between that world and our own. Here the sky repeatedly and rapidly crashes against the earth, making it impossible to cross. This sort of border is widespread in mythology, and in Greek mythology is called the Symplegades. I use this name once in my translation; other references to it are more descriptive in Mr. Heck's narration, and I have translated them accordingly.

Of the characters in this myth, Moon is by far the most important, even though he does not appear until well into the story. Mr. Heck refers to him throughout the story merely as "chief's son," a designation that is never explained, but can be understood when the Lushootseed myth, where he is the son of a star, is taken into account. One time Mr. Heck calls him Nukwimalh, which is the Chehalis rendering of Lushootseed Dukwibalh (Dúkʷibał), the Transformer in their Star Child myth. Only at the end of Mr. Heck's story is he finally called Moon. Other versions call him Moon (or Sun) throughout, foretelling his final manifestation. The use of the name Moon in Upper Chehalis is ambiguous because there is a single word for "moon" and "sun" in the language. When a speaker wants to refer specifically to the moon, the circumlocution "night-sun/moon" must be used.

As noted earlier, x̣ʷə́n only appears at the beginning of the myth. This character's name is difficult to render into English; Jackson (1906) writes it "Whun," Palmer (1925) writes it "Honne." (These spellings will give the reader unfamiliar with phonetic transcription a fairly good idea of the Upper Chehalis pronunciation of the name.) All other sources write it phonetically. Furthermore, it has at least three variants in Upper Chehalis. Mr. Heck always used x̣ʷə́n, but others used either x̣ʷə́ni or x̣ʷə́néx̣ʷə́ne as well. The salmon women are unnamed. The baby's mother in other versions is named Malé (written Mar-lhee in Jackson 1906), but here is turned into Crow after she and her grandmother give up their pursuit, and her mother becomes Pheasant (actually Ruffed Grouse, the name for which was extended to introduced pheasants and chickens); other versions have the mother turned into Earthquake and the grandmother either a swamp or rotten wood. Moon's younger brother is known as Diaper Child, particularly in Lushootseed, reflecting the manner in which he was created; he nevertheless ends up as the sun. Bluejay and Frog are simply those creatures.

In my judgment, Silas Heck gives a very good rendition of this myth. He took great care in the telling of stories, and analysis of other stories told by him show considerable skillful organization (see Kinkade 1987). I have chosen to present this story in a way that helps to reflect this organization, and have used a format more or less following that promoted and exemplified by Dell Hymes (particularly D. Hymes 1981 and V. Hymes 1987). Alternative arrangements of the text are certainly possible. Two features of narration, however, are important both for telling an Upper Chehalis story and for presenting it in printed form. One is the use of the particle *húy* (translated here consistently as "and then") to begin each new important section, and I have allowed the occurrence of this particle to determine most divisions of the text. The reader can easily see that these divisions are natural breaks in the narrative. (Other instances of *húy* do occur, sometimes in clusters at important places, and a very few sections do not have it.)

The other important narrative feature is the occurrence of objects or events in groups of five, just as in English folktales they must be in groups of three. That there must be five of something is often explicitly stated, and events often occur in a series of five. In section II.B, one might expect there to be five instances of catching up with the kidnappers, but there are only four; the fifth part of this section is instead the introduction to the chase. The songs of the grandmother are not arranged in fives, although the second consists of three identical lines plus one different one, and threes and fives are often correlated in Upper Chehalis narratives.

Three sections stand out for their complexity and further reflect the artistry of this telling. The first of these is part 4 of section II.A when the women plan and carry out the kidnapping. The second is section II.B (entitled "Pursuit of the Kidnappers"), which demonstrates the use of repetition common in Upper Chehalis stories, while still employing considerable variation in detail within these repetitions. The third is section IV.B, the transformation of Deer.

Some sections of the story are quite short, and reflect Mr. Heck's choice as to what he wanted to emphasize, while retaining enough structural elements to provide proper form of the overall text. The creation of suckers (section IV.A) and the episode in which Fire pursues the hero (section IV.C) are examples of this reduction of episodes that are fleshed out considerably in other versions of the story (for a presentation of Jonas Secena's version of the Fire episode, see Kinkade 1983a). The detail of Moon's younger brother imitating or mocking him (IV.D) is found in an episode about the transformation of Tapeworm in the Boas-Secena version, and the sticking hat detail of IV.E is part of an entirely separate episode of transformation there.

The Kidnapping of Moon

Once upon a time x̣ʷə́n lived there.
He stayed there a long time and he gets lonely.

> *Why am I alone?*
> *I could have children by a woman,*
> *and they could be good for me.*

And then he goes salmon fishing.
Then he is told by his spirit power,
　　"Take the milt of a salmon
　　and hang it on a tree close to where you turn back."

And then he does this.
Every time x̣ʷə́n goes salmon fishing,
he takes a look at that milt.
Nothing happens.

> And on the fifth time he passes that milt,
> then he hears a girl's laughter.
> Then he turns off there and sees two girls,

the most beautiful girls there could be on this earth.

The milt of the salmon became girls.

And then the girls grew to become adults after a while.

And then xʷə́n wants to marry the women.
But the women don't want that.

Therefore the women make a plan and say,
"Well, then, we will leave this bad person."

II.A. THE KIDNAPPING OF THE CHIEF'S SON |

And then they make a plan.

They agree on a plan,
and say,
"Let's go to the east."

And then they travel.
They leave xʷə́n.

They go a long way,
then they hear singing
that says,

"Sleep, sleep, little master.
Sleep, sleep, little master.
Nice, nice is your little canoe.
Nice, nice is your little canoe.
Sleep, sleep, little master.
Sleep, sleep, little master.
Good, good is your little canoe.
Good, good is your little canoe."

And then the women turn off
and they see an old woman pushing a cradle-swing.
And there is a baby there in that cradle-swing.
And the old woman keeps pushing the cradle-swing.

It would come to a stop far away from her,
and it would come back to her.
And then she pushes it again.

And then the women make a plan,
"Well, we will kidnap the baby."
They make a plan
and one says,

"Get some rotten wood,
you prepare it.
However big the baby is,
that's how big the rotten wood is to be.
When the cradle-swing gets here,
I will pick up the baby,
at that time you will lay the rotten wood down where the baby was
    lying,
without stopping the cradle-swing."

They do this.
The cradle-swing comes to a stop by them,
and one of the women takes the baby
while the other lays down the rotten wood,
and they go.
And the women keep traveling to the east.

The cradle-swing arrives again from the other side,
and the old woman watching the baby keeps singing,

The little master smells like rotten wood now.
The little master smells like rotten wood now.
The little master smells like rotten wood now.
Oh! Oh! Oh! the little canoe.

That's what she sings.

And then the mother of the baby is out on the prairie digging roots,
and she hears her.

What is happening at home?

She goes home to the house.
She goes to the old woman, who is blind,
she is told,
"Here is what was your child.
He is rotten wood now.
Your child was kidnapped by two women."

And the mother begins to cry continuously . . . the baby's
mother,
how will she get her child back?
She gives up.

II.B. PURSUIT OF THE KIDNAPPERS |

And then the old woman says,
"Don't give up.

I have my packstrap.
When I throw it down on the ground,
the ground shrinks.
And doing thus, after this,
we will overtake the women.
Then I will get back your baby.

I will carry you on my back.
Climb onto my back,
I will carry you on my back. [No, I got that wrong.]
So carry me on your back!"

The mother says then,
"Then come onto my back,
I will carry you."

And then they walk quite a while,
and they come out onto a prairie.

There the old woman takes her packstrap,
strikes down on the ground with it.

The ground keeps shrinking,
and they get near the women.

      And then they chase them.
      And they are still far behind them
      and the women get across the prairie.

            And then they go.
            The women go into the woods
            and they disappear.

And then the old woman says,
"Don't give up!
Carry me on your back and we will go on."

      And then they go a while,
      and they come out onto another prairie.
      There they are!
      The women are in the middle of the prairie,
      they are walking.

            The old woman throws her packstrap down on the ground,
            and the ground keeps shrinking.
            And they keep getting somewhat near the women.

                  And they are still far behind,
                  the women get across the prairie again,
                  they keep disappearing.

And then the old woman says again,
"Don't give up!
We will overtake them."

      So they go.
      They come out on a prairie.
      There are the women
      far away on the other side of the prairie.

And then she is told,
"Well, throw it down!"
She throws down her packstrap,
the ground shrinks up a lot.

     And here they are getting near;
     they chase them,
     and the women get across the prairie again
     and disappear.

          Now then the mother says,
          "We cannot overtake them."
          The old woman says,
          "Don't give up!
          We'd better try once more now!"

And then they go on,
and come to another prairie.

     There she throws her packstrap down on the ground again,
     and the ground keeps shrinking up a lot.

          And now they chase the women.
          And they are near enough now so they can grab the women,
          but they get across the prairie again.
          They always disappear.

          There now they give up.
          When they have finally given up,
          the old woman says,
          "I will turn myself into Pheasant.
          You will become Crow."

          And then they do this.

III. Recovery of the Chief's Son |

And then they stay there a long time.
A long time.
Then the people gather.

They make a plan.

> A long time ago a baby, son of a chief of the people of this land, was
> kidnapped.
> "Well, we will go
> to where he was taken by the women
> so we can bring him here to this land."

And then the people travel.
They go there where the sky and the earth come together.
They will arrive there.
And then the people travel,
they get to where the earth and the sky come together,
the blue sky.

> At that place there is no way they can pass through,
> because the sky keeps coming together hard with the earth.
> No one could jump to the other side.
> They would be struck and be annihilated.

Then they say to Bluejay,
"Well, it is to be you.
When the sky has raised,
jump to the other side;
it may be there that the chief's son lives."

> Then Bluejay says,
> he says,
> "*káčə káčə káčə.*"
> That's all.
> And he disappears to the other side.

And then Bluejay goes now,
he walks,
then he gets to a house.
A big house.
He peeks in.
The door is open.

He peeks in.

A person is sitting there,
scraping a hide.
He pulls the scraper,
and it keeps breaking.
He takes another,
it breaks.

When on the fifth time the scraper breaks, he says,
There must be someone peeping at me.
Then it would be Bluejay.

And he throws the scraper behind him, toward the
door.
The scraper hits,
and he hears someone moan.
The person turns around to see,
and it turns out to be Bluejay who was hit.

And then he asks Bluejay,
"What have you come to this land for?"

"Oh, your people have missed you for a long time.
You were kidnapped from us by the women a long time ago when
you were a baby.
You are big now,
and people want you to come back to your country."

And the chief's son gets ready.
He consents.

IV. THE CHIEF'S SON'S DEEDS |

A. Suckers |

And then after that
he says to his children (who are) made of mud,

he says to them,

"You, the suckers, will be in the water.
You will stay at the edge of the water.
You will suck the earth,
there you will be food.

And whenever someone gets hungry,
he will take a pole to punch you on the head.
You will die
so I can eat you.

That will be your job forever after."

And then now the chief's son does this.
Now he walks all over the earth,
changing everything.

He gets to a person (an old man now) sharpening a tool, a rock.
He sharpens it,
making it good.

Then he asks him from behind,
"Well, Grandfather,
what are you making?"

"Oh, I am making this
to be ready to hit that Nukwimalh, who is coming, on the head.
He is upsetting everything to . . . to be things,
so they will not be people."

"Oh, Grandfather.
So that's what you are making.
Will you hand it to me?"

And the chief's son takes the sticks.
Two long ones, one short one.

He says to the old man, his grandfather,
"Well, Grandfather,
stand up!"

The old man stands up,
he sticks the weapons that the old man had made onto one side of
his head.
And then he sticks another on the other side.
He sticks the weapons on.

And then he tells the old man,
"Well! Look the other way!"

And then the old man looks the other way,
And then he sticks the short one of the person's weapons on,

and says to him,
"Well! Jump forward five times!"
And then the person jumps around five times.

"The fifth time you jump
you will stop and look back.

Then a person will kill you—you will be killed
because you will be food for people then."

This which he stuck on one side of his head,
that will be an ear.
And the short piece that was stuck on the buttocks,
that will be a tail.

This who was an old man,
who had threatened him—
the chief's son who keeps on coming,
changing everything—

he will be a deer
to be food now for people.

c. Fire |

And then he goes on a long way,
and then the earth is burning.
Where can he go?

It is burning around him.

> Then an old man says to him,
> "Well, Grandson!
> Come lie on top of me!"

And then the fire just reaches there where the old man is,
and the fire dies out.
The earth stops burning,
and it turns out to be Trail.

> It is Trail who saves him.
> Now then the chief's son says,
> "From this day on,
> a trail will not burn forever after."

D. Younger Brother |

And then he goes on.
He goes down to a river.

> And on the other side a person is fishing.
> He catches water dogs (salamanders).
> Everything bad in the water,
> he catches it.

> > And he puts it into his mouth.
> > Whatever he catches,
> > he puts it into his mouth.
> > Now he has become nothing but stomach
> > from being full of everything that might be bad.

And then the chief's son asks him,
"What are you doing?"
And he doesn't get answered.
He just keeps getting imitated.

> He asks him many times,
> and the person just keeps mocking him.
> The people just keep telling him.

And it is Echo.

> And this person, the chief's son, knows he is his younger
>> brother.
> A person was made—
> rotten wood became a person;
> they made the chief's son a younger brother.
> And he's not worth anything.

And then the chief's son says to him,
because he holds his younger brother upside down
(whom he knew to be a relative),
he shakes him,
so that everything that he swallowed that ought to be bad comes out.
It comes out of his mouth.

> He is empty,
> and now he stands him up again,
> and they go on, both of them now.

E. Hat |

And then the chief's son gets to a stump.
That thing—its bark became wrinkled
so that it seems to be a hat.

And then the chief's son says,
"Well, Grandmother!
Give me your hat,
I like it,
I want it."

> "Oh, I cannot give it to you.
> It would not be good for you.
> I cannot give it to you."

> And then he says to the old lady,
> "And then, Grandmother,
> give me your hat;
> I want it."

And then the old lady takes it off,
and puts it on the chief's son,

    and the hat gets stuck on the head of the chief's son,
    he can't take it off.

        How can he take it off?

And then he is told by the people . . .
The chief's son says,
"Whoever can take this hat from my head
I will marry her daughter."

    Whoever can come tries.
    The one with the greatest spirit power
    cannot take the hat off.

        Then Frog comes,
        leading her daughter by the hand.

And then the people are saying,
"Is she going to take the hat off now?
Her daughter cannot be married to the chief."

    Without saying anything
    Frog goes there,
    and sings her spirit power song.

        As soon as she sings her spirit power song
        his hat comes off.
        His hat comes off.
        The person is victorious.
        Her daughter marries the chief's son.

V. Sun and Moon |

And then the chief's son and his younger brother make a plan now.

    The chief's son says,
    "You will travel up above the earth.

You will be the moon.
I will travel above the earth during the day."

       The younger brother says,
       "All right."

And then he goes to the Symplegades,
and his older brother asks him,
"How was the night travel for you?"

       He says,
       "Oh, I didn't like it.
       I was frightened looking at the earth,
       there were shadows of everything,
       and there might have been monsters.
       I was afraid.
       I saw nothing but people outside committing adultery.[1]
       It isn't good for me
       that I should look at such things.

       I don't want to go again."

"Well, Younger Brother.
Well, I will go up now."

       And he is just barely sticking up at daybreak,
       and the earth starts to get hot,
       it burns,
       water boils.

       And the chief's son goes back down.

And then he says to his younger brother,
"All right, you will work during the day,
and I will work at night.

       I am too strong
       to work during the day,
       because the earth could burn;

but you do not have as much strength as I.
So you will work during the daytime."

And then they finish their plan for the moon.

And when you can see the moon,
Frog is there,
because the chief's son took his wife, Frog, there with him.
To this day, Frog is there.

That is the end of the story
of the kidnapping of Moon.

Notes

1. This motif occurs in (Interior Salish) Spokane and Thompson River Salish narrative, where Coyote becomes the Moon for a time and sees people committing adultery. See Egesdal 1992. Also see the (Oregon Coast Salish) Tillamook story of "South Wind's Journeys," in this volume.—Eds.

Sun's Child
A Traditional Bella Coola Story

Told by Agnes Edgar

Edited by Dell Hymes

Stories of escape by creating barriers behind oneself ("magical obstacle flight") are found throughout the world. Stories of a child who learns that his father is the Sun, and joins him, are well-known in native North America. The Bella Coola of British Columbia have stories with one or the other plot, and two have been recorded that combine both, and only both (Boas 1898b:100–103; Davis and Saunders 1980:95–126). "Sun's Child," told by Agnes Edgar, is integrated by parenthood, parallel, and contrast.

In the first part a girl leaves in anger a house in which she has no parent, and succeeds in reaching the Sun. Her child, the Sun's child, having no father on earth, and being teased, determines to reach his father and succeeds. Both return home, the girl meeting doubt then acceptance, the boy punishment and transformation.

The joining seems not quite perfect, in that the girl reaches the Sun overland to the east (as in a number of other Northwest myths), while the boy reaches the Sun by making and climbing a chain of arrows to the sky. Perhaps both routes were considered possible—alternatives that convey something about the girl and boy. Travel to and from the house of the Sun was thought instructive of the difference between them at the end: the girl rescuing people threatened by the boy's mistake, and he being made into a source of pests.

Four is the pattern number of the Bella Coola, and it pervades the organization of this telling. Here is an outline.

Part One: The Foster Child and Stump
  I. At Stump's House
    i. A girl goes off angry and is taken to the house of Stump
    ii. The girl runs away and is brought back
  II. Magic Flight
    i. The girl runs away again: preparation
    ii. The girl runs away again: comb undergrowth

iii. The girl runs away again: wool lake

iv. The girl runs away again: whetstone mountain

III. At the House of Sun

  i. The girl is accepted by Sun

  ii. End of Stump

IV. The Girl Returns Home

  i. The girl has a boy

  ii. She thinks of her foster parents

  iii. She arrives home: her mother can't believe a daughter

  iv. Another daughter goes: fresh sand

Part Two: The Sun's Son Tries to be the Sun

 V. Her Son Goes to His Father

  i. The boy is teased about his father

  ii. He grows rapidly

  iii. He makes an arrow chain

  iv. He takes leave of his mother and reaches his father

VI. He Gets to Be Sun

  i. He wants to be the Sun

  ii. He disobeys instructions

  iii. The sky burns

  iv. His father punishes him

Mrs. Edgar remarks that she has forgotten one of the four magic obstacles, but organizes what she says so that there is formally no gap. While four underlies so much, there are points at which three and five are called upon expressively. Notice the three parallel verses reiterating that the girl is pregnant (IV.i), the three pairs of lines about the rapid growth of the boy (V.ii), and the three lines each about the clam and the weasel in (VI.iii). Before that, the scene in which the son disobeys is marked with parallelism such that it inescapably has five groups of lines, three pairs within an opening and closing verse.

A special point about this translation: it follows the recurrent marking of relationships among lines or groups of lines by a suffix, $-k^w$, a quotative with the effect "they say" or "it is said." I first translated the story always including "they say," but the result was very awkward. I could not find a way to have its presence fade into the background, as has seemed possible in texts in some languages. Here "they say" is omitted, with the result that a reason for a certain relation among lines and groups of lines is not always evident. In compensation, perhaps, I have always retained a recurrence of an expression at the end of lines translated "then." It often appears to point up a line, or a pairing of lines. And I have regularly attempted to follow the parallelism of phrases in the original.

Sun's Child

Okay, I'll just tell about these things. Preface |
It's been really a long time since it's been told how the
   world was formed.

Part One: The Foster Child and Stump |

I. At Stump's House |

i. A girl goes off angry and |

is taken to the house of Stump |

A young girl went away,
     she got mad.
She was the adopted child of her foster parents.
She got mad about something.
It happened,
     she wandered about, then,
         she followed the edge of the river.
She got mad then.

It happened, then,
     that she heard someone pounding poles upriver.
She went,
     she began to walk faster, then,
        she wanted
           to see him.
It turned out to be a person,
     he was pounding in the middle of the river.
Maybe he was making fish traps.

The young girl hollered out to be fetched.
It was heard, then,
     the hollering then.
She was gone to by him,
     to be fetched.
She was actually taken to his house,
     made to go inside.

She was fed by him, that person.
She was fed, then,
    by him then.
She finished eating then.

ii. The girl runs away and is brought back |

He went off, then,
    outside,
        to pound poles at the river.
That was when
    she was hollered to by a woman in front of the house.
The woman was making floor mats.
"You won't be any good
    if you do like me,
        staying here forever,"
            the girl was told by the woman.
"Leave him.
Go on this path."

She thought the path was clear to the back of their house.
She started now,
    to run away from the man.
She ran away then.
She got pretty far away then.

That person's water pot hollered.
"Stummp!
    Come here!
        Your wife is running away,"
          Stump's water pot said.
That one started, then,
    he followed the other one
        to return her, then
            to his house.
That was when
    she was made to eat
        inside his house.
The man was good,
    keeping the young one sated then.

He went as before
 to pound poles in the river,
  to finish what he was doing.
He was making a fish trap.
 He was doing that then.
"All right, come here.
 Look in his toolbox.
 Drill holes around the edge of his water pot.
 Maybe it won't be able to holler,"
  the woman told the young girl.

The young girl went
 to look in the person's box.
She began
 to drill holes around the water pot.
She finished, then,
 to be called as before by her.
She was handed something, then . . .
 a comb and some wool and a whetstone were handed her.
 (I forget one of them.
 There are four of them.)
"Okay, you can go.
 When you're just about caught by him,
  he's catching up to you,
   you throw this one behind you,"
    she was told by that woman.

She started to run then.
She got just so far, then,
 when the water pot succeeded in hollering to Stump then.
Hulu hulu hulu hulu, he said,
 that water pot trying to holler then.
In a little while the water pot was able to speak.
"Come here, Stump!
 Your wife has gone running away again,"
  that water pot said.

The young girl then had done just that.
Just as she was about to be caught, then,
        she threw it down behind her.
The woman, instructing her,
        had said to do just that.
The young girl threw it on the path behind her.

The comb became dense growth.
Okay. The place behind the young girl got all bushy.
This one, Stump, got caught up here and there on his way,
        trying to follow the young girl.

This one got loose now as before.
The young girl had gotten far
        by the time that person got untangled.
That was when
        he ran as before
                to follow her.

Again he was just about to catch her
        when she threw down the second thing
 I don't remember what it was[1]
        but it slowed him down
                and she got away.

iii. The girl runs away again: wool lake |

It happened as before then,
        she was just about to be caught.
She began as before,
        throwing the wool on the spot behind her.
The path she had taken became a pond.
The pond became a really big lake.
Maybe it became an ocean then.

Stump did as before,
        walking along the edge of the young girl's path.
As before he got loose, then, . . .
        from where she had last gone through.

iv. The girl runs away again: whetstone mountain |

She threw something as before,
>   when she was just about to be caught.
It was then it turned into a mountain.
It was a whetstone she threw, then,
>   on the path behind her.
It became a mountain.

He managed, then,
>   Stump, not to be locked up then.
She kept trying to climb the mountain,
>   the little girl.
There were four of these.
But I've forgotten what one of them was like.

III. At the House of Sun |

i. The girl is accepted by Sun |

She must have gotten close to the Sun now!
She ran and ran then.
She reached his house.
She stopped in front of it.

She was hollered to by him.
>   "Come here!
>   Come inside,
>   if you are the one who got angry,"
>   she was told by him.
She opened the door to the house.
And heat struck her hard.

She closed the door hard.
"Come here!
>   Don't be afraid,"
>   she truly was told by him.
That was when it began to be done to her by the Sun,
>   having her body rubbed by him.
Her body was rubbed by him then.

It happened then

that she got inside.
She was made to eat by him.
Inside the house,
> there was nothing on the walls inside the house,
>> . . . nothing.
She went to sit down now,
> she was fed by Our Father.

ii. End of Stump |

It was when she had in fact finished eating,
> he who followed her showed up.
He who followed her arrived—
> Stump.

It was then that person went inside.
The Sun did not go
> to rub the body of that one.

It really happened, then,
> Stump burned the back of his head.
He burned the back of his head then.
Maybe that is why it happened, then,
> he died, then . . .
>> Stump.

That's when
> that one was cast away, then.
Stump was charcoal.
(This is the one, okay,
> "Stump" in our village is named after.
Maybe it's from that he's called "Stump.")

IV. The Girl Returns Home |
i. The girl has a boy |

The young girl didn't in fact know
> okay, what she was (doing) with him
>> . . . with the Sun.
It happened, then,
> she was pregnant then.

She didn't know
        she would be pregnant from the Sun.
She was pregnant.
She was pregnant then.

She wasn't in fact as long as expected, then . . .
        okay, giving birth to her boy.
It was a boy she gave birth to.

Right from the beginning it was given a name.
The boy knew what he had been named by our father.
He was Kankthli [kankłi].
She had her first child with Kankthli.

                                        ii. She thinks of her foster parents |

It happened then with her.
Suddenly she thought of her foster parents.
Maybe she was lonely for them then.
Her thoughts were heard by the Sun.
"Be brave,
        go in the morning,"
                he said to her.

They,
        the sun's eyelashes,
                are the sunbeams to the earth on which we live.
It is those
        the young girl walked the center of.

She went then.
It happened
        that one started to be afraid then.

"Can I really walk on this sunbeam?"
        they say that one said.
"Yes, you can really go.
        You can really go.
                Go on!"

She walked the center of the sunbeams
    down to us where we dwell,
        we live.
She led by the hand her child . . .
    Kankthli.
Her mother was crying in their bedroom.
She reached, then,
        the back.
Her path led to the back of their house.
The woman hollered to one of her daughters
    to see who was playing tricks on her.
"Go see who's at the back of the house,"
        their mother said.

The little girl went,
    running outside.
"It's Laqamuts," [ƛaqamuc] she said,
    returning to her mother.

"Oh no!" their mother said.
"You must be teasing me.
  It's been a long time
    since she left us.
  She must be dead now,"
    the woman said to her daughter.

She hollered indeed to another one.
    She didn't believe her.
The other one went, indeed,
    to see.
She said (the same) indeed as the first.
    "It's her all right," she said.
    "It's her indeed.
        She's got a child . . ."
Okay. She had said
    to put sand on the floor here.

"When there is fresh sand,
  she'll come inside the house,"
    the little girl said to their mother.
They went to get fresh sand.
They actually rushed, then,
  to get their houses spread with sand.

      Part Two: The Sun's Son Tries to be the Sun |
        V. HER SON GOES TO HIS FATHER |
         i. The boy is teased about his father |

The mother's children and her child's son went to play, then,
  outside.
The boy would begin to be rolled by his playmates.
He would explain
  that it was the sun who was his father.
"I am called 'Kankthli,'"
  the boy would try to say to his playmates.
His playmates said,
  "Ha . . . he is called 'Kankthli.'
  He has good looking eyes."
The boy had tears in his eyes.
"This one keeps saying the Sun is his father . . .
  But he's no good nevertheless,"
    they said to him.
They made fun of him.

          ii. He grows rapidly |

The boy,
  he grew by leaps and bounds.
It would dawn,
  he would be even bigger.
It would dawn,
  he did the same then.

        iii. He makes an arrow chain |

It was then he decided
  to have his Grandfather make him arrows.
And he decided
  to have his Grandmother make him a quiver.
(The quiver is where his arrows will be kept.)

The boy would begin

to shoot arrows into the sky then.
When he used up his arrows,
      he would return to his Grandfather.

He went again
      to ask him politely
            to make arrows.
"What are you really doing to your arrows
      that you use them up so fast?"
            he said to him.
"They get hung up on the tree branches.
 There's no way I can get them,"
      he said,
              . . . his Grandchild.
He began again to make arrows for him.

It dawned the next day again,
      that one went hunting again.
It was then,
      he was just able, then,
            to hang on to the arrows.
They (the chain) came down closer toward him.

iv. He takes leave of his mother and reaches his father |

He was not seen by the people.
Okay.
"Be brave,"
      he said to his mother.
"I'm going to leave you when day comes,"
      he said to his mother.
"Don't cry when I have left you.
 Maybe I'll see you where I go,"
      the boy said to his mother.

And it happened then in fact like that.
It dawned.
She went with him
      to the place from which he was going to leave.
He began to climb
      to the place where he and the Sun would meet.

The Sun arrived
        to meet him then.
That's when
        the Sun stopped, then,
                arriving there
                        where he was.

A boat is the Sun's transportation.
Then it happened that he got in.
He started to move again, then,
        to where the Sun goes down.

VI. He Gets to Be Sun |
i. He wants to be the Sun |

The boy had a plan.
"I want to be the Sun tomorrow,"
        he said.
                "I'll be the Sun tomorrow."
"No way!"
        his father said to him.
"No way!
    You might not do it right,"
        he said to his son.

"Let me be the Sun tomorrow,"
        the boy said to his father.
He did not agree at the time.

Okay.
He began now
        to say all right.
He made him bundles of kindling, then,
        to use for light.

"Be brave,"
        he said, then,
                to his son.
"Use this for your light,
        when you first appear.

When you get a little further downstream,
        you add a bundle,"
                    his father said to him.
"When you get a little further downstream again,
        you add the third bundle.
When you get to the middle of the sky,
        you add the fourth bundle.
It's there you add the fourth bundle for your light."

ii. He disobeys instructions |

But the boy did not in fact do so, then,
        as he began to move.
From the beginning he had two bundles lit
        when the Sun came up.
From the beginning the world was hot then.
Not far downstream, then,
        he added a bundle again.
He had three bundles.
Again a little further downstream,
            again he added a bundle.
That is what he did, then,
        until the lights given him by Our Father were gone.

iii. The sky burns |

That is when the sky burned.
The sky burned.

The people began to run around, then,
        on the ground.
They were looking for a place to hide, then.
They tried to throw themselves into the water, then.
It was they who died.
The water was hot.

This is what she did, then,
        the woman.
Her friends went to her
        to have their bodies rubbed by her.
And she rubbed their bodies.
They did not feel the heat of the Sun.

These were in fact the only ones alive.

It happened that the sky burned.
That's when the tip of the clam's penis was showing.
That's when its tip became black.

The tail of the weasel was sticking out then.
The weasel tried to get inside a hole.
That's when its tail became black.

They used to tell us this,
    telling us stories . . .
        the old people.

iv. His father punishes him |

He got back to his father.
His father began to spank him.
"You have caused pain to those human beings,"
    his father said.
He began to be spanked by him.

He actually made his child a cloud of dust.
That's when he did it to human beings,
    he was angry at them.
His father actually made a cloud of dust.

He gathered his child's bones.
He began to blow them into the sky.
Okay.

Maybe he will be the Mosquitoes to those who come after us,
    his father said to himself.
They say he is the Mosquito . . .
    the Sun's son.
Okay.

Notes

  1. Perhaps her packstrap, which turned into a prairie, as in some other versions of this story.
—Eds.

Star Husband

Two Brothers' Versions of a Traditional Skokomish-Twana Story

Told by Frank Allen and by Henry Allen

Edited by William W. Elmendorf and Steven M. Egesdal

Elmendorf gathered many Skokomish-Twana myths and folktales during fieldwork in 1939 and 1940. The stories were narrated in English by two brothers, Henry Allen and Frank Allen. Their father and their Native cultural background was Skokomish,[1] although their mother was Klallam. Elmendorf reports that the Allen brothers' personalities differed greatly. "Frank Allen was strongly and self-consciously 'Indian' in most of his attitudes." Henry Allen, conversely, showed a "much more apparent adjustment to the norms of the dominant white society." Henry Allen was more objective and critically analytical about both white and native belief systems, "by a kind of cross-cultural cancellation." Frank Allen's accounts of religious matters were more of a knowledgeable direct participant, while Henry Allen's were those of a knowledgeable observer (Elmendorf 1961:5).

The stories below are different versions of the same "myth," which relates events that occurred during the myth period (*sábu*). The myth period was set before the magical change of the world known as "the capsizing" (*sṗəláč'*), when "the world turned over," and "when we were animals" (Elmendorf 1961:20–21). Elmendorf (1993:lii) further explains: "The people of the sábu are animals, or at least they bear animal names and have some of the attributes of animals. Yet they are also more or less human in personality and motivations. Informants [Frank and Henry Allen] consistently refer to the sábu period as "when the animals were people," but also as "when the people were animals." The subsequent fate of these myth-time animal people is variously described as change into the animals of today, and change into the guardian spirits (*c'šált* and *swádaš*) of today."

The general plot of the myth concerns two women who wish for stars to be their husbands, and the events that follow when their wishes come true. They venture to the star world, marry and become pregnant, become homesick, and return home. The two versions differ greatly in the events that happen after the women return to Earth and bear their children.

In Frank Allen's version, the women give birth to two children, a boy and a girl. The celestial father of the star boy feels threatened, so the father has the boy kidnapped and taken to a remote place in the north. Different characters try to rescue the boy, but only Wren succeeds. The star boy eventually introduces roots, berries, and salmon to the people.

In Henry Allen's version, the star boy is similarly kidnapped. But instead of a successful rescue, Bluejay finds him already a grown man. The star man then has adventures on Earth—his "mother's land"—during which he shows its inhabitants all he knows. It turns out that this star man is Dúkʷibaɬ,' the Transformer. Numerous characters are brought into his adventures, including Mink and Snake Basket Witch. After he shows the people all he knows, he departs homeward for the star land. He takes Frog as his wife, and he ultimately becomes the Moon.

In both versions, the star boy is important in engineering "the way things are" in the world. For Frank Allen, the star boy introduces what would be the principal foods of the people, roots, berries, and salmon. For Henry Allen, the star boy is specifically identified as the Transformer, "destroyer of dangerous monsters" and "establisher of techniques and customs for the coming human race" (Elmendorf 1961:11).

Star Husband

(First Version, Snoqualmie)[3]

Now a story I heard the Snoqualmie tell when I was up Cedar River. Doctor Jack told it to me there. Those people say of themselves *udúkʷdukʷul*, we say *bidúkʷdukʷukʷ*, "miracles were done there." And that is why they are called *sdukʷálbɪxʷ*.

Now as you come to Snoqualmie Pass, on the left hand there is a big high rock mountain, and on it there is a big white spot every four hundred yards or so. Now these were the pictures of the Snoqualmie chiefs that Dúkʷibaɬ put there in the beginning. SɬXélčXqédəb was the first one, and then yá•qédəb and then c'əl'qédəb and ɬəbášqédəb and lots more. And as they died those pictures dropped off and left those white spots. They call that mountain *saXʷaɬsXálacut as dúkʷalbɪxʷ ti'iɬbá•dət*, "mountain where the head people of the Snoqualmie are counted."

Now the Skokomish in their language call stories like this *sábu* or *sxʷiyáb*, and the Snoqualmie call them the same.[4]

Now two girls slept outside on a nice clear night. One said, "I wish I had that bright star for my husband." And the other said, "No, I wish I had that dark-looking star for my husband." They went to sleep. And when they woke up two men were sleeping with them. Good-looking young men they were. One of them was that bright star, he had red eyes, and the other was dark.

They asked the girls, "You want us, don't you?" And they said, "Oh, yes! We wished for husbands." And the men said, "Well, you wished for stars and here we are. We're those stars you wished for." And they told the girls, "You shut your eyes." And the girls shut their eyes. And they told them, "Open your eyes, you women." And the girls opened their eyes and they were in a different world. And the two men took their wives to their two houses. And people lived there, just as on this earth. And the girls dug camas roots and lived with their husbands.

Now those people that lived there in that star world couldn't talk to each other. They just made motions. And the two girls followed the other women out and dug roots with them. Now these star men told their wives, "You're going to stay here, you're not going back to your country any more." And those girls felt bad when they heard that.

So those two women talked to each other. "What are we going to do?" They're getting homesick already. They know now that they're way up in another world above their own. So they say to each other, "You dig that camas and you give me half of your camas." So every day they went off and one dug and the other twisted cedar limbs into a long rope. Every day they worked that way. Well, one day they said, "Now we have enough rope." So they dug a hole till they got through the bottom of the star world and they let down their rope till they reached the world below with it. And they tied the upper end to a big rock. And now they started to climb down that rope, one at a time. And one said, "When you get down, pull on that rope so I'll know that you got down."

And there was one old woman there that was good to them. She's helping those two girls. They both have babies in their bellies now. They told this old woman, the last one to go down told her, "When I get down there I'll pull on this rope and then you untie it and throw it down." So they climbed down and the last one down pulled on the rope and the old woman threw it down to them. And that rope coiled up on the ground and it is a big pile of stones there now, in a prairie above Snoqualmie Falls.

And those two women got home now. Their bellies are getting big now. And those babies are born on the same day, one of them a boy, one a girl. And those women went out to dig roots. And they tied their babies up in a *yák^{w}təd* (spring halter) and left an old blind woman to watch after them. And the old woman jiggled the babies back and forth in their *yák^{w}təd*.

The star that was father of one of those children sent a message to the farthest north, to the north end of the world. Now there was a thing there that went up and down all the time.[5] The Snohomish call that thing *biƙéƙap̓q*ʷ*ab* or *x*ʷ*ádix*ʷ*adi*. And beyond that, farther north, there were people. Now that star father of the boy was afraid that when that boy grew up he'd do something great. So he sent to this place beyond that thing that went up and down and he got a person there to go and take that boy baby and take him down north to that place. And he did that.

Now all the people gathered where the two girls had come down. They're all going to look for that child.

Now that person from the north had taken the boy from the cradle board and he put rotten wood in his place. And when the baby's mother came home, there was the old blind woman juggling that rotten wood. She didn't know the baby was gone. And the mother saw the rotten wood, and she said to her old grandmother, "Where is my child? Who put that rotten wood there?" And the old woman said, "I don't know anything about it. I didn't know the baby was gone." And that old woman sang:

*udák*ʷ*adax*ʷ*čád*[6]	I'm shaking
*tə yuyúƙ*ʷ*ay*	The rotten wood
ú• ú• ú•	Oh, oh, oh!

And now those Snoqualmie people called the animals from all over to come. Those animals were people then. And the people gathered, and Bluejay said, "I'll go through to get that baby!" And everybody said, "All right, you go."

And ahh, now Bluejay comes back with his head all flattened on the sides. And he came back crying. That thing that goes up and down had caught his head when he tried to get through.

Now Eagle said, "I'll go and get that baby." And then he came back and told the people, "Well, I just sat down and watched that thing. I couldn't make it. It's too dangerous for me."

And now Seagull said, "I'll go." So he went down north and he came back and said, "I can't make it. I'm too slow for that thing."

And Mallard Duck said, "Well, I'll go and try to get that baby." But he came back and said, "I was too scared to try it. I'll get killed if I try to go through there."

And now Loon said, "I'll go and get him." And he's a smart man, Loon. He went and he was away a long time. And now he came back with his nose all flat. That *x*ʷ*ádix*ʷ*adi* had caught his nose when he tried to get through.

And now those small birds we call *t'əbt'áb'* and the Puget Sound people call *spícxʷ*.[7] That t'əbt'áb' laughed. "Oh, I'll go and get that baby." And he went. And now the Snoqualmie got drumming planks and sticks to beat on them, all ready to have a big time when they get that baby. And ha! t'əbt'áb' comes back now with that baby and he lays it down. And now the people are happy, And that old blind woman made a song now:[8]

uɬčíldubaxʷ	They've brought it back,
tə húyuyúk̓ʷ'ay	what was made of rotten wood.

And all the people danced and sang with her. And now all the animals went home except spícxʷ. They told spícxʷ to stay there.

And they told *spícxʷ*, "You're going to stay with the Snoqualmie now. Your name is Snoqualmie now." So *spícxʷ* said, "All right, I'll go and bring my family here." And there are lots of *spícxʷ* in that country right today.

And now that boy and girl grow up now. They become a man and a woman. Now the head men at Snoqualmie said, "We're not going to give our blood away from this place. You two marry people right here." And after a while sɬXélčXqédəb married that star girl. And they had children. And the star boy went down to the falls. He dived down the falls and washed and came home. And he did that two or three times and then he disappeared, he's no more to be seen.

Now that star father was afraid that boy would do something. That's why he had him stolen and taken beyond the *xʷádixʷadi* when he was a baby. And now that young man is going to do something big. And he disappeared and people began to think he was dead or had gone back beyond the *xʷádixʷadi*.

One morning that boy comes back with a girl. He had gone home to his father's place and had married a girl there, and now he came home to his mother.

And after a while that wife he had brought back told the Snoqualmie women, "You shut your eyes now." And they shut their eyes and when they opened them, there were all kinds of roots, camas and all kinds. Where had that come from? Those women didn't know where those roots had come from. And the woman from the star world said, "Get all your baskets, you women. We'll go out in the mountains here and get berries." When they got up in the mountains the star woman said, "Shut your eyes." And they shut their eyes and when they opened them, the baskets were all full of berries. So they went home.

And now that star boy said to the people, "Come on everybody, let's go down to the falls." And they went to the falls. And he told them, "You look up in the air, and you look all around [counterclockwise] till you come back to where you first looked." And the people all did as he told them. And when they looked down on the ground again there was a big pile of salmon by each man. And they packed that salmon home.

And now słXélčXqédəb is breeding children now by that star woman. And that star boy and his wife are having children too, and they marry one another's families. They didn't marry anywhere else, they married among their own families. And they kept on that way and became a big tribe now. And in those times those Snoqualmie just married in their own tribe.

And that is why those people are called *sdukʷábɪxʷ*, because they are the people who were there when those wonderful things happened.

Now at the end of those story times, at the end of *sábu*, Dúkʷibáł went all over everywhere and changed the world to the way it is now. And those people became animals.

Star Husband

(Second Version)[9]

Two sisters went out to dig roots. They camped out for the night. One said, "I wish that star was my husband!" The other said, "I want that other one." They went to sleep and found themselves in the sky land, a flat earth above the sky. And there they were the wives of those two stars. After a while one had a boy, the other no child. They began to want to get back to this earth, so while they were digging for roots they dug a hole through the bottom of the sky land. They made a rope out of cedar limbs and climbed down, baby on back. And after they got down everybody went to see that rope, and had a big time playing and swinging on it.

There was an old man bachelor living alone in the woods. He made a fish trap in the river and caught one male steelhead. He'd never eaten fish before, so he wondered if the milt was eatable. He discovered each roe had an eye, and thought he'd better leave it alone. It incubated and after a while there were two girls. That old man had to raise them until they became grown; he called them "my daughters," and they helped him. After a while he wanted to call them "my wives," but they ran away. And as they went on they came across this hallelujah good time everybody was having, all the people swinging on the rope. And off to one side was the sky baby, with its old blind grandmother taking care of it, rocking it in its cradle with her toe. And those girls stole the baby and put a piece of rotten wood in its place.

After a while the people discovered the baby was gone, and now every-body was looking for the child. Someone got a doctor to put breath into the rotten wood and it became a human child. And they got Hummingbird and Cougar and all the animals to go hunt the lost child. They came back one at a time, and none of them could find it. But a long time later Bluejay went as far as he could go, where the earth got thin, and there was something going up and down. Bluejay had a hunch the thief had made that. Then Bluejay came back to the middle and he took out his watch and noticed one stroke was longer than others every so often. That thing was like a gate going up and down. Bluejay watched his chance and slid through feet first on the long stroke. But just as he got through the thing caught his head. You'll notice Bluejay has a flat head if you look carefully.

Bluejay went on and saw smoke after a while. It was a man making arrow points. And that was the lost child grown up. So Bluejay told him all about the case, that he had been stolen and who he was. So the man told Bluejay to go on home and tell his mother that he was found and would come as soon as he could. Then Bluejay left him.

And the man put arrow points into a bag and set out for his mother. He had children now by those two women who had stolen him. So he called them together and told him he was going back to his mother. He called his oldest son, Cedar Tree. I guess there were no people yet. "I leave it with you, my dear son, that you will be used for making canoes and for baskets." And he told him all the other things cedar would be good for. Fir Tree was his next son. He called him and told him what he would be used for. And so with the other trees. Then he called all the fishes of the sea and said, "I am leaving you, my dear children." They cried when he said that, and so some fish have wide open mouths.

Now he went along and the first thing he saw was a man who had rain coming through his roof. That man had the shakes on all wrong. And he showed him how to put the shakes on right.

Then he saw Raven, a big chief with lots of slaves. He had a fish trap and the slaves were standing there acting as supports to the trap. Now Dúkʷibał showed them how to make the three sticks as supports to a trap. And Raven had to be black after that.

Now he went on and he heard people singing:

> dəbá•łčad qʷi sát sát sát[10]
> We are the sons of fire.

And he went up and asked them what all that meant. "Oh, we can start a fire and burn the earth!" But he wouldn't believe that, he told them to go ahead. So they sang and had power and the earth started to burn. And Dúkʷibał had to run. He asked a big rock to save him but it couldn't. "I crack when fire comes!" He came to water and it said, "I boil!" But the trail he was running on said. "I don't burn. Lie down! Lie down!" So he lay down and was saved.

Then Mink. Mink had been trying to make love to his niece. She died, so he took her down north to where there was a strong doctor. And the doctor brought her to life. Mink was a miracle man too. He had slaves he made out of rotten wood to paddle for him. As they came back in the canoe Mink's other niece said, "That looks like Mink and my sister." But her sister didn't know her husband was Mink, her uncle. Mink played at being a big chief. He had lots of rotten wood slaves. After a while his wife began to catch on who he was from her sister, so Mink moved on with her.

They saw sea urchins. They had no way to get them, but Mink was a diver. The slaves couldn't get them, so he dived down and got some. He kept doing this. His wife knew now from this that he was Mink, her uncle. Mink was always a glutton for sea urchins. So she threw the baby overboard and told the slaves to paddle her back home. Mink told the child to swim to shore. They swam ashore and there they were, homeless.

Now a salmon came ashore dead. So Mink and his son sharpened a stick and built a fire and cooked him. Mink lay down while the fish was cooking, downhearted. They fell asleep. And when they woke up the fish was all eaten up. Mink wondered, who has done this? He knew the Dúkʷibał was around by this time, so he set out to find him. But Dúkʷibał just kept ahead of him. Finally Mink got disgusted and quit.

Then Dúkʷibał saw a child swimming out from shore, diving far out to tease his mother. That mother was worried and kept asking the child to come in to shore. But the child just laughed. Dúkʷibał changed him to Loon.

Then Deer sang:

      bɪsya'qyáq čəd[11]   I'm filing and filing.

This was to kill Dúkʷibał. And Dúkʷibał said, "Let me see that." It was a sharp bone Deer was filing. So Dúkʷibał stuck it in Deer's leg, and you can find it there now. And Dúkʷibał said, "You will be food for the hereafter."

Beaver had an ax he was sharpening to kill Dúkʷibał. He sang the same song as Deer. And Dúkʷibał stuck it on his tail, so it became flat like a blade.

And Dúk^{w}ibəł went on. He found a big bad animal, Bát'qs ("suck-nose"), was that monster's name. It could draw in a canoe and people at a breath. Now there is a bluff near Lilliwaup sticking out into the Canal. This is what Bát'qs was changed into.[12]

And he turned all these bad animals into rock points along Hood Canal. Except for this you couldn't use the Canal today.

Then he came to a little creek below Hamma Hamma. There were so many salmon in that creek that he slipped around trying to cross it. He said, "You will have no fish." Today we call that creek qačqá•ƛ̓ədəs, "No Salmon Go Up." That is Wake Tiki creek.[13]

Near Dewatto, Dúk^{w}ibəł turned a first-time menstruating girl into a big piece of rock like cement. That was because she wasn't bathing or tending to business. Today we call it a•ták̓^{w}čəd ("girl at first menses").

He tried to get rid of the disk game, *slahál*. He threw the disks away several times, but they kept coming back, so he let them remain. And we still have that game.

The little wrens (*spícx^w*) were using an elk-horn wedge. Dúk^{w}ibəł saw one of them banging it with his head for a hammer. Wren sang:

bɪspáẃpáẃpáẃ[14]	I'm banging and banging
təcilάladi	the side of my head.

Then Dúk^{w}ibəł taught him to use a stone for a mallet, the way they do now.

There was a bad old witch who would steal children and roast them. She had a live snake basket, woven of snakes, to carry the children in. She drank at a little creek near Hamma Hamma, habibiəlqó ("Cascara Bark Creek"). She sang:

səbqɔ•čɪ səbqɔ• '[15]	I'm going to drink
ax^{w}óačɪd aƛ̓ídqoqɔ•´	to my little creek,
habíbíawó	habibiəlqó
habáy' qé ó	(meaningless)

Now Dúk^{w}ibəł told the old Snake Basket Witch he'd show her something. He saw Butterball Duck out catching crabs. He had a whole canoe full. Dúk^{w}ibəł called Butterball over to shore and asked the old witch if she liked crabs. She said no, she was afraid of them. But Dúk^{w}ibəł told her to go catch crabs with Butterball. He told Butterball not to hurt her, but gave him the wink. So they went out and Dúk^{w}ibəł watched. The crabs in the canoe went toward that old witch. And Dúk^{w}ibəł and Butterball called to them to stop, but of course they didn't. So the old witch backed up and they tipped her out into the water. Today you see little freshwater springs out from shore in some places. That's the old witch, bubbling up out of the water.

Then when he finally did all his work he came home to his mother.

He saw a young man coming to get water. And the young man asked Dúkʷibaɫ lots of questions. And it turned out this was his brother; this was that rotten-wood child. Then Dúkʷibaɫ knew he was at his mother's. He didn't tell his brother who he was. And that brother needed fixing. He was knock-kneed, cross-eyed, had a big belly, and was all deformed. And Dúkʷibaɫ said to him, "Tell my mother I have arrived. Tell her to clean the house." And now the brother knew him. And he fixed his brother all up and made him good looking and gave him a haircut and a shave. "Now my mother will know it is me, when she sees you."

Soon the brother came back and said the mother was ready. All the animals and birds were there and they feasted and had a big time. Dúkʷibaɫ knew just where they could get game, so they had lots to eat. They kept on feasting and having a good time, and everyone came to see the Dúkʷibaɫ. That went on for some time.

Then he said, "I've showed my mother's land all I know, how to live. Now I think I will go to my father's country." So he put his arrow points in a bundle and said he would take his brother with him. And any woman who could lift his bundle could be his wife and go with him. And all the big animals nudged each other and said, "This'll be easy!" But none of them could lift it.

Now grandma Frog had *duxʷč̓əláxʷ* [compulsive magic] power. She was over in a corner singing to her poor little granddaughter so she could win Dúkʷibaɫ for a husband. And poor little Frog held up the bundle first try! So she became his wife, and they went up to the star land.

Now there had been no Sun or Moon up to that time. So Dúkʷibaɫ said, "I will rule in the daytime and my brother will rule in the night." But in the daytime he saw that he was making too much heat; all the people were digging holes in the ground and going into the water. So he changed places with his brother. And you can still see Frog, his wife, in the Moon, holding the bundle.

Notes

Professor Elmendorf died in 1997. We are grateful to his wife, the late Eleanor Elmendorf, for sending a contribution from his notes for inclusion in this volume.—Eds.

1. Twana refers to a speech community of Coast Salish Indians in the Hood Canal region of western Washington, between Puget Sound and the Olympic Peninsula. Before 1860, the Twana were divided into nine village communities, of which the Skokomish was the largest (Elmendorf 1993:xxix).

2. This is the Twana name for the Transformer.

3. For comparative references see the second version of "Star Husband" below.

4. The Twana (Skokomish) term is *sábu*, the Lushootseed (Puget Sound) *sx̌ʷiyáb*; Snoqualmie would use the latter (Elmendorf 1961:27n32).

5. This was the sky-earth border, described in Kinkade's Upper Chehalis story about "The Kidnapping of Moon" in this volume.—Eds.

6. The song is sung in Lushootseed (Puget Sound) (Elmendorf 1961:29).

7. Warren Snyder (1965:165) gives "snowbird," probably *Junco hyemalis* or *Oregon junco*, a winter resident of the area.

8. This song is sung in Lushootseed (Elmendorf 1961:30).

9. Adamson (1934:374–78), "Moon and Sun." Curtis (1913:117–21) gives a Lushootseed (Puyallup) version of this Transformer myth with a star-husband introduction, in which Transformer's adventures closely parallel the Skokomish versions. A detail supplied in the Curtis story is identification of Transformer's grandmother, from whom he is stolen in infancy, as Toad. (Elmendorf 1961:31n33.) This version contains very abbreviated accounts of many of the story themes in other stories in this book.—Eds.

10. This song is sung in Lushootseed (Puget Sound) (Elmendorf 1961:33).

11. This song is sung in Lushootseed (Elmendorf 1961:35).

12. Henry Allen remarks that sucking-monster's name, Bátʼqs, "suck-nose," is Lushootseed (Puget Sound). Twana would be Bútʼqs, but it is never used in the story. The place name is also Bátʼqs, a rock on the Hood Canal shore into which the monster was changed. Cf. Lushootseed and Twana song words in the story (Elmendorf 1961:35n35).

13. First creek north of Cummings Point, on west side of Hood Canal (Elmendorf 1961:41 [item 57], 1961:35n36).

14. This song is sung in Lushootseed (Elmendorf 1961:35).

15. This song is sung in Twana (Skokomish) (Elmendorf 1961:35).

Maiden of Deception Pass

A Traditional Samish Story

Told by Victor Underwood Sr.

Edited by Brent Galloway

This traditional Samish story of Qʷəlʾásəlʾwət—Maiden of Deception Pass—was told by Victor Underwood Sr., of the Tsawout Reserve, East Saanich, Vancouver Island, British Columbia, in July 1984. Mr. Underwood was born on Orcas Island, Washington, in about 1914. It was the only traditional Samish story that Mr. Underwood remembered completely in Samish.

Samish speakers aboriginally dominated a cluster of islands around Samish and Guemes Islands (Thompson, Thompson, and Efrat 1974:184), probably including Samish, Guemes, Cypress, Burrows, Allen, Blakely, Decatur, and part of Lopez, San Juan, and Fidalgo islands. They lived in plank longhouses and made their living from products of the sea.

The story of the "Maiden of Deception Pass" is now quite well known, thanks to Victor Underwood's work and that of the Samish tribe. A totem pole was raised at Deception Pass, Washington, in the early 1980s that shows the maiden changing from human to sea creature (or vice versa). The story fits into a series of stories about the origins of islands and places in Samish territory. It belongs to a genre of stories called *sxʷíy̓əm'* or *sxʷíy̓im̓* ("legend from way back; rock with a spirit in it"), contrasted with *ʔəw̓ səʔít sqʷəl'qʷəl'* (a "true story") and *xʷqéyəxqən̓ sqʷəl'qʷəl'* (a "made-up story"). The story is transcribed in Samish and analyzed linguistically with a word list and grammatical sketch in Galloway 1980.

Three versions of the story are presented here. Two versions were originally told in English, with the second somewhat longer than the first. Both are presented in prose style. A third version was told in Samish and translated into English, presented here in an ethnopoetic style. The first English version was told before the Samish version, and the second English version was told after the Samish version. They are presented below in that order of telling, reflecting how each version leads organically to the next.

Maiden of Deception Pass

[1. Short English version, before telling the story in Samish.]

Well, the way the old people used to tell me, you know, they lived right there, you know, at Deception Pass. They lived there for fishings and all that stuff. They had a place, a whole village there. And she used to go down, down to the beach, alone. And that's when this man come up, come up to get her. Because when she did go down below . . . She went down below; they took her down there, and it was just like this; you can see the village. There was a village. You can see all their people. Didn't bother her any. And she stayed there and she come back up.

This man was a monster, went right up, asked their [her] parents—I'm just cutting it short, you know—asked her, asked their [her] parents if they [he and his people] could take her down. Parents says "No." They can feel everything got cold in the house, you know, got cold when he was coming up. You know, he's from down in the sea. When he got up there and he asked and they says [that], and he says, "Well, if you don't let me have your daughter," he says, "we'll starve you people." He says, "I'm the king, king of the sea." Well that's the way, close as I can say in English, "I'm the king of the sea, down there." But *Ɂə́sə siẏéms tə x̌ix̌əč tə sɁiɫən* ["I am the chief/head-man of the food down below."]. That means, well, as close as I can say it, "king of the sea." "I supply all the food, you know, everything down below. If you don't give me your daughter you people will starve; everything will go."

Well they answered him that he took their daughter away, people will get a lot of fish, everything they need, everything they eat from the sea. They can get it anytime, anytime, you see. And barnacles and mussels, anything that they can eat down at the sea, they have it. And this guy done it for oh, quite a while. I don't know how long it is.

And when she comes and visits her parents, well she comes by herself, and soon the barnacles start to grow, you know, a barnacle on her face, [sea]weeds. Her parents says, "You better not come up no more." That's why you see that, how they got that barnacle [on her face on the totem pole carving at Deception Pass]. It was real . . . I don't have to tell them when they called me. They [the carvers] had everything, everything, you know. Well them days I didn't care. I should have taken it all in, but I never know I was going to be telling people, you know.

[2. English version based on translation of the Samish version.]
The biggest tribe then were the Samish,
Well-respected people.
They're big.
So they're there.

Those that go aren't just sitting around home.
They go to a place where they go to fish.
They're looking to eat fish.
They get to the place where they're going.
That's where they were working.
All of them want to get some food for the children.
Those people are gathered there.
They get the fish, anything, everything on the sea-bottom right here, the
     sea-bottom food.
The Samish never get hungry.
They always get their food for their children.

Then she saw a powerful monster right here on the sea bottom.
He wished for the woman.
She went into the water to bathe.
So she was grabbed.
Then he went taking her down to put her at the sea bottom.
He wanted to get as a spouse a woman from here, out of the water.

He went to go to her parents.

Then he asked, "I want to take your daughter as my wife.
She is a good child."

So the mother said, "I don't want my daughter to go.
I want her here with us."
So the monster from here on the sea bottom said, "I want to take your
     daughter.
If you don't give me your daughter, then it will be impossible for you to
get any food from here down on the bottom, anything.
I am the king of what's on the bottom here where I am.
I am the one supplying you folks's food.

If you won't give me your daughter, then therefore lots will be hungry.
Then your people will be all the same."

And so they answered for their own daughter.

So their daughter was taken away.
And then all their many relatives got the food easily.
It was just easy for them to get the food from down there at the bottom.

So when their daughter comes up out of the water she sees them.
Whenever their daughter is ready to come up out of the water it gets cold
       inside.
It gets cold.
Then her own parents already know it.

"My dear daughter must be coming here.
She got here,
it's really true."

And he saw green seaweed growing from her face.
Everything was growing,
coming,
coming out,
growing from her face.
Mussels too.

So he said, "Child, it's enough.
You can't always come see us.
You're always staying home and resting there.
Look at us because we're showing
And don't worry about anything there.
I know that you are all right where you're at when you are there.
I guess that's the way you're being taken when you're going to where
your relatives are at.
You've helped them (your relatives).
He's feeding them every kind of food.
You can leave us alone.
Really, you're going to be happy when you're there down below."

That's all I'm going to say.
The story is over

[3. Longer English version, after telling the story in Samish.]
As I say, Samish was the biggest tribe, you know. It's the biggest tribe they
ever had that I was told. I was told by my grandfather. It was the biggest
tribe. They had houses, houses all around, that's in Guemes. And I seen . . . I
lived in Guemes when I was a kid. But I seen the poles but I never seen the
houses. And the Samish used to be together all the time.

And they went to Deception Pass, that's where their fishing grounds was.
There was a big village there; they stayed right there. They do a lot of fishing. Everything is what they eat from the sea, everything they want. They
had everything there, mussels and all that, everything of seafood they can
eat. They have always had it there.

One day this girl, daughter of this, one of the old people, went down the
beach. She would stay down on the beach for . . . goes down every day.
Every day she goes down there. Pretty soon she went down the beach and
went into the water, washing. Somebody grabbed her and she looked and it
was a hand. So they dragged her down, dragged her down the beach, down
under the water. When she got down there she felt the water when she was
going, but after she got down it was just like the way we are now, you see.
She looked back and seen all her people, seen the village; everything was,
you know, it was just the same as we are today. So this man told her—he was
a nice looking man—"I been watching you. I been watching you every day
when you come down. And I had kind of worked on you so you can come
down." Well them days people used to work on somebody that they want
to get ahold of. They work on them. I wouldn't know how to say it, but the
Indians had their own way. They had their own power. If they want anybody,
well, they work on it so they can come down. So they talked and he says,
"Well I want to marry you. So I'm going to go up and ask your parents if you
can, you can come down with me."

So they went up. They got up and people were kind of worried about their
daughter and can feel that cold cold in the house before he walked in. He
walked in and they seen him, a good-looking man, and he talked to the parents. He says, "I had your daughter down below." He says, "I'm the king of
the sea." He says, "I'm the king of everything that you eat, everything, the
fish, everything that you got down below to eat." And he says, "I look after
it. I'm the king. And if you don't let me have your daughter," he says, "your

people are going to starve. You wouldn't get nothing out of me. There'll be no fish or anything that you eat." So they talked it over and says, "Well yeah, I guess you can go."

So they took her daughter down, and she comes up to see their parents. They done that for I wouldn't know how long. It just took quite a while, in a way to go down, up, up and see their parents. Pretty soon the barnacles started to grow, the weeds started to grow on her thigh. So the old man says, "You better not come back." He says, "We're okay. You say you can see us, so we're all fine here." He says that to her because she felt bad her daughter was turning to sea, like. That's why they told her not to come back.

So Samish had lots to eat, everything they need; everything they need they go get out, even after, after-time people, Samish, used to go over and call her name, "Qʷəlʼásəlʼwət, we want something to eat." They čʼíːtəŋ (thanked her) when I want something that's going to come we need. Now the Samish people never starve. They get all the food they want. They go out and get it. Even if they're traveling through there's supposed to have been real swift water, and they talk to her, kind of talk to her that they're from the tribe. The water settles down; they can go right up with their canoe. No trouble at all because they believed her, she's down there. They called her name. That's how people used to go. That's all far as I can remember. Yeah.

Kakantu, the Chief's Daughter Who Married a Blackfish

A Traditional Klallam Story

*Told by Amy Allen, translated by Laurence C. Thompson and
Martha Charles John*

Edited by Steven M. Egesdal

Amy Allen, of Jamestown, Washington, told this story to Laurence C. Thompson in the late 1960s. She tape-recorded it for Martha Charles John of Little Boston, Washington, and Thompson and Mrs. John later translated the story. That context allowed it to be a performance of sorts, albeit with a temporally removed audience. The extensive moralizing explanation that ends the story, however, might appear more directed at an outsider, here a linguist. Thompson later used "Kakantu" as a linguistic puzzle in his courses on Salishan linguistics at the University of Hawaii, and what began as a linguistic puzzle eventually would become an even more elusive cultural one.

"Kakantu" is similar to the story of the "Maiden of Deception Pass" found in other Coast Salish groups.[1] They share the motif of a daughter leaving her family to live with a husband in the sea world. In the Klallam version, a young maiden decides to marry a killer whale, or "blackfish" as they are better known in the Klallam area. A slave tries to take Kakantu's place, unsuccessfully. Kakantu leaves with her groom and then begins to change features, such as seaweed growing on her face. Eventually, her family asks her not to return home anymore. She haunts that place near Port Townsend (Washington), where her family bade her a final farewell.

The story raises several interesting cultural points. First, the story reflects something about the traditional Klallam view on the proper behavior of young women toward potential mates. Kakantu showed an unusual lust, animal-like to the point of wanting an animal. She refused to have a slave take her place; inappropriately, she wanted him for herself. Amy Allen warns that young women ought to keep quiet, not wishing for "that fellow"; that is, they should keep their budding sexual desires in check.

Second, the story may reflect something about marriage in traditional Klallam culture. On the Northwest Coast was the notion of "bride wealth." Incident to the marriage would have been some exchange of wealth, instigated with gifts by the groom's family but reciprocated in kind by the bride's family.

It is unclear why the father consented to the marriage of his daughter to a killer whale; perhaps he expected a special exchange of wealth through Kakantu's marriage. That explanation is clearer in other versions of this Coast Salish story, where a maiden's marriage to a sea creature brings her family bountiful gifts of the sea.

Third, the story may reflect something about social hierarchy and the place of the killer whale in the ethnozoological cosmology of the Klallam. The Northwest Coast culture that enveloped the Klallam was hierarchical, even developing hereditary slavery. Against that backdrop, a killer whale bids successfully for the hand of a chief's daughter who correspondingly wanted him as a mate. Killer whales were perceived as very special beings, evidenced by the parity of the marriage pair. Killer whale spirit power was very strong in Klallam culture. Kakantu becomes a supernatural being, *sxʷnáʔm*, by associating with the killer whale. Moreover, when a slave, a person of lower rank, tried to take Kakantu's place, Seagull reported what the audience knew: "Not the right one!" The killer whale was not to marry beneath his station.

The role of slave subtly reminds of the traditional practice of taking and keeping slaves prevalent on the Northwest Coast. When the attempt to replace Kakantu with a slave failed, Kakantu took the slave's place—an interesting role reversal, perhaps. Kakantu also was "enslaved" by an unnatural desire. She was taken to a far-off, alien place, as a captured slave would have been. Her face was marked with seaweed, a stigma symbolically reflecting a change in status, not unlike the blot of slavery. When a person was taken as a slave in a raid, the captive's family might ransom him; but sometimes the stigma of slavery was too great, and he was abandoned. In this story, Kakantu was marked with an ignoble fate, one perhaps better fit for a slave. Her family then rejected her for the stigma her status may have brought her family, not unlike if she had been taken a slave. Wealth, rank, and social stature were so important. A daughter with seaweed on the face just would not do.

Kakantu, the Chief's Daughter Who Married a Blackfish

Now I'm going to tell you the old legend about the place there at
Port Townsend,
and the former chief there.
There was a daughter of that chief.
She was with one of her slaves one night,
when she saw the killer whales.

The chief's daughter said,
>"They have handsome faces.
>I wish that particular one were my husband."

That evening, that very evening,
he went there and asked for the chief's daughter for his wife.
The slave said,
>"He's the very one you wanted!"
Then the chief's daughter was not sure she wanted him.
Then the slave said,
>"Let me take your place!"
When the time came that evening for the marriage, she said,
>"I'll be the one."

When it was settled and accomplished, Seagull cried:
>"Not the right one! Not the right one!"[2]
So they took the slave back.

The next morning the chief said,
>"Let her go and be taken, my daughter.[3]
>It's not right for you to take her place."

So Killer Whale took her and went away with her.
It was several days before she was brought out of the water and taken
ashore.
Now she didn't observe how her husband, Killer Whale, was playing
around.
Then the one she left home for took her away again, deep into the sea.

Then the chief's daughter was brought out of the water again.
Seaweed already had begun to grow on her face.
So then her mother told her,
>"You've already left behind my urging you to come back.
>It's no longer what you want, no longer.
>You've become a supernatural thing.
>It's already all over now.
>So whenever it was to be that you go, then go!"

If you are traveling there by canoe, you have to go straight and keep
silent.
For if you go talking, then it comes floating up[4] just like the cattail mat,
and you won't be able to paddle.
Only if you take along some dried salmon,
and throw a little into the water there, then you'll be able to paddle,
because of Kakantu there, the chief's daughter.
And that's the way the story went from 'way back.

That's why young girls ought to keep quiet—not talk about wishing for
that fellow.
He was good looking. That was why she was taken, the chief's daughter.
She wouldn't permit herself to be replaced by the slave.
The chief's daughter wanted to have him herself, Killer Whale.
She wouldn't permit herself to be replaced by the slave.
And so she, the chief's daughter, was taken by Killer Whale.

That's why it's named after Kakantu.
And when you go there, it's Kakantu that goes along beside you.

Notes

1. See the previous story from Northern Straits Samish.—Eds.
2. Seagull was a notorious tattletale, playing the role that Meadowlark plays in Interior Salish.
3. He called the slave his daughter as a term of familiarity.
4. The seaweed from the chief's daughter's face.

References and Suggested Further Reading

Abbott, Donald, ed. 1981. *The World Is as Sharp as a Knife: An Anthology in Honour of Wilson Duff*. Victoria: British Columbia Provincial Museum.

Abraham, Otto, and Eric M. Von Hornbostel. [1906]. 1977. Phonographierte Indianermelodieen Aus Britisch-Columbia. In *Boas Anniversary Volume*, 447–74. New York: G. E. Stechert. Reprint; Klaus P. Wachsmann et al., eds., English translation by Bruno Nettl. Indian Melodies from British-Columbia Recorded on the Phonograph. In *Hornbostel Opera Omnia* 1:310–22. The Hague: Martinus Nijhoff.

Adamson, Thelma. 1934. *Folk Tales of the Coast Salish*. Memoirs of the American Folklore Society 27. New York: G. E. Stechert.

Allen, Paula Gunn. 1974. The Mythopoeic Vision in Native American Literature: The Problem of Myth. *American Indian Culture and Research Journal* 1:1–3.

Allen, Paula Gunn, ed. 1989. *Spider Woman's Granddaughters*. New York: Fawcett Columbine-Ballantine.

Amoss, Pamela. [1975.] Manuscript Catalogue of the Marian Smith Collection of Fieldnotes, Manuscripts, and Photographs in the Library of the Royal Anthropological Institute of Great Britain and Ireland. Ms. in Amoss's possession.

———. 1978. *Coast Salish Spirit Dancing: The Survival of an Ancestral Religion*. Seattle: University of Washington Press.

Andrade, Manuel J. 1931. *Quileute Texts*. Columbia University Contributions to Anthropology 12. New York: Columbia University Press.

Anonymous. 1906. *An Illustrated History of Skagit and Snohomish Counties*. Chicago: Interstate Publishing Company.

Aoki, Haruo. 1979. *Nez Perce Texts*. University of California Publications in Linguistics 90. Berkeley, Los Angeles, London.

Aoki, Haruo, and Deward Walker. 1989. *Nez Perce Oral Narratives*. University of California Publications in Linguistics 104. Berkeley, Los Angeles, London.

Babcock, Barbara, and Jay Cox. 1994. The Native American Trickster. In *Dictionary of Native American Literature*, ed. Andrew Wiget, 99–105. New York: Garland.

Bahr, Donald. 1994a. Dreams, Song, and Narrative. In *Dictionary of Native American Literature*, ed. Andrew Wiget, 119–23. New York: Garland.

———. 1994b. Oratory. In *Dictionary of Native American Literature*, ed. Andrew Wiget, 107–17. New York: Garland.

Baker, Marie Annharte. 1992. Coyote Trail. In *An Anthology of Canadian Native Literature in English*, ed. Daniel David Moses and Terry Goldie, 168–69. Toronto: Oxford University Press.

Ballard, Arthur C. 1935. Southern Puget Sound Salish Kinship Terms. *American Anthropologist* 37:102–12.

———. 1950. Calendric Terms of the Southern Puget Sound Salish. *Southwest Journal of Anthropology* 6:79–99.

Banks, Judith Judd. 1966. *Comparative Biographies of Two British Columbia Anthropologists: Charles Hill-Tout and James A. Teit*. Master's thesis, Anthropology, University of British Columbia, Vancouver.

Barbeau, Marius, and Chief Tiɬńíče?. 1913. Recording, Canadian Museum of Civilization, Hull, Quebec; on Bobine (Cylinder) No. 8.

Barnett, Homer G. 1938. The Coast Salish of Canada. *American Anthropologist* 40:118–41.

———. 1955. *The Coast Salish of British Columbia*. University of Oregon Monographs: Studies in Anthropology 4. Eugene: University of Oregon Press.

Basso, Keith H. 1984. "Stalking with Stories": Names, Places, and Moral Narratives among the Western Apache. In *Text, Play, and Story: The Construction and Reconstruction of Self in Society*, ed. Edward M. Bruner, 19–55. Washington DC: American Ethnological Society.

———. 1996. *Wisdom Sits in Places: Landscape and Language among the Western Apache*. Albuquerque: University of New Mexico Press.

Bates, Dawn. 1997. Person Marking in Lushootseed Subordinate Clauses. *International Journal of American Linguistics* 63(3):316–33.

Bates, Dawn, Thom[as M.] Hess, and Vi [T.] Hilbert. 1994. *Lushootseed Dictionary*, ed. Dawn Bates. Seattle: University of Washington Press.

Beaumont, Ronald C. 1985. *she shashishalhem: The Sechelt Language. Language, Stories and Sayings of the Sechelt Indian People of British Columbia*. Penticton, BC: Theytus Books.

Berman, Judith. 1996. "The Culture as It Appears to the Indian Himself": Boas, George Hunt, and the Methods of Ethnography. In *Volksgeist as Method and Ethic: Essays on Boasian Ethnography and the German Anthropological Tradition*, ed. George W. Stocking Jr., 215–56. Madison: University of Wisconsin Press.

Bierhorst, John. 1985. *The Mythology of North America*. New York: Morrow.

———. 1987. *Doctor Coyote: A Native American Aesop's Fables*. New York: Macmillan.

Bierwert, Crisca, ed. 1996. *Lushootseed Texts: An Introduction to Puget Salish Narrative Aesthetics*. Studies in the Anthropology of North American Indians. Lincoln: University of Nebraska Press.

————. 2004. Coyote and His Son. In *Voices from Four Directions: Contemporary Translations of the Native Literatures of North America*, ed. Brian Swann, 171–94. Lincoln: University of Nebraska Press.

Boas, Franz. n.d. [BPC]. Franz Boas Professional Correspondence. American Philosophical Society Library, Philadelphia.

————. n.d. [BPP]. Franz Boas Professional Papers. American Philosophical Society Library, Philadelphia.

————. [1886.] Pentlatch Materials. (Manuscript No. 30[S2j.3] Freeman No. 3090), in American Philosophical Society Library, Philadelphia.

[1890a.] Handwritten Copies of Linguistic Field Notebooks, Lexical Files, and Grammatical Notes from Approximately Three Weeks' Fieldwork among the Tillamook Salish, Siletz, Oregon, given to his student, May Mandelbaum Edel. May M. Edel Papers, Manuscript Division, University of Washington Libraries, Seattle.

————. [1890b.] Miscellaneous Items on Tillamook, Siletz, Nehalim. (Ms. No. [30(S4.3)] Freeman No. 3744), in American Philosophical Society Library, Philadelphia.

————. 1890c. Shuswap. *Report of the British Association for the Advancement of Science* 60:688–92.

————. [ca. 1890.] Lower Chehalis Vocabulary and Text. (Ms. No. 30[S2b.1] Freeman No. 593), in American Philosophical Society Library, Philadelphia.

————. 1891. The Coast Salish of British Columbia. *Report of the British Association for the Advancement of Science* 61:679–715.

————. 1892. Sagen aus Britisch-Columbien IX. Sagen der PE´ntlatc. *Verhandlungen der Berliner Gesellschaft für Anthropologie, Ethnologie und Urgeschichte, Jahrgang* 1892:65–66. Berlin: Verlag von A. Asher.

————. 1894. The Indian Tribes of the Lower Fraser River. *Report of the British Association for the Advancement of Science* 1894:453–63.

————. [1895a.] 2002. *Indianische Sagen von der Nord-Pacifischen Küste Amerikas. Sonder-Abdruck aus den Verhandlungen der Berliner Gesellschaft fur Anthropologie, Ethnologie und Urgeschichte*. Berlin: Verlag von A. Asher. Reprint; Randy Bouchard and Dorothy I. D. Kennedy, eds. Translated by Dietrich Bertz. BC Indian Language Project, *Indian Myths and Legends from the North Pacific Coast*. Victoria BC: Talonbooks.

————. 1895b. Salishan Texts. *Proceedings of the American Philosophical Society* 34:31–48.

————. [1896.] 1940. The Growth of Indian Mythologies. *Journal of American Folklore* 9:1–11. Reprinted in Boas's *Race, Language and Culture*.

————. [1898a.] 1969. Introduction to James Teit's *Traditions of the Thompson Indians of British Columbia*. Memoirs of the American Folklore Society 6:1–18. Boston and New York. Reprint; Krause Reprints.

———. 1898b. The Mythology of the Bella Coola Indians. *The Jesup North Pacific Expedition* II, *Anthropology* I:25–127, with plates. Memoirs of the American Museum of Natural History 2. New York.

———. 1898c. Traditions of the Tillamook Indians I. *Journal of American Folklore* 11:23–38.

———. 1898d. Traditions of the Tillamook Indians II. *Journal of American Folklore* 11:133–50.

———. 1899. The Ntlakya'pamuQ. *Report of the British Association for the Advancement of Science* 68:654–63.

———. [1900.] Tillamook and Siletz Folkloristic Texts (copies of 1890 texts) (Ms. No. [30(S4.2)] Freeman No. 3745), in American Philosophical Society Library, Philadelphia.

———. [1911.] 1966. Introduction. *Handbook of American Indian Languages*. Bureau of American Ethnology Bulletin 40, Part I:5–83. Washington DC: Government Printing Office. Reprint; Lincoln: University of Nebraska Press.

———. [1914.] 1940. Mythology and Folk-Tales of the North American Indians. *Journal of American Folklore* 27:374–410. Reprinted in Boas's *Race, Language and Culture*.

———. 1917. *Folk-Tales of Salishan and Sahaptin Tribes*. Collected by James A. Teit, Livingston Farrand, Marian K. Gould, and Herbert J. Spinden. Memoirs of the American Folk-Lore Society 11. Lancaster PA: G. E. Stechert.

———. 1923. Notes on the Tillamook. University of California Publications in American Archaeology and Ethnology 20:3–16.

———. [1927–35.] Chehalis Field Notes. (Ms. No. 30[62] Freeman No. 586); (30[7] Freeman No. 587); (30[S2c.1] Freeman No. 589), in American Philosophical Society Library, Philadelphia.

———. 1934. A Chehalis Text. *International Journal of American Linguistics* 8:103–10.

———. 1940. *Race, Language and Culture*. New York: Macmillan.

———. [1985.] *Coeur d'Alene, Flathead, and Okanagan Indians*. Fairfield WA: Ye Galleon Press.

Boas, Franz, and A. Chamberlain. 1918. *Kutenai Tales*. Bureau of American Ethnology Bulletin 49:1–387. Washington DC: Smithsonian Institution.

Boas, Franz, and James A. Teit. [1987.] [ATM] Cylinder Collection of Thompson River Indian Songs, Recorded by Franz Boas and James A. Teit, Spences Bridge, British Columbia. Indiana University Archives of Traditional Music, Bloomington.

Boyd, Robert. 1990. Demographic History, 1774–1874. In *Handbook of North American Indians* 7:135–48. *Northwest Coast*, ed. Wayne Suttles. Washington DC: Smithsonian Institution Press.

Bouchard, Randy, and Dorothy Kennedy. 1977. *Lillooet Stories. Sound Heritage* No. 16. Victoria BC.

Bouchard, Randy, and Dorothy Kennedy, eds. 1979. *Shuswap Stories*. Vancouver: CommCept Publishing.

———. 2002. *Indian Myths and Legends from the North Pacific Coast*. Translated by Dietrich Bertz. BC Indian Language Project. Victoria BC: Talonbooks. Reprinted from Boas, Franz. 1895a. *Indianische Sagen von der Nord-Pacifischen Küste Amerikas. Sonder-Abdruck aus den Verhandlungen der Berliner Gesellschaft fur Anthropologie, Ethnologie und Urgeschichte*. Berlin: Verlag von A. Asher.

Bright, William. 1980. Coyote's Journey. *American Indian Culture and Research Journal* 4(1/2):21–48.

———. 1984a. Literature: Written and Oral. In *American Indian Linguistics and Literature*, 79–89. Berlin: Mouton Publishers.

——— . 1984b. Poetic Structure in Oral Narrative. In *American Indian Linguistics and Literature*, 133–48. Berlin: Mouton Publishers.

———. 1984c. The Virtues of Illiteracy. In *American Indian Linguistics and Literature*, 149–59. Berlin: Mouton Publishers.

———. 1987. The Natural History of Old Man Coyote. In *Recovering the Word: Essays on Native American Literature*, ed. Brian Swann and Arnold Krupat, 339–87. Berkeley: University of California Press.

———. 1993. *A Coyote Reader*. Berkeley: University of California Press.

Bright, William, ed. 1978. *Coyote Stories*. International Journal of American Linguistics, Native American Texts Series. Monograph 1. Chicago: University of Chicago Press.

Brown, Robert. 1873. The Indian Story of "Jack and the Bean Stalk." In *The Races of Mankind, Being a Popular Description of the Characteristics, Manners, and Customs of the Principal Varieties of the Human Family* 1:131–32. London, Paris, and New York: Cassel, Petter and Galpin.

Capoeman, Pauline K., ed. 1990. *Land of the Quinault*. Taholah WA: Quinault Indian Nation.

Carlson, Barry F., ed. 1977. *Northwest Coast Texts: Stealing Light*. International Journal of American Linguistics, Native American Texts Series. Monograph 2(3). Chicago: University of Chicago Press.

———. 1978. Coyote and Gopher (Spokane). In *Coyote Stories*, ed. William Bright. International Journal of American Linguistics, Native American Texts Series. Monograph 1:3–14.

Carlson, Barry F., and Pauline Flett. 1989. *Spokane Dictionary*. University of Montana Occasional Papers in Linguistics 6. Missoula.

Center, Ellen. n.d. Reminiscences of Ellen Center. Unpublished notes in "Clatsop Indian" files of Lewis and Clark National Historical Park, Fort Clatsop, Oregon.

Clifford, James. 1985. Objects and Selves—An Afterword. In *Objects and Others: Essays on Museums and Material Culture*, ed. George W. Stocking Jr. Madison: University of Wisconsin Press.

————. 1988. *The Predicament of Culture: Twentieth-Century Ethnography, Literature, and Art*. Cambridge, MA: Harvard University Press.

Cole, Douglas. 1999. *Franz Boas: The Early Years*. Vancouver and Seattle: Douglas and McIntyre and the University of Washington Press.

Collins, June McCormick. 1952. The Mythological Basis for Attitudes toward Animals among the Salish-Speaking Indians. *Journal of American Folklore* 65(258):353–59.

Collins, Lloyd R. 1953. *Archaeological Survey of the Oregon Coast from June 1951–December 1952*. Eugene: Oregon State Museum of Anthropology.

Compton, Brian D., Dwight Gardiner, Mary Thomas, and Joe Michel. 1994. The Sucker: A Fish Full of Bones, Coyotes, Coots, and Clam Shells. Working Papers of the 29th International Conference on Salish and Neighboring Languages, 54–78. Pablo MT: Salish Kootenai College.

Crawford, Ailsa E. 1983. *Tillamook Indian Basketry: Continuity and Change as Seen in the Adams Collection*. Unpublished master's thesis, Anthropology, Portland State University, OR.

Czaykowska-Higgins, Ewa, and M. Dale Kinkade, eds. 1997. *Salish Language and Linguistics: Theoretical and Descriptive Perspectives*. Trends in Linguistics: Studies and Monographs 107. Berlin and New York: Mouton de Gruyter.

Davis, Henry. 2001. *Kayam*: An Early St'at'imcets Text. *Anthropological Linguistics* 43(3):288–347.

Davis, Philip W., and Ross Saunders. 1980. *Bella Coola Texts*. British Columbia Provincial Museum, Heritage Record 10. Victoria BC.

De Smet, Pierre-Jean. [1905.] 2005. *Life, Letters, and Travels of Father De Smet*. Reprint; Crabtree OR: Narrative Press.

Deur, Douglas E. 1996. Chinook Jargon Placenames as Points of Mutual Reference: Discourse, Intersubjectivity, and Environment in an Intercultural Toponymic Complex. *Native American Geographic Names: Problems, Practices, and Prospects* (Special Issue). *Names* 44(4):291–321.

————. 1997. Was the Northwest Coast Agricultural: Ecological, Archaeological, and Ethnographic Evidence. Paper presented at the 1997 Annual Meeting of the American Association for the Advancement of Science, Seattle WA.

————. 1999. Salmon, Sedentism, and Culture: Toward an Environmental Prehistory of the Northwest Coast. In *Northwest Lands, Northwest Peoples: Readings in Environmental History*, ed. Dale D. Goble and Paul W. Hirt, 129–55. Seattle: University of Washington Press.

————. 2005. Community, Place, and Persistence: An Introduction to Clatsop-Nehalem History since the Time of Lewis and Clark. Unpublished report. Salem: Oregon Heritage Commission, and Turner OR: Clatsop-Nehalem Confederated Tribes.

Dicken, Samuel N. 1978. *Pioneer Trails of the Oregon Coast*, 2nd ed. Portland: Oregon Historical Society.

Dixon, May, Mary Palmantier, and Aert H. Kuipers. 1982. *A Western Shuswap Reader*. Leiden: University of Leiden.

Driver, Harold E. [1961.] 1969. *The Indians of North America*, 2nd ed., rev. Chicago: University of Chicago Press.

Drucker, Philip. [1955.] 1963. *Indians of the Northwest Coast*. Garden City NY: The Natural History Press. Originally published in Anthropological Handbook for The American Museum of Natural History.

―――. 1981. Ronald Leroy Olson. *American Anthropologist* 83(3):605–7.

Duff, Wilson. 1952. *The Upper Stalo Indians of the Fraser River of B.C. Anthropology in British Columbia*. British Columbia Provincial Museum Memoir 1. Victoria.

―――. 1969. *The Indian History of British Columbia: The Impact of the White Man*. Victoria BC: Ministry of Provincial Secretary and Government Services.

Dundes, Alan. 1965. *The Study of Folklore*. Englewood Cliffs NJ: Prentice Hall.

―――. 1967. North American Indian Folklore Studies. *Journal de la Société des Américanistes* 56:53–79.

Edel, May Mandelbaum. [1931.] Field notebooks, lexical files, folklore texts, based on fieldwork among the Tillamook Salish, Oregon. May M. Edel Papers, University of Washington Libraries, Seattle.

―――. 1939. The Tillamook Language. *International Journal of American Linguistics* 10:1–57.

―――. 1944. Stability in Tillamook Folklore. *Journal of American Folklore* 57:116–27.

Efrat, Barbara S. 1969. *A Grammar of Non-Particles in Sooke, a Dialect of Straits Coast Salish*. Published PhD dissertation, University of Pennsylvania. Ann Arbor: University Microfilms International.

Egesdal, Steven. 1991. Margaret Sherwood's Badger and Skunk: A Spokane Traditional Legend with Commentary. Working Papers of the 26th International Conference on Salish and Neighboring Languages, 97–118. Vancouver: University of British Columbia.

―――. 1992. *Stylized Characters' Speech in Thompson Salish Narrative*. University of Montana Occasional Papers in Linguistics 9. Missoula.

Egesdal, Steven M., and M. Terry Thompson. 1994. Hilda Austin's Telling of Qʷíqʷƛ̓qʷəƛ̓t/Nɬeʔképmx Legend (Thompson River Salish). In *Coming to Light: Contemporary Translations of the Native Literatures of North America*, ed. Brian Swann, 313–31. New York: Random House.

―――. 1998. A Fresh Look at Tillamook (*Hutyéyu*) Inflectional Morphology. In *Salish Languages and Linguistics: Current Theoretical and Descriptive Perspectives*, ed. Ewa Czaykowska-Higgins and M. Dale Kinkade, 235–73. Berlin and New York: Mouton de Gruyter.

Eigenbrod, Renate. 1995. The Oral in the Written: A Literature between Two Cultures. *Canadian Journal of Native Studies* 15(1):89–102.

Elliott, T. C. 1936. Religion among the Flatheads. *Oregon Historical Quarterly* 37:1–8.

Elmendorf, William. 1961a. Skokomish and Other Coast Salish Tales (Parts 1–3). *Research Studies of Washington State University* 29(1):1–37; 29(2):84–117; 29(3):119–50.

———. 1961b. System Change in Salish Kinship Terminologies. *Southwest Journal of Anthropology* 17:365–82.

———. 1993. *Twana Narratives: Native Historical Accounts of a Coast Salish Culture.* Seattle: University of Washington Press; Vancouver: University of British Columbia Press.

Erdoes, Richard, and Alfonso Ortiz, eds. 1984. *American Indian Myths and Legends.* New York: Pantheon Books.

Fabian, Johannes. 1983. *Time and the Other: How Anthropology Makes Its Object.* New York: Columbia University Press.

Farrand, Livingston. [1897–98.] [Quinault Field Notebook No. 12. (Ms. No. [30(S2a.1)] Freeman No. 3198), in American Philosophical Society Library, Philadelphia.]

———. 1902. Traditions of the Quinault Indians. Assisted by W. S. Kahnweiler. *The Jesup North Pacific Expedition* II. *Anthropology* 1:77–132. Memoirs of the American Museum of Natural History 4(3). New York.

Fisher, Robin. 1977. *Contact and Conflict: Indian-European Relations in British Columbia, 1774–1890.* Vancouver: University of British Columbia Press.

Flathead Cultural Committee. 1979. *A Brief History of the Flathead Tribes*, 2nd ed. St. Ignatius MT: Flathead Culture Committee, Confederated Salish and Kootenai Tribes.

Fleck, Richard. 1993. *Critical Perspectives on Native American Fiction.* Washington DC: Three Continents.

Frey, Rodney, ed. 1995. *Stories That Make the World: Oral Literature of the Indian Peoples of the Inland Northwest. As Told by Lawrence Aripa, Tom Yellowtail, and Other Elders.* Norman: University of Oklahoma Press.

Frey, Rodney, and Dell Hymes. 1998. Mythology. In *Handbook of North American Indians* 12:584–99. *Plateau*, ed. Deward E. Walker. Washington DC: Smithsonian Institution Press.

Frey, Rodney, in collaboration with the Schitsu'umsh. 2001. *Landscape Traveled by Crane and Coyote: The World of the Schitsu'umsh-Coeur d'Alene Indians.* Seattle: University of Washington Press.

Galloway, Brent D. 1977. *A Grammar of Chilliwack Halkomelem.* PhD dissertation, University of California, Berkeley.

———. 1980. *Tó:lmels Ye Siyelyólexwa (Wisdom of the Elders)*, (consisting of The Structure of Upriver *Halq'eméylem*, a Grammatical Sketch, and Classified Word List for Upriver *Halq'eméylem*). Sardis BC: Coqualeetza Education Training Centre.

———. 1996. *An Upriver Halkomelem Mink Story: Ethnopoetics and Discourse Analysis*. Working Papers of the 31st International Conference on Salish and Neighboring Languages, 159–74. Vancouver: University of British Columbia.

Gunther, Erna. 1925. *Klallam Folk Tales*. University of Washington Publications in Anthropology 1(4):113–69. Seattle.

Hajda, Yvonne. 1990. Southwestern Coast Salish. In *Handbook of North American Indians* 7:503–17. *Northwest Coast*, ed. Wayne Suttles. Washington DC: Smithsonian Institution Press.

Hanna, Darwin, and Mamie Henry, eds. 1995. *Our Tellings: Interior Salish Stories of the Nlha'kapmx People*. Vancouver: University of British Columbia Press

Harrington, John P. [1942–43.] Tillamook Field Notes: Vocabulary, Texts, Grammatical Notes, from Bay Center, Washington, and Siletz, Oregon. John P. Harrington Papers, National Anthropological Archives, Smithsonian Institution, Washington DC. Microfilm edition (with Guide, Elaine L. Mills, ed.), Reel 20, 1981.

Hess, Thom[as M.] 1976. *Dictionary of Puget Salish*. Seattle: University of Washington Press.

———. 1979. Central Coast Salish Words for Deer: Their Wavelike Distribution. *International Journal of American Linguistics* 45:5–16.

———. 1982. *Traces of Abnormal Speech in Lushootseed*. Working Papers of the 17th International Conference on Salish and Neighboring Languages, 89–97. Portland OR: Portland State University.

———. 1993. A Schema for the Presentation of Lushootseed Verb Stems. In *American Indian Linguistics and Ethnography in Honor of Laurence C. Thompson*, ed. Anthony Mattina and Timothy Montler. University of Montana Occasional Papers in Linguistics 10:113–25. Missoula.

———. 1995. *Lushootseed Reader with Introductory Grammar I: Four Stories from Edward Sam*. University of Montana Occasional Papers in Linguistics 11. Missoula.

———. 1998. *Lushootseed Reader with Intermediate Grammar II: Four Stories from Martha Lamont*. 2 volumes, with glossary, accompanied by a recording of Mrs. Lamont narrating the four stories. University of Montana Occasional Papers in Linguistics 14. Missoula.

Hilbert, Vi Taqᵂšəblu. 1980. *Haboo: Lushootseed Literature in English*. Privately printed for use in class at University of Washington.

———. 1991. When Chief Seattle (si-alh) Spoke. In *A Time of Gathering: Native Heritage in Washington State*, ed. Robin Wright, 259–66. Seattle: University of Washington Press.

Hilbert, Vi [T.], ed. 1985. *Haboo: Native American Stories from Puget Sound*. Seattle: University of Washington Press.

Hilbert, Vi [T.], and Thom[as M.] Hess. 1977. Lushootseed. In *Northwest Coast Texts: Stealing Light*, ed. Barry F. Carlson. International Journal of American Linguistics, Native American Texts Series. Monograph 2:4–32.

Hill-Tout, Charles. 1899. *Notes on the N'tlakapamuq of British Columbia.* Report of the British Association for the Advancement of Science 69:500–505, Appendix 2.

———. 1900. *Notes on the Sk.qomic [Squamish] of British Columbia, a Branch of the Great Salish Stock of North America.* Appendix II of the Ethnological Survey of Canada. Report of the British Association for the Advancement of Science 70:471–549.

———. 1904. Report on the Ethnology of the *Síciatl* of British Columbia, a Coast Division of the Salish Stock. *Journal of the Royal Anthropological Institute of Great Britain and Ireland* 34:20–91.

———. 1905. Report on the Ethnology of the *StlatlumH* of British Columbia. *Journal of the Royal Anthropological Institute of Great Britain and Ireland* 35:156–76, 206–18.

———. 1911. Report on the Ethnology of the *Okanak'en. Journal of the Royal Anthropological Institute of Great Britain and Ireland* 41:130–61.

———. [1978.] *The Salish People: The Local Contribution of Charles Hill-Tout,* 4 vols. Ed. Ralph Maud. Vancouver: Talonbooks.

Hines, Donald. 1984. *Tales of the Nez Perce.* Fairfield WA: Ye Galleon Press.

Hinkson, Mercedes Quesney. 1999. *Salishan Lexical Suffixes: A Study in the Conceptualization of Space.* PhD dissertation, Simon Fraser University, Vancouver.

Holbert, Harry. 1941. *Ethnography of the Kootenai.* Memoirs of the American Anthropological Association 56.

Hopson, Gerry, ed. 2002. *Ralph Maud's Transmission Difficulties.* Vancouver: Talonbooks.

Hukari, Thomas E., R. Peter, and E. White. 1977. Halkomelem. In *Northwest Coast Texts: Stealing Light,* ed. Barry Carlson. International Journal of American Linguistics, Native American Texts Series. Monograph 2(3):33–68.

Hunn, Eugene, with James Selam and family. 1990. *Nch'i-Wána "The Big River": Mid-Columbia Indians and Their Land.* Seattle and London: University of Washington Press.

Hymes, Dell. 1979. How to Talk like a Bear in Takelma. *International Journal of American Linguistics* 45:101–6.

———. 1981. *"In Vain I Tried to Tell You": Essays in Native American Ethnopoetics.* Studies in Native American Ethnopoetics. Philadelphia: University of Pennsylvania Press.

———. 1985a. Language, Memory, and Selective Performance: Cultee's "Salmon's Myth" as Twice Told to Boas. *Journal of American Folklore* 98:391–434.

———. 1985b. Some Subtleties of Measured Verse. In *Proceedings of the 15th Spring Conference, Niagara Linguistics Society,* ed. June Iris Hesch, 13–57. Buffalo NY.

———. 1987. Anthologies and Narrators. In *Recovering the Word: Essays on Native American Literature,* ed. Brian Swann and Arnold Krupat. Berkeley: University of California Press.

————. 1990. Thomas Paul's *Sametl*: Verse Analysis of a (Saanich) Chinook Jargon Text. *Journal of Pidgin and Creole Languages* 5(1):71–105.

————. 1993. In Need of a Wife: Clara Pearson's "Split-His-(Own)-Head." In *American Indian Linguistics and Ethnography in Honor of Laurence C. Thompson*, ed. Anthony Mattina and Timothy Montler. University of Montana Occasional Papers in Linguistics 10:127–62. Missoula.

————. 1994a. Coyote, Master of Death, True to Life. In *Coming to Light: Contemporary Translations of the Native Literatures of North America*, ed. Brian Swann, 286–306. New York: Random House.

————. 1994b. Seal and Her Younger Brother Lived There. In *Coming to Light: Contemporary Translations of the Native Literatures of North America*, ed. Brian Swann, 307–10. New York: Random House.

————. 1994c. The Sun's Myth. In *Coming to Light: Contemporary Translations of the Native Literatures of North America*, ed. Brian Swann, 273–85. New York: Random House.

————. 1998. *Reading Takelma Texts*. Bloomington IN: Trickster Press.

————. 1990. Mythology. In *Handbook of North American Indians* 7:593–601. *Northwest Coast*, ed. Wayne Suttles. Washington DC: Smithsonian Institution Press.

————. 2004. *Now I Know Only So Far: Essays in Ethnopoetics*. Lincoln: University of Nebraska Press.

Hymes, Dell, and Henry Zenk. 1987. Narrative Structure in Chinook Jargon. In *Pidgin and Creole Languages: Essays in Memory of John E. Reinecke*, ed. Glenn G. Gilbert, 445–65. Honolulu: University of Hawaii Press.

Hymes, Virginia. 1987. Warm Springs Sahaptin Narrative Analysis. In *Native American Discourse: Poetics and Rhetoric*, ed. Joel Sherzer and Anthony C. Woodbury. Cambridge Studies in Oral and Literate Culture 13:62–102. Cambridge: Cambridge University Press.

Idaho Centennial Commission. 1990. *Idaho Indians: Tribal Histories*. Boise: Idaho Centennial Commission.

Ignace, Marianne Boelscher. 1990. *Passive and Agency in Shuswap Narrative Discourse*. Working Papers of the 25th International Conference on Salish and Neighboring Languages, 61–70. Vancouver: University of British Columbia.

Jacknis, Ira. 1996. The Ethnographic Object and the Object of Ethnology in the Early Career of Franz Boas. In *Volksgeist as Method and Ethic: Essays on Boasian Ethnography and the German Anthropological Tradition*, ed. George W. Stocking Jr., 185–214. Madison: University of Wisconsin Press.

Jacobs, Elizabeth Derr. [1933–34.] Ethnographic notes: Field notebooks, folklore, and ethnography mss., based on three months' fieldwork among the Tillamook Salish, Garibaldi, Oregon. Melville Jacobs Collection, University of Washington Libraries, Seattle.

———. 1959. *Nehalem Tillamook Tales*, ed. Melville Jacobs, told by Clara Pearson. University of Oregon Monographs, Studies in Anthropology 5. Eugene: University of Oregon Books.

———. 2003. *The Nehalem-Tillamook: An Ethnography*, ed. William Seaburg. Corvallis: Oregon State University Press.

Jacobs, Melville. 1929. *Northwest Sahaptin Texts* 1. University of Washington Publications in Anthropology 2(6):175–244. Seattle.

———. [1933–34.] 2 wax cylinder and 10 acetate disc recordings of texts and music in Garibaldi and Nehalem Tillamook Salish, from Ellen Center and Clara Pearson, Garibaldi, Oregon. Melville Jacobs Collection, University of Washington Libraries, Seattle.

———. [1934.] 1969 *Northwest Sahaptin Texts*, Part I. Columbia University Contributions to Anthropology 19. New York: Columbia University Press. Reprint; New York: AMS Press.

———. 1936. *Texts in Chinook Jargon*. University of Washington Publications in Anthropology 7(1). Seattle: University of Washington Press.

———. [1937.] 1969. *Northwest Sahaptin Texts*, Part II. Columbia University Contributions to Anthropology 19. New York: Columbia University Press. Reprint: New York: AMS Press.

———. 1939. *Coos Narrative and Ethnologic Texts*. University of Washington Publications in Anthropology 8(1):1–126. Seattle: University of Washington Press.

———. 1940. *Coos Myth Texts*. University of Washington Publications in Anthropology 8(2):127–260. Seattle: University of Washington Press.

———. 1958. *Clackamas Chinook Texts*, Part I. *International Journal of American Linguistics* 24(2). Indiana University Research Center in Anthropology, Folklore, and Linguistics Publication 8.

———. 1959a. *Clackamas Chinook Texts*, Part II. *International Journal of American Linguistics* 25. Indiana University Research Center in Anthropology, Folklore, and Linguistics Publication 11.

———. 1959b. *The Content and Style of an Oral Literature: Clackamas Chinook Myths and Tales*. Viking Fund Publications in Anthropology 26. Chicago: University of Chicago Press.

———. 1960a. Humor and Social Structure in an Oral Literature. In *Culture in History: Essays in Honor of Paul Radin*, ed. Stanley Diamond, 181–89. New York: Columbia University Press.

———. 1960b. *The People Are Coming Soon: Analyses of Clackamas Chinook Myths and Tales*. Seattle: University of Washington Press.

———. 1962. The Fate of Indian Oral Literature in Oregon. *Northwest Review* 5(3):90–99.

———. 1967. Our Knowledge of Pacific Northwest Folklores. *Northwest Folklore* 11(2):14–21.

Jules, Mona, et al., eds. 1994. *Spetekwles re Oelmucx: Stories of the People*. Kamloops BC: Secwepemc Cultural Education Society.

Kennedy, Dorothy [I. D.], and Randy Bouchard. 1983. *Sliammon Life, Sliammon Lands*. Vancouver: Talonbooks.

Kinkade, M. Dale. [1958–2004.] Papers and sound recordings, M. Dale Kinkade Sub-Collection, Northwest Linguistic Collection, Manuscripts Division, University of Washington Libraries, Seattle.

———. 1963–64. Phonology and Morphology of Upper Chehalis. *International Journal of American Linguistics* I 29:181–95; II 29:345–56; III 30:32–61; IV 30:151–60.

———. 1967. On the Identification of the Methows (Salish). *International Journal of American Linguistics* 33:193–97.

———. 1978. Coyote and Rock (Columbia Salish). In *Coyote Stories*, ed. William Bright. International Journal of American Linguistics, Native American Texts Series. Monograph 1:15–20. Chicago: University of Chicago Press.

———. 1981. *Dictionary of the Moses-Columbian Language*. Nespelem WA: Colville Confederated Tribes.

———. 1983a. Daughters of Fire: Narrative Verse Analysis of an Upper Chehalis Folktale. In *North American Indians: Humanistic Perspectives*, ed. James S. Thayer. Papers in Anthropology 24(2):267–78. University of Okalahoma Department of Anthropology.

———. 1983b. Salish Evidence against the Universality of "Noun" and "Verb." *Lingua* 60:25–40.

———. 1984. "Bear and Bee": Narrative Verse Analysis of an Upper Chehalis Folktale. In *1983 Mid-America Linguistics Conference Papers*, ed. David S. Rood, 246–61. Boulder: Department of Linguistics, University of Colorado.

———. 1986. *Narrative Art, Narrator Skill*. Working Papers of the 21st International Conference on Salish and Neighboring Languages, 135–46. Seattle: University of Washington.

———. 1987. Bluejay and His Sister. In *Recovering the Word: Essays on Native American Literature*, ed. Brian Swann and Arnold Krupat, 255–96. Berkeley: University of California Press.

———. 1990. *Prehistory of Salishan Languages*. Working Papers of the 25th International Conference on Salish and Neighboring Languages, 197–208. Vancouver: University of British Columbia.

———. 1991. *Upper Chehalis Dictionary*. University of Montana Occasional Papers in Linguistics 7. Missoula.

———. 1992a. Salish Languages. In *International Encyclopedia of Linguistics*, ed. William Bright, 3:359–63. Oxford: Oxford University Press.

———. 1992b. Translating Pentlatch. In *On the Translation of Native American Literatures*, ed. Brian Swann, 163–75. Washington DC: Smithsonian Institution Press.

———. 1993. Salishan Words for "Person, Human, Indian, Man." In *American Indian Linguistics and Ethnography in Honor of Laurence C. Thompson*, ed. Anthony Mattina and Timothy Montler. University of Montana Occasional Papers in Linguistics 10:163–83. Missoula.

———. 1994. Native Oral Literature of the Northwest Coast and the Plateau. In *Dictionary of Native American Literature*, ed. Andrew Wiget, 33–45. New York: Garland Publishing.

Kinkade, M. Dale, and Anthony Mattina. 1996. Discourse. In *Handbook of North American Indians* 17:244–74. *Languages*, ed. Ives Goddard. Washington DC: Smithsonian Institution Press.

Kinkade, M. Dale, and William R. Seaburg. 1991. John P. Harrington and Salish. *Anthropological Linguistics* 33(4):392–405. Special Issue, *John P. Harrington and His Legacy*.

Kroeber, Karl. 1989. Technology and Tribal Narrative. In *Narrative Chance: Postmodern Discourse on Native American Literatures*, ed. Gerald Vizenor. Albuquerque: University of New Mexico Press.

———. 1998. *Artistry in Native American Mythology*. Lincoln: University of Nebraska Press.

Kroeber, Karl, ed. 1981. *Traditional Literatures of the American Indian: Texts and Interpretations*. Lincoln: University of Nebraska Press.

Kroeber, Paul D. 1999. The Salish Language Family: Reconstructing Syntax. In *Studies in the Anthropology of North American Indians*. Lincoln: University of Nebraska Press.

Krueger, James R. 1961a. Miscellanea Selica II: Some Kinship Terms of the Flathead Salish. *Anthropological Linguistics* 3(2):11–18.

———. 1961b. Miscellanea Selica III: Flathead Animal Names and Anatomical Terms. *Anthropological Linguistics* 3(9):43–52.

Krupat, Arnold. 1992a. *Ethnocriticism: Ethnography, History, Literature*. Berkeley: University of California Press.

———. 1992b. On the Translation of Native American Song and Story: A Theorized History. In *On the Translation of Native American Literatures*, ed. Brian Swann, 3–32. Washington DC: Smithsonian Institution Press.

———. 1993. *New Voices in Native American Literary Criticism*. Washington DC: Smithsonian Institution Press.

Kuipers, Aert H. 1967. *The Squamish Language: Grammar, Texts, Dictionary*. Janua Linguarum. Series Practica 73. The Hague and Paris: Mouton.

———. 1969. *The Squamish Language: Grammar, Texts, Dictionary*, Part II. The Hague and Paris: Mouton.

———. 1974. *The Shuswap Language: Grammar, Texts, Dictionary*. Janua Linguarum, Series Practica 225. The Hague: Mouton.

———. 1975. *A Classified English-Shuswap Word List*. Louvain: Peter de Ridder Press.

———. 1982. Towards a Salish Etymological Dictionary II. *Lingua* 57:71–92.

———. 1983. *Shuswap-English Dictionary*. Leuven: Peeters.

———. 1989. *A Report on Shuswap, with a Squamish Lexical Appendix*. Langues et Sociétés d'Amérique Traditionnelle 2. Paris: Peeters/SELAF.

———. 1996. *Towards a Salish Etymological Dictionary*. Working Papers of the 31st International Conference on Salish and Neighboring Languages, 203–10. Vancouver: University of British Columbia.

———. 2002. *Salish Etymological Dictionary*. University of Montana Occasional Publications in Linguistics 16. Missoula.

Laforet, Andrea, and Annie Z. York. 1981. Notes on the Thompson Winter Dwelling. In *The World Is as Sharp as a Knife*, ed. Donald N. Abbott, 115–22. Victoria: British Columbia Provincial Museum.

Laforet, Andrea, Nancy J. Turner, and Annie [Z.] York. 1993. Traditional Foods of the Fraser Canyon Nɬeʔképmx In *American Indian Linguistics and Ethnography in Honor of Laurence C. Thompson*, ed. Anthony Mattina and Timothy Montler. University of Montana Occasional Papers in Linguistics 10:191–213. Missoula.

Lamb, W. Kaye, ed. 1960. *Simon Fraser Letters and Journals, 1806–1808*. Toronto: Macmillan.

Langen, Toby C. S. 1989. The Organization of Thought in Lushootseed (Puget Salish) Literature: Martha Lamont's "Mink and Changer." *Melus* 16:77–93.

———. 1992. Translating Form in Classical American Indian Literature. In *On the Translation of Native American Literatures*, ed. Brian Swann, 191–207. Washington DC: Smithsonian Institution Press.

Lerner, Andrea. 1990. *Dancing on the Rim of the World: An Anthology of Contemporary Northwest Native American Writing*. Tucson: University of Arizona Press.

Lincoln, Kenneth. 1983. *Native American Renaissance*. Berkeley: University of California Press.

Malan, Vernon D. 1948. *Language and Social Change among the Flathead Indians*. Master's thesis, Montana State University.

Marr, John Paul. [1941.] Aluminum Disc Recordings of Texts, Vocabulary, and Music in Tillamook Salish, from Mabel Burns and Louey Fuller, Oregon. John P. Harrington Papers, National Anthropological Archives, Smithsonian Institution, Washington DC.

Mattina, Anthony, ed. 1985. *The Golden Woman: The Colville Narrative of Peter J. Seymour*. Trans. Anthony Mattina and Madeline de Sautel. Tucson: University of Arizona Press.

———. 1987a. *Colville-Okanagan Dictionary*. University of Montana Occasional Papers in Linguistics 5. Missoula.

———. 1987b. North American Indian Mythography: Editing Texts for the Printed Page. In *Recovering the Word: Essays on Native American Literature*, ed. Brian Swann and Arnold Krupat, 129–48. Berkeley: University of California Press.

————. 1987c. On the Transcription and Translation of *The Golden Woman*. Studies in American Indian Literature 11:92–101. Center for American Culture Studies. New York: Columbia University Press.

————. 1989. Interior Salish Post-Vogt: A Report and Bibliography. *International Journal of American Linguistics* 55(1):85–94.

————. 1994. Blue Jay and His Brother-in-Law Wolf. In *Coming to Light: Contemporary Translations of the Native Literatures of North America*, ed. Brian Swann, 332–45. New York: Random House.

Mattina, Anthony, and Clara Jack. 1992. Okanagan-Colville Kinship Terms. *Anthropological Linguistics* 34(1–4):117–37. Florence M. Voegelin Memorial Volume.

Mattina, Anthony, and Timothy Montler, eds. 1993. *American Indian Linguistics and Ethnography in Honor of Laurence C. Thompson*. University of Montana Occasional Papers in Linguistics 10. Missoula.

Mattina, Nancy, ed. 2001. *Nxa7amx!In Nwwawelxtnt Dictionary*. Nespelem Language Preservation Program. Nespelem WA: Colville Confederated Tribes.

Maud, Ralph. 1982. *A Guide to B.C. Indian Myth and Legend: A Short History of Myth-Collecting and a Survey of Published Texts*. Vancouver: Talonbooks.

————. 2000. *Transmission Difficulties: Franz Boas and Tsimshian Mythology*. Vancouver: Talonbooks.

Maud, Ralph, ed. 1978. *The Salish People: The Local Contribution of Charles Hill-Tout*. Volume I: *The Thompson and the Okanagan*; Volume II: *The Squamish and the Lillooet*; Volume III: *The Mainland Halkomelem*; Volume IV: *The Sechelt and the South-Eastern Tribes of Vancouver Island*. Vancouver: Talonbooks.

————. 1994. *The Porcupine Hunter and Other Stories: The Original Tsimshian Texts of Henry Tate*, annotated. Vancouver: Talonbooks.

Mayes, Sharon, and Yvonne Hebert. [1978.] Tape recording of Elders Day stories, Quilcene, British Columbia. L. C. and M. T. Thompson Sub-Collection, Northwest Linguistic Collection. Manuscripts Division, University of Washington Libraries, Seattle.

McIlwraith, T. F. 1948. *The Bella Coola Indians*, 2 vols. Toronto: University of Toronto Press.

McMillan, Alan D. 1988. *Native Peoples and Cultures of Canada: An Anthropological Overview*. Vancouver: Douglas and McIntyre.

————. 2000. *Since the Time of the Transformers: The Ancient Heritage of the Nuu-Chah-Nulth, Ditidaht, and Makah*. Vancouver: University of British Columbia Press.

Merriam, Alan. 1967. *Ethnomusicology of the Flathead Indians*. New York: Wenner-Gren Foundation.

Metcalf, Leon V. [1951.] Tape Recordings of Texts, Vocabulary, and Messages in Tillamook and other Salish Languages. Ethnology Archives, Thomas Burke Memorial Washington State Museum, University of Washington, Seattle.

Miller, Harriet, and Elizabeth Harrison. 1974. *Coyote Tales of the Montana Salish*. Rapid City SD: U.S. Department of the Interior, Tipi Shop.

Miller, Jay. 1990. An Overview of Northwest Coast Mythology. *Northwest Anthropological Research Notes* 23:125–41.

Miller, Jay, and Vi [T.] Hilbert. 1996. Lushootseed Animal People: Mediation and Transformation from Myth to History. In *Monsters, Tricksters and Sacred Cows: Animal Tales and American Indian Identities*, ed. A. James Arnold, 138–56. Charlottesville: University of Virginia Press.

Minor, Rick. 1991. *Archaeology of the Nehalem Bay Dune Site, Northern Oregon Coast*. Eugene: Oregon State Museum of Anthropology.

Monroe, Jean Guard, and Ray A. Williamson. 1987. *They Dance in the Sky: Native American Star Myths*. Boston: Houghton Mifflin.

Montler, Timothy. 1986. *An Outline of the Morphology and Phonology of Saanich, North Straits Salish*. University of Montana Occasional Papers in Linguistics 4. Missoula.

———. 1991. *Saanich: North Straits Salish Classified Word List*. Canadian Ethnology Service, Mercury Series 119. Ottawa: Canadian Museum of Civilization.

———. 1996. A Reconstruction of the Earliest Songish Text. *Anthropological Linguistics* 38(3):405–38.

———. 2003. Auxiliaries and Other Categories in Straits Salishan. *International Journal of American Linguistics* 69(2):103–34.

Moses, Marya, and Toby C. S. Langen. 1998. Reading Martha Lamont's Crow Story Today. *Oral Tradition* 13(1):92–129.

———. 2001. Reading Martha Lamont's Crow Story Today. In *Native American Oral Traditions: Collaboration and Interpretation*, ed. Larry Evers and Barre Toelken. Logan: Utah State University Press.

Moulton, Gary, ed. 1990. *The Journals of the Lewis and Clark Expedition*, Volume 6: *November 2, 1805–March 22, 1806*. Nebraska: University of Nebraska Press.

Mourning Dove. [1927.] 1981. *Cogewea, the Half-Blood*. Boston: Four Seas. Reprint; Lincoln: University of Nebraska Press.

——— (Humishuma). [1933.] 1990. *Coyote Stories*, ed. Heister Dean Guie, with notes by L. V. McWhorter (Old Wolf). Caldwell ID: Caxton Printers. Reprint; With Introduction and Notes to the Bison Book Edition by Jay Miller. Lincoln: University of Nebraska Press.

———. 1976. *Tales of the Okanogans*, ed. Donald M. Hines. Fairfield WA: Ye Galleon Press.

Nater, Hank F. 1984. *The Bella Coola Language*. Mercury Series 92. Ottawa: National Museums of Canada.

———. 1989. *A Concise Uxalk (Bella Coola) Dictionary*. Mercury Series 115. Ottawa: Canadian Museum of Civilization.

Nettl, Bruno. 1975–76. Indian Melodies from British-Columbia Recorded on the

Phonograph. Translation and reprint of Abraham and Von Hornbostel 1906. In *Opera Omnia,* ed. Klaus P. Wachsmann et al., 1:301–22. The Hague: M. Nijhoff.

Newman, Stanley. 1976. Salish and Bella Coola Prefixes. *International Journal of American Linguistics* 42:228–42.

———. 1977. The Salish Independent Pronoun System. *International Journal of American Linguistics* 43:302–14.

———. 1980. Functional Changes in the Salish Pronominal System. *International Journal of American Linguistics* 46:155–67.

Newman, Thomas M. 1959. *Tillamook Prehistory and Its Relation to the Northwest Coast Culture Area.* Unpublished PhD dissertation, Anthropology, University of Oregon, Eugene.

Niatum, Duane (McGinnis). 1970. *After the Death of an Elder Klallam, and Other Poems.* Santa Fe: Baleen.

———. 1973a. *Ascending Red Cedar Moon.* New York: Harper and Row.

———. 1973b. *A Cycle for the Woman in the Field.* A Chapbook. Baltimore: Laughing Man Press.

———. 1975. *Carriers of the Dream Wheel.* New York: Harper and Row.

———. 1977a. *Digging Out the Roots: Poems.* Native American Series. New York: Harpers.

———. 1977b. *Turning to the Rhythms of Her Song.* A Chapbook. Seattle: Jawbone Press.

———. 1978. *To Bridge the Dream.* A Story Chapbook. Laguna NM: AP Ltd.

———. 1981a. *Pieces.* New York: Strawberry Press.

———. 1981b. *Songs for the Harvester of Dreams.* Seattle: University of Washington Press.

———. 1983. *Raven and the Fear of Growing White.* Amsterdam: Bridges Press.

———. 1984. History in the Colors of Song: A Few Words on Contemporary Native American Poetry. In *Coyote Was Here: Essays on Contemporary Native American Literary and Political Mobilizations,* ed. Bo Schöler. Special Issue of *The Dolphin* 6. Aarhus, Denmark: Seklos.

———. 1987a. On Stereotypes. In *Recovering the Word: Essays on Native American Literature,* ed. Brian Swann and Arnold Krupat, 552–62. Berkeley: University of California Press.

———. 1987b. *Stories of the Moons.* Marvin SD: Blue Cloud Quarterly Press.

Niatum, Duane, ed. 1988. *Harper's Anthology of 20th Century Native American Poetry.* San Francisco: Harper and Row.

Nicodemus, Lawrence. 1975. *Snchitsu'umshtsn: The Coeur d'Alene Language,* 2 vols. Spokane WA: University Press.

Olson, Ronald L. [1925–27.] Quinault Field Notebooks. Ronald Olson Papers, Manuscripts and University Archives, University of Washington Libraries, Seattle.

————. [ca. 1927.] Typescript of Quinault Field Notebooks. Ethnology Archives, Thomas Burke Memorial Washington State Museum, University of Washington, Seattle.

————. [1936.] 1967. *The Quinault Indians*. University of Washington Publications in Anthropology 6(1):1–190. Reprint; Seattle: University of Washington Press.

Orchard, Imbert. [1965.] Interview with Annie (Z.) York. Audio-tape 678:1–2, Imbert Orchard Collection, Accession 4103. Provincial Archives of British Columbia.

Palmer, Andie. 1994. *Maps of Experience: Shuswap Narratives of Place*. PhD dissertation, Anthropology, University of Washington, Seattle.

Palmer, Gary. 1975. Shuswap Indian Ethnobotany. *Syesis* 8.29–81.

Palmer, Gary, Lawrence Nicodemus, and Lavinia Felsmen. 1987. *Khwi Khwe Hnlmikhwlumkhw: "This Is My Land."* Plummer ID: Coeur d'Alene Tribe.

Palmer, Katherine Van Winkle. 1925. *Honne: The Spirit of the Chehalis*. Geneva NY: Press of W. F. Humphrey.

Peltier, Jerome. *Manners and Customs of the Coeur d'Alene Indians*. Spokane WA: Peltier Publishing.

Peterson, Jacqueline. 1993. *Sacred Encounters: Father De Smet and the Indians of the Rocky Mountains*. Norman: University of Oklahoma Press.

Phinney, Archie. 1934. *Nez Perce Text*. Columbia University Contributions to Anthropology 23. New York.

Point, Nicolas. 1967. *Wilderness Kingdom: Indian Life in the Rocky Mountains, 1840–1847*. New York: Holt, Rinehart and Winston.

Post, Richard, and Rachel S. Commonst. 1938. *The Sinkaietk or Southern Okanogan*. General Series in Anthropology 6. Menasha WI: George Banta Publishing.

Powell, Jay, Vickie Jensen, and Phyllis Chelsea. 1979. *Learning Shuswap*. Book 1. Kamloops BC: Shuswap Language Committee.

Radin, Paul. 1956. *The Trickster: A Study in American Indian Mythology*. With commentaries by Karl Kerényi and C. G. Jung. New York: Bell Publishing.

Ramsey, Jarold, ed. 1977. *Coyote Was Going There: Indian Literature of the Oregon Country*. Seattle: University of Washington Press.

————. 1979. The Indian Literature of Oregon. In *Northwest Perspectives: Essays on the Culture of the Pacific Northwest*, ed. Edwin R. Bingham and Glen A. Love, 3–19. Seattle: University of Washington Press.

————. 1983a. "The Hunter Who Had an Elk for a Guardian Spirit," and the Ecological Imagination. In *Smoothing the Ground: Essays on Native American Oral Literature*, ed. Brian Swann, 309–22. Berkeley: University of California Press.

————. 1983b. *Reading the Fire: Essays in the Traditional Indian Literatures of the Far West*. Lincoln: University of Nebraska Press.

————. 1983c. Uncursing the Misbegotten in a Tillamook Incest Story. In *Reading the Fire: Essays in the Traditional Indian Literatures of the Far West*, ed. Jarold Ramsey. Lincoln: University of Nebraska Press.

————. 1983d. The Wife Who Goes Out Like a Man, Comes Back as a Hero: The Art of Two Oregon Indian Narratives. In *Reading the Fire: Essays in the Traditional Indian Literatures of the Far West*, ed. Jarold Ramsey. Lincoln: University of Nebraska Press.

————. 2001. Telling Stories for Readers: The Interplay of Orality and Literacy in Clara Pearson's *Nehalem Tillamook Tales*. In *Native American Representations: First Encounters, Distorted Images, and Literary Appropriations*, ed. Gretchen M. Bataille, 120–31. Lincoln: University of Nebraska Press.

Raufer, Sister Maria Ilma, O.P. 1966. *Black Robes and Indians on the Last Frontier, a Story of Heroism*. Milwaukee: Bruce Publishing.

Ray, Verne F. 1932. *The Sanpoil and Nespelem: Salishan People of Northwestern Washington*. University of Washington Publications in Anthropology 5. Seattle.

————. 1933. Sanpoil Folk Tales. *Journal of American Folklore* 46:129–87.

————. 1936. Native Villages and Groupings of the Columbia Basin. *Pacific Northwest Quarterly* 27:99–152.

————. 1937. The Bluejay Character in the Plateau Spirit Dance. *American Anthropologist* 39:593–601.

————. 1939. *Cultural Relations in the Plateau of Northwestern America*. Publications of the Frederick Webb Hodge Anniversary Publication Fund 3. Los Angeles: The Southwest Museum.

Reichard, Gladys A. 1938. Coeur d'Alene. In *Handbook of American Indian Languages* 3:517–707, ed. Franz Boas. Gluckstadt, Hamburg, and New York: J. J. Augustin.

————. 1947. *An Analysis of Coeur d'Alene Indian Myths*, With a Comparison by Adele Froelich. American Folklore Society Memoirs 41. Philadelphia: American Folklore Society.

Riley, Patricia. 1993. *Growing Up Native American: An Anthology*. New York: Morrow.

Roberts, Helen, and Herman K. Haeberlin. 1918. Some Songs of the Puget Sound Salish. *Journal of American Folklore* 31:496–520.

Robinson, Harry. 1992. *Native Power: In the Spirit of an Okanagan Storyteller*. Seattle: University of Washington Press.

Rohner, Ronald P., ed. 1969. *The Ethnography of Franz Boas: Letters and Diaries of Franz Boas Written on the Northwest Coast from 1886 to 1931*. Chicago: University of Chicago Press.

Ronan, Peter. 1890. *History of the Flathead Nation*. Minneapolis: Ross and Haines.

Ruby, Robert, and John Brown. 1989. *Dreamer-Prophets of the Columbia Plateau: Smohalla and Skolaskin*. Norman: University of Okalahoma Press.

Ruoff, A. LaVonne Brown. 1990a. *American Indian Literatures: An Introduction, Bibliographic Review, and Selected Bibliography*. New York: Modern Language Association of America.

————. 1990b. *Redefining American Literary History*. New York: Modern Language Association of America.

Sapir, Edward. 1909. *Wishram Texts*. Leiden: Publications of the American Ethnological Society 2.

————. n.d. [SPC] Edward Sapir Professional Correspondence, Canadian Ethnology Service, Canadian Museum of Civilization, Hull, Quebec.

Sapir, Edward, and Leslie Spier. 1930. *Wishram Ethnography*. University of Washington Publications in Anthropology 3. Seattle.

Schlick, Mary Dodds. 1994. *Columbia River Basketry: Gift of the Ancestors, Gifts of the Earth.* Seattle: University of Washington Press.

Seaburg, William R. 2000. Two Tales of Power. In *Voices from Four Directions: Contemporary Translations of the Native Literatures of North America*, ed. Brian Swann, 209–25. Lincoln: University of Nebraska Press.

Seaburg, William R., and Pamela T. Amoss, eds. 2000. *Badger and Coyote Were Neighbors: Melville Jacobs on Northwest Indian Myths and Tales*. Corvallis: Oregon State University Press.

Sherzer, Joel. 1987. A Discourse-Centered Approach to Language and Culture. *American Anthropologist* 89:295–309.

Sherzer, Joel, and Anthony C. Woodbury, eds. 1987. *Native American Discourse: Poetics and Rhetoric*. Cambridge: Cambridge University Press.

Simonds, Ann G., and Richard L. Bland. 1999. Native Legends of Oregon and Washington Collected by Franz Boas. *Northwest Anthropological Research Notes* 33(1):100–101.

Siska, Heather Smith. 1988. *We Are the Shuswap*. Kamloops BC: Secwepemc Cultural Education Society.

Slickpoo, Allen, Sr., Leroy Seth, and Deward Walker Jr. 1972. *Nu Mee Poom Tit Wah Tit (Nez Perce Legends)*. Lapwai ID: Tribal Publications.

Smet, Pierre-Jean de. 1905. *Life, Letters, and Travels of Father Pierre-Jean de Smet, S.J., 1801–1873*, also a Life of Father de Smet by H. M. Chittenden and A. T. Richardson. New York: F. P. Harper.

Smythe, Willie, and Esme Ryan, eds. 1999. *Spirit of the First Peoples: Native American Music Traditions of Washington State*. Seattle: University of Washington Press.

Snyder, Sally. 1964. *Skagit Society and Its Existential Basis: An Ethnofolkloristic Reconstruction*. PhD dissertation, Anthropology, University of Washington, Seattle.

Snyder, Warren A. 1968. *Southern Puget Sound Salish: Texts, Place Names, and Dictionary*. Sacramento Anthropological Society Paper 9.

Speck, Brenda J. 1980. *An Edition of Father Post's Kalispel Grammar*. University of Montana Occasional Papers in Linguistics 1. Missoula.

Spier, Leslie. 1930. *Klamath Ethnography*. University of California Publications in American Archaeology and Ethnology 30. Berkeley.

Spier, Leslie, ed. 1938. *The Sinkaietk or Southern Okanagan of Washington*. General Studies in Anthropology 6. Menasha WI: George Banta Publishing.

Spinden, Herbert Joseph. 1908. *The Nez Perce Indians*. Memoirs of the American Anthropological Association II, Part III. Lancaster PA New Era Printing.

Sprague, Roderick. 1991. A Bibliography of James A. Teit. *Northwest Anthropological Research Notes* 25(1):103–15.

Steedman, Elsie Viault, ed. 1930. *Ethnobotany of the Thompson Indians of British Columbia*. Based on field notes by James A. Teit. Bureau of American Ethnology Annual Report 45:441–552.

Stern, Bernhard J. 1934. *The Lummi Indians of Northwest Washington*. Columbia University Publications in Anthropology 17. New York: Columbia University Press.

Stewart, Hilary. [1977.] 1982. *Indian Fishing: Early Methods on the Northwest Coast*. Seattle: University of Washington Press. Reprint; Vancouver: Douglas and McIntyre.

Stuart, Wendy Bross. 1972. *Gambling Music of the Coast Salish Indians*. Canadian Ethnology Division Paper No. 3. National Museum of Man, Mercury Series. Ottawa: National Museums of Canada.

Suttles, Wayne, ed. 1990. *Handbook of North American Indians 7. Northwest Coast*. Washington DC: Smithsonian Institution Press.

Suttles, Wayne, and William W. Elmendorf. 1963. Linguistic Evidence for Salish Prehistory. Symposium on Language and Culture, 41–52. American Ethnological Society.

Swadesh, Morris. 1949. The Linguistic Approach to Salish Prehistory. In *Indians of the Urban Northwest*. Columbia University Contributions to Anthropology 36:161–73.

———. 1950. Salish Internal Relationships. *International Journal of American Linguistics* 16:157–67.

Swan, James. [1857.] 1972. *The Northwest Coast, or Three Years Residence in Washington Territory*. New York: Harper and Brothers. Republished; Seattle: University of Washington Press.

Swann, Brian, ed. 1983. *Smoothing the Ground: Essays on Native American Oral Literature*. Berkeley: University of California Press.

———, ed. 1992. *On the Translation of Native American Literatures*. Washington DC: Smithsonian Institution Press.

———, ed. 1994a. *Coming to Light: Contemporary Translations of the Native Literatures of North America*. New York: Random House.

———. 1994b. Introduction. *Coming to Light: Contemporary Translations of the Native Literatures of North America*, ed. Brian Swann, xiii–xlvi. New York: Random House.

———, ed. 1996. *Wearing the Morning Star: Native American Song-Poems*. New York: Random House.

————, ed. 2004. *Voices from Four Directions: Contemporary Translations of the Native Literatures of North America*. Lincoln: University of Nebraska Press.

Swann, Brian, and Arnold Krupat, eds. 1987. *Recovering the Word: Essays on Native American Literature*. Berkeley: University of California Press.

Tedlock, Dennis. 1972. *Finding the Center: Narrative Poetry of the Zuni Indians*. New York: Dial.

————. 1983. *The Spoken Word and the Work of Interpretation*. Philadelphia: University of Pennsylvania Press.

Teit, James A. n.d. [TCF]. James Teit Correspondence File, Anthropology Archives, American Museum of Natural History, New York.

————. [1898.] 1969. *Traditions of the Thompson Indians of British Columbia*. Memoirs of the American Folklore Society 6. Boston and New York: Houghton Mifflin. Reprint; Krause Reprints.

————. [1900.] 1975. The Thompson Indians of British Columbia. *The Jesup North Pacific Expedition* IV. *Anthropology* I, ed. Franz Boas. Memoirs of the American Museum of Natural History 2(4) with plates. New York. Reprint; New York: AMS Press.

————. [1906.] 1975. The Lillooet Indians. *The Jesup North Pacific Expedition* II(V). Memoirs of the American Museum of Natural History 4(5). New York. Reprint; New York: AMS Press.

————. 1909. The Shuswap. *The Jesup North Pacific Expedition* II(VII). Memoirs of the American Museum of Natural History 4(5):447–758. Leiden and New York.

————. [1912a.] 1975. Mythology of the Thompson Indians. *The Jesup North Pacific Expedition* II, 8(2):199–416. Memoirs of the American Museum of Natural History 12. Leiden: E. J. Brill, and New York: G. E. Stechert. Reprint; New York: AMS Press.

————. 1912b. Traditions of the Lillooet Indians of British Columbia, *Journal of American Folklore* 25:287–371.

————. [1915–18.] [CMC]. Cylinder Collection (Interior Salish) recorded by James A. Teit, Spences Bridge, British Columbia, and accompanying field notes: Songs of the Indians of British Columbia. Canadian Museum of Civilization (CMC). Hull, Quebec.

————. [1915–21.] Ms. Songs from the Salish Area. Recordings sent to National Museum of Canada. (Ms. [30(S.6] Freeman No. 3208), in American Philosophical Society Library, Philadelphia.

————. 1916. European Tales from the Upper Thompson Indians. *Journal of American Folklore* 29:301–29.

————. 1917a. Coeur d'Alene Tales. In *Folktales of Salishan and Sahaptin Tribes*, ed. Franz Boas. Memoirs of the American Folklore Society 11:119–28. Boston: Houghton Mifflin.

———. 1917b. Okanagan Tales.In *Folktales of Salishan and Sahaptin Tribes*, ed. Franz Boas. Memoirs of the American Folklore Society 11:65–97. Boston: Houghton Mifflin.

———. 1917c. Pend d'Oreille Tales. In *Folktales of Salishan and Sahaptin Tribes*, ed. Franz Boas. Memoirs of the American Folklore Society 11:114–18. Boston: Houghton Mifflin.

———. 1917d. Tales from the Lower Fraser River. In *Folktales of Salishan and Sahaptin Tribes*, ed. Franz Boas. Memoirs of the American Folklore Society 11:129–34. Boston: Houghton Mifflin.

———. 1917e. Thompson Tales. In *Folktales of Salishan and Sahaptin Tribes*, ed. Franz Boas. Memoirs of the American Folklore Society 11:1–64. Boston: Houghton Mifflin.

———. [1927–28.] 1930. The Salishan Tribes of the Western Plateaus. *Annual Report of the Bureau of American Ethnology* 45:25–396. Washington DC. Reprint; Washington DC: Government Printing Office.

———. 1928. The Middle Columbia Salish. *University of Washington Publications in Anthropology* 2(4):89–128. Seattle.

———. 1930. *Ethnobotany of the Thompson Indians of British Columbia. Annual Report of the Bureau of American Ethnology*, 1927–28, No. 45.

———. 1937. More Thompson Indian Tales, ed. Lucy Kramer. *Journal of American Folklore* 50:173–90.

Teit, James A., Livingston Farrand, Marian K. Gould, and Herbert J. Spinden. 1917. *Folk-Tales of Salishan and Sahaptin Tribes*, ed. Franz Boas. Memoirs of the American Folklore Society 11. Lancaster PA: G. E. Steichert.

Tepper, Leslie. 1987. *The Interior Salish Tribes of British Columbia: A Photographic Collection*. Mercury Series 11. Ottawa: Canadian Ethnology Service. Canadian Museum of Civilization.

———. 1994. *Earth Line and Morning Star: NLaka'pamux Clothing Traditions*. Hull QC: Canadian Museum of Civilization.

Thompson, Laurence C. [1972.] Ms. Thompson Field Notebook D, pp. 234ff.; Thompson tapes No. 71–73, CT79.26B and CT79.27. Thompson Sub-Collection, Northwest Linguistic Collection, Manuscript Division, University of Washington Libraries, Seattle.

———. 1979. Salishan and the Northwest. In *The Languages of Native America: Historical and Comparative Assessment*, ed. Lyle Campbell and Marianne Mithun, 692–765. Austin: University of Texas Press.

———. 1985. Control in Salish Grammar. In *Relational Typology*, ed. Frans Plank, 391–428. The Hague: Mouton.

Thompson, Laurence C., and M. Terry Thompson. [1948–2003.] Class notes, field notebooks, sound recordings, manuscripts, and correspondence. L. C. and M. T. Thompson Sub-Collection, Northwest Linguistic Collection, Manuscript Division, University of Washington Libraries, Seattle.

————. 1966. A Fresh Look at Tillamook Phonology. *International Journal of American Linguistics* 32(4):313–19.

————. 1972. Language Universals, Nasals, and the Northwest Coast. In *Studies in Linguistics in Honor of George L. Trager*. The Hague: Mouton.

————. 1992. *The Thompson Language*. University of Montana Occasional Papers in Linguistics 8. Missoula.

————. 1996. *Thompson River Salish Dictionary*. University of Montana Occasional Papers in Linguistics 12. Missoula.

Thompson, Laurence C., M. Terry Thompson, and Barbara Efrat. 1974. Some Phonological Developments in Straits Salish. *International Journal of American Linguistics* 40(3):182–96.

Thompson, Laurence C., M. Terry Thompson, and Steven M. Egesdal. 1997. Sketch of Thompson, a Salishan Language. In *Handbook of North American Indians* 17:609–43, *Languages*, ed. Ives Goddard. Washington DC: Smithsonian Institution Press.

Thompson, M. Terry. [1985–92.] Ms. field notebooks and sound recordings of the Thompson River Salish (Nɬeʔképmx) language. L. C. and M. T. Thompson Sub-Collection, Northwest Linguistic Collection, Manuscripts Division, University of Washington Libraries, Seattle.

Thompson, M. Terry, and Steven M. Egesdal. 1993. Push-Back-Sides-of-His-Hair, Nʔikʔikñincút: A Traditional Thompson River Salish Legend with Commentary. In *American Indian Linguistics and Ethnography in Honor of Laurence C. Thompson*, ed. Anthony Mattina and Timothy Montler. University of Montana Occasional Papers in Linguistics 10:279–302. Missoula.

Thompson, M. Terry, and Mabel Joe. [1989.] Ms. Field notes, text transcription and translation of Mayes and Hebert 1978 tape recording. L. C. and M. T. Thompson Sub-Collection, Northwest Linguistic Collection, Manuscripts Division, University of Washington Libraries, Seattle.

Thompson, Stith, ed. 1929. [1968] *Tales of the North American Indians*. Bloomington: Indiana University Press.

————. [1946.] 1977. *The Folktale*. New York: Dryden Press. Reprint; Berkeley: University of California Press.

————. [1953.] 1965. The Star Husband Tale. *Studia Septentrionalia* 4:93–163. Reprint; in *The Study of Folklore*, ed. Alan Dundes. Englewood Cliffs NJ: Prentice Hall.

Turner, Nancy. 1973. The Ethnobotany of the Bella Coola Indians of British Columbia. *Syesis* 6:193–220.

————. 1975. *Food Plants of British Columbia Indians*. Part One: *Coastal Peoples*. Handbook No. 34. Victoria: British Columbia Provincial Museum.

————. 1978. *Food Plants of British Columbia Indians*. Part Two: *Interior Peoples*. Handbook No. 36. Victoria: British Columbia Provincial Museum.

————. 1979. *Plants in British Columbia Indian Technology*. Handbook No. 38. Victoria: British Columbia Provincial Museum.

Turner, Nancy J., Randy Bouchard, and Dorothy Kennedy. 1980. *Ethnobotany of the Okanagan-Colville Indians of British Columbia and Washington*. British Columbia Provincial Museum Occasional Paper 21. Victoria.

Turner, Nancy J., Laurence C. Thompson, M. Terry Thompson, and Annie Z. York. 1990. *Thompson Ethnobotany: Knowledge and Usage of Plants by the Thompson Indians of British Columbia*. Memoir No. 3. Victoria: Royal British Columbia Museum.

Turney-High, Harry Holbert. 1937. *The Flathead Indians of Montana*. Memoirs of the American Anthropological Association 48. Menasha WI: American Anthropological Association.

————. [1941.] 1974. *Ethnography of the Kootenai*. Memoirs of the American Anthropological Association 56. Reprint; Millwood NY: Krause Reprints.

van Eijk, Jan P. 1985. *The Lillooet Language*. Amsterdam: University of Amsterdam.

————. [1993.] 1998. Reduplication and Infixation in Lillooet. In *American Indian Linguistics and Ethnography in Honor of Laurence C. Thompson*, ed. Anthony Mattina and Timothy Montler. University of Montana Occasional Papers in Linguistics 10:317–25. Reprint; in *Salish Languages and Linguistics: Theoretical and Descriptive Perspectives*, ed. Ewa Czaykowska-Higgins and M. Dale Kinkade, 453–76. Berlin and New York: Mouton de Gruyter.

————. 1997. *The Lillooet Language: Phonology, Morphology, Syntax*. Vancouver: University of British Columbia Press.

van Eijk, Jan P., and Lorna B. Williams, eds. 1981. *Cuystwi Malh Ucwalmicwts: Lillooet Legends and Stories*. Mount Currie BC: *Ts'zil* Publishing House.

Vizenor, Gerald. 1993. *Narrative Chance: Postmodern Discourse on Native American Indian Literature*. Norman: University of Oklahoma Press.

Vogt, Hans. 1940. *The Kalispel Language*. Oslo: Det Norske Videnskaps-Akademi.

Walker, Deward. 1980. *Myths of Idaho Indians*. Moscow: University Press of Idaho.

————. 1982. *Indians of Idaho*. Moscow: University Press of Idaho.

————. 1994. *Blood of the Monster: The Nez Perce Coyote Cycle*. Worland WY: High Plains Publishing.

————, ed. 1998. *Handbook of North American Indians* 12. *Plateau*. Washington DC: Smithsonian Institution Press.

Watanabe, Honoré. 1994. A Report on Sliammon (Mainland Comox) Phonology and Reduplication. In *Languages of the North Pacific Rim*, ed. Osahito Miyaoka. Hokkaido University Publications in Linguistics No. 7. Sapporo.

————. 1998. Sapir's Research on Comox. *Bulletin of the Edward Sapir Society of Japan* 12:15–30. In Japanese.

Weisel, George F. 1960. The Osteocranium of the Catostomid Fish, *Catostomus macrocheilus*. A Study in Adaptation and Natural Relationship. *Journal of Morphology* 106(1):109–29.

Wells, Oliver. 1987. *The Chilliwacks and Their Neighbors*, ed. Ralph Maud, Brent Galloway, and Marie Weeden. Vancouver: Talonbooks.

Wells, Oliver, ed. 1966. *Squamish Legends by Chief August Jack Khahtsahlano and Dominic Charlie*. Printed privately.

Wells, Oliver, comp. 1970. *Staw-Loh Indians: Myths and Legends of South Western British Columbia*. Privately printed posthumously.

White, Richard. 1980. *Land Use, Environment, and Social Change: The Shaping of Island County, Washington*. Seattle: University of Washington Press.

Wickersham, James. 1898. Nisqually Mythology. *Overland Monthly*. Series 2, 32.

Wickwire, Wendy C. [1977–90.] Field notes and recordings in author's files.

———. 1985. Theories of Ethnomusicology and the North American Indian: Retrospective and Critique. *Canadian University Music Review* 66:186–222.

———. 1988. James A. Teit: His Contribution to Canadian Ethnomusicology. *Canadian Journal of Native Studies* 8(2):183–204.

———. 1992. Women in Ethnography: The Research of James A. Teit. *Ethnohistory* 40(4):539–62.

———. 1994. To See Ourselves as the Other's Other: Nlaka'pamux Contact Narratives. *Canadian Historical Review* 75:1–20.

———. 1998. "We Shall Drink from the Stream and So Shall You": James A. Teit and Native Resistance in British Columbia, 1908–1922. *Canadian Historical Review* 79(2):199–236.

———. 2001. The Grizzly Gave Them the Song: James Teit and Franz Boas Interpret Twin Ritual in Aboriginal British Columbia, 1897–1920. *American Indian Quarterly* 25(3):431–52.

———. 2003. Beyond Boas? Re-Assessing the Contribution of "Informant" and "Research Assistant" James A. Teit. In *Constructing Cultures Then and Now: Celebrating Franz Boas and the Jesup North Pacific Expedition*, ed. Laurel Kendall and Igor Krupnik. Washington DC: Smithsonian Institution.

———. 2004. Prophecy at Lytton. In *Voices from Four Directions: Contemporary Translations of the Native Literatures of North America*, ed. Brian Swann, 134–70. Lincoln: University of Nebraska Press.

Wiget, Andrew. 1985. *Native American Literature*. Boston: Twayne.

———, ed. 1994a. *Dictionary of Native American Literature*. New York: Garland Publishing.

———. 1994b. Native American Oral Literatures: A Critical Orientation. In *Dictionary of Native American Literature*, ed. Andrew Wiget, 3–18. New York: Garland Publishing.

Woodcock, Clarence, ed. *Stories from Our Elders*. Pablo MT: Flathead Culture Committee, Confederated Salish and Kootenai Tribes.

———. 1996. Salish Tradition. *Journal of the Oregon Historical Society* 39:3 and 4, 8–9.

Yanan, Eileen. 1971. *Coyote and the Colville*. Omak WA: St. Mary's Mission.

Young, Stanley Paul, and H. H. T. Jackson. [1951.] 1978. *The Clever Coyote*. Harrisburg PA: Stackpole; Washington DC: Wildlife Management Institute. Reprint: Lincoln: University of Nebraska Press.

Zenk, Henry. 1988. Chinook Jargon in the Speech Economy of Grande Ronde Reservation, Oregon: An Ethnography-of-Speaking Approach to a Historical Case of Creolization in Process. *International Journal of the Sociology of Language* 71:107–24.

Index

Pitch Boy, 55n68
pitch/pitchwood, 31, 54n66, 107, 108, 113, 115, 251, 307
The Place of Coyote, 149–53
Plains culture, 141, 172, 225
plank houses. *See* cedar
Plateau culture: geographic area of, xxi; hunting and fishing, xxi, 141; mixture of Plains and Northwest Coast cultures, xxi
Pope, Bob, 60, 61, 202, 203, 204
Port Gamble, 110
Port Townsend, 401, 402
potlatches, xx
Powell, Jay, 213, 214
Powell, Luke, 213
Powell River, xix, 121
Prairie Chickens, 190
Priest Rapids, 177
prosodic phrasing, 228
Proto-Salish: kinship systems, xxii; language and grammar, xvii, xli, xlviiin3; origins of Northwest Coast cultures, xv
Pǝtcinéyt, Chief, 301n4
pubic hair, 161, 175n5
Puget Sound, xviii, 107, 119, 219, 266, 277
Puget Sound Salish people, xviii
Puyallup people, 203

Qálqaliɫ, the Basket Ogress, 113–16
Qápnats, 102
Q̓ʷáti, 215
Qeqals, 201
Qeyqeyší's Marriage, 223–34
Quileute culture, 213–16
Quileute Texts (Andrade), 213
Quileute Tribal School, 214
Quinault culture: Bluejay cycle, 60–77; Sun and Moon Are Brothers story, 202–9; Tsamosan Salish language, *xvi*, xviii
Quintasket, Charles, 193
Quintasket, Christine, 193

raconteur/raconteuse, xxviii, xxix, xxx, xxxi, xxxii–xxxiii, xxxiv
Raufer, Sister Maria Ilma, 294
Raven: daughter of, 72–74; feces of, 98; Jesuits and, 287–89; killing Ts'ítsixwun, 270; in Myth Era, 3, 340; Seal and, 200–201; siblings of, 98, 270; slaves of, 390; stealing Skunk's "asset" (*ahso*), 196, 197; stylized speech, xxvi; as Trickster-Transformer, 60
"Raven and His Sisters," 85, 87, 98–99
Ray, Verne, xxxv, 149
red arrow, 241
Red Cedar, 86
red cloud, 329
red snapper, 121
red willow, 212, 250
Reichard, Gladys, xxxv, xxxvi, 210
A Report on Shuswap (Kuipers), 249
Roberts, Charlie, 200
Rock, 79–80
rocks, 25, 31, 45, 49, 52n45, 55n68, 59n113, 175n16, 215
Rock Squirrel, 193, 199
Rocky Mountains, xxi
Ross, Alexander, 295
Rotten Log, xxvi
rotten wood, as decoy, 43, 58n97, 258–59, 261n1, 353, 356, 387, 390, 391, 393
Ruffed Grouse, 159, 353

Saanich culture: four as pattern number, 235–39; historical story of, 235–39; Straits Salish dialect, xviii
sábu, 384, 385, 389
Sahaptin language, 133
The Sailor Who Jumped Ship and Was Befriended by Skagits, 277–86
St. Ignatius Mission, 223
St. Ignatius Community Center, 225
St. Joseph River, 287
St. Mary's, 225
St. Mary's Mission, 294, 297
Salishan languages: Bella Coola, *xvi*; Central Coast Salish, *xvi*; characteristics of, xli–xlviii, 317, 318n1, 319n4; elderly speakers of, xxiii; family of, xv, *xvi*, xvii; grammar of, xlvi, xlviiin5; imperiled status of, xxii–xxv; Interior Salish, *xvi*; North American and Salish territory, *l*, 2; pattern number in, xxvii–xxviii; pronunciation guide of,

In the Native Literatures of the Americas Series

Pitch Woman and Other Stories: The Oral Traditions of Coquelle Thompson, Upper Coquille Athabaskan Indian
Edited and with an introduction by William R. Seaburg Collected by Elizabeth D. Jacobs

Inside Dazzling Mountains: Southwest Native Verbal Arts
Edited by David L. Kozak

The Complete Seymour: Colville Storyteller
Peter J. Seymour
Compiled and edited by Anthony Mattina
Translated by Madeline DeSautel and Anthony Mattina

Algonquian Spirit: Contemporary Translations of the Algonquian Literatures of North America
Edited by Brian Swann

Born in the Blood: On Native American Translation Edited and with an introduction by Brian Swann

Sky Loom: Native American Myth, Story, and Song
Edited and with an introduction by Brian Swann

Voices from Four Directions: Contemporary Translations of the Native Literatures of North America
Edited by Brian Swann

Salish Myths and Legends: One People's Stories
Edited by M. Terry Thompson
and Steven M. Egesdal

To order or obtain more information on these or other University of Nebraska Press titles, visit nebraskapress.unl.edu.